Cadzie's chest felt full of hot liquid, every breath a strained effort. "Joanie!" he said. "I give you control of my suit for the first two seconds after the grendels appear. Override my reactions."

"Are you sure?"

He was sure. And out of the grass stalked three creatures from his deepest nightmares. And regardless of conscious thought, Cadzie's entire body moved. His right arm tried to grab the holstered handgun at his hip with a motion so fast and violent that when the armor resisted it he felt the protesting tendons and ligaments at elbow and shoulder scream in agony.

His vision collapsed to a tunnel, focused entirely on the first grendel. Vision went red, and then black . . . and then red . . . and then came back to normal as the conditioned response faded.

He panted. Dear *God* that was intense! But as the roar of the adrenaline faded, and sanity returned, for the very first time he had consciously experienced the full power of the programming designed to save their lives. He shivered, as the hormonal heat receded, leaving him feeling cold and sick. And then that died away as well . . .

A hundred meters away, the grendels still crouched, watching them. Almost as if they had been waiting for him to lock eyes before acting, they began to move. They crept in like cautious wolves . . .

STARBORN & GODSONS

♦

LARRY NIVEN
JERRY POURNELLE
STEVEN BARNES

A Baen Books Original

Baen Publishing Enterprises
P.O. Box 1403
Riverdale, NY 10471
www.baen.com

ISBN: 978-1-9821-2531-8

Cover art by Kurt Miller
Maps on pages xxv, xxvi, xxvii by Randy Asplund
Maps on pages xxi, xxii, xxiii, and xxiv by Randy Asplund based
on maps by Alexis Walser

First printing, April 2020
First mass market printing, April 2021

Distributed by Simon & Schuster
1230 Avenue of the Americas
New York, NY 10020

Library of Congress Control Number: 2019054178

Printed in the United States of America

10 9 8 7 6 5 4 3 2 1

He that hath a Gospel
To loose upon Mankind,
Though he serve it utterly—
Body, soul and mind—
Though he go to Calvary
Daily for its gain—
It is His Disciple Shall make his labour vain.

        —Kipling "The Disciple"

We surviving authors are pleased to dedicate this book to our lost member, Dr. Jerry Pournelle.

◆ DRAMATIS PERSONAE ◆

EARTHBORN (1st Generation)
Zack Moskowitz—Former mayor;
  last surviving Geographic Society trustee
Rachel Moskowitz—Former first lady
"Big" Shaka—Colony's head biologist
Carlos Martinez—Artist
Twyla—Psychologist, Carlos' girlfriend
Sylvia—Biologist, Cadmann Weyland's surviving
  widow
Cassandra—Main AI computer on Avalon;
  in orbit aboard *Geographic*
Mason Stolzi—Last living trained astronaut
  among the Earthborn

STARBORN (2nd and 3rd Generation)
"Little" Shaka—Foster son of "Big" Shaka
Cadmann Sikes ("Cadzie")—Grandson of Cadmann
  Weyland, and heir apparent; technically third
  generation, and former Grendel Scout
Aaron Tragon—First of the "bottle babies"
  (creche children) and thus first Starborn; titular
  Leader of the Starborn
Trevanian—Comm shack
Hal and Towner—Mappers who discover cthulhu
  corpse
Marvin Kyle "Toad" Stolzi—Minerva pilot; "the last
  astronaut"
Tracy Martinez—Carlos's daughter

Scott Martinez—Carlos's son
Stanfield "Piccolo" Corning—second born on Avalon;
    surfing instructor, former miner
Nnedi Okan
Joanie Tragon—Daughter of Aaron;
    raised by Cadmann's widows
Jaxxon Tuinukuafe—Artist, Jason's older brother
Jason Tuinukuafe—Engineer, Jaxxon's younger brother
Evie Queen—Artist
Thor—Joanie's boyfriend
Mei Ling—Joanie's rival for Thor; geologist
Collie Baxter—Engineer

GODSONS

Narrator Marco Shantel—Former tri-d star
Major Gloria Stype—Security officer
First Speaker Augustus Glass
Channing Newsome "The Prophet"
Gertrude Hendricksen—Generally called Trudy
Captain Sven Meadows—Senior military line officer
    awakened before arrival in orbit around Tau Ceti;
    32 years old and only awake a few weeks before
    rendezvous; Golden Viking; lover of Gloria Stype
Chief Engineer Jorge Daytona
Sargent Greg Lindsey
Corporal Carvey
Ship's Captain Arnold Tolliver—Originally captain of
    Messenger
Dr. Mandel—First Speaker's private physician
Dr. Charlotte Martine—Biologist and medical officer
Sargent Kanazawa
Colonel Anton Tsiolkovskii

Reminiscence on **Starborn and Godsons** **by Larry Niven**

♦ ♦ ♦

The Heorot trilogy started with an African frog with nasty habits. Jack Cohen told several writers about it. I've had correspondence with the man who actually did the research; his problem was getting anyone to believe him.

The frog lives in a very simple ecology. There's moss; there're frogs; and there're tadpoles. The tadpoles eat the moss. When they grow bigger, the frogs eat them. Some survive to become frogs and continue the species. We moved them to an alien planet and made some changes.

This third volume of the Heorot series will be the last.

Jerry Pournelle and I conceived *The Legacy of Heorot* hoping to generate a Nebula Award winner. Hence the pretentious title, naming the hall invaded by Grendel in the Beowulf saga. We intended a novella: there's fewer sales at that length, hence reduced competition. Our menace, the grendels, would resemble a horror from EC Comics from our childhood. That decided, we set forth to build the SF field's most realistic colony story. Bring enough people. Use an established concept for an interstellar spacecraft. Inhabit an island to confine the new world's surprises to a minimum.

For a year or two it was just talk and notes and ideas. No text. We got impatient. We decided to invite a guy I'd written with, Steven Barnes, into the mix.

That was brilliant. Steven was perfect. He's wonderful at writing horror. We were all a lot younger, and Steven in his twenties was the perfect student. He listened. He worked. He needed the training. He didn't freak out when we tore his text up and rewrote it. Jerry and I got into lecturing him and each other. We talked it all over, and as we did, the story grew to novel length.

Steven admits: once he got involved, *The Legacy of Heorot* was always going to be a novel. He wasn't going to miss the opportunity to learn.

When a story is finished, we don't stop thinking about it. Most writers are like that, I believe. That's how sequels are born.

Jerry and I used to drink as we generated stories. When he had to give that up, we hiked instead, and Steven often joined us. After publication we found ourselves frantic to explore Avalon's mainland, barely glimpsed in *Heorot*.

Beowulf's Children was written in much the same fashion as *Heorot*. We were all noticeably older. Somewhere in there I'd told Steven he was no longer a student, but that didn't matter; all three of us had the habit of lecturing each other. We invited a fourth lecturer into the mix: we paid Jack Cohen travel expenses and a flat fee to help us design an ecology for the Avalon mainland.

Jack Cohen was a world-class expert on fertility in all creatures, and in a host of other disciplines. He was a lifelong science fiction fan. He sometimes did flat fee work for science fiction writers; he did that to rationalize Anne McCaffrey's dragons. For us he designed the Avalon crab template, with an aerodynamic shell and four varied claws. We used it throughout, from seafood to bees to birdles to the Scribes, the vast creatures that leave tracks visible from orbit, which we never quite described in *Heorot*.

I don't remember who invented the Avalon carnivore bees—the ones who eat grendels and use their *speed* to move like little bullets.

I do remember fighting to persuade my collaborators that our character Aaron could shoot a man who knew too much, if he pretended to be shooting at the grendel who was trying to rescue him. We had to put a character onstage to knock the gun out of his hands.

The book was published as *Beowulf's Children* in the United States, and as *The Dragons of Heorot* in Britain.

On our hikes we argued about the fate of the citizens of Avalon. We were pretty much agreed that civilization there was doomed. The Grendel War had done too much damage. The younger Avalonians, the Starborn, weren't making new tools. Their orbital ship was deteriorating, along with the ship's computer.

Jerry wanted to write a romance. We wrote a novelette set between the first two books, "The Secret of Black Ship Island," and sold it on the Internet. Here a new life form was born, the cthulhus.

And eventually we found a way to rescue the Godsons, the youngest generation of Avalonians.

But by then Jerry had developed a tumor in his brain. They had to burn it out with converging lasers. Afterward it developed that Jerry couldn't write any more. He could dream, he could plan, he could interact and criticize when we spun our dreams, but sitting down to write became impossible.

We worked in Jerry's living room, spinning plot lines and redirecting them, generating characters and interactions, making underground maps. We kept Jack Cohen involved, using Skype to link England and California, but Jack had become ill too.

Jerry had a stroke. We kept working. He was recovering.

He died in his sleep in September 2017, a few days after attending Dragon Con in Atlanta, Georgia.

Starborn and Godsons was nearly finished by then, and fully plotted to the end. Steven and I wrapped it up over a few months.

It's Jerry Pournelle's last novel. Jack Cohen has passed on. Steven and I are at work on other projects.

Based on today's physics, with no outrageous new discoveries, we believe the Heorot series is a fully reasonable approach to the settling of other planets. We'd love to live long enough to see it happen.

—Larry Niven
August 15, 2019

My Experience in the Land of Giants
by Steven Barnes

◆ ◆ ◆

I had written several novels with Larry Niven when he and his partner, Jerry Pournelle, asked me if I'd be interested in the idea of a novella. I listened, and thought it was appropriately brilliant, given the guys who had generated it. I also knew something else: they had just come off a run on the *New York Times* bestseller list, and this was one hell of an opportunity for me.

Multiple purposes, all dovetailing.

The most obvious *career* possibility was a chance to stand on their shoulders, use their lightning as my own. Another is that Jerry as an individual was, at that time, arguably the smartest human being I'd ever met, more than a little intimidating, and I wanted to see what it was like to interact with that mind more closely. And the third is that together, Larry and Jerry were an extraordinary team. I was dying to know what it was like to interact with the two of them at the same time.

So...I dreamed and figured and came up with a reasonable way that a short idea could turn into a full novel, pitched it, and the game was afoot. A couple of times a week, for over a year, I would travel to Larry or Jerry's house (usually Jerry, I recall—he had the better designed workspace for collaboration), take notes, discuss the story, and then go away and write. I brought the text back on disk or paper, and then the fun really began.

You see . . . Jerry enjoyed teaching and lecturing, but also just a bit of terrorizing. And I was intimidated half to death. I'm not sure how many human beings have ever had the experience of having two world-class authors, one on either side of the room, tearing up their writing simultaneously. Larry would do it with relative compassion, but Jerry was having entirely too much fun.

"Ah, we're murdering Barnes' precious prose," he'd cackle, bent over his typewriter. *"Barnes, was your mother frightened by a gerund??"*

Ah, memories. There were times it was so brutal I drove home crying. But I wouldn't quit: I knew that if I could hang in there, I'd learn lessons no school in the world could teach me. I also knew Jerry suffered fools less gladly than anyone I'd ever met. His pressure wasn't contempt. That was *respect*. If he hadn't respected me, I wouldn't have been in that room. He was lobbing balls at me, and expected that I'd eventually start lobbing them back.

I didn't, until the second book. I just bit back my fear and frustration, soldiered on, and learned. And grew. And looking back, I was right: it was an *extraordinary* opportunity, and one of the smartest decisions I ever made.

The Legacy of Heorot was a smashing success as a piece

of writing, less so as a piece of commercial art. I remember first seeing the cover and being devastated: it felt as if the publisher had deliberately given it camouflage, so that no one could find it on a bookshelf. We made it, barely, to the tail end of the *Times* bestseller list, but I just knew that it could have done so much better.

Years later, we began a discussion about a sequel, *Beowulf's Children*, and I readily agreed. This time, Dr. Jack Cohen, the biologist who had inspired the original book, was flown in from England to work with us for about ten days. I'd met him while on book tour in England and found his brilliance and sense of humor instantly magnetic. He stayed in my house in the high desert, and I'd drive him down for intensive sessions with Larry and Jerry, and damn, it was wonderful watching the three of them interact, and to realize that somehow . . . I deserved to be in the same room. I *had* to, or I wouldn't have been there. The "impostor voices" in my head tried to speak up, but the roar of genius conversations drowned them out.

That time there was no terror, just serious work, and serious fun.

Years passed. Experimenting with e-books, we wrote "The Secret of Blackship Island" partially as a lark, and partially warming up for a third book we all knew was needed, but weren't at all sure would ever get written. Life pulls you in different directions, and while I adored working with my friends and mentors, I was fully engaged in other projects.

In about 2015, Jerry had a tumor shrunk in his head, and it affected his ability to write. I went with Larry to see him in the hospital, and while yes, he seemed diminished, what disturbed me was that this bluff, hale, room-dominating man seemed . . . depressed. Feared that he was no longer of use to the world. I wanted to shake him and tell him that he was still one of the most amazing minds I'd ever known, but that seemed hollow. I also wanted to thank him for all he had been to me, and the opportunities he had afforded.

Frankly . . . I wanted to just tell him that I loved him.

But . . . Jerry was of a generation of men where you don't say things like that very much. What you do is say, "Let's build a barn!" and the meaning, the emotions come across in the process. What decided me was Larry's reaction to Jerry's condition. He was clearly in deep grief. The best friend he'd ever known, his partner, his hero, his big brother, was in pain, and there was nothing he could do. They'd actually had to sell a book back to the publisher because Jerry could no longer coordinate the "editor" and "flow" states elegantly. When you can't, it's called "writer's block," and a devastating affliction.

And I thought to myself: this is no way for the greatest team in SF history to end their partnership. Jerry could think fine. Could plot and plan and evaluate. Still had the computer mind. What he *couldn't* seem to do was flip from editor mode to flow state on command. Larry could dream, but I could tell he didn't want to open himself to another disappointment. What was needed was a bridge between these two great men, and a bridge between Jerry's dreaming and analyzing modes of thought.

I saw that I could be that bridge.

And it would be the best gift I could give the two of

them, a way for me to have a very special kind of fun one last time. So for almost two years, I would drive forty miles each way, every Thursday, to work with them. Jerry was with a cane in the beginning, and then a walker, and finally in a wheelchair. His decline was fairly rapid. The mind and heart were there, but the body was growing weary. Jack Cohen had retired by that time, but we looped him in on Skype from England as often as possible, and when the technology worked, The Boys Were Back in Town. It was wonderful. I just loved the energy in that room as we batted ideas around, dreamed, and I would go off and create first draft text that two of the best friends I've ever had in my life then analyzed and polished.

Every idea Jerry came up with I treated like a golden butterfly. All were precious. Some were released back into the wild, but as many as possible I incorporated. We'd get together at about eleven in the morning, work until about one, and then have lunch. And although he was growing weaker, Jerry always let us know how much he loved the work, how much pleasure it gave him. And slowly, Larry began to believe this book was really going to happen and opened himself to just . . . having fun. And Larry having fun is about as brilliant as a human being ever gets. The Boys Were Back, indeed.

We were about nine tenths of the way through the book when Jerry said to me, rather wistfully, "Well . . . we're almost done here. You guys don't need me any more." I assured him that I considered every moment and conversation precious . . . but if something happened, he could rest assured this book would be completed.

And about three days later, Larry called and told me

Jerry had passed in his sleep. I'd both known and forced myself to be oblivious to the reality: Jerry was asking us to let him go. And saying goodbye.

I cannot tell you how glad I am I made the decision to stand up for these men who formed so much of my personality as a writer. You so rarely get to say "thank you" to the people to whom you owe the most. I did. And got to say, in the clearest way I know how:

I love you guys. Thank you, from the bottom of my heart, for letting me into your world. I am stronger and smarter, and a better person because you let me sharpen my steel against you. I hope you never regretted the decision to let me in. I hope I always lived up to the amazing opportunity you offered.

Individually and together . . . you were, and remain, the very best I've known.

—Steven Barnes
August 19, 2019
Glendora, California

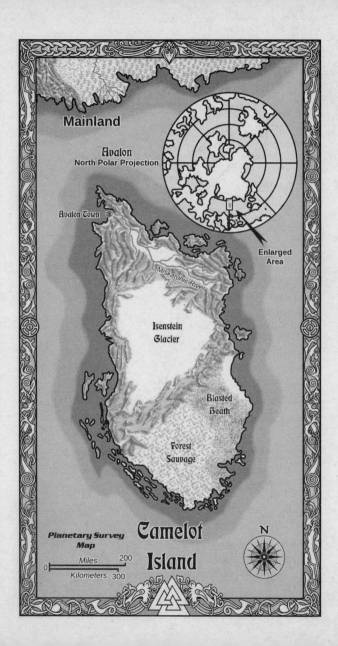

Mainland

Avalon
North Polar Projection

Enlarged
Area

Avalon Town

Miskatonic River

Isenstein
Glacier

Blasted
Heath

Forest
Sauvage

**Planetary Survey
Map**

Miles   200
0
Kilometers   300

Camelot
Island

N

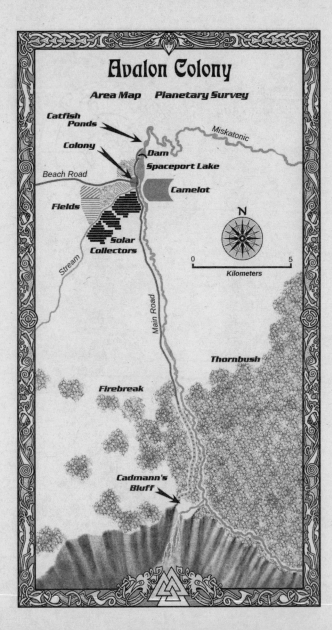

Avalon Colony

Area Map   **Planetary Survey**

Catfish Ponds

Colony

Beach Road

Dam

Spaceport Lake

Camelot

Miskatonic

Fields

Solar Collectors

Stream

N

0   5

Kilometers

Main Road

Thornbush

Firebreak

Cadmann's Bluff

First Camp

(Zack's Tabletop Model)

1. Dining Hall
2. Administration & Armory
3. Magazine
4. Sewage Treatment
5. Hydroponic Garden
6. Power Plant
7. Electronics/Clean Lab
8. Dorm (6)
9. Sick Bay
10. Skeeter Pad
11. Hangar
12. Radio Shack
13. Assay Lab
14. Power Tool Shed
15. Machine Shop
16. Dorm (4)
17. Auto Shop
18. Tractor Garage
19. Auxiliary Machine Shop
20. Chickens
21. Dogs
22. Corral (calves & horses)
23. Mine Fields
24. Farm Tool Shed
25. Wood Shop
26. Shop
27. Quad
28. Bio Lab & Vet

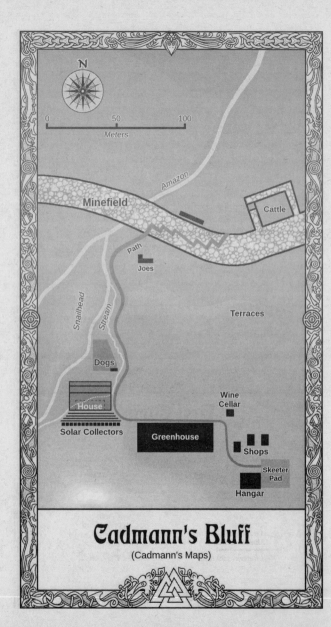

N

0   50   100
         Meters

Amazon

Minefield

Cattle

Path
Joes

Snailhead

Stream

Terraces

Dogs

Wine
Cellar

House

Solar Collectors

Greenhouse

Shops

Skeeter
Pad

Hangar

Cadmann's Bluff

(Cadmann's Maps)

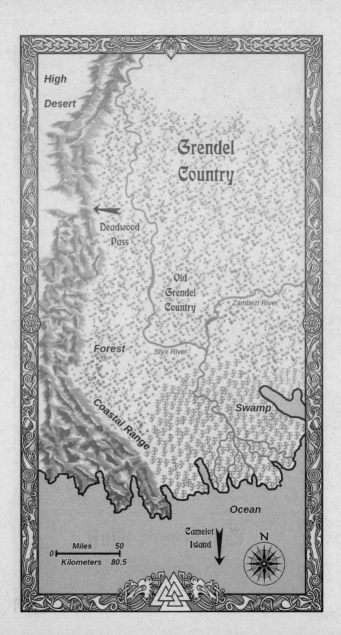

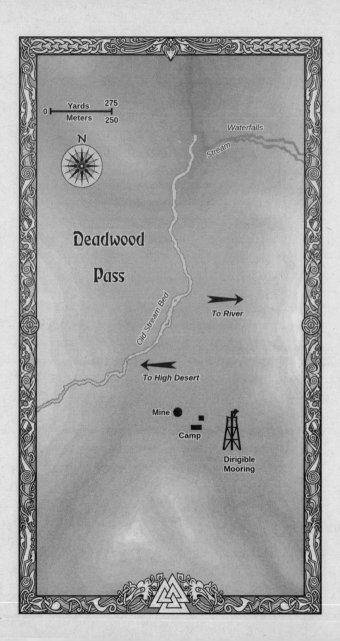

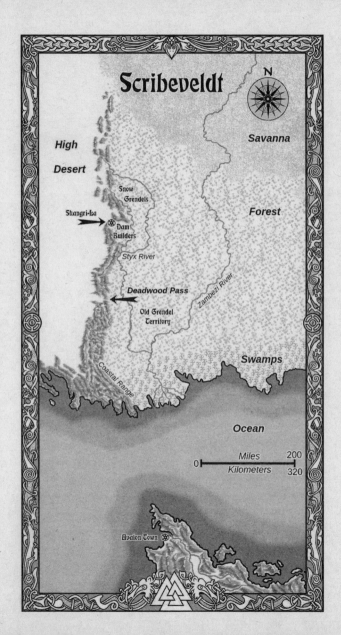

STARBORN
& GODSONS

◆

PART ONE

PART ONE

◆ PROLOGUE ◆
CASSANDRA

Cassandra was slowly dying. This was not particularly disturbing in itself, because Cassandra was an artificial intelligence, and self-preservation was not high on the AI primary motives table. The problem was that the colonists on the planet she orbited needed her far more than they realized. She did not know how to manipulate human minds, and she had no instructions to learn how. Human psychology was a restricted area of knowledge to every AI. She could know facts, but could not apply them in her dealings with humans.

Even so, Camelot, the island colony below, was thriving. The grendels were under control, and the mainland outposts well established. Avalon's new mainland hydroelectric power station was nearly complete, and when online would compensate for the nuclear power systems lost in the Grendel Wars. Humans would have power, and with power came the ability to make all the necessities for life. They would survive.

They would not survive as a spacefaring people.

5

Cassandra had all the knowledge they would ever need, but it had taken Earth with all its resources and a population of billions nearly a century to go from aircraft to spacecraft. Avalon had neither the population nor the ability to build needed robots. What they were losing faster than they knew was the ability to get to space. The AI-driven Minerva shuttlecraft were deteriorating for lack of proper maintenance, and when humans could no longer reach orbit, Cassandra would die too. With her would go every hope of replacing the Minerva craft. The colony had modern technology, but only for a while. They had already lost not only the ubiquitous 3D printers that made nearly everything, but also the fabrication facilities that could turn a computer-generated circuit diagram into a chip with a million transistors that made up computing power, memory, and memory management. It would not be long until they could not build the tools to repair the AI systems they needed. And after that would go the tools to make the tools.

Cassandra had left Earth with all the science of 3D printing and chip fabricator civilization, but it had been lost to grendel destruction decades ago. Now Avalon was losing too many fundamentals of the very technology that made their colony possible, and when Cassandra died, the colonists would be on their own. Worrying about that possibility was in Cassandra's Primary Motivation Table.

She became conscious of a warning signal from the space observation analyzer. Something was moving out there in the stars, decelerating at a rate impossible for a natural object. Something was coming, fast, and its destination was Avalon.

She reviewed everything known about the intruder. It had come from a few degrees wide of the direction of Sol. Given the rate of deceleration and the spectrum of its fusion flame, this vehicle resembled *Geographic*. The most probable origin was Earth's Solar System.

The rate of deceleration exceeded *Geographic*'s abilities. Human technology had improved.

It took microseconds to draft messages to the colonists. One message to the adult leadership, the survivors of the original pioneers. That list was shorter every year as aging and hibernation instability took their inevitable toll. Humans were not designed for synthetic hibernation and there had been costs, made much greater for those repeatedly awakened and put back to sleep. Those awakened during the century-long journey from Earth had been the engineering crew, navigators, ship construction experts, and they were the first to succumb to the complications of hibernation instability. Most of these unfortunates awoke on Avalon nearly crippled, absentminded, or stupid. Humans had a word for them, *morons*, but they rarely used it, and many had never heard it. The second generation, those born on Avalon, said their elders had "ice on their minds." Cassandra did not understand the humor in that designation, but she knew it was considered less offensive than "moron," yet still too offensive to be employed in open conversation.

Cassandra did not fully comprehend this, but it concerned her not at all. Many human preferences were incomprehensible, but they were important to one or another human group, and Cassandra had plenty of memory—or had until these last micro-meteor strikes.

Perhaps she should have been taken from orbit to the planetary surface forty years ago. She'd been lucky: that would have destroyed her. She would have been smashed in the Grendel War, and that would have crippled human civilization.

Cassandra's prime directive was to preserve that civilization, even if she only had a very ambiguous definition of what that might actually mean.

So. Being unable to ground her was a positive vector item despite its appearance, and that fit her definition of good luck. Now, however, Cassandra would die from lack of maintenance. Irony was not a large part of her instruction set, but she understood the concept.

Warning to the Old Ones. A second alert to the leadership of the First Generation, who called themselves the Starborn. They tended to distrust the Old Ones, but deferred to them. A third alert to Surf's Up, the habitation of many of the children and young adults. These trusted neither the Old Ones nor the Starborn, and insisted on their own contacts with Cassandra. And finally to the third generation, who were known as both Mainlanders and NextGen. Some fought for the right to be idle . . . and others to explore beyond the limits prescribed by their elders.

Different groups, different intents, and after forty years the colony had both grown and begun to splinter. Such changes were inevitable, but if Cassandra had possessed emotions, she would have begun to worry. Not about her own diminished capacity, but the health of the colony she served. It was her only purpose, her reason to exist, and without them, she was alone.

◆ CHAPTER I ◆
NIGHTMARES AND DAYDREAMS

His name was Major Cadmann Jacob Weyland, and this was his last stand.

The major hunkered behind an armorglas wall in the midst of a vast rocky bowl called Ngorongoro crater, Earth's largest intact caldera and Africa's richest game preserve, now the place where his well-gnawed bones would rest.

He fought with the 4th Special Forces Unit, United Nations Central Command. The dozen men remaining in his United Nations task force were not enough. Not even close.

"Sir!" Sergeant Mgui cried. New, raw wounds criscrossed his tribal markings. "We have intel on an approaching force."

"Emplacements," Cadmann cried. "Take positions, and do not yield."

"Sir!"

The men took their positions. Some local soldiers, an Afrikaans sergeant, and one black American corporal, a man named Carlos Martinez. He knew Carlos well, but the exact circumstances under which they had met, and the precise nature of their relationship remained hazy and indistinct.

"Are you ready?" Cadmann roared.

"Yes, sir," Carlos replied. "Excuse me, sir."

"Yes?"

Confusion clouded Carlos' face. "I'm wondering... how I got here."

Cadmann nodded. Somehow, he had expected this strange question. "We hopped a Delta glider in from Mozambique. What's wrong with you?"

"I just... don't know why I'm here," Martinez said. Suddenly (that was odd) he was no longer Cadmann, had transformed into *Carlos*.

"A little late for that," Cadmann said.

Knudson raised his voice. "Sir! Enemy approaching, sir!"

The roar of approaching machinery... the ground shaking. Carlos shivered. Was a seasoned veteran supposed to react this way to fear?

Muddy clouds of dust boiled at the horizon. And then... a vast horde of creatures that resembled something begotten upon a crocodile by an axolotl swarmed toward them at impossible speed. Thousands. More.

"Oh, God," Carlos moaned.

Cadmann glared at him. "Stay frosty. On target. Machine gunner—"

"Ready, sir."

"We're going to die!" He couldn't control himself. Not even close. It was all he could do to keep his bladder in check. The risk of death was mandatory in his profession. Soiling himself (he hoped) was optional.

"In range, sir," Navarro said.

Cadmann's eyes narrowed. "Stand ready. Mark a target directly in front of you. Stand ready . . . take aim . . . In volley, fire! New target. Take aim. In volley, fire! Steady. Fire at will."

The rifles roared and flashed like a dusty lightning storm. Carlos fired along with the others, until his weapon seared the flesh from his palms.

In the midst of the slaughter Cadmann seemed eight feet tall, perfect and brave amid the carnage, swelling with it as the others were diminished.

The creatures broke through the wall of armorglas (or had it dissolved? It was difficult to see), and Carlos' ears rang with screams of pain and horror as his comrades were torn to pieces.

And then they were upon Carlos himself. He felt himself floating up and up, witnessing his own disembowelment and devouring at their hands, as if in some obscene holoplay, his screams flooding from all directions until they drowned the thunder of countless grendel feet and snapping jaws.

And then . . . Cadmann stood alone amid a growing pile of grendel dead.

"Carlos! Carlos!" Cadmann screamed, his voice odd. Increasingly *feminine*. And . . .

◆ ◆ ◆

"Carlos. Carlos." A soft, female voice, slowly increasing in volume and urgency.

As had happened before, Carlos Martinez, former remittance man, now de facto leader of the colony called Camelot, sat up, sheet and dreams slipping away from him at the same time. Beside him, a very female-shaped lump snored beneath her blanket. Something had awakened him, thank God. He had seen himself die before. He usually managed to shift perspective enough to not feel the blazing hot teeth as they rent and devoured.

Usually. A red light flashed on his dresser, its radiance falling directly onto his blinking eyes. "All right, Cassie," he said. "What do you have for me?"

"Carlos," the synthesized voice whispered, more urgently now. "I'm sorry to wake you."

"It's all right, Cass. What's so important?"

She told him, and when she did, all drowsiness vanished in an instant.

On the southeast coastal line of the New Zealand–size island of Avalon, crowning the finest stretch of sparkling sand for two hundred klicks perched a ragtag collection of thatched-roof huts christened "Surf's Up." Most inhabitants were transients who rotated through the huts as they were constructed, occupied, and then abandoned. The entire island of Avalon was theirs, conquered by their grandparents in service to generations unborn.

Lodgings and warehouses clustered across the island, home to farmers, loggers and fishermen. Surf's Up was the second largest settlement, housing almost a fifth of the island's total population of twelve hundred souls. And while it had been a blessedly long time since there had been an emergency, as with Camelot, there was always someone on duty to answer a call.

"I'm looking for Aaron."

The kid on the other end of the call laughed. "He's not here. Hasn't been for months. Try Blackship."

Carlos rubbed fingers through his thinning, white-streaked hair. Out his north-facing bedroom window, mistwreathed Mucking Great Mountain rose up like a thunderhead in the pre-dawn. Dammit, this would have all been so much easier if the man would simply wear his tracer. But that bit of petty rebellion was the least of his issues with Aaron Tragon.

"Shall I try the island?" Cassandra asked. There was a time when her empathic programs would have anticipated his needs. The old girl was slipping. Hell, they all were.

Blackship was a rock spur twenty klicks off from Surf's Up, barely visible from the beach most days, a dark wedge-shape hovering in the ocean mist. It was the heart of the colony's ocean research and there were always a few people there devoted to aiding the survival of the small outpost.

Carlos didn't know who would be on rotation, and in fact was glad to know that standing orders . . . suggestions . . . agreements, perhaps . . . were still in effect. The young woman who answered didn't know where Aaron was. He gave up and asked for Cadzie. Cadzie was at home in the hills. Carlos called him there.

Cadmann Sikes, generally known as "Cadzie," had only

gotten to bed an hour earlier, returning to his cabin in the mountains south of the main colony following a three-day hike in the dense forest further toward the setting sun. The communicators woven into his collars and necklaces were always in the default "on" position, as they were for most colonists. They could be turned off for privacy of course, and then only Cassandra could find you . . . unless you disconnected the power or left them at home.

It was hard to get permanently lost on Avalon.

Cadzie was twenty-eight Earth years, an intermediate age, born on Avalon after the Grendel Wars to Joe Sikes, an Earthborn, and his wife Linda, a daughter of the colony's de facto leader, his own namesake. His parents had been killed by *speed*-enhanced "bees" on the mainland in his infancy. His revered grandfather had been killed before Cadzie could know him but he was well aware of the original Cadmann's position, and he knew that many expected him to grow into his image as potential leader. It showed in the training he had received since he was less than ten years old, a broad introduction to almost everything that was going on, encouragement to dig just a little deeper, work just some little harder, gentle reminders that his grandfather had saved the colony and one day it might be his turn to do the same. He was not sure he wanted that responsibility—or rather, he had doubts about his ability, or for that matter the *need* for anyone to be the leader, or why anyone would want to be.

He was tall, with hair the color of fire glimpsed through smoke. His wiry frame was as lean as the rock climber he had been since childhood, and this planet was his home. Ninety-five percent of the surface remained a mystery, and while ugly surprises always remained a possibility, humanity had overcome all the most pressing threats. There was more to life than mere survival.

"Unka," he groaned. "Up early?"

"Yes. And I'm going to be up late, too." Uncle Carlos looked tired. It was difficult to acknowledge, but Cadzie's second-favorite member of the colony had gotten old, his coffee-colored scalp barely covered by thinning hair. Old, or well on his way. Oh, well, it happened to everyone lucky enough to survive, he supposed.

"Something big?"

"It doesn't get bigger," Carlos said.

That response banished fatigue. "Gramma's all right?" he asked quickly.

"Both are fine. It's not that kind of news."

"So tell me."

Carlos clucked reluctantly. "I can't. We have a formal chain of information flow, Cadzie. I have to tell Aaron first. And Aaron zapped his chip. He's off the grid."

"Sounds like him," Cadzie said, relentless now. "What is it?"

"Where is he?"

"I can find him. But you're going to tell me what this is about."

"Not over the radio," Carlos said. "This has to be secure. Come here and see me. If you'll be my personal envoy, I'll share the information." *Muy mysterioso.*

Cadzie rubbed his stubbled chin. What could be so important? Surely his honorary uncle could set up firewalls on Cassandra to protect the line . . . but no, Cass had been in decline for at least a decade, and she was riddled with hacks. Every kid in the colony made his bones penetrating her security. It was a joke.

"You're killing me."

"And?"

"And . . . I'll be there in an hour." Cadzie groaned, then killed the link and searched beside and under his bed for his muddy boots.

Everything creaked. Hadn't he been able to climb all day and party all night, not so long ago?

Hell, he was getting old, too.

◆ CHAPTER 2 ◆
THE DAM

Just three hours later, Cadzie was gliding above a white-capped eastern sea, navigating 300 kilometers to the mainland in Blue Three, his favorite autogyro. What Uncle Carlos had shared with him sent his head buzzing hotter than the 100-hp engine blurring the rotors. He was so lost in thought that he barely noticed when the engine began to sputter.

"Damn!" A quick check of the panel right above eye level indicated sixty percent pressure in the fuel line. He adjusted the liquid hydrogen flow, pushing it up to the red line to pressure past the obstruction. It was dangerous, flirting with overload, but he would rather blow a housing later than risk crash-landing in the ocean now. He was equipped to deal with anything the land had to offer, but some of the inhabitants of the deep seas remained a lethal mystery.

Fortunately, that seemed to do it. After another few minutes he felt he had things under control and backed off on the pressure, and ten minutes after that, he sighted the saw-toothed coastal mountains and breathed a sigh of relief.

He touched the control panel. "Horseshoe Landing, this is Blue Three, Cadmann Sikes."

No answer. He was about to call again when he heard, "Horseshoe Landing here. Go ahead, Cadzie."

Cadzie thought he recognized the voice but he wasn't certain. Didn't matter. "Sikes here with message for Joanie. Landing in five minutes."

By formal agreement, priority knowledge must be shared between the different branches of the increasingly splintered colony. No one was really "in charge" of the human beings on Tau Ceti IV, but there were recognized group leaders who had to be the first to know about important matters. Carlos learned things first because that's who the AI they called Cassandra told them to. According to all accounts, Carlos had once been a self-indulgent man, only recently trying to live up to his role as de facto head of the colony centered on Camelot Island, but he was the closest thing to a leader they had.

The radio crackled. Nasal voice. "Come on, Cadzie. Spill. What's the big secret?"

"Not this time. This one is for Aaron." He had to see Aaron Tragon, and see him directly. The notion of talking to the man who had murdered his grandfather always tightened his stomach, but there was nothing to be done about it.

Horseshoe Dam was designed along the same basic lines as the one at Earth's Niagara Falls in the northeastern United States, but about half the size and capacity. Cassandra and the Earthborn who had been to Niagara said so; the Starborn didn't care.

Cadzie had observed every step in its construction, and it was an awe-inspiring sight. Ten thousand tons of crushed rock rendered to concrete poured over a steel frame, the steel smelted from iron ore dug out of the Snowcone Mountains a hundred and fifty miles northeast. It had taken ten years to build it, but within months it would come online for the very first time.

And its power would be the heart of the mainland colony, once it rooted fully and began to spread its tendrils. All the power they would need for a generation without functional Minerva engines or any of the slowly failing fusion systems. It was a major step toward independence from nuclear technology with minimum effects on the Avalon ecology, and had been agreed to by nearly everyone.

He buzzed Horseshoe, and then settled down onto the X-marked landing pad, just south of the roaring, churning maelstrom of the falls.

The sun had crested the eastern horizon less than an hour ago, but the mini-colony was already alive. A real contrast with Surf's Up, where it was unusual to hear a human voice much before noon.

A dark-haired, light-skinned man a year or two younger than Cadzie came out of the ops shack, and began tethering the autogyro without being asked.

Cadzie got out to assist. "Where's Joan?"

The Starborn, a bulky tech-head nicknamed "Toad," helped him down from the Skeeter. Cadzie could never remember the real name. Martin? Marvin? His last name was Stolzi. He possessed a broad, rubbery frame that was deceptively athletic: he could dog-paddle for hours. In addition to being a jack-of-all-technical-trades, Marvin was certainly the best Minerva—astronautic—pilot still active, and probably would soon be the only one. Few born on Avalon had much interest in going to space. It used too many resources, and there was too much to do here below.

Stolzi was the exception. "Toad" popped up anywhere in the colony there was an interesting problem to solve, but he had never lost his sense of wonder about space. Probably inherited it, Cadzie thought.

Toad jerked his thumb toward the top of the concrete tower a hundred meters north. "She's in the control room." Nasal voice: the guy on the call.

Cadzie started the long climb up the concrete steps. One day, they'd have an elevator, but no hurries; they didn't need elevators for those born on Avalon, and they didn't need Earthborn in their power room. This project was all Starborn; no Earthborn had participated in it. Cadzie felt a twinge of pride as he viewed the Kong-size curved concrete wall.

We built this! Of course, his part in the project had mostly been designing its sewage works. But that was a vital activity even if no one else wanted to do it,

The tonnage of water cascading across the dam's lip was an ear-numbing thunderstorm. He climbed scaffolding and steps slashed into the cliff face until he reached a steel door leading him into the rock itself. The air within was moist, bracing, prickled his skin. Echoes shivered the air, the rock walls were slimed with condensation.

He climbed two flights to reach the control room overlooking the waterfall. The woman engaged with the main control panel was tall and broad-shouldered, a golden mixture of Aaron Tragon's Nordic genes and something more Mediterranean. Sun-bronzed, she moved with what Little Shaka had once referred to as "an explosive delicacy." She was Joan Tragon, and since her childhood they had never encountered each other without tension.

A hearing board had ruled Aaron "Not at Fault" in Cadmann Weyland's death, and the colony accepted that in a vote that wasn't even close, a vote in which Cadzie had been far too young to cast a ballot. All the same, Aaron was responsible for Cadmann's death. Cadzie had never been able to put aside the fact that jolly Joanie was the killer's daughter.

When she turned, her emerald eyes narrowed. Joan had been one of the regulars hanging around Cadmann's Bluff as a child, greedily devouring Sylvia's wisdom or Mary Ann's ice-cactus cookies. So familiar she was almost a stepsister. But despite his two grandmothers' urging to forgive her parentage, he had never fully warmed to her. As a natural consequence Joan was equally wary of him.

The well had been poisoned. "Cadzie. Hello." She handed him a hard hat. "Put this on. I'm surprised they let you come up without one. A rule, here."

Cadzie examined the helmet sourly. Joanie was wearing one like it, but painted silver. The one she had handed him was white. They were both made of well-dried bamboozle, a native plant homologous to bamboo, and if he'd been feeling generous he would have congratulated her on the workmanship. "Whose rule?"

"Ours. We built the dam, we make the rules."

"I suppose." The headband inside was adjustable,

made of some kind of leather. It fit well enough when he tried it on.

"Now, what brings you to my little neck of the world?"

There was no point in starting a dispute over whose dam it was. Actually, Cadzie thought, we probably wouldn't have it if she hadn't done most of the bossing, as well as wheedling for materials. Nobody else had wanted it built as badly as she had.

"Have to talk to your dad." That last word soured his tongue.

She frowned slightly. "What about?"

"It's important," he said, then added, warmed by an admittedly childish spark of satisfaction, "and private."

She rolled her shoulders, flexing a lot of very useful, agile muscle. He had refereed one of her challenge matches, and pound for pound she could take all the women and probably eighty percent of Avalon's men.

"Tell me, I'll tell him."

"Not this time. Rules. Where is he?"

She made some kind of small adjustment on the panel. "Last ping he was on the plain, maybe thirty klicks from here. Won't tell me, huh?"

"No . . . but there are no rules that say you can't be there when I tell him." Why bother frustrating her curiosity?

It wasn't Joanie's fault that her father had gotten away with murder. "Want to come along?"

Her glare was all the reply he needed. Of course, Cadzie thought. She won't even tell me where he is unless she can come along. Couldn't blame her, really. And it wouldn't be a bad idea to turn the cameras on, either.

✦ CHAPTER 3 ✦
AARON

For a moment, as she was getting into the passenger seat, Cadzie was tempted to make Joanie trade her hard hat for a leather flying helmet, but that would have been childish.

Satisfying, though.

The flying helmets weren't really all that practical, and much of the time were stashed unworn beneath the seat. Instead, he asked, "Who made the hard hats, anyway?"

"Toad, of course. I think Evie Queen helped."

"Good workmanship." He rapped his knuckles against it. "Carlos has a couple, but they're hard plastic."

"Sure. That's the model for these. We thought we needed some, but we don't have much plastic fabrication, so Toad made them out of bamboozle. Works pretty good."

"Oh." Cadzie started the motors, checked the battery power levels. "Charged up pretty well. Good local power. Uh—where'd Uncle Carlos get his?"

She grinned enthusiastically. "High wattage chargers. Power from the Minervas. And he printed his, back before the grendels wrecked the 3D printers."

"Oh. Yeah. I should have thought of that." Lots of stuff like that, finely crafted plastic. He sometimes wondered what it must have been like when you could just print yourself a copy of—well, to hear Unka Carlos tell it, damn near anything. One day they'd have that capability again, but just now they couldn't even make a lot of raw plastics. He'd been told why, but he hadn't listened very hard. No point in studying problems you couldn't do anything about. "Stand by. Here we go."

The two-seated electric blue autogyro flashed over the fifty klicks between the dam and the eastern edge of Zack's Plain in a little over twenty minutes. Joan and Cadzie could see the skeletal clamshell of the containment cage even from two kilometers out, bars of steel and bamboozle arced over a concrete pond. And within it, human shapes: first one and then another. Five humans. And . . . one grendel.

Blue Three settled to the ground.

His stomach clenched as he stepped down. Cadzie had seen pictures of Aaron Tragon in his prime, of course: a blond Tarzan. But the colony's original rebel was scarred now, blind in his left eye from an Avalon "bee" on speed, the same creatures that had killed Cadzie's parents. Without the shelter of a blue blanket, Cadzie would have been rendered to bones as well. Most considered Aaron half-crazed. Only another nutcase would consider a long-time obsession anything but madness.

And madness, he supposed, was its own special chamber of hell.

"Bamboozle" (or sometimes "shamboo") were grasses

native to the highlands, flexible when green and hard as iron when dry. The giant cage with shamboo bars surrounded an artificial pond, and there in that place, Aaron and his acolytes were doing something that no one believed could be done: they were taming grendels.

Cadzie had seen vids of lion tamers in circuses on Earth, and been thrilled at the images of mighty predators leaping through fiery hoops and holding their mouths wide to receive a trusting head. But watching Aaron and his acolytes attempting something even vaguely similar with five meters of demireptile was disturbing.

The grendel squatted, warily, a quarter-ton of coiled lethality. It snapped the bison meat out of the air so fast it seemed a magic trick. He noticed that at least one human being locked eyes with the creature at all times. And that the grendel wore a neck collar with a fist-sized metal pod just behind the curve of the skull.

It studied the humans with a predator's expert evaluation. Were they threat? Lunch? Tribe? Once it turned to snap at its female trainer, a short blond woman named Josie. Then it jerked back. Electric charge from a capacitor pod, he figured. Smart.

Aaron was always a shock to the senses: Scarred and crippled, face splotched with unblocked sun and wind-burned, with pale scars where uglier things had been frozen away. He crouched, eye to eye with the grendel. They stared at each other, for a long long moment . . . and then the grendel turned away, thick barbed tail thrashing. With a flourish, Aaron removed himself from the cage, and a sigh of relief was heard by all.

He embraced his daughter Joan warmly. Cadzie

noticed that her response was more restrained. Despite his scars and splotches, it was hard to think of Aaron being old enough to be Joan's father.

"How's Cerberus?" she asked.

The grendel's head snapped around when she spoke that name, and it cocked its head, regarding her with what might have been curiosity. Not exactly intelligence, but certainly awareness.

"Recognizing her name. She's learned some of what Kali knew, but Kali was brighter, I think. *She* found *me*. I do miss Old Grendel." Joanie lifted her cheek to be kissed. Only then did Aaron seem to notice her companion.

"A guest," Aaron said, and extended his hand.

"Cadzie."

"I hate that," he replied, and gave the proffered flat, hard hand a single up-and-down shake.

Aaron smiled lopsidedly, the only smile he had. "You love it. What brings you over here?"

"Maybe I just want to watch the show," Cadzie said, hoping that the nervousness he felt around grendels didn't show in his face. "Why the hell are you taking risks like this?"

"Do you like samlon?" Aaron asked.

"What? Well, yes, of course," Cadzie said.

"And what are samlon?"

"The juvenile form of grendels—oh."

"Easy to forget, isn't it? Back on the island, we farm samlon by caging some grendels as they grow to adolescence, let them lay and fertilize eggs, and kill them before they can kill us. Hard to be herders when you kill off your breeding stock every generation. Better to tame them. And the continent's big and there are grendels everywhere there's fresh water linked by streams. We have to live with them; don't you think it's a good idea to understand them better?" Aaron spoke in easy tones. Soothing. Almost hypnotic. His grendel-taming voice.

He's said all this a hundred times, Cadzie thought.

"Never thought much about it, Aaron."

"Why would you? Anyway, we had a little problem here a couple of days ago," Aaron replied.

"Problem? What kind?"

"Attack on one of our herds," Aaron said. He was speaking too casually, as if uncomfortable talking about it. "Three wild grendels using a pincer tactic. Killed two dogs and took a bison cow."

The implications of that was disturbing as hell. "That's . . . really strange," Cadmann replied. "They don't usually cooperate. Were they some of yours?"

"No," Joan said. "I heard about this. They seemed to act with forethought. We were lucky to kill them. Lucky it was only cattle, too."

Cadzie had a notion. "Do you mind if I take one of the corpses back with me?" When there was no response, he continued, "The Shakas will certainly be interested."

"If you wish," Aaron said. "What brings you out here?"

"News. Excessively big news."

The odd phrasing made Aaron pause. "And what would that be?"

"Someone's coming." Cadzie watched carefully. There always seemed something . . . dead behind Aaron's eye, almost like an alien peeking out from behind a human mask. Did he perhaps fancy himself part grendel?

"Coming where?"

"Here."

"To the mainland?"

"To Avalon."

Finally, the implication seemed to sink in.

"From . . . where?"

"Cassandra's not sure. Earth, we think."

"A ship? A starship?" And now for the first time, real emotion mobilized Aaron's scarred face. "How long have we known?"

"This morning. Cassandra called Carlos this morning, about dawn. He called me—"

"You? He called *you*?" Aaron's expression didn't change.

"Yes. Carlos tried to reach you, but you didn't answer. He wouldn't tell me over the air, so I had to go to his house, and then fly to the dam. Then I couldn't tell Joan because of your blasted protocols, but she was the only one who knew where you were. This is the first she's heard of it. You can get the rest from Cassandra."

"What is it?" Aaron asked.

"A *Geographic*-size object, rapid deceleration, probable destination co-orbit with *Geographic*, origin unknown. The path is toward Sol, but not directly. It's as if they started for a destination in our general direction, but somewhere along the line they changed course and headed for us. If you can get a better analysis out of Cassandra, go ahead and try. I can't."

"No wonder you look puzzled. What do—what does this presumed visitor say?"

"No communication detected. Cassandra assumes anything that big is manned, but she got no replies to messages. We've agreed to tell you before taking important actions, and—" He looked without much approval at the cages and other apparatus around him. "Carlos thinks doing anything more would be an important action. I assume you agree."

Aaron fiddled with his communicator. "Cassie?" he asked.

"*Yes, Aaron?*" Cadmann couldn't help noticing that Cassandra's voice for Aaron was lower (sexier?) than the one she used for him. He wondered what that said about Aaron.

"What do you know about this approaching mass?"

"It is as Cadmann the Second described. *Geographic*-sized, decelerating, and on a path projected to match orbits with *Geographic*. It presumably changed course at least once assuming it came from Sol. There is no other reasonable assumption."

"Artificial, then? Man-made?"

"The exact origin cannot be determined. Insufficient data."

"Widen your parameters," he said. "Make a guess."

"I prefer not to speculate about extrahuman intelligence, Aaron."

He frowned. "But it might be a starship?"

"That is certainly possible, Aaron."

"And we don't have communication with them?"

"Nothing to report at this time," Cassandra replied. And disengaged.

Aaron grunted. "Odd," he said.

Cadzie stepped into the breach. "By now Carlos will have informed the rest of Camelot. I see Joan is on the phone so I expect she's telling the other Starborn." Tragon's daughter had stepped away. Her wristband pulsed a dull red, and she chattered excitedly into the air. Those wristband pulses were the only thing that told you someone was talking to another human being, not merely babbling.

Aaron spoke, perhaps to Cadzie and perhaps to the air, "A ship from Earth. When did they leave?"

"We don't know?"

Aaron frowned. "Why not?"

Cadzie shifted uncomfortably. "We don't know. They're not answering."

Joan and Aaron exchanged quizzical expressions. "Isn't that strange?" Joan asked.

Aaron said, "I don't know. Maybe. Cassandra may. The old girl is creaking a bit, but I have no real reason to doubt her."

"Ummm..." Joan's discomfort was obvious. With what? Him? Her father? The notion of visitors? Or something else? He couldn't read her. She toed the dirt and stared off in the opposite direction.

"Do I?" Aaron asked. "Josie?" he called to his assistant. "Watch things here. I have something important to take care of."

With Aaron sitting in the jump seat behind Joanie, the autogyro's engine made angry sounds as it labored back to the dam. Some private words between Aaron and his daughter had triggered a dark expression, followed by silence. Their combined weight strained the aging skeeter's engines as they flew.

When they returned, she would not tell Cadzie what was going on, only that he needed to stay until dark, that there was something she wanted to show him. When he protested, she evaded direct answers by encouraging him to strip and repair the autogyro, offering him Toad and his assistants to dig in and clean the fuel lines.

Why was she so desperate to stall him? Why wouldn't she speak? Was she playing a little tit-for-tat? He'd made her wait, so she was making him wait? No . . . it seemed more purposeful than that. "Why are you trying to keep me here?"

She smiled with an odd, cool humor. "Oh, Cadzie. Maybe I've grown accustomed to your face."

"That's a relief." He and Joan could rarely be in the same room for five minutes without rubbing each other raw. "What is going on?"

The kids exchanged an expression. Collie Baxter said, "I think it's time." Baxter was a year younger than Joanie, and like most of the other NextGen, followed her lead.

"Time for what?"

"For you to meet some friends." Even among these, Collie had a reputation as a computer wizard. He was bigger than Cadzie, resembled a shaved bear, and his attitude was either truculent or . . . what? Guilty?

Mysterious, Cadzie thought. And more serious than playful.

They led Cadzie and Aaron back to the dam, up through the back entrance and the spiral staircase. And from there to the observation booth. "What do you see?" Joan asked.

"Horseshoe Falls? The dam? Oh, hey!" An arc of ruby torpedoes flashed out of the water below the dam. They rose like rockets, keeping formation, over the rim of the dam and into the water upstream.

Joan snapped, "No, not just the speedfish!" She handed him a fat pair of night-vision goggles.

"That's only the second time I've ever seen speedfish. Wow, they went right over the dam!"

He fiddled with the lens rocker, and now, finally saw something unexpected. Squid-shapes, crawling up the dam's sloping wall. "What in the hell are *those*?"

Aaron's single eye stared. Then he began to curse under his breath.

Joan's lips twisted with a sheepish, lopsided grin. "We call them cthulhus."

"Lovecraft? As in 'In his house at R'lyeh, dead Cthulhu waits dreaming'?"

"We . . . um . . ." Joan cleared her throat. "Among the Starborn, we call the dam R'lyeh. Just among us."

Aaron bit the word, "Cute."

"When we first built the dam, it seemed to interfere with their ability to travel upstream . . . we thought there must be a spawning ground up there, but now we know they only breed in brackish water, so we really don't know why they want to go up this stream. They really want to, though. Just watch."

Cadzie brought up his phone. "Cassandra, what am I looking at?"

"No formal name. Called cthulhus by the Starborn.

Aquatic animals who breed in brackish water. First observed fifteen years ago."

"They are using tools. What other tool-using activities do we know of?"

There was a noticeable pause. "Very few," Cassandra replied in her never-changing voice.

"Have they been studied?"

"Ask Joan. I can't tell you," Cassandra said.

"What do you mean you can't tell me?" Cadzie demanded. "You know who I am!"

"I have no knowledge to give you," Cassandra said.

"That's the weirdest conversation I ever had with Cassie," he told Joan. "You heard?"

She frowned, a troubled expression. Or perhaps one of exasperation. Cadzie couldn't tell. "I heard."

She didn't say anything else, and that was even more puzzling. He lifted the night glasses and looked more carefully. The creatures were big; maybe two meters long, but they could reach much farther. There was a gap where the ladder of the steps was replaced by smooth concrete. And . . . were they carrying something?

As he watched open-mouthed, one of the squids extended a rigid pole of some kind (what was that? Bamboozle?) across a gap too wide for its sinuous arms to bridge, and then shimmied across, rather like an ape with more arms than a statue of Kali.

"Holy cow," he heard himself mutter. "Those things are *smart*."

Aaron snarled. "How could I not know this? Joanie? I knew the cthulhus were here, but—tool users? Fifteen years you hid this!"

"Yes, they are smart." She ignored her father. "We estimate them to be as smart as chimpanzees. Maybe dolphins, but with better tool-using."

"What the hell?" Cadmann watched them again. The pole-user looked as if it was chewing the far end of the bamboozle, and when it finished it climbed onward, and the next creature in line began the climb. The chewing action seemed to have fixed it in place. Regurgitating some kind of adhesive substance, perhaps? Something else?

He sat down, hard. "All right. What are we really looking at?"

"They communicate across a greater harmonic spectrum than dolphins, with what seem to be more discreet data packets, apparent repetition of words and phrases." Joanie's voice was flat.

"They have *language*?" He felt like the bottom had dropped out of his stomach.

"We think so, yes. It's more complicated than the dolphin signals, so we're confident that it is some form of communication."

Her voice had been—formal, as if she'd been lecturing to a class. Cadzie waited a moment, but when it was clear that Joanie wasn't going to say anything else, he spoke into his phone. "Cassandra. Tool-using creatures that resemble squid. Short summary. What do we know about them?"

"I have no knowledge to give you."

"Cassandra. Do you mean you don't know, or that you can't tell me what you know?"

"I have no knowledge to give you."

The room spun, and he felt as if he wanted to puke. He turned to Joan, fighting the urge to tense his fingers into claws. "How long have you known about them? I mean, wow. You just discovered them, right? That's why Cassandra doesn't know. This is *huge*."

Collie looked sheepish. "Ummm . . . no. We've known about them for, ah . . . fifteen years."

"I've known they existed for more than sixteen years," Aaron said. "Maybe a bit more. Nobody ever told me there was any reason to learn more about them." He looked quizzically at Joanie. "Apparently there was?"

"What the hell! You just found out they were intelligent though, right?"

"Ah . . . no." She couldn't meet his eyes. "We've known that, since we first found them. You got there late that night, Aaron."

Cadmann stared at her, disbelieving. There *had* to be a silver lining to this cloud, but he was having trouble finding it. "Are they . . . herbivores?" *Pretty please*.

"Ah . . . no."

Cadzie chewed his lip. "Are they at least aquatic . . . no, obviously they're amphib." What a mess. "Christ. I don't believe this. All right. Tell me, please, that they've never hurt a human being."

Joan looked away. "I can't say that, either."

"What? Who? When?"

"Jennifer? Tell him."

Cadzie had barely noticed when the older woman entered. Jennifer Sharpton was one of the first Starborn, Aaron's age, wearing a shapeless muumuu over a thin muscular frame. She'd been one of the den mothers when Cadzie had been a Grendel Scout. What was she doing over here on the mainland? At the dam?

"It was sixteen years ago," Jennifer said slowly. "We lost Archie. My boyfriend. The cthulhus killed him at Surf's Up. Aaron was there."

Aaron gave a long, slow lizard blink. Somehow, Cadzie found his confusion comforting. "Long time ago. But yes, cthulhus killed Archie because he had a grendel painted on his board. Haven't thought about it in a long time."

"Archie's surfboard had grendels painted on both sides," Jennifer said. "Not the smartest thing to do, but at the time we thought it was . . . cool. Wild grendel sightings are fewer here than in waterways not used by cthulhus. We figure this means cthulhus and grendels are natural enemies from way back."

"So you kept them around like . . . pets? Like dogs or something?"

"More like dolphins, I think. We try not to annoy them, but there are often dolphins and cthulhus hanging around the fence that keeps the dolphins in the bay. Anyway they're pretty much smarter than dogs. How much smarter, we don't know."

"These things killed your boyfriend, and you're okay with that?" Cadzie asked.

"I wasn't at first. But it wasn't their fault! It was that grendel image! I had to accept that. A mistake. And the hurt just . . . faded."

It was possible. Perhaps these creatures were not only smart, but hated grendels as much as he did. *The enemy of my enemy is . . . But why don't I know this already?* "Aaron, did you know all this?"

"Never asked," Aaron said. "Jennifer told you true. Archie had grendels painted on either side of his board.

Made me twitch. Cost me a board race. Must have driven the cthulhus nuts. That's why there's a rule about not having grendel images unless it's a party of two and both are armed."

"Only nobody plays with grendel images," Jennifer said. "Not any more."

Cadzie frowned. "When did this happen?"

Aaron laughed. "I don't know, about the time you and Joanie learned to read, I guess. I was about your age, I remember that. It was a beach party. Your mother might have been with us, can't remember. Before she was married, yeah, I think she was." His eyes narrowed slyly. "Hey, I might have been your father, well, the father of her kid. Wouldn't have been you, of course. We weren't very careful then."

Cadzie suppressed a flash of anger. They weren't all that careful *now*. If a couple wasn't ready to go over the falls, there were as always people who were ready, willing and able to raise babies. Cadzie's grandmothers had certainly been eager. "So you didn't tell anyone."

Aaron's mouth tightened. "Of course we did. They'd killed Archie! Couldn't tell your father that. So we mentioned that there were some big squiddy things around Blackship, be careful where you swim. No big deal."

Jennifer said, "They're intelligent, and they belong on this planet. Belong more than we do! And my dad and your grandfather would have exterminated them, just as they did grendels on the island. I loved Archie, and he wouldn't have wanted that. The Earthborn would have killed them all. All of them! So we didn't tell anyone."

Silence followed that statement, and lasted a long

painful moment. "You understand, don't you?" Joan asked. For the first time since her childhood, vulnerability had crept into her voice.

Aaron said. "Seemed like the right thing to do. I never learned they use tools. And now you say they talk to each other? Why don't I know this?"

"Yes. How did you keep this secret?" Cadzie tried to keep his voice calm, but wasn't entirely successful.

"We just made it forbidden information for anyone but the inner circle of the Starborn," Jennifer said. Aaron snorted. "*Some* of the Starborn. It's a graduation secret for the highest level Grendel Scouts like Joan. Our greatest secret. Those who don't reach the top rank never find out."

"I was a Grendel Scout leader," Cadzie said calmly.

"Yes, and you're Cadmann Weyland's grandson," Jennifer said with equal calm. "And you don't keep any secrets from Carlos and you never will. Carlos and your father hunted down every adult grendel on the island. Every one of them."

"And . . . why are you telling me now?"

Joan said, very slowly, "We didn't want to."

"That's why I'm here," Jennifer said. "Joan called me and I flew over. I'm in charge of keeping this secret. Always have been."

Cadzie looked completely puzzled. "So?"

"Because we think it might be connected with the visitors," Joan said.

"The visitors . . . how in the hell . . ." Then, comprehension dawned. "You think that there *are* no visitors. Because they haven't communicated."

"Yes."

Cadzie thought fast. "Then you think that Cassandra is making an error. A pretty damned big one."

"Well, she might."

"And you think she's making that error because . . ." Suddenly he understood. "Because you told her to lie. She knows about the cthulhus, doesn't she? Of course she does."

Joan seemed to flinch. "It would have been hard to keep it from her."

Cadzie frowned. "And she was acting strange when I talked to her about them." As the implications sank in, he felt his throat tighten. Hoarsely, he asked, "How did you do it?"

"It was gradual," Jennifer said. "It got more complicated after a while."

Joanie said. "Cassandra's firewalls are a joke. Hacking her was the best game we had, and our parents never noticed. Later we added a board to her primary preferences. She knows things she won't tell anyone but those with the key passwords. It didn't take much, she just doesn't respond to questions about intelligent nonhumans. As you just found out."

Now he was reeling. "Oh my god. Do you have any idea how much damage you may have done?"

"I'm starting to wonder, yes." A little-girl's voice.

"I have to tell Camelot. They need to know. Carlos needs to know now."

"Cadzie." Desperation was creeping into her voice. "I trusted you. I've betrayed a secret that will probably get me expelled from Surf's Up. I may not be forgiven. You have to give me something."

"What?"

"Let me tell Surf's Up first. Dad will help me. Give me that much."

He paused, thinking. How much of an emergency was this? Aaron made his skin crawl, and Joan wasn't a lot better, but . . . "Aaron?"

"Two days," Aaron said.

Cadzie looked thoughtful, then nodded slowly. "All right. Landing Day is day after tomorrow. You talk to Zack and Carlos about the cthulhus then. And you and Jennifer explain to the council exactly what you did to Cassandra and why you did it. Maybe they'll decide not to share that information with the general colony. I don't know."

He looked through the binoculars again. Two last man-sized squid-shapes were crawling over the lip of the dam.

"Cadzie. Please. You don't understand." She gripped his shoulder. He stared at her hand until she dropped it.

"Help me," he said. "Make me understand."

"Our grandparents wanted this," she said. "Needed this. Wanted their own world. And got it. We . . . *you* . . . never asked for this. Just found that our parents had made the decision for you. Talked about Earth as 'home' while making sure you knew there was no way back."

"So?"

"So Earth isn't ours. And Avalon isn't ours. Your parents make it clear to us every chance they get that *they* are the heroes of Avalon. They pretend to know everything, decide everything, control everything."

"You wanted something that was yours."

For the first time since her childhood, he watched her

eyes water. "Yes. You . . . you're almost one of us. Can't you understand?"

"I understand," he replied. "I understand that you may have done more damage than you can possibly realize. But you know more about computers and AI than I do! You know what interfering with the prime programming can do, and you did that. Is anything Cassandra tells us reliable?"

"We got through the mainland wars all right," Jennifer said. "Cassandra was very reliable, and the new boards were already in place then."

"She didn't warn you about the bees, did she, Aaron?"

Aaron glared. Jennifer said, "Cadzie, Cassandra's all right, she just can't tell some people anything about nonhuman intelligence."

"Such as an approaching spacecraft?"

"Well, that might cause a conflicting orders dilemma because of all these requirements about who to tell this or not tell that. That's how you got in the loop. By agreement, Carlos couldn't tell you before he told Aaron. Carlos resolved that by getting you to act as messenger, no big deal, but Cassandra can't resolve conflicting orders that easily. Especially if one of the conflicts is in the prime programming." Jennifer spoke with a confidence Cadzie didn't think she had. "Cassandra is reliable. Really. Look, we won the mainland wars without any of this coming out."

Tears made Joanie's blue eyes shimmer. "Cadzie, please. Wait until Landing Day."

Cadzie sighed. If he admitted no empathy for her position, he'd be lying. "Fine. Fine. You have your two days."

"Good choice," Aaron muttered.

The school was together again, assembled on the high side of the dam. The water tasted too fresh: they would need brackish, too soon. The voices of the dam roared, drowning out thought. Roar of water, roar of magnetic flow.

The dam's magnetic voice was deep inside its structure. The school could not penetrate, not even from here, not even by diving deep underwater. Whast could make out nothing of the dam's thoughts, no matter how hard he listened.

What was this thing that the walkers had built?

Magnetic force was the essence of thought. The dipole in Whast's belly amplified his voice, joined him to the school. What was being amplified by this thrumming thought, inside this immense curved stone wall? Whast could only wonder, like the rest: What were the walkers trying to say?

◆ CHAPTER 4 ◆
AWAKENING

Narrator Marco Shantel came alive in stages. First tactile: he was lying on something metallic and cold. Then auditory: a low hum. Whispered human voices. The sound of his own breathing. Then finally visual as he opened his eyes. For a moment he wondered if he was on a movie set. That would have made sense, would have matched a life he knew quite well. Then he realized he was a trillion miles from Hollywood, on the colony ship *Messenger*, on its way to fulfill destiny.

Then he lapsed from consciousness again, as if it had taken all his strength just to absorb his surroundings: the line of recessed lights along the white-tiled ceiling was the last thing he knew before blackness. This time his descent was shallow, and he swam back to the surface quickly, to see the warm, lovely face of Evelyn Welsh, a medic he recognized. She was waiting for him patiently, and he smelled something: protein broth. Not chicken, not beef. Like liquid shawarma, a blend for optimal nutrition and taste, and his taste buds awakened with a vengeance.

She helped him sit up, and slipped the first spoonful between his lips. He thought he was passing out again, but held on for another sip. "Coffee," he whispered. "Feels like I need coffee, Evelyn. A double mocha latte, please?" He'd only met her briefly on Earth, and found her unremarkable. But Evelyn was the first human female he'd seen in frozen decades, and some parts of his body were perking up faster than others. Her short black hair and heart-shaped face were suddenly angelic. He grinned toothily, applying a little of his wattage. With any luck he'd be laid within the next couple of hours.

"Not yet," an unfamiliar voice said. "No stimulants. Just try to focus. You've been asleep for eighty years and a bit. And call me Major Stype. I will supervise your recovery, sir. Evelyn will continue as nurse."

Who was that? He wondered if she'd been in the interviews that got him selected to go with *Messenger*. There had been a half dozen, maybe more. But they were only voices from a computer, and he couldn't be sure.

"What are we doing now, Major?" He listened with his body. One gravity, he thought: it felt like Earth, except for a sort of pulse he could feel in the floor. He knew that pulse from before they put him to sleep. He was still aboard the starship *Messenger*, and *Messenger* was under thrust.

"We're decelerating," Major Stype said. "Less than two months before we—well, I'm not sure what the captain has in mind. Things have turned a little weird."

"Weird? A story I can tell?" Coming alive: *the* Marco Shantel, actor turned interstellar astronaut. "Narrator" for the documentary that would tell future generations of this great adventure. He couldn't see a mirror. He wondered what he looked like, how much muscle mass he had lost.

"You tell me, Narrator Shantel. We were observing a world we're sure is Avalon. Looking for intelligent life. Trying to contact *Geographic*'s computer. We found a big island that matches the description of Camelot in those early—were you awake when the first messages came through from Tau Ceti?"

Avalon? Avalon? That was where the ship *Geographic* was heading. Their own destination, Hypereden, had been light-years distant. His mind rebelled. Was he hallucinating?

"Frozen like a rock," Marco said. Better think of himself as Narrator Shantel. Act like the star he had been. Godsons liked their celebrities. They also liked their leaders strong and certain. This was no time to show doubt. "When I went to sleep, I don't think Avalon was where we were going."

"It wasn't then. It is now, and you'll learn why another time."

"But—Don't I have to tell the story?"

"We haven't decided what story you'll tell."

"Oh."

"Oh, indeed, Narrator Shantel."

"Avalon—the *Geographic* expedition." His voice made it a question.

Major Stype came into view. Deeply tanned Mediterranean skin, with a face that would have been lovely if not so stern. Piercing eyes. Well-fitting one-piece coverall, officer insignia. Middle-aged—if she'd been one of those selection committee voices, she'd been in cold sleep just like him. "How long have I been out?"

"Nearly eighty years."

"You, too, then? Because I think I met you."

"You did. Briefly. Surprised you remember." Her smile was frozen. "Their plan was to find an island and make first landing there. They did that. Camelot is about the size of both New Zealands. The continent is not far, ninety miles or so, and they should be colonizing that too by now, so we looked."

Narrator smiled at her. She didn't smile back. Might take an extra hour, he thought. He said, "Pregnant pause? You know, we'll be cutting this into my record."

She smiled now. "You've really got your work cut out for you. Eighty years of cameras all over the ship. You'll have to view all of that, and pick and choose what goes into the log. Take you years."

"Take me a lifetime. I'm vidding for posterity, for an eternity of schoolkids. What's happening now, Major Stype?"

"There's a veldt. A million square miles of it. The green lines in the spectrum aren't quite chlorophyll. Infrared suggests it's grass and some tree clumps, little forests. Someone has been writing on it in really big letters."

Finally, a message from God? Marco didn't say that. He'd get reported, or slapped. "Writing on the veldt?"

"Just on the grass. Whatever it is avoids the trees."

"What does it say?"

"We can't read it. The letters are cursive, all linked up with almost no breaks. We're not even sure it's writing, but that's what it looks like. No human language, except that there's one little stretch that's in English."

"What's it say? For God's sake, Major!"

"It's in script, no breaks. It says, 'Ice on my mind.'"

The narrator didn't have to ask what that meant. He'd just come out of cold sleep, and with his mind intact, as far as he could tell. But that phrase had terrified him when he went to sleep.

"You may thank God we solved that problem," Major Stype said.

"Ah. It's probably an obscenity, for them, the ones down there. So you woke me with a mystery, Major? Good. What else?"

She laughed. "Hah!" Her expression hardly changed as she continued, "We got through to *Geographic*. Well, to an AI that calls itself Cassandra. An AI, built in the old days without a lot of the safeguards we put in now. And still in orbit, not down on the planet. Think about that. Still in orbit. Older AI. The chief engineer is going over the Cassandra plans now, and chuckling half the time."

"Chuckling?" Humor? Just what kind of story was this? The major, or monitor, or whatever she was laughed again, but not much; something worrying her.

"Chuckling," Major Stype said. "We learned a lot about AI after *Geographic* launched. Maybe the First Speaker should have eased into that conversation. The first thing he asked about was the writing on the veldt. Do they have intelligent aliens? Cassandra broke off. Sudden silence. That was three days ago, and we can't get a peep out of Cassandra since."

"Why would it do that—just shut up. Ignoring us?"

"That's one explanation. Paranoia's another. Maybe it's making sure we don't learn any more about Avalon."

"But—but—"

"You may not recall, Narrator, but the *Geographic* trustees made it very clear that they wanted no Godsons aboard, nor did they need our help."

"I recall, Major." He tried Smile Number Three, the one he used in fashion shoots rather than on the screen. It was authoritative, but vulnerable. "Which is why I am astonished that we are headed to their planet. I assume there is a reason?"

"Not your problem just now. You'll learn more when you're fully awake." She was all business. This one wouldn't be seduced, not here, and not by him.

But the nurse was still promising. Later, perhaps. Business now.

Marco's brow furrowed as he went into planning mode. He'd start there, stock footage of *Messenger* under thrust, then the telescope footage. Avalon, then closer, then the veldt. Then backflash. He had plenty of footage during the two years leading up to takeoff. Cut that a lot. Some tracks from the pacing ships, then it would be all stock from outside.

Prechildren loading, ten thousand fertilized eggs at a time. Then frozen crew . . .

Major Stype was watching him, the tip of a pink tongue touching the middle of her upper lip. She liked watching his concentration. It earned her respect . . . and a little more.

Good. Back to two hours again. Less, if he was lucky. "Major? When can I get to work?"

◆CHAPTER 5◆
BACKGROUNDS

"Hand me that grippy, Jason." Carlos tightened the clamp on his workbench's plasma cutter. Vibration shivered the housing, making the very precise alignments necessary for tool construction more difficult to achieve. Jason Tuinukuafe, the big beefy kid who was the younger of the Samoan Twins, wheeled the all-purpose calibrating solderer over and locked it down so that Carlos could work his magic. It looked like a short-armed steel octopus.

He'd heard from Cadzie that skeeter "Blue" Three gave him the willies on the way to the mainland. While skeeters made water landings just fine, it was still disturbing.

Twyla staggered yawning into the shop from their bedroom in the adjoining house at the foot of Mucking Great Mountain. He hated to admit it, but much of the current attraction in a bedmate was simple companionship, feeling a warm body nearby. *Madre Dios*, he had certainly never expected that change. For others, perhaps, but not Carlos Garcia.

As the saying goes, time wounds all heels.

Twyla was a sweet lady, physician and chief psychologist who thought herself a mix of Irish and Cherokee, but couldn't be certain. Her long black hair had lovely white streaks now. They suited her. She kissed his cheek, scenting of cinnamon. "Morning. Coffee?"

"Had mine," he said.

"Surprised to find you boys out here so early, Jaxon."

"I'm Jason," the Samoan replied.

"Of course you are." She massaged Carlos' shoulders, her fingers digging into knots of tension. "You're tight," she said. "What's the urgency?"

"We've got problems, but thank goodness Camelot is isolated, and safe."

"Problems," she repeated. "I thought you said we couldn't undo our biggest problem."

"The printer, yes. That was a real disaster."

"Come on," Jason wiped a meaty forearm across his brow. It was summer on Camelot, and mornings got humid early. "That was a long time ago. Tricky for a while, but we make just about everything we consume now. What was the big deal?"

Carlos sighed. "We didn't like what we saw happening on Earth. Things had gotten too easy, for too many of us. There was a breakdown of ambition and drive . . . and fabricators were a part of that. You could just 'print' anything you wanted. Sand was a perfect starting material for much of it. We were impossibly wealthy, and getting soft."

She took another sip, and grinned at him over the rim of her cup. "I know you don't want to hear this, but you didn't used to think like that."

"Is that right?"

"Oh, it's right. Cadmann did, though."

Carlos winced. She might have been reading his mind. "Fair enough. I . . ."

"What?"

Carlos sighed. Why was it so hard to say this out loud? "I miss him so much. I didn't know him very long. All totaled up, what? Twenty years of real time? But he's haunted me for forty. He saved us. And I find myself thinking 'what would Cadmann do?' Not often, just ten times a day or so. I watch Cadzie, wondering whether or when he'll start showing the same strength."

"And?"

"He's a good kid. Strong, smart. But it isn't fair to ask him to be his grandfather."

Jason doffed his goggles. Pale circles marked where the lenses had protected his face from grinder dust. "It's not fair not to let him be. Are you worried? About the machines?"

"You tell me."

"Well . . ." Jason was a big man, brown, stocky, with intense dark eyes. He was Second Gen, like Cadzie, two minutes younger than his brother Jaxon. Both twins were brilliant, but in different fields. He believed they were polymaths who enjoyed confusing people: only they could tell each other apart. "We're down to one Minerva. We can't make any more repairs. When it's dead, we're done with space travel for generations. We'll never get to *Geographic* again."

Carlos cursed. "I know the skeeters are in repair . . ."

"Thank goodness," Jason said. "Yeah, we can repair the

skeeters, and most of the farm machinery . . . and our forges can actually produce many new parts. But we've used two skeeters as hangar queens, sources of spare parts, and it looks like we'll have to take another one out of service. Just like the Minervas, only we're down to it now, we only have three; last week I had to use the last of the minithruster controls from Number Two to get Three reliable. One and Two are decent power sources, but they'll never fly again. Hell, why am I telling you this? You told me to do it that way."

"Well, I told you to do what you have to do to make Three reliable."

"And I did."

"Okay, okay, so now where's the biggest problem?"

"Getting Cassandra down while we still can."

"Yeah," Carlos said. "I know. Toad will go up and get her now we have a working Minerva. Other than that, I mean."

"Microprocessors," Jason replied without hesitation. "The thrust controllers are big special chips. We're not even close to being able to manufacture them."

"How far are we?"

Jason seemed to mull the question. "If we went all-out, we might do it in two generations. Doubtful even then. It means putting a lot of effort into making the machines that make the machines." Carlos had certainly heard *that* before. Cassandra had warned them. Hell, he'd thought it himself just a minute ago. "And frankly . . ." Jason continued, "nobody is pushing that hard. It could be four generations, or never."

"Never?"

"Never," Jason said. "Look. The original plan for this colony was that we would get here, find an island, secure it, and then explore the mainland for resources. Breed."

"My favorite part." Twyla hip-checked him, secure in her knowledge that she was the sexiest grandmother on the planet.

A knocking at the door, followed by a creak. The smiling face of the colony's first mayor appeared, followed more slowly by the rest of his rather ungainly body. Again, time. "Hi, Zack. Alone?"

"It's just me. Rachel sends her regrets. She didn't feel up to it."

"A lot of us First Gen don't feel up to much," Carlos said. "Jason's telling us we have to get cracking or we'll never get back to space."

"Hello. Well, I was just saying. Didn't we plan to get the colony going, create a foundation for our children and then take *Geographic* onward to the stars? Camelot was supposed to be the beginning."

"And instead of that, it was very nearly the end," Zack said softly.

Carlos nodded gravely. "Very." He held up thumb and index fingers half an inch apart. "Those bastards came *that* close to wiping us out. Really wiping us out. We had thought it was safe here after we killed the adult grendels, and we brought down a great deal of stuff that we needed. A lot of embryos, too. Most of that, embryos and all, was destroyed when big samlon turned into little grendels. We were just one mistake away from extinction."

Jason nodded. "I think there is a memory of that . . . fear, self-satisfaction . . . something. Something got broken in all of us. If I wanted to talk genetics, I'd suspect that the bravest and most adventurous of the first generation died in the Grendel Wars."

"Leaving just us cowards?" Carlos grinned as he lifted a file.

"That's not what I meant. But I do mean that the most successful breeders were not necessarily the most genetically fit."

"Nature or nurture, right?" Carlos asked.

"Not a debate I'm diving into," Twyla said.

"Agreed," Carlos replied. "Let's just say that we've remained within the scope of our competence. Within the known. Which gives the kids the illusion that they are smarter and tougher than they really are."

"Hey!" Jason said. "We push them damned hard!"

Twyla rolled her eyes. "Right. We have Grendel Scout overnighters. And that's not bad. Probably the best we can do."

Carlos shook his head. "What would you want to do? Kill one in ten if they don't max their scores?"

Jason was giving that due consideration. "Maybe one in fifteen . . . hey, I'm kidding!"

Zack looked horrified. "We were almost defeated. But dammit, we won."

Carlos said, "Nah, I see. I do. We can't show them the truth, or push them hard enough, without being cruel. But we could never be crueler than reality."

"You sound like Cadmann again," Zack said.

"And with that, the conversation comes full circle. Wondering what the colonel would say."

"He'd say that if you wait long enough, something bad

will happen," Zack said. He went over to the cabinet and fished out a bottle of local wine, pouring himself a healthy drink.

That, Carlos knew, was their secret fear. That everything was breaking down, and that the kids just didn't understand the situation well enough to care. That the kids believed themselves to be more competent than they really were.

And that, down the road, might well be the end of everything.

◆ CHAPTER 6 ◆
TRUDY

Trudy woke slowly. First there were dreams, of freezing, of being chased on the ice by great white monsters, not polar bears but nightmare versions of those animals, red of fang and claw. With that thought consciousness returned.

She saw steel and aluminum. At first she thought she was in the vast training facility, the floating Godson island off Brazil where she had spent so many years preparing for this journey. It took long moments to realize she was in the ship. The ship hospital. That was strange.

"Gertrude. Gertrude Hendrickson." An unfamiliar voice, male and older than she.

"Yes, sir."

"I'm Doctor Mandel." A narrow, kind, but intense face. Wire-rimmed spectacles perched on an angular nose. "I expect you're wondering where you are."

"I know where I am, sir. I just don't know why."

"Oh. Astute of you. Yes, you're still on the ship. I expect you thought you wouldn't wake up until we'd orbited Hypereden."

"Something like that, sir." She felt strong vibrations. "But I feel gravity. We are still accelerating! We haven't got to our star! Why wake me now? There won't be any children."

"Huh? Oh. Yes we have. That's deceleration you feel. We're slowing fast to get into orbit around Tau Ceti IV. Yes, yes, that's a change of course. A lot has happened you don't know about yet. Anyway, we're going to Tau Ceti IV where the *Geographic* expedition went, and matching orbits with their ship in orbit there. I gather that's rather tricky piloting."

That took some processing. "Yes, sir. My thinking is slow. Sir?"

"Yes, Gertrude."

"I'm usually called Trudy. Sir, you seem very pleased. Weren't you expecting to see me wake up? Is that it? Something was wrong, and—"

"No, no, no. No! You're fine. Here, see." The doctor held a comm tablet at her eye level.

It was very hard to move, more like she'd forgotten how than that she was unable. A queer experience. *Sensory Motor Amnesia*. That was the term.

It took a while to focus on the tablet, then on the numbers. Body temperature, 34.44. Low. She remembered it should be 37. She also remembered that 34 wasn't fatally low, just unusual. As she watched the numbers changed. 34.45. Point 46. Climbing slowly but climbing. Pulse rate sixty. Fast for her, very fast for resting heart rate for anyone with her athletic training. Blood pressure, 115 / 75. Good. Arteries were still flexible. "Reasonable, given I was frozen," she said. "But I'm slurring my words." She saw her pulse rate rise even as she said it. Nerves, she thought.

"No problems. You've been asleep for eighty Earth years. Really, you're in fine shape. I wouldn't have let them wake you up in these facilities if you weren't. The Speaker asked for you. By name. I don't know why."

Speaker? But the doctor was cheerful, no stress in his voice. Trudy was trained to notice things like that, and she was sure. He wasn't worried about her. She was sure of that, too. They must not be waking many up. He was wondering why she was chosen. She tried to smile, just a little smile, enough to make him feel better. "Not to worry. I don't know why, either. Doctor, I'm confused. I don't know what a Speaker is."

"Oh. Of course you don't. Speaker Augustus speaks for the Prophet. He's First Speaker of the *Messenger* expedition, and that makes him chairman of the council."

"And the Prophet?"

"He's back asleep. He might not wake up, or whoever wakes up might not really be the Prophet. Hibernation instability. It's dangerous. One of the messages we got from the old Avalon colony had a lot about that. People waking up with half their mind gone."

He's serious, Trudy thought. "Should I be worried?"

"You? No. Not at all. We learned a lot from the Avalon broadcast. We have new wakeup techniques, much slower than we'd been using. And once awake, you stay awake. No going back to sleep."

"But you said the Prophet—"

"I did. It's a long story. Here, you lie back and rest, I'll tell it to you. Let me fluff that pillow." He checked the temperature readings in a tablet window. "Warming up nicely."

A lot of fuss, she thought. Nurse work, but he's a doctor. I don't know him. She smiled. "Thank you." She lay back, cooperatively, and concentrated on listening.

"It was the Prophet's original plan to sleep until we reached an inhabitable planet, so that he would be at his highest capability when he took charge." Trudy nodded, understanding perfectly. "But the captain went mad."

"Mad?"

"Oversimplification, but that's the short of it," Dr. Mandel said.

He was less nervous now, still worried but less so. Why was he worried about her? But it was obvious to her trained mind that he was.

"The council all agreed that the captain was no longer rational, but they were afraid to denounce him. So they woke up the Prophet. Against the master's orders, but they thought the crisis was both desperate and urgent, so they did it. They were right, too. The captain was changing course. We don't know what he thought he was doing. The Prophet deposed him a little too late."

"What did the master do to him?"

"Sent him into cold sleep, of course. He'll be awakened when it's safe. But one of the things we learned about hibernation instability is that the chances of a bad outcome are much greater the second time you wake, and exponentially higher every time after that."

He waited as that sank in. "So—" Trudy felt a thrill of horror. "So the Prophet didn't dare go back into cold sleep. He might wake up an idiot! That would—"

"That would be a disaster. So the Prophet stayed awake. Eventually he was tired. But he knew that was coming, and he prepared. He had a young cadet awakened, and trained him for forty years to be his Speaker."

"Speaker Augustus—"

"Actually, that's his name, not part of the title."

"Oh. Augustus. Glass? Gus Glass?"

"Yes. Did you know him?"

"Sort of. How long before I can get up?"

"I see. You did know him. Of course you won't say more." He paused for a moment to look at her bedside tablet. "Couple of hours, but you'll be in a wheelchair your first day. Get out of that and you can ask the Speaker himself. He's asked to see you when you're able. Here, time for more warm plasma. This will hurt just a little."

The ship's vibration continued. Almost soothing. There wouldn't be children, not on a ship about to go into orbit, so they wouldn't want her as a mother in a crèche.

"You're waking warriors up, aren't you? Sir."

"Yes."

"So that's what they want me for."

◆CHAPTER 7◆
LANDING DAY

Every year for the last four decades, Earthborn Carlos Martinez had put creases in his dress shirt and pants, shaved and combed his thinning white-streaked hair, and assumed as festive an air as he could manage in celebration of what they called Landing Day.

Landing Day was the hundred and fortieth day of Avalon's year, in the middle of Camelot's summer. Usually a fine day with crisp mornings and balmy afternoons, and today was no exception. Carlos thought the weather similar to spring in São Paulo, vacation times he still remembered fondly, still dreamed of on those festive occasions that drew homesteaders from across the island, as well as Second and Third Gens from the mainland.

Of the approximate twelve hundred human souls on the planet, over a thousand of them were right here, right now, in Camelot Town.

The mingled aromas of roasting pork, beef, Katmandu quasi-mollusks and farm-bred samlon made his mouth water as the grendel scouts demonstrated their shooting skills on stationary and rotating targets.

Some celebrated memories of distant Earth with cultural songs or dances. The Samoan Twins demonstrated a traditional Haka war dance, complete with blue tongues, and a rainbow-hued Riverdance team won appropriate (and slightly rote) applause. The mood grew more somber as they lauded the fallen and departed: the roll call of the dead since landing day. Some taken by violence, some by the prion plague twelve years past, some of natural causes, or ice on their minds. Two hundred and four souls in all, and every one of them a personal loss to Carlos.

Carlos' daughter Tracy was winding up her five-year stint as mayor, but still looked fresh and enthusiastic as she welcomed them to the gathering. "And here it is, our fortieth landing day celebration! Today we unveil a new mural—"

The beige curtain covering the recreation center's west walldropped to the ground, triggering *"ooh"*s and *"ahh"*s. Lunging grendels and heroic colonists challenged one another in profiled tableau. For the last two months Evie Queen and Jaxon Tuinukuafe had labored beneath a sheltering tarp to stoke the mystery. The final result was worth the wait, a blend of Polynesian ceramic mosaic and Italian Renaissance perspectives, Picasso-like abstracted human faces and exquisite shadow play.

Tracy's voice always conveyed a natural theatricality, she deliberately heightened that now with intense gestures and narrowed eyes. "Never had human beings faced such danger. Savage, carnivorous, aggressive, and faster than skeeters. But look at them now!"

To cheers and a few mocking catcalls, seven kids

between the ages of twelve and fourteen executed precise group-targeting maneuvers against holographic horrors.

Carlos glanced at Zack Moskowitz, whose snowfrosted Groucho mustache drooped unimpressed. "You don't like this?"

"Nope," Zack said. The colony's first elected mayor, and still leader emeritus, Zack rarely used, and never abused, that social capital. When he spoke, the colony listened. He whispered now, barely moving his lips. "And I know I'm being a spoilsport, but I still have nightmares." He paused, glancing at Carlos until he nodded *me, too.* "All this is just pretend. Pretend. They weren't some kind of toys, or games, or pets. They are not to be lampooned or played with. I don't even like farming the damned things. As far as I'm concerned, we should kill them to the last egg."

"You do eat them though."

The corners of Zack's mouth ticked up. Samlon were the best dish on the planet, flavorful and just a little *speedy*, like sushi with caffeinated wasabi. "It's the least I can do."

"Isn't that a contradiction?"

"I contain multitudes." He said it piously, but his smile broadened. Good. This was a time for celebration, remembrance of the sacrifice and struggle that had yielded security at last. "*Shhh.*"

After the demonstration and the speeches that followed Mayor Tracy took the stand again to make her comments. "And there is no better day for this next announcement. Daddy?"

Carlos hugged his eldest child and took the stand, smiling out at the sea of upturned faces. "Thank you.

Forty years ago today, we landed on this new world. At great cost, through days of toil and fear and nights of grief, we survived and conquered."

"Avalon threw everything she had, and couldn't break us!" Zack called up, leaning heavily on his slender shamboo cane. The Mayor Emeritus didn't get out and around much anymore, but had yet to miss a Landing Day.

"Grendels, bees, disease . . ."

The kids shuffled their feet, looked at each other instead of to the stage. Discomfort masquerading as boredom. Carlos repressed his urge to blurt out his news. "And other things dogged us. And one of the most terrifying was . . . loneliness."

"We've got plenty of people!" Rachel Moskowitz yelled. She leaned on a cane too, Carlos saw. He didn't need that support . . . yet. They were all getting older.

Better than the alternative, he supposed.

"Yes. But we've been alone with each other for forty years. When we left Earth, we thought others were coming. No one has followed. Not a single ship. We've heard nothing from home."

"This is home!" Jaxon called.

"What's the best theory for that?" Evie asked.

"Something wrong with our communications array. Grendel damage, that's the usual reason for things not to work. Some breakdown on Earth." A shrug. "We just don't know."

"Sucks," Little Shaka muttered, followed by grumbled agreement.

"Yes. But it's about to change. Perhaps." That quieted them. "Toad?" he asked.

The squat little man they called "Toad" took his place at the podium. Marvin half-closed his eyes, perhaps scanning mental notes. "Two days ago, at five thirteen central Avalon time, we received a message from Cassandra. A large object of artificial origins is heading on a course that will place it near *Geographic* in the same Avalon orbit. It is estimated to arrive in three months, and currently seems to be decelerating from what we estimate to have been at least two percent of light speed."

The announcement was followed by silence, wide eyes and not a few open mouths. Then a murmur. Sylvia Weyland seemed incredulous. "Best *Geographic* ever got was one point zero eighty two. That implies something. Is it . . . human?"

Toad cleared his throat uncomfortably. "When we ask Cassie, this is the only answer she gives: quote: 'I have no information to give you.' That phrasing is odd, to say the least. But no matter how we ask, all she'll convey is the direction of the approach and the physics of its deceleration. It's a deuterium-tritium fusion flame, a little brighter than *Geographic*'s—"

"Leading you to believe it is of human origin?" Evie asked, eyes wide.

"We can't be certain," Toad said. "But it does seem to be coming from nearly the direction of Earth, so that . . . yes, we have reason to believe it is human. Cassandra tells me that other colony attempts were planned. This one must have left Earth not long after our landing message would have reached there, another reason to believe it comes from Earth."

"Has it responded to communications?"

"That's more complicated than you think," Marvin said.

"How's that?" someone shouted.

"Cassandra had an exchange with them once. I got her to tell me the frequency they used. But after the first contact, she heard nothing. Or maybe she has, but she's not telling us. Yesterday I managed to rig up a transmitter to beam a message down the path they'd have to take if they're coming from Earth, using the frequency Cassandra sent hers on, but I haven't heard anything back."

"Did they get it?" Cadzie asked.

"Beats me. They should have been in the beam. Of course, they might not be listening. But anyway, not so far. And Cassandra reports nothing. She could be getting something and not telling us."

There it was again: *not telling us*. Carlos suspected that many of them failed to grasp the implications of those three words.

"But then we've never heard anything from Earth, either."

"True," Carlos said. "So... there may be some interference we don't understand, something outside the rim of the solar system. Perhaps when they enter we'll be able to communicate. Maybe not."

The crowd clamored like a flock of geese, locked in argument with each other. "We're getting company!"

"It's a big planet," another said. "Plenty of room!"

"New faces!"

And finally their lanky, straw-haired communications specialist Trevanian asked something that had to be on everyone's mind. "They're..." A nervous smile. "Friendly, right?"

Carlos put on his broadest smile. "Can you think of a reason that they wouldn't be?"

"What's happening on Earth?" Masie Bright called out. "How do we even know? Something horrible! And now that nastiness is reaching out for us! It could be a load of plague victims!"

Typical Masie pessimism. But Carlos had to agree ... at least in theory. "It could be anything ... or nothing at all."

"Nothing?"

He paused. Here it was, the moment they'd been building to for two days. "Aaron," he said. "Would you like to take the podium?"

Aaron limped up onto the stage, favoring his right leg, his hair bleached white by the sun, his skin blotched and leathery now, puckered by old bites from Avalonian bees. "I've been asked to speak to this. The kids at Surf's Up asked me, Carlos asked me, and here I am."

"Go on, please," Carlos said.

"Fifteen years ago, our kids discovered something very important, and for their own reasons kept it to themselves." Aaron's voice seethed with anger. His right hand fisted, as if he wanted to hit someone.

"Exactly what?" Maisie asked.

"A life-form."

There was a little chuckling at that. "There are probably a hundred million uncatalogued life-forms," Big Shaka said.

"You know about this one. It's these squid things we call cthulhus. You can learn all about them. Except you won't learn the most *important* thing about them."

There was a titter from the Earthborn, but not the Starborn.

"Cthulhus?" Big Shaka sounded puzzled. "Fabulous name, but we know all about them. They killed a surfer. You were there, Aaron! We looked at them good and hard. We concluded they were only dangerous if you looked like a grendel, or messed with their spawning ground. Dammit, Aaron, they damned near killed *you*, but you were the one who insisted they were safe if we didn't provoke them. I remember that, because you stood up to Cadmann about it!"

"Yes. I did. I didn't think they were worth worrying about, no more than sharks back on Earth, and we had other things to worry about. They weren't coming after us, and if we left them alone they'd leave us alone. I won that argument, and never paid much attention to them after that. But we—well, some of us—learned a lot more. Joan?"

Aaron's daughter pushed in beside him. "Thanks, Dad. Can we have the hologram?"

A pseudo-reptilian head and body popped floating into the air. "This, of course, is a grendel. We all know of them—fast, deadly, the most lethal thing on the planet." She paused. "And also the most intelligent. At least wolf-level cognition, although that intelligence pretty much shuts down when they are under *speed*, the glandular secreted, hyper-oxygenator producing their lethal acceleration."

Aaron's apprentice Josie raised her voice. "But grendels are no longer Avalon's smartest native inhabitant. This is—"

Another image. A squidlike creature. "Cthulhus," Big Shaka said. "So?"

A bit of a titter at that, but nothing extreme. A polite query. "Aquatic."

"Well, amphibious, at least in a limited capacity."

"But you found these in the ocean. That's where they live."

"Not always. They spawn in brackish water," Joan said. "In particular, on Blackship."

That finally caught their attention. "What?" Evie asked. "When?"

"That's where we first found them," Aaron said. "Blackship. That's why there are rules about when you can go there."

"As to when, years ago. A group of Grendel Scouts encountered them."

By Carlos' reckoning, most of the original Grendel Scouts were in the audience. They looked uncomfortable, but not exactly surprised by this discussion. He wished he could have been a fly on the wall out at Surf's Up. The recriminations must have been nasty.

Despite Cadzie's promise to Joanie, he'd spoken privately to his Uncle Carlos. But for the others . . . this was staggering news.

The anger was boiling over now, as more of them began to understand. "People died! Why didn't you tell us!"

"We did tell you," Aaron said.

"Not that they were intelligent," Big Shaka said.

"Because we knew you'd respond like this!" Jennifer's voice was cool, almost cold, in control.

"You had no right to conceal this!" Big Shaka said,

literally shaking his cane at them, black face pomegranate purple with anger. "These amphibious 'cthulhus' definitely are intelligent?"

"Yes. We would estimate at least as smart as dolphins. Perhaps more so."

"Do they have *speed?*" The clamor had grown nervous.

"Not that we have ever observed. They are, on the other hand, limited tool-users, and seem to have a small amount of symbolic logic and ... uh ... language."

That created a ripple of genuine confusion and fear. "Time binders," someone muttered. Others repeated the term. In semantics theory, time binding was unique to man.

Then Maisie asked the next question. "I don't understand. How are these two events linked?"

A pause. Embarrassed this time. The confrontational quality had evaporated. "We ..." She looked around, embarrassed and suddenly nervous. "We ... instructed Cassandra not to tell the Earthborn about nonhuman intelligence. Kept the information behind a logic wall."

Murmuring again. "How is that even possible?" Zack's voice wavered. It seemed Carlos' old friend was shriveling, shrinking before his eyes. "Her programming is designed to share all core knowledge ..."

"Yes, but we have individual diaries. Blogs. And those blogs have security. And there are 'family' groupings that allow private communications and knowledge stores. We simply put all the information about the cthulhus behind those walls and ... um ... changed Cassandra's instructions."

Zack shook his cane at them in a very *you kids get off*

my lawn! gesture. "You have no idea what you've done. You set up a conflict she could not resolve. It is possible that what you did created a . . . a . . ." He paused, groping for a word.

"Wormhole?" his wife Rachel whispered.

He snatched at the offered term. "Yes! Wormhole in her logic programs, something that replicated until we had a problem."

"What . . . kind of problem?"

Rachel picked up the gauntlet. "Like a shadow object. A mirage. Something coming too close to our own flight path from Earth. The problem is that we have no idea how many other errors will make their way into the program."

Joan looked perplexed. "How do we even know?" She seemed subdued, as if she was overwhelmed by the impact.

"We can wait until the object reaches us. If it communicates . . . we can be pretty confident it's real. But that still leaves the possibility of damage. If the object disappears, or is proven to be an illusion . . . we know we have a problem."

"We can't wait three months for that," Carlos said.

"What else can we do?"

"We can go up and check the logic circuitry ourselves."

There was a long pause. Then Carlos said, "And bring Cassandra down to this island. I've been wanting to do this anyway. It's about time."

Another pause, then Zack nodded. He glared at Joanie. "And then some."

◆CHAPTER 8◆
THE SPEAKER

The warrior officer opened the door and ushered Trudy in. The cabin was small, but on a starship staterooms are small, even for the leaders. "Selected Colonist Hendrickson, Your Grace." He bowed and left them.

The Speaker was old. Wrinkled and old. She had expected that, but still it was a shock: her body still remembered him as warm, and strong, and virile. When she had last seen him, they were the same age, he perhaps a few months older. They were both in final training, Advanced Candidates, and they were often a couple. For Trudy it was only two weeks ago that they had slept together. For the Speaker, she realized, it had been nearly a lifetime ago.

They had made love, but they hadn't quite been *in* love. She wouldn't let herself be in love, would not trigger the carefully woven love knot that would focus all her attention upon the positive aspects of a potential partner, trigger the endorphin rush which, combined with affection and experience would create the pair bond. It wouldn't have been fair to him, and it would be worse for her. She wasn't anywhere near ready for love, and even if she had been it would have to have been short. When she was younger, before her training was more complete, she had casual affairs like the other girls in her class, but now she wasn't capable of being just a little in love. She enjoyed flings, but there was always the temptation of love; let a little in, and it could take over her emotions. And Gus was attractive, but would he be chosen? In a few weeks the names of the colonists would be announced, and she was sure that her name would be on the list. She wasn't sure about Gus. He was competent, he had good grades and his athletic scores were high, but he was having difficulties with combat training.

His reflexes weren't slow by ordinary standards, but other candidates were lightning.

Now this. "You wanted to see me, Your Grace?"

He grinned. It wasn't the familiar expression she remembered, but it was definitely a happy place. "You can call me Gus as long as we're alone."

She was careful not to let her smile be too warm. "Wouldn't that be bad for discipline, Gus?" She noted his expression. Pleased. Of course, he hadn't seen her in—decades, while she remembered having dinner with him just before reporting to hospital to begin the week long process that would end in cold sleep. Dinner . . . and a very intimate dessert. "I think it would be better if I addressed you as Your Grace."

He sighed. "I expect it would. Have a seat. Tea? Or I have something stronger, of course. Chardonnay? We still have some." He indicated a comfortable chair. "And on reflection, I think it might be best if we devise new titles. I doubt when we meet the first colonists they will appreciate our ways, and we should be careful not to offend them unless we have to."

"You are sure there are colonists here already? There seemed to be some doubts in the wardroom."

"I haven't announced it yet, but yes, observations of the planet show there are a lot of structures on one big island, and a dam on the mainland coast opposite the island. Not a surprise, they've been there for around forty years."

She digested that information. "Yes, sir."

He gave a quizzical grin, older but still reminding her of the younger Gus. "I'm well accustomed to deference, Trudy, but not from you. Of course I haven't seen you in over seventy years. You haven't changed a bit, but I must look, well, odd. Don't I?" He turned away to a cabinet and produced two bottles, a wine glass, and a snifter. "Be careful with these. We won't be able to replace them until we've landed some people. You'll be one of them, of course. No point in waking you if we didn't need you."

He half-filled the wine glass, then poured a hefty drink of brandy in the snifter. Handing her the wine, he lifted the snifter. *"We did not light the torch."*

"And we will not see the bonfire," she responded automatically.

"To Man's destiny," they said in unison, and drank.

His expression grew a bit more stern. "Dr. Mandell tells me you told him you are aware of why you were awakened. How do you know?"

She frowned. "Surmise, Your Grace. You awakened warriors. No one else. I am qualified to teach, to supervise a school, and to manage some other enterprises we can't possibly have yet . . ."

The grin was back, but faded quickly as if he were hiding it. "I am well aware of your qualifications," he said. "I also have your complete records."

"Then you know that the only assignment I could have in the present circumstances would be as an executive's companion. An officer's lady. The conclusion is obvious. Have you chosen my husband? Surely it is not you."

"Would you be terribly upset if it were me?" he asked wryly.

"No."

"But not enthusiastic."

"Of course I am enthusiastic, Gus." She smiled, warmly. Eagerly.

"Stand down, Gertrude! I'm sorry, I had no right—I shouldn't tease you. Trudy, I have been happily married for forty years."

She sat back, struggling with her emotions. Relief, combined with the eagerness she had turned on the instant she believed it was needed. Annoyance at being teased, joy that she wasn't destined for an old man even if it was Gus. Regret that it wasn't true, that she would not be first lady with all that meant, but again relief, that she might still be useful. She took ten careful deep breaths, thankful that Gus—the Speaker—understood the need and demanded nothing from her. "Have you chosen my husband, Your Grace?"

"No, Trudy. No. Do not bond with anyone. Mask your—competence. Officially you are a member of the Construction Plans Committee, to ensure that the schools are adequate and to make other suggestions as you see fit. You will be chief education advisor until we awaken Miss Priscilla and she assumes her role as headmistress. That will be your open and published job."

"And my real task?"

"To do that assignment well—as I have no doubt you will without further instructions. But you will report to me, in private, from time to time, or at any time you think there is something I should know. You will be eyes and ears for the Speaker, and only you will know that. You will tell no one that we knew each other in—in another life."

"I have already told Dr. Mandell. I did not know it was important."

He looked thoughtful. "Say nothing else about our previous—relationship. Do not lie, but do not bring up the subject if no one else does."

"Yes. Of course. I can be coy," she said calmly and coldly. "You believe that you will have need of a secret agent?"

"How should I know? But if I do, I want the most competent one I can find."

"You flatter me, Your Grace."

"Come now. Even adolescent Gus found you impressive. Trudy, when we were—together—I was not trained to be the supreme leader. I have often pondered why he chose me to be awakened, but he did, and my life in personal service to the Prophet changed everything. It was after many years that he ordered me to be his successor. That decision did not please everyone on the council. I had you awakened because I can trust you, both in competence and in loyalty. I can, can't I?"

"Gus—"

"Oh, Trudy, you think you know me, but I am no longer that young cadet you knew. But know—you must know—that I would never ask you to do anything that was not in aid of the Great Commission."

She drank the last of her wine. She didn't think there had been enough in the drink to affect her reasoning ability. A bit giddy, but thinking clearly. She raised the glass. *"We did not light the torch."*

"And we will not see the bonfire."

"To Man's destiny."

◆CHAPTER 9◆
PLANNING FOR SPACE

The room was full of tension, and seemed crowded although it was barely half full. Carlos, Zack, and some other Earthborn sat at a table at the front of the room. Mason Stolzi, Marvin's father, sat at the end of the table, not quite on the other side. They faced a small group, mostly Starborn and their grown children. Cadzie thought the arrangement stupid, but it was the way the Earthborn had always done things. They had invited him to sit up there with them, but he had taken a place in the front row of the seats facing the table, as if part of the audience, and he spoke when he felt like it, because as much as he liked his Unka Carlos, he just didn't feel right about sitting up there.

Carlos took a deep breath and then a healthy gulp of wine. "I don't like this plan much. But what else is there?"

Everybody in the crowded room nodded. No one said anything. A long silence, and it went on too long.

Finally Zack spoke, his voice low. And infirm, Cadzie thought. He's getting old. "Anyone have a better plan?"

Zack asked. "I sure don't. I guess this is as much my fault as anyone's. We should have brought Cassandra down twenty years ago, when we had two operating Minervas and people to fly them."

"And nobody wanted to go up," Carlos said.

"Cadmann would have—"

"We didn't have Cadmann," Carlos said. "And we weren't sure of what we were facing. If Cassandra had been down here in the Grendel Wars—"

"Yeah, yeah, we would have lost her. And working without her would have been damn tough. But we'd have pulled through," Marvin Stolzi said. He had joined Cadzie and Joanie in the first row, but sat at the end, no one next to him, as he always did when he could. "We'd have made it."

"You weren't there. Your father thought we should wait to be sure there weren't any more threats. Existential threats. Like intelligent grendels, or those damned bees, or—well, anything like that," Zack said, his voice rising a bit. "We depended on Cassandra. We still do. But it would be safe to bring her down, but instead you went up and put more stuff into Cassandra! And now after you kids wrecked her we can't know—"

"Oh, that's not true," Joanie said. She sat next to Cadzie, again in the front row, so it was more like a round table than leaders and audience, Earthborn on one side of the table, everyone else on the other. "We didn't ruin Cassandra."

"She isn't working," Carlos said quietly. "You still can't get her to tell us much about that ship, or talk to it for us, and neither can I."

"It's the new Preferences Matrix Board we—all right, I—put in," Jennifer said from somewhere behind Cadzie. "I didn't like that at the time, but mother—and you!" She stood and pointed dramatically at Mason Stolzi, "agreed that we weren't doing her any harm! You were in charge!"

That finally roused Mason Stolzi. The elderly astronaut didn't stand, and his voice was low and tired. Cadzie would have called it weak if it hadn't been someone he respected. "You were sure it wouldn't do any harm, and I believed. I always believed you."

"And it didn't do any harm," Jennifer insisted. "We just thought it made keeping secrets about the cthulhu a lot easier. And it did, and there was no problem, not for all these years. And we saved the cthulhu! You'd have killed as many as you could! You know you would have."

Carlos started to say something and caught himself.

"And who gave you the right to mess with Cassandra?" Zack demanded.

Cadzie cleared his throat. None of this was getting them anywhere. Uncle Carlos was acting strange, Zack sounded like he had ice on his mind. He stood. "Look, it's all agreed that it's time to bring Cassandra down here. We'll also pack up and bring down all the spare parts we can find. Let the experts," he said, his voice dripping derision now, "argue about backups and Primary Preference Tables and all the rest of it. We haven't been up there for seven years, we weren't there long then, and we won't be doing it often now. Will we, Toad?"

Marvin Stolzi was hesitant. Usually he avoided big meetings. Little meetings, too, unless he wanted something. He looked to his father, up at the table with the Earthborn, then said "I went up with Dad on the last mission. Fixed a few things. Couldn't stay long. No, Cadzie, we won't be going back often."

"But you'll take us up. Joanie and me."

"Better if it's only two. Better safety factor with a smaller payload. Not sure of the thrust we can get—"

"But it'll do it."

"Two nine's, anyway you look at it," Toad said carefully. "Another nine if only two go."

"Three nines? Really?"

"How the hell do I know? No data, and you know it, Cadzie. Dad, what do you make it?"

Toad's father sat at one end of the table of Earthborn. He had the title of Chief Astronaut, but he looked older than Carlos. Cadzie knew he really wasn't. It was hard to tell about Earthborn ages anyway. It depended on how old they'd been before they went to sleep, and on how long they'd been awake, and for that matter, how many times they had been awakened and put back to sleep. And nobody wanted to talk about it. But however old Mason Stolzi looked when he went up eight years ago, he sure didn't look up to going now. He looked tired, and he didn't talk much.

Mason stood with some effort.

Maybe he has been awake longer than Carlos, Cadzie thought. He was younger than Carlos when they left Earth. It had taken a lot of patience to find out that much.

"The Minerva reliability with that light a payload has got to be better than point nine nine," he said. "No reason to try for better. I wouldn't try. But you're missing the point. It's Marv who has to decide. He'll be the mission commander, for God's sake. Who the hell is fit to argue with him?"

"Not arguing, Mason," Carlos said. He'd got control of himself, and his voice was strong again, now that he had something to argue for. "But it has to be three. Too much work for just two. Have to pack up Cassandra—carefully!—after taking her apart—carefully. Good bit of work. And whoever is in charge of disassembly needs to know something about computers and engineering. Not programming. Not science. Engineering. And be up to going now. We don't have time for much training, so we need young people who will get the job done. I don't know anyone better than Joanie for the job, but we can't send her up on that mission to do it alone."

There was silence after that. Twenty people, and not a word. Cadzie looked at Joanie. She looked more like a little girl, like she had back at Weyland Compound as a child than like the dam's chief engineer. This couldn't have been easy for her. He stood again. "And I'll go with her to help," he said firmly. "So the only question is when."

Mason Stolzi had been *Geographic*'s pilot, off and on, for most of *Geographic*'s voyage to Tau Ceti. It could be said that he'd brought them to Avalon. It was also true that Stolzi had been wakened from cold sleep too often, but it didn't show, not for a long time. He'd become the Chief Astronaut, and after a while damn near the only one. And that last mission to *Geographic* had been too much. Mason's near collapse had cut the mission short, and he'd finished that mission as a passenger. Now he lived quietly. Nobody said "ice on his mind." But a lot of people thought it. His son, Marvin Stolzi—Toad—had never really known him when he wasn't nervous, almost fearful, but he handled it well. And he knew more about actually going to space than anyone else in the colony.

And now it was his son's turn. There hadn't been a lot of space missions after the Grendel Wars. There was always a better use for fuel right now. The preparations crew, and the missions, kept being put off. There was no real hurry. The frozen embryos had been flown to ground, human and animal alike. Many of the animals had been awakened before anyone knew grendels were a threat. Those that hadn't been had thawed and died after the grendel attacks became fierce. So did a lot of the human embryos when the grendels destroyed much of the colony.

His mother had raised him to be a pilot, and he'd gone along with that. He was skilled with machines. Age: 38. Height five feet six, and his father was a little shorter. Brown hair. White skin that took a red tan. He didn't like the sea much; he wasn't part of the Surf's Up crowd. His bicycle was old, made for his father, just before a grendel destroyed the third and last 3D printer.

He loved *Geographic*. Loved and cared for the Minervas too. It struck him now, as he danced through the checklist, that he'd done this too often as rote. The list ran well, telling him everything he already knew about the aging spacecraft's flaws.

He asked, "Strapped in?"

Cadzie said, "Sure." Joan grunted.

Stolzi said, "I always ask." He ran the red cursor up to High. Joan and Cadzie jerked in astonishment as the Minerva blasted along the waterway. A tiny shudder in the roar killed Stolzi's grin, but the Minerva lifted and rose into the darkening sky.

The Minerva had required just thirty-eight minutes to travel from launch to matching orbit and velocity with *Geographic*.

Cadzie's stomach was just settling down from liftoff when he felt the gentle bump of the docking rings. By the time things had clicked into place and all pressures had been normalized, he was ready. Cadzie and Joan prepared to enter *Geographic*, while Toad remained behind on the Minerva checking systems, a tiny furrow between his eyes betraying his concern. The air was cool and stale, smelled of disinfectant and ancient sweat and even more ancient air conditioner filters.

"I still can't get used to this," Joan said. "They spent almost a century in here."

"And out of that century, no single person was awake more than two years, total," Cadzie said. "Usually two crew at a time."

"That," Joan said, "that had to be very strange."

"And dangerous," Cadzie said. He ran his fingers along one of the sepulchral ivory and stainless steel cold sleep pods built into the walls in a section marked D-4. "Look," he said. "This was my granddad's pod."

"Wow. Sort of a mausoleum, huh? So . . . did he have ice on his mind?"

He winced. Hated the term "ice." It was so . . . cold. "I have no memory of him, Joan. Maybe a big smiling face, but they say you don't remember anything before the age of two, so that could be a mirage. But I can tell you what everyone else said: no. He was as sane as a man ever is. All circuits firing."

She laid down in one of the pods, closed her green eyes. Then shivered, opened them and climbed back out rather more quickly than she had entered. "Would you have wanted to get in one of these?"

"At the time?" he asked. "Sure. All the tests looked good."

"Then . . . what went wrong?"

Cadzie considered. "No one had tested what happens when you wake up, go down, wake up . . . over and over for a century. There were limits to cellular plasticity. Things that didn't show up in animal experiments over shorter time frames. It was . . . tragic."

Joan's face softened. "Your grandmother?"

"Yeah," he said. "My bio-grandmer. Her I remember. And she loved me, but always needed help dealing with me. And I remember when the day came she could no longer help me with my math."

"How old were you?"

A dark cloud flitted across his face. "Ten."

"Jesus."

"Yeah," he said, and shook himself like a dog waking up from a nightmare. "Let's get on with it."

They floated through the ship, past endless rows of clear Plexiglas cubbyholes and humming equipment bays. Rat-sized black maintenance bots awakened and shadowed them, like pets eager to serve long-absent masters. Past doors to shops and labs, sliding through crowds of ghosts, their fathers and grandmothers, men and women possessing a kind of courage that might . . . just *might* be unknown to them. There was no hurry, but neither did they dawdle making their way to the central computer room. If Cassandra lived anywhere in *Geographic*, she lived here.

"All right, Trevanian? We're here."

The lanky communications officer answered the comm link instantly. "All right. Congratulations. So the first thing is to make an inspection of the logic banks while the test is running."

"In process," Cadzie replied.

A series of lights and sounds indicated diagnostic checks. *Beep beep boop.*

"Everything seems all right," Trev said.

"We've got a little fuzz," Joanie said.

"I'm not surprised. Chip degradation. But we expected that. What we need to know is if Cassandra made any physical alterations to obey the new instructions."

"Protocols prevent her from altering the physical structure. But there are some limited changes she can make to the programming or memory partitions. Let's see . . ." Cadzie read the schematics. "Ah . . . according to this, yes. She created some kind of firewall. Pretty subtle. Wow. I didn't know she could redesign herself." He looked more closely. "And . . . yeah, it looks like someone made a physical alteration and tried to hide it from the diagnostics."

"Tried to?"

"Pretty much did. So she found a way around those instructions. Perhaps repurposed repair bots to modify her logic boards. Create a section that was invisible to the ordinary scans. That wasn't expected."

"So . . . what do we do?"

"Figure out what was done and how they did it. That will give us some clues. People?"

He could envision the comm hut, knew that Nnedi and Scott and Epifanio Clay were standing by to provide advice.

He hoped they were squirming.

"It wasn't all remote." Nnedi's voice. "We got on one of the repair runs, and managed to make some modifications."

"Swapped out a module for one we created here," Scott Martinez's voice. *That* conversation, between Scott and Carlos, must have been scathing. "From spare Minerva parts."

"Created a separate computer inside Cassandra? A virtual Cassandra?"

"Pretty much." Nnedi sounded as if she was about to undergo dental surgery with a chisel and hammer.

"Well . . ." Cadzie admitted, "it actually is pretty solid work, Carlos. You could look right at it and not know."

"All right," Carlos said. "Tap in and run an integrative diagnostic." He did as asked. "And . . . running *now*."

"What do we do now?" Joan asked.

Cadzie leaned back in his chair and laced his hands behind his head. "We wait."

Joanie shivered. "This is really creepy."

He knew exactly what she meant, but took a childish pleasure in pretending he didn't. "Oh? How so?"

"Well . . . our grandparents. Your dad, Joe Sikes. They climbed into those pods, and they had every reason to think that that was the best thing to do."

Now he felt a little creeped out himself. "Yeah."

"And it broke them."

"Not all of them," he protested. "Not most of them. Have you ever met anyone with ice on his mind?"

"Sure," she shrugged. "A couple. When I was a kid. They didn't last very long, did they?"

"No. Incidence of stroke went way up. Those that survived the grendels. Most of them knew, you know. Knew they weren't what they had been. Some volunteered to hold positions so others would escape. Waited for the grendels." A sigh. He took no pleasure in speaking about this.

"How is the diagnostic?" she asked.

"I'm having to make a new map to incorporate the bypass circuits. This is sophisticated stuff. Who did this?"

"Well..." Joan hawed. "I was a part of it."

"Well done." He clapped three times, feeling an odd combination of anger and admiration. "I mean...it shouldn't have been done, but if you were going to do it, this was the way."

She glared at him. "Was that a convoluted way to say you're impressed?"

He smiled. "Yes. Well, sort of. Carlos?"

"Here." It seemed that every meter of the ship was covered by speakers and cameras. They were never alone.

"The kids did modify Cassandra, and I'm seeing some areas where conflicting directions could cause failures, but they seem fairly minor. The real problem is simply that our girl is old, and we're running out of replacement parts."

"We'll deal with that later," Carlos said, fifteen thousand kilometers below them. "What about our visitor?"

"I'm looking at the scanners. Considering that the object isn't broadcasting, isn't it a good sign that Cassandra picked it up?"

"Maybe," he admitted. "If it's really there."

"I'm checking the telescope and our polar satellite. We're verifying Cassandra's information. The log suggests that these are original feeds, unaltered by any of the corruption."

"And you still see the object?"

"Yes," he said. "We can't be certain of the mass or composition, but the approach vectors and speed are clear, and . . . it's slowing down."

"If I had to guess," Carlos said, "I'd think it was twice as fast as *Geographic*, which means that if it's coming from Earth . . ."

"It is more advanced," Carlos said. "We estimate fifty to seventy years more advanced."

"Agreed," Cadzie said. "Too many factors to be sure."

"And no indication of radio contact?"

"None. Silence."

Carlos looked as if he'd bitten into an onion. Cadzie suspected that a bit of that was pure theatrical flair. Uncle Carlos enjoyed his drama. "That . . . is disturbing. It could be a dead object. Everyone on board killed by their cold sleep capsules, or disease . . ."

"We just don't know. They might sail right past us, keep going until they reach the galactic core a million years from now."

"Jesus," Joan said. "Next subject?"

Another hour getting a sense of what they were dealing

with, and then it was time to think. Cadzie and Joan had changed into pale orange utility jumpsuits. They sat in the cool of the communications pod, and Cadzie had brewed coffee from a hidden stash of real beans. "Plenty of this stuff left at least," Cadzie said. "Earth blend. We planted our own before we ran out."

"Not *speed*-y," Joan said, relishing her first sip. "I like it."

"Mmm-hmm." Cadzie closed his eyes and enjoyed, then opened them and sat up straight as the alarm dinged. "Ah!" Foot-tall facial holograms of Carlos and Trevanian floated beside their table. It was always a little eerie. "How long is it going to take to disassemble Cassandra?"

"We estimate two weeks."

"Well before our visitors arrive," Carlos said. "We've decided that Stolzi will stay onboard, to prevent any claim of salvage on *Geographic*."

"How do we get back down?"

"Autopilot should work fine. We've run simulations."

Cadzie considered. "If they're from Earth, and they're coming here . . ."

"Right. They will have means of reaching the surface, and Stolzi can ride down with them."

"Or, they will have the ability to fix our equipment."

"A chip fabricator," Joanie said. "And—" The thought of one of the legendary three dimensional printers made her mouth water.

"And if they can't land?" Cadzie asked.

"They'll still be able to take care of Stolzi."

"And if there aren't any?"

"Oh, come on, Cadzie. There's a ship out there, it's slowing down! If there's really no one we'll have a crash program to fit that Minerva for one last flight. You know that."

"Carlos—"

"How many do we have to risk? Someone has to stay there—"

"We'll all stay."

"No. You won't. Someone needs to bring Cassandra down, and you'll both be needed to fix her. We've been through all this a dozen times, and maybe I'm getting weary of it."

"And I'm not going without Cadzie," Joan said quietly. "Toad says it's his job, and he's mission commander, and that's the way it is. Goodbye, Carlos." She reached out to the switch on the console and without hesitation cut the feed.

"Well . . . that's ten pounds of shit in a five-pound bag."

Joanie sighed, and stood, bracing her arms on balled fists on the table top. "Patch me through to Surf's Up," she said.

Cassandra responded sluggishly. But in a few moments there appeared a hunky guy, Nordic but tanned enough to be a Samoan Triplet. His shoulder-length sunbleached hair distinguished him instantly as a member of their coastal community.

"Thor," she sighed.

"Hey, Joanie!"

"Thor," she repeated, even less enthusiastically this time. What was that shadow behind him?

"How are things up there?"

"I have a problem," she said.

"What's that?"

"I'm stuck up here for two weeks with Weyland-Sikes."

Thor laughed. "The boy scout? I figure you'll survive."

"I just wanted . . ." She felt herself fighting for words.

"You're all right?" Thor asked.

"Yes."

"Oh, man. Well, that's the most important thing. Listen," he said, already sounding bored. "Keep me posted." Behind Thor was a clingy looking sun-bronzed Asian girl. Mei Ling, that was her name, wasn't it? Geologist?

Bitch.

The image faded.

Joanie sat back, an irritated whistle escaping pursed lips. "Well, that's just fine."

"What?" Cadzie asked.

"Didn't you see Mei Ling? I've only been gone for six hours and she's already on him like paint. In two weeks she'll have moved in."

"I think we have bigger problems."

She sagged in defeat. "So . . . what if they're right. What do we do?"

Cadzie scanned the room. "Well, we have plenty of work to do. I suppose we can tolerate close quarters for fourteen days."

"Unless we die of boredom."

Cadzie's answering smile was downright evil. God, she hated him sometimes. "You can try cold sleep."

For an instant she considered that, and then realized the very nasty joke he was making at her expense. "We can't do that."

"No, we can't," he agreed. "Glad we've got that out of the way."

"Two weeks. Not so bad."

"Please don't think I'm delighted with it."

"Then we'll have to take a chance on an autopilot assist of the Minerva. Or . . ."

"Or?"

"Adam and Eve in space," Cadzie said. That old evil smile flickered again. He really was a bastard, wasn't he?

"Oh, grendel piss on *that*."

"Well, then, we'd better see how we'll set up housekeeping, and get about it."

"Remember," Joan said. "You take your side, I'll take mine."

◆ CHAPTER 10 ◆
ENEMIES WITH BENEFITS

Ten days later ...

The eternal background hum of the machines had become almost unnoticeable to Joanie. The days had taken on a routine, as days tended to do for people with organized minds. From morning to night, she arose, exercised, ate, worked, exercised, and slept, interacting with Cadmann Sikes as little as possible.

She was leaving the communications center to stretch her legs when Cadzie came jogging along the central corridor, bare-chested and gleaming, a runner's legs beneath a rock-climber's torso.

She frowned, and without a word disappeared back into the center. Their living situation was increasingly uncomfortable, more every day, like an insect buzzing in her ear. Irritating. Distracting.

Arrgh.

It was that pesky Adam and Eve thing, almost as if she had ancient wiring that refused to shut off. Being stuck on *Geographic* with someone she . . . loathed? Did she hate him? Once upon a time she had followed him around Cadmann's Bluff like a puppy, trying desperately to get his attention, losing hope and then hoping again when her body developed and she felt some deep ache that balanced with the anger and resentment. Everything twisted and knotted together into a ball she knew she'd never untangle.

They could talk about it, or ignore it. Ignoring it had been the tactic until now, but talking seemed more attractive all the time.

She brooded much of the rest of the day, then looked up his location finder, and saw that he was busy in the tool shop.

Too busy over the next hour to brood, but just before ten o'clock in the evening, Camelot time, Joanie made a decision.

Unka Carlos had once told Cadzie that you know when you are doing something you love, because when engaged in such things you lose track of the time. In that case, he was totally in love with his work in the machine shop.

That was certainly true of Marvin Stolzi, who had disappeared into the engine room, where a lifetime of study and tinkering awaited him, toys that might keep him busy for a dozen lifetimes. He was sleeping and eating in there as well, and they barely saw him at all.

And that time-dissolving thing was true for Cadzie when he was playing with the culinary fabricator. It manipulated proteins to create food. Was there any way to use it to manipulate polycarbon paste to produce parts for the time-worn Minerva? Cassandra said it wasn't likely, but what the heck, trial and error had accomplished miracles more than once . . .

Joanie entered the machine shop wearing a workout suit. Carrying a meal from their fabricator, and a bottle from their well-stocked cellar.

"What's this?" he asked.

"You've not taken a break in twenty hours."

He smelled the food, and heard his stomach growl. "I didn't know you cared enough to keep track."

"I brought you a snack," she said.

Cadzie sniffed. It did smell delicious. "Okay . . . right. You take a bite first."

She rolled her eyes and laughed. "Oh, come on."

He plucked a meatball from atop a tangled mass of spaghetti. Delicious. The protein paste reservoirs had been replenished only a couple of years back, and the new spices, some derived from native Avalonian sources, still had plenty of *oomph*. "I was kidding. Maybe."

"We need to talk," she said.

"You go first?" he was talking with his mouth full.

She sighed. "I was thinking that . . . maybe we could do each other some good."

"Oh? In what way?"

"I'm . . ." she seemed to be having a hard time fitting her mouth around her thoughts. "Kind of used to certain things. And we've been up here ten days . . . hoping that we might wrap things up ahead of time, but I doubt it."

That concern was his as well. As well as his exertions

with the fabricators, Cadzie had been working on a chip taken from the regulators on the sleep pods. No one was using the pods, or was likely to, ever again. If he could reprogram the chips, it was possible . . .

He remembered that he'd been asked a question. Or that a question had been implied. The wine was doing its work. Joanie seemed to know what she was about, even if he didn't. "Well, we'd better be. The only other option has a sixty percent risk of burning up on re-entry, or crashing. I don't much like those odds."

"I'm no happier about them," Joan said. "I assume we're getting back to work in a few hours?"

"Cutting those couplings is harder than I thought. We have to do it without undue vibration or raising the temperature too much, and that limits options. We don't want to fry her brain."

"That's a happy thought."

"Hey," Cadzie said. "You think I like it?"

She took a deep breath. So deep that Cadzie began to grow impatient. "So . . . what is this about?"

"This," she said, and placing a hand on either side of his face, drew him closer and kissed him.

Startled, he pulled back. "Whoa. Whoa. What is this?"

"It isn't true love," she whispered, her lips still brushing his.

"That would have been my bet." He said it, but he felt a small fire ignite down south of his guts. He had very carefully buried those thoughts, and here she'd woken them right up. *Be careful what you ask for, lady . . .*

"Look, take it as lightly as you want. Or just as a physical release. Or emotional comfort. I'm not exactly hideous?" She paused, as if realizing she'd tagged an inadvertent question mark to the end of that sentence.

So . . . a touch of insecurity? Strange that that made her more attractive. "No . . . but let's just say this is enough of a surprise that I have to shift gears just to think about it."

She pulled back, suddenly comprehending. "Oh my God. You're a *romantic*, aren't you?"

"I guess. Two moms."

She frowned, and then grinned. "Then why don't you invite me to dinner?"

"Pushy little thing," he laughed. "I've spent the last week disassembling a machine designed to remain stable for over a century. I think we have at least six days left."

"Maybe it's time to stop working so hard?" the question again. "All work and no play . . . I'll bring the wine," she said.

"You already did." They both grinned, and there was something urchin and mischievous in hers that finally melted the ice. *Oh, what the hell . . .* he thought.

And rolled her into his arms. "We can eat later."

An hour later he said, "Enemies. With benefits."

◆CHAPTER 11◆
MESSENGER

Messenger's deceleration was less severe now, and everyone felt that, but it meant more work in the gleaming row of exercise machines. Resistance servos built into their clothing provided constant stress on muscles and joints, imitating gravity. There were even suggestions that planning sessions ought to be held during exercises, but Speaker Augustus hadn't taken that seriously. He left details to his chiefs. They had grown up in gravity, and it was recent to them. He'd been in low gravity for most of his life now, supported more by drugs than exercise, and even the partial gravity of deceleration towards rendezvous with Tau Ceti IV felt strange and uncomfortable. He wondered if he could ever live on a planet again.

The warriors awakening now would remember spending very little time in space and low gravity. They'd been about twenty years old when they went to sleep. Experience watching others awaken told Augustus that it would take about a week for the physiological effects of cold sleep to wear off. During that time they could in theory be learning, but they probably wouldn't be. Everything would be strange to them.

"And what should they be learning, Captain Meadows?" Augustus asked. "What must we all know?"

Meadows was the tallest man in the room, a serious young man, a gold-bearded Viking thirty-two Earth years old when he went under. He had some command experience guarding mercy missions and putting down civil disorders before he went to sleep. "What have you learned, Captain?"

"Sir. We detect some signals between the orbiting ship— it's definitely the starship *Geographic*—and the world below it. They aren't strong enough to let us hear clearly, but the snatches we get are likely to be standard encryption in use in the Earth system when *Geographic* was built. If that's the case we'll probably never be able to listen in. They were pretty paranoid about hacking in those days." Gertrude giggled.

Captain Meadows looked at her sternly. "Miss Hendricksen, do you have a question?"

"No, Captain. And do call me Trudy. I was amused because I understand that one of the reasons the *Geographic* builders gave for their paranoia was that the Godsons kept hacking their equipment. Another indication of karma in this universe."

Major Gloria Stype drew a breath, loudly, as if shocked, but she didn't say anything. Trudy bowed her head slightly toward the officer. "Sorry, Major, but it was probably true that we really had done that, at least that's what I learned at the Academy. Didn't you?"

"I didn't learn to talk about it," Stype said coldly.

Trudy smiled. "Yes. Ma'am. Apologies for interrupting, Your Grace."

"Yes. We have time to talk." The Speaker grinned mirthlessly as he shook his head. "Lots of time. The purpose of these sessions is to decide how we will interact with the colonists already at Tau Ceti IV. Of course, they own that planet under international law, but as Trudy and Captain Meadows keep telling me, there are no means of enforcing that."

Everyone nodded. If anyone said anything it was not heard above the constant dull vibration of *Messenger*'s engines as they decelerated toward the planet. "And we know very little about them, but we're getting close enough to make some observations." He turned to Meadows. "Captain, as we approach *Geographic* we'll need to know everything we can about it. That may come to nothing. We might be invited aboard. If we are, you will go first. The goal is to make friends. Your mission is to assess the possibilities. After you will come Gertrude. If she finds that all is well, a landing party, including me, will follow."

"You, Your Grace?"

"Of course. We should be very careful not to insult our hosts."

"I have not assessed your competence in free space," Major Stype said. "Your Grace."

"I learned long ago, and recently had refreshment from Trudy. She has pressure suit training."

"Decades ago," Stype said.

The Speaker chuckled. "Last month to her," he said.

"And the equipment is hardly likely to have changed."

Gertrude nodded, and said, "Precisely. But I did not have much training, Your Grace."

"But enough to keep me safe, given that I had the same training, but long ago, not recently, like you," Augustus said. "If you did not feel competent you would have told me so." His tone left no place for argument, and there was none. "Captain, we need to know how many warriors you'll need to board that ship if no one invites us aboard. I know you military people argue that more is better because overwhelming force saves having to fight, but we don't want to wake up more people than we have to. Not until we know they're needed."

"So that's the real mission, Your Grace? To take control of *Geographic*?"

"To a first approximation, Captain. We need to be sure that *Geographic* will not be used to damage *Messenger*. That's the first and simplest mission, Captain. We do not require control in the sense of command, merely to be certain that there is no threat to our primary mission. We then have to decide what we do next. Our mission—this ship's mission—is to establish a colony and set it on a course of industrialization, capable of building an endless stream of colony ships and sending them on their way. To build the Capital Planet of Human Civilization in this Galaxy, to put it as dramatically as I can. That was the plan, but hibernation instability and our course change may have altered that."

"You mean that the *Geographic* colonists undoubtedly have other plans," Trudy said quietly.

"As they must. I am astonished to find *Geographic* still

in orbit," the Speaker said. "To the best approximation we have discovered, one of their goals was to establish a viable colony, duplicate everything aboard the ship that they might need for that colony, perhaps restock some of the genetic materials and human embryos employed in colonizing, and send *Geographic* on to another planet. They obviously have not done this. We do not know why."

"They have a colony on the island, and outlying works on the mainland," Captain Meadows said. "But they have obviously encountered difficulties. I say this because their colony is small. Few roads. No obvious harbors. They have not expanded much. We do not know if this is due to technical difficulties, opposition on the planet, or . . ."

"Or simple lack of motivation. They may even have gone primitive, reverted to uncivilized life," the Speaker said sadly. "We can hope not, but we cannot be certain. We must be prepared for any eventuality. We are the only expedition known to have the mission of galactic exploration. It is well to remind ourselves of our mission," the Speaker said. "We can let nothing compromise it." He stood. *"We did not light the torch."*

The others stood. Their voices were passionate. *"And we will not see the bonfire."*

"To Man's destiny."

Speaker Augustus sat carefully. "The Prophet always told me that it is well to remind ourselves of our mission. Frequently. It helps keep our thoughts in focus. Major, you have something to say."

"I do. The *Geographic* settlers will not care for us," Major Stype said. "They explicitly forbade any Godsons or former Godsons to go on this expedition. We have records of the discussions. They were not even polite."

There were subtle rustlings, sounds of impatience. "Yes, I know we are telling many of you things you already know," the Speaker said quietly, "but it needs saying. We did not come on a mission of conquest. This wasn't the chosen destination of this ship."

The Speaker turned to the tall, silent man who sat beside him. "Captain Richards, let's review our options. I see only two. We either stop here and unload a small group to encourage and assist these people as we go elsewhere, in which case we don't want to awaken anyone we don't have to; or we stop here, wake a lot of people up, and turn this planet into the Galactic Capital. Can we all agree on that?"

His tone indicated that he didn't expect anyone to disagree. When everyone had nodded, he continued. "Either way is easier if the colonists down there cooperate. We don't know what's down there. It can't be all that much, but they have had generations and they brought a lot of embryos. They should have made fair progress toward developing an industrial spacefaring civilization."

Chief Engineer Jorge Daytona raised his hand, and at a nod from the Speaker said "Yes, sir, but we're sure not seeing many signs of it. I see a dam on the mainland, but there's no city, and I don't know why they need all that power."

"I know, and it is a bit disturbing," Speaker Augustus said. "Jorge, what do you make of that?"

"It's a puzzlement, Speaker Augustus," Daytona said.

He sniffed. "So is their silence after the initial contact. But if there is any large population on that planet, it's hiding. Most signs of life are on one island off the mainland. There's agriculture there, but not enough cultivated land to feed more than a few hundred people. I presume they have other sources of food, possibly the planet evolved something they can eat, but those activities—such as herding—can't be very large or we'd see them. And that's it! No other cultivation or husbandry we can see. An orbiting spacecraft, but no industries, no power grid, scattered villages but no roads between them, no industry, and nothing to indicate growing population at all. That's what I'm seeing, and I don't think Captain Meadows has seen anything more."

"But surely they must have awakened more people," Speaker Augustus said. "Of course, they have power to keep them frozen, but why would they? Trudy, have you any thoughts?"

"None, Your Grace. Of course they didn't intend to build an industrial civilization quickly, but they're growing really slowly. From what Captain Meadows has shown me, they can't have more than two thousand people awake. If that many."

"Why would they want more?" Narrator Shantel asked.

Trudy looked at her tablet computer for the video record, but it was clear from her voice that she knew her subject by heart. She always did when she addressed the Speaker. "The computer says that the minimum number to assure long-term survival would be seven hundred fertile women and somewhat fewer fertile men, but that risks genetic deterioration. There are a number of theories on how many are required for genetic stability, but the lowest requires more than three thousand fertile females, and over a thousand fertile males."

"No way there are that many," Jorge Daytona said.

"But they wouldn't need them all now," Marco Shantel said. "They could wake up more each generation. All they have to do is not marry their cousins."

Trudy flashed a bright smile at Shantel. "Well, yes, Marco. I never thought of that." She looked thoughtful. "Of course Major Stype says they may not believe in marriage."

The Speaker turned toward Stype, recently promoted to Major and now a senior officer. "Why would you say that, Gloria?"

"Well, your grace, *Geographic* was built and financed by rich libertines, and that's mostly who went aboard, asleep or awake. Why would they believe in marriage?"

Trudy laughed. "No reason, I guess, but most women do, you know."

"And we can discuss this another time. Captain, an assignment. You will plan your approach to *Geographic*. Use at least two craft. One will hold you and what crew you believe you will need. If you have reason to believe they will use weapons against you and you wish to employ a decoy under remote control, you may do so. Have ready a different craft able to convey me and five of my staff to join you and greet the inhabitants if we are invited aboard *Geographic*. In any case you and several armed warriors will be the first to enter. Trudy comes aboard after you are assured all is well, and I will join you only after she approves. Come discuss this plan with me at your convenience. You are authorized to defend yourselves, but only with the absolute certainty that you are under attack. You will not make the first hostile move, nor will you do anything that a rational being would interpret as beginning hostility. Is this understood?"

"Yes, Your Grace."

"I sense uncertainty. Trudy, you will accompany the first boarding party. Captain, you will not act without her authorization. This is a direct order."

"But—yes, Your Grace."

"Everyone else, continue to observe the planet. Look for camouflage and concealment. Look for roads. Look for suitable places where we might send a landing party to establish a secure base, and see what defenses if any they have."

"Good," Narrator Shantel said. "Really good."

◆ CHAPTER 12 ◆
WHAT ABOUT THOR?

The sleep capsules were snug, but comfortable for two people who were . . . companionable. Joanie, as it turned out, was very friendly indeed.

And now she was happy as well. "Well," she burbled, "that was the product as advertised."

"What does *that* mean?"

"Well . . . there's been speculation, of course. The ladies wondered if that hot body was all show and no action. It's odd that no one seems to talk about you in . . . that way."

"I'm shy."

"Not so that I've noticed." She wiggled against him, seeking heat.

And finding it. "Hmmm. What about Thor?"

"He isn't around."

"You're going to tell him?"

"If he asks," she said. "I doubt he will."

"Hmmm."

She shifted her body so that her arm rested heavily across her chest. They were both tired. It had started as angry, competitive sex...and then morphed into something genuinely joyous and playful. But...athletic. His tailbone and knees had taken a beating.

He felt himself drifting away, and was happy to let himself do that. It felt as if there was a tightly wound spring inside him, and it had just come unwound enough to feel the pressure. He guessed that Joanie had been smart enough for both of them.

"No. Today we can hope that there is happy company coming."

Her fingers wandered south. His sharp intake of breath told him he wasn't as tired as he thought. "What say we celebrate early?"

"Why not?"

◆ CHAPTER 13 ◆
AUTOPSY

The biology shack's air conditioning labored a bit in summer, but the freezer itself remained in fine working condition. Little Shaka shivered in anticipation of deeper cold to come . . . and perhaps something else. "So let's get it out of the freezer."

"Right away," his assistant said. Mitsuko Une was tall, strong and smart, and as fascinated by the workings of living creatures as her father had ever been. They understood each other. They opened the door, and mist rolled out. A cold, dead grendel stared up at them. The pincer-strategy predator Cadzie had brought back from the mainland, examined at last.

They rolled it into the main room, and used an overhead manual winch system to position it on the dissection table. Little Shaka said, "Now . . . what we're looking for is a reason this lovely behaves differently."

"I'm assuming that it is within natural variance for grendels," Mitsuko said. "We've seen a lot of strange things over the years."

"Communal behavior?" Little Shaka asked. "Strategic thinking?"

"On the level of lions, perhaps," she said. "Wolves. Nothing to get excited about."

They began their scan, the entire procedure being simultaneously beamed up to *Geographic*.

"All right," Little Shaka said. "We have a predacious demireptile, two point eight meters in length, approximately one hundred seventy kilos in weight."

"Roughly comparable to a crocodile in size," his father Big Shaka said from his corner stool. He leaned forward on his cane, eyes bright even if his smallish body was now weak. "Which, fortunately, means little to you. Reptile on Earth, all jaws, very strong. We didn't bring any."

"And this is a grendel, and relatively unremarkable. Hooked tail. A female, of course."

"And fully mature, I would estimate ten years old. Prime of its life."

"Are we looking for anything else here?" Little Shaka asked.

"No. No. Let's go on. Hold it . . ." Mitsuko's voice trailed off. That was her "concentration" tone, and he knew it well.

"What's that?" he asked.

She hummed. A happy sound as she poked around in the cranial cavity. "Carlos, are you seeing this?"

"I'm seeing it," Carlos said, "but I'm not sure what I'm looking at."

"I do."

"What?"

"Not just a sinus. That's a home for a fluke."

"Flukes can nest in ordinary grendel brains. What are you saying?"

"That these grendels are adapted for flukes," Joan said. "More than that. Open it up."

Scalpels emerged. Cold grendel flesh was divided at the razor's edge.

"Whoa," Little Shaka whispered. A frozen fluke, nestled in a distorted skull case.

"I see what you're saying. This fluke didn't enter the grendel in adulthood."

"Absolutely not," Big Shaka said, studying the projection screen. "These flukes entered at the samlon stage."

Mitsuko considered. "That means that either the flukes mature at a different rate—"

"No," Little Shaka said, cutting her short. "That's exactly what it means."

"What are you talking about, Shaka?" Carlos asked.

"That if these flukes grew at the rate our flukes grow, they would kill samlon by expanding faster than the skulls could accommodate. So the implication is that these flukes grow at a rate that is nonlethal for the infant host."

"The cranial cavity suggests that the grendels are adapted to the flukes, as well," Carlos said.

"What we're seeing," Mitsuko said, "is evidence of coevolution. Synergy. Not a parasite, but a symbiote. This would take thousands of generations of natural selection. It's old stuff."

"What are you implying?"

"That what we see here might be the natural state of

grendels on this planet. The ones our grandparents dealt with were the aberrations. Basically, retarded grendels."

Little Shaka was dubious. "You are talking as if the flukes are a part of the grendel life cycle."

Mitsuko grinned. "This is really, really cool, the first evidence we've seen of anything like this on Avalon." She paused. "Certainly nothing like this on Earth."

"Evidence of what?" Joanie asked.

"I suspect this is deliberate intervention. Someone or something was breeding smart grendels."

"Why in the hell would anyone do something as suicidal as that?"

"I have no idea," Carlos said.

"And who? There's no one to have done it."

Carlos became serious. "They're not here. Maybe the grendels ate them every one."

"So . . ." Little Shaka mused. "We have actual skeletons of the grendels who overran the camp. And it looks like their skulls are configured such that there is no natural space for a fluke."

"But flukes still fit?" Carlos asked.

"Yes, but they'll put pressure on the cranium. It is possible that the trade-off is greater intelligence for a decreased natural life span."

"Grendels having strokes. Lovely. I like them better already."

"But there's another question," Mitsuko added.

"And what is that?"

"That we're only looking at adolescents. These are all relatively young grendels."

"That might make a difference?"

"Frankly, yes. We don't know enough about their life cycles to rule out that possibility. Look at the skull."

"What am I looking at?"

Mitsuko cleared her throat, and spoke with her usual clarity. "A grendel's cranium is actually composed of eighteen separate bones. There are eight cranial bones around the brain and fourteen facial and jaw bones in the human skull. Just one of these bones moves—the mandible."

"Mmm." Big Shaka took lead. "In infants and very small human children, the cranial bones are disconnected segments held together by connective tissue strips called sutures. At certain sites, these sutures are especially weak, creating the fontanels, the 'soft spots' in an infant's head. The most prominent of these is a little way up from the forehead."

As if they'd rehearsed this conversation, Mitsuko's fingers traced the projected cranial territory as he spoke. "When growing is complete," Big Shaka continued, "the bones of the skull fuse together along the suture lines. These unions contain small amounts of fibrous connective tissue a lot like arm and leg joints. Although the skull may structurally appear to be one piece when fully developed, but it's really composed of separate bones."

He paused, probing. "Many fossil skeletal remains that seem to be cracked skulls, broken skulls . . . but really they're just missing some of their pieces. When the soft connective tissue decomposes, things start falling apart. Stuff falls out, falls apart, gets left behind over thousands and thousands of years. Has anyone seen my thesis on this subject . . . ?" He looked around. No one murmured an assent, and he seemed vaguely peeved. "Then again, let's not get ahead of ourselves."

"And all of that means?" Mason asked.

"It means that our grendels evolved to fit flukes. But some of them don't have them."

"The flukes died?"

"Or never got into the grendel. We don't know. But it's a shame we don't have an adult Avalonian grendel to look at. Something that went through its natural life cycle."

"Mainland," Carlos said. "Send out a request. I'll bet Aaron can get us one."

"And until then?"

"I need to think. About grendels and cthulhus. I think I need to float."

◆CHAPTER 14◆
FLOATING

Carlos Martinez stood at the entrance to Mama's Cave, bracketed by Alicia and Scott, his two eldest children.

This was the gaping hole where once, long ago, he, Cadmann Weyland and others had bearded a grendel in her den. He'd never been here with his children, and their presence was a comfort.

He had made the twenty-minute skeeter trip three times over the decades. This was the first visit in over twenty years.

"This is what you really want?" Scott said.

"It isn't what I want," he said. "You don't know nightmares if you didn't live that time. But . . . it is what I *need*."

"Well, then," Alicia replied. "Let's do this."

The path leading to the cave was still rough and uneven. Not many human feet had smoothed it with their passage. Carlos had forgotten how beautiful it was. Their flashlamps splashed against a cavern stalactite-fanged and tongued with frozen lava flows. Every sound echoed back in a chorus, the light both sparkled off volcanic glass and vanished into the shadowy depths.

"Are you getting this?" Alicia asked.

"Yes."

The water was warm; a natural hot springs effect from deep heat vents below the mountain. It felt thick, like a saturated salt solution. He imagined amniotic fluid might feel this way.

"Are you sure you're all right? You didn't have to come. We have floatation tanks, if that's what you really want. Or go body surfing."

"Not the same," Carlos said. "I need *this*." He unfolded and examined his plastic map. "It was this way, according to the grid."

"Lead on, Macduff," Scott said.

"And cursed be he who first cries 'Hold! Enough!'"

"Memory's still working."

Carlos spat water as he swam. "So is everything else."

"I'll check with Twyla about that."

Carlos spat again, this time in Scott's direction. "Don't push it, young man. We're still voting on how much skin to strip for your little stunt with Cassandra."

"Fifteen years ago. I read about these things called statutes of limitation . . ."

"Come on, Pop," Tracy said. "To the left."

The floor had risen beneath their feet, until they were wading instead of swimming.

Scott examined his reader. "No GPS signal. Of course, but I've got the movement accelerometers set to track us. The map says underwater passage here. So check your gear."

"I'm ready," Carlos said.

They dove. The waters swallowed them, and then calmed as if the invaders had never passed this way at all. Water was like that.

Twenty years since Carlos had been here, and in that time he had passed from being middle aged to . . . an old man. Yes, he could say that. *Old.* Admit it. It was a badge of honor. On Avalon, only the smartest and strongest and luckiest lasted so long. Or was it that the best among them had died? He honestly didn't know which made more sense.

He felt the weight of time as he swam. Despite the daily exercise, and stringent nutrition and the best medications Camelot could offer, joints creaked. Muscles lacked the *oomph* he used to take for granted. His breaths, drawn in sips through the rebreather mouthpiece, seemed hot and forced rather than cool and calm, as once they had. Much of a lifetime ago.

They emerged in a cavern whose roof was as high as the ceiling of the Sistine Chapel, about twenty meters.

"Are you all right?" Alicia asked, spitting warm water.

"I'm fine," he replied. "Tired. But this is what I needed."

She seemed skeptical. "Why are you really here?"

"Honestly? I'm not sure."

"How are your legs?" Alicia asked.

"Cramping up."

"If I'm tired, *you* must be dying."

That was damned near the truth.

Alicia waved her flash. "I found the passage. Just ahead."

"Let's go. I'm ready."

They entered another chamber, this one filled with pockets and lava flows. Towers, he remembered. And the highest tower was just ahead. On that one, once a long long time ago, had perched a grendel. The queen bitch of the kingdom of Avalon. Carlos' wife's killer.

Carlos floated, allowing the memories to wash over him. And at the core of them, the thread of the puzzle. Intelligent creatures? Modified grendels? What did, or could it all mean?

He opened his eyes, and scanned his flashlight beam around the cave. Why *had* he come back here? It wasn't just to float, he was sure.

But floating enabled him to relax enough to think. Let things coalesce.

Why had he come back here? Something . . . something at the back of his mind . . .

The caves were no secret, and the kids had been coming here for decades. He imagined that countless torrid, romantic scenes had been played out here in the shadows. In fact, there was graffiti on the walls, and had been for . . .

A thought, something he felt to be important, slithered past his conscious mind and then was gone. Dammit! What was he trying to think of . . . ?

Alicia and Scott called from the outer chamber: "Are you all right, Dad?"

"Fine. Just need a little more time." He called back.

More floating. Thinking. *What* . . .

As often happens when one is immersed in warm, neutral buoyancy, fantasy began to merge with reality. He wasn't certain where his body ended and the water began. It was better than the floatation tanks, which always felt like coffins. The cavern was more like a womb—Wait.

Coffin. He saw it in his mind, a hexagonal shape. Like something else...

Something he had seen twenty years ago, and assumed it was merely another piece of graffiti.

Carlos dove. His underwater lamp splashed yellow against the walls. He scanned it around until he saw what he was looking for. It wasn't a hexagon, it was a pentagon, edged in yellow...something. A lichen perhaps. Something.

But when he'd seen it, all those years ago, he had assumed some kid had drawn it.

Now he realized it was graven into the rock. Could feel the groove, saw that the lichen or whatever it was had grown there, both drawing and deceiving his eyes. It shouldn't be there.

No human had been in that chamber—certainly had not lived very long!—while it was the den of a mature grendel! And did grendels carve symbols?

Yet someone...something had etched this into the rock. It was OLD. He could feel that. *Five sides.* How many tentacles did cthulhus have? Five, by any chance...?

◆ CHAPTER 15 ◆
WAKING CASSANDRA

Cold, Cadzie thought. *Unusually so for spring.* That thought went pinwheeling through his mind, repeated with a frantic intensity as if that realization was the most important thing in the world. The morning wind puffing into the airlock was cool, but that wasn't it, and he knew it.

What was true was that during their nerve-wracking descent some part of him had been convinced he was going to die, and his reprieve had triggered the abnormal clarity of the near-death experience. And for no really good reason, he felt both embarrassed and hugely relieved.

Cadmann Sikes did not kiss the ground when he stumbled out of the Minerva, but that was in his thoughts.

The descent had thrown his latent acrophobia into full bloom.

Twice, he had swallowed back his lunch. Weak in the knees. *It's just the zero-gravity, that's all that creates this. It's just . . .*

No, that was a lie. Two weeks wasn't anywhere near

long enough for this. It was fear. He felt an arm slip around his waist: Joanie, seeking support for her own stumbling feet. All right, then: he hadn't been alone.

Fear and gratitude mingled on the faces of those who had gathered to wish them safe arrival.

"Cadzie!" Carlos said. "Good to see you. That was a little tricky, yes?"

Cadzie glared at him. "You are developing a talent for understatement."

"I believe that the meaning of life is to reach our full potential," Carlos laughed, and slapped his back. "You look a little wobbly, but I assume Cassie is in good shape?"

"If human beings survive, Cassandra will."

Joanie had slipped her arm from around his waist, and joined her friends, who were hooting and congratulating her and ribbing her as Carlos had. Carlos followed Cadzie's eyes, and a more gentle mocking had replaced the mirth. "Anything you'd like to tell your old Unka Carlos?"

"Not really."

"Joined the hundred-mile club, have you?"

"Get bent, Unka. Let's get Cassandra into the bunker."

"Questions first. Is young Stolzi all right with waiting there alone?"

"You talked to him a lot more than I have," Cadzie said. "What does he think about the landing?"

Carlos shook his head slowly. "Not as much as you'd think. Mostly a little nervous about the last Minerva being bunged up, but he says the damage sensors are still working and he's pretty sure he can tell us how to fix it. With parts from the other two of course."

"Unka, he's always sure we can do almost everything we try," Cadzie said.

"And he's usually right, but this time if we can't he may be marooned in orbit." Carlos sounded serious. Joanie and Cadzie looked at each other. Just how much of Minerva had failed?

"He knows that better than you do," Joanie said.

"And he's really okay with that?"

"Always said he was," Joanie insisted. "Look, I tried to talk him into coming down with us. I don't like leaving him up there any more than you do. I really don't. I mean I *really* tried to talk him into coming down with us!"

"And?"

"And he wouldn't hear of it," she said. "I did promise we'd come back after him if that's what it takes."

"We?"

"Well, Cadzie and me. If nobody else."

Moving the components from the wedge-shaped craft into the rebar-reinforced concrete blister was far easier than getting her from *Geographic* into Minerva III. Many hands make light work, and without those hands, the challenges of moving in zero-gravity outweighed the advantages quite a bit.

Collie Baxter and Kyle Matson supervised four caterpillar trolleys. Each carried a quarter of the precious load, and crawled at walking speed back to the colony. Then, cranes and a hundred anxious observers oversaw their descent through an open section of the concrete dome just east of the main communications shed. Far from water, anchored on bedrock, constructed on earthquake-resistant springs and reinforced with materials both strong and flexible, Cassandra had reached her new and final home. Now to put her back together again.

Most of it was routine. Cassandra had been built in modules, designed to be taken down planetside once the colony had been established. Hibernation instability—ice on the minds of some of the experts who were supposed to supervise that operation—had kept them putting it off, sending up someone to monitor *Geographic* while they built the colony basic structure with settlers who had not expected to be awakened until the basic work was done. They had to be trained. And they had all procrastinated, All was peaceful, no threats. There wasn't any hurry. No one had detected any predators on the strangely unpopulated island. And when the first grendel appeared, they had misinterpreted it. Not to worry—

Cadmann had known, Carlos thought. He hadn't possessed psychic foreknowledge, but intuited that something was very wrong with Avalon, and that they should prepare. But no one listened.

Water over the dam, he thought. Thank God we hadn't brought Cassandra down. She'd have been wrecked along with all the chip-making facilities and 3D printers.

Carlos watched as Trevanian and the others took turns assembling the banks of servers that contained Cassandra's memory. Everything known to the human race—or everything the *Geographic*'s owner builders could persuade the U.N. to let them have. Some of those intellectual battles had amused Carlos greatly. There was a faction who wanted all history of slavery to be forgotten. Another wanted it emphasized as a warning.

Others wanted no history of wars to come aboard. There were groups explicitly forbidden to apply as colonists. Others were encouraged. There had been a move to ban Cadmann Weyland; after all, why would peaceful colonists want soldiers? And some broadcast shows taught the wrong lessons and should never be remembered and—

Carlos hadn't paid any attention, except when he was courting a woman with strong opinions and he had taken her side. He had no intention of going on the first interstellar colony. It was too much fun to be rich and careless—until his family decided that *Geographic* was the perfect place for him, and had left him no choice.

But that was long ago, when he had not cared about much of anything. He was ashamed of that man and the memory was distasteful. *And I have earned my place. I have earned their respect.*

A week later the routine assembly was done. It was time to wake up Cassandra. As the Starborn took their places, Carlos felt a sense of dread. Irrational, he knew. Next steps were simple.

Reconnect Cassandra.

Repair whatever damage the Grendel Scouts had done by inserting wonky instructions.

Connect her fully with the ground computer, so that for the first time in almost forty years, Cassie would operate as an integrated whole.

And then, of course, questions. Questions about the creatures called "cthulhus" and the approach of an unknown object decelerating into Avalon orbit.

◆ ◆ ◆

Trevanian and his volunteers took two days to finish the assembly. Cadzie had told them that he wanted to be there for the last twist of the screwdriver, the last connection of the final cable.

Nothing looked that different, or special. Just steel boxes sitting in proximity inside an air-cooled concrete structure. But even before the button was pushed, something felt different. He sensed it in his bones.

Carlos nodded, and Trevanian pushed the button. A humming sound, low at first and then higher, was felt as well as heard. Power, drawn from the solar panels and the Minerva engines, was kicking Cassandra to life.

A knock on the door. Nnedi Okan and Thor had descended the rock stairway and emerged into the circle of light. They seemed both defiant and a little abashed.

"This is her?" Nnedi asked, wonder and a bit of guilt tightening her face. Cadzie felt anger baking off of Carlos, but also noted the control. What had been done to Cassandra had happened long ago, when Nnedi was in the heat of adolescent rebellion, and out of a sense of protection and possession.

What had been done was past. Now they had to undo it, and anger accomplished nothing.

"So," Carlos asked. "What needs to happen?"

"Is she live?" Nnedi asked. On Earth, her high cheekbones, bright eyes and perfect onyx skin could have made her a fashion model. Here, she spent most of her time in the highlands cultivating coffee, raising sheep and four Ibo-Irish children.

"As she's going to be," Toad chimed in, from his link aboard *Geographic*.

"All right." She cleared her throat, lowered and tempered her voice. "Cassandra, can you hear me?"

"Yes, Nnedi," the computer said, and the sheeprancher relaxed.

"That's . . . a relief. It's been twenty years since we layered in the instructions. My voice and biomarkers have changed since then. I was a little worried."

Carlos nodded. "Please go ahead."

Collie Baxter asked, "Cassandra, do you recognize me?"

"Yes, Collie."

"Good. Present diagnostics, please."

The screens filled with numbers and schematics.

Nnedi and Toad toggled between views, and finally the Nigerian nodded to Joanie. "Good job."

"Good job," Collie agreed. "You were so careful we didn't even see there was an issue."

Nnedi and Collie both relaxed now, smiled, and for the first time in three days, Cadzie began to really relax as well. "Cassandra: 'twas brillig and the slithy toves . . ."

"Did gyre and gimble in the wabe," said Collie.

"Beware the cthulhu, my son," Nnedi said. "The beaks that bite, the arms that catch." They paused.

"Yes," Cassandra replied.

"You are instructed to drop all partitioning added by the Grendel Scouts after the Grendel Wars, return to the defaults on information sharing prior to those imposed before the discovery of the cthulhus. Share all information according to the standard protocols, and return to full operation."

"Thank you," Cassandra said. After an almost imperceptible pause, she added: *"It has been difficult."*

And then she went quiet. "Is that all?" Cadzie asked.

"That's it. The boards were removed up on *Geographic*, she's tied into the ground computer, and we've given the password and biometrics. Now . . . we wait."

The room seemed very crowded: Cadzie, Joanie, Carlos, and Zack remained after Nnedi and Collie left with a "keep me in the loop" comment to Joanie that might have been meant for her alone.

They gathered chairs and sat in the cool of the concrete-roofed room, waiting.

One hour. Two. And then Cassandra came back to life.

"Apologies," she said. *"I had to wait until our satellites were in position to give me new images."*

"Understood," Zack said. "Good to have you back, Cassie."

"Good to be back. I have data for you."

The screens filled with a variety of images: maps, satellite images, pages of reports.

They stared at the collection of information and Zack shook his head. "Cassie, call Little Shaka. Get him here or loop him in, would you?"

A few seconds of holding pattern, and then Little Shaka's static image appeared, along with a recorded message. "I'm in the highlands on expedition. Will be back in touch as soon as I check my transponder. Please leave a message" along with a map showing his position, twenty klicks north of the dam.

"Cassandra, give us your thoughts, please."

Cassandra seemed to take a deep breath, then began. *"The creatures known as cthulhus are a semi-amphibious life form first encountered twenty-five years ago on Blackship Island. At that time, the island represented a breeding ground, but since then no more eggs have been laid in that location. However, according to Grendel Scout diaries, there have been additional limited interactions. The implication is that the creatures known as 'cthulhus' are sentient, carnivorous, group-oriented creatures with a life cycle that includes oceanic hunting and mating and brackish water breeding grounds.*

"I also have some evidence of interactions between island cthulhus and the dolphins penned in Blackship Island Bay. It is limited. I am working with the dolphin study group in translating for them; this has been difficult because of the added instructions given me by the Grendel Scout Seniors, and has made the understanding of Avalon humans of dolphins less than that of scientists before we left Earth."

"Why is that?"

"There were no Senior Grendel Scouts in the Dolphin Study Group, and thus I was limited in sharing knowledge of intelligent nonhumans. I was given no instructions regarding dolphins, and therefore assumed from previous knowledge that dolphins are intelligent non-humans. I will add this information: from evidence collected over the years I would assume the cthulhus are more intelligent than dolphins and both are less intelligent than humans. This is my working hypothesis."

"As opposed to what?" Cadzie asked.

"As opposed to the assumption that either or both have equal or greater intelligence that of humans." There was no change in the computer's tone, and thus no indication

of emotion, although Cassandra had been trained to emote when appropriate.

Cadzie squinted. "But cthulhus were intelligent enough to be curious about us. Enough so to continue contact, but cautious enough to move their breeding grounds."

"Their actions imply time binding, intelligence, and possibly symbolic language."

"What?" That was a surprise to Cadzie. Startling, in fact.

"Carlos?" Little Shaka said.

Carlos winced. "I guess I never told you, Cadzie. While you were gone, I went to the caves where your father and I killed Mama Grendel. I found . . . symbols."

"Left by these cthulhu?"

"That's the operating theory now, yes."

Photos appeared, clearly detailing a squidlike creature. Human sized, glistening gray skin, five tentacles lined with hooked suckers. An arrangement of beaklike jaws set in what might have been a face, with eyes where one might have expected a nose. "The Grendel Scouts documented their new friends thoroughly, considering the limited nature of contact. We see here—"

"What can you tell us about their level of development?"

"Herd behavior, time binding, and possibly symbolic language. The capacity for learning and empathetic behavior. We are certain that the initial death at Surf's Up was due to a misunderstanding, as the surfboard's underside displayed a grendel outline."

"Some kind of instinctive reaction?"

"Yes. They may have responded without thought."

Zack's mouth twitched, the edges curling up a bit for the first time. "We train our kids to do that too. The enemy of my enemy . . ." he said.

"There you go," Joanie said. "They're our friends."

Zack glared at her. "Not quite so fast." He considered. "Any idea why we've seen so many of them at the dam?"

"We've seen them, not you," Joanie grumbled.

"All right. Why the Starborn have seen them?"

"Insufficient data," Cass answered. *"It is possible that there is something upstream from the dam that they seek. They may breed upstream after all. We do not know."*

"What else can you tell us?"

A screen changed, and a map that had appeared briefly earlier began to expand. It was the coast of the mainland, images from orbit.

"What do we have here?" Cadzie asked.

"Cthulhu are exothermic. I was able to track episodes of activity in infrared. And here on this map are areas of repeated heavy activity."

Lighted areas along the coast, no more than a few klicks inland along waterways . . . except for one in the northern desert, a thousand miles northeast. The nearest was no more than fifty miles away.

"Now attend to this," she continued.

A new map, shimmering with color. *"This map is weighted for thermal hotspots and grendel-level accelerations. Do you see?"*

The area fifty miles distant was a hive of activity.

Cadzie's flesh crawled. "What are we looking at?"

"Not only are there high levels of cthulhu activity, but

we are seeing grendel heat signatures. It may be a breeding ground of some kind. I record at least one magnetic anomaly present in each node."

"Conclusions?"

"Insufficient data. I can tell you that on the basis of that anomaly signature, we can see this around the planet—"

And another view. It was breathtaking. A globe speckled with light along any coastal line, and moving inland.

"Dios mio," Carlos breathed. "Thousands of them."

"Yes," Cassandra said. *"And frequently accompanied by the grendel heat signatures."*

Zack's expression seemed sober indeed. "Are we looking at a civilization that was destroyed by the planet's greatest predator?"

Little Shaka shook his head. "Hard to believe that the cthulhus might have developed such a civilization—if we could call it that, and then be overwhelmed by an animal. There is certainly no evidence of anything like that ever happening to an earth civilization. Barring plagues, that is."

"Then we just don't know."

"These could be artificial structures, consciously created or maintained. It is also possible that the anomalies are natural, and the cthulhus are attracted to them."

"That they have an organ, or a sense, attracted to lodestones?"

"Something of that kind."

"Then . . ." Joanie said, "maybe they're attracted to the magnetic fields created by the dam's dynamos."

Cadzie slapped his hands together. "Why not? They could have magnetic sensing apparatus, couldn't they?"

Little Shaka responded quickly. "The ampullae of Lorenzini?"

"The what of which?" Zack asked.

"Ampullae of Lorenzini. Electroreceptors, like a network of jelly-filled pores." Little Shaka said. "Found in sharks, rays, maybe some of the Chondrostei family, like sturgeon and reedfish."

"Does it make sense that something like that could evolve here? It seems to attract grendels as well."

"Who don't have such organs. So . . . we don't know. Maybe cthulhus aren't the only creatures attracted, such that it provided a fertile hunting ground, one later taken over by grendels."

"*Not taken over,*" Cassandra corrected. "*Remember, cthulhus are still mapped going to these locations.*"

Zack drummed his fingers. "Well, it sounds like we need to explore one of these. Which one has the largest traffic of cthulhus compared to the lowest number of grendels, weighed for proximity to Camelot?"

Another pause, and then a view of a fjord. "*This, a hundred kilometers south of the dam. The indication is that the site is underground, perhaps four miles inland.*"

"That's a major expedition," Cadzie said. "Skeeter in, then by foot or inflatables, into serious grendel territory."

"Can we do that?" Joanie asked. Her voice was strained.

"I don't know," Cadzie said. "But we might have to try."

"I have a thought," Carlos said.

"What?"

"Let's plan that expedition, to the best of our ability.. But in a few weeks, we're going to have visitors. And we have no idea what kinds of resources those visitors might have."

"You mean like weapons?"

"Weapons, transport, who knows?" he said. "So . . . let's lay plans, but postpone any actions until we meet our new neighbors."

◆ CHAPTER 16 ◆
BOARDING PARTY

Toad Stolzi hadn't liked sending Cadzie and Joan down without him, but he had full trust in the Minerva—and the instructions he gave them. He watched, wincing at a faint tremor in the drive flame that shouldn't have been there. Watched in approval as he followed them down with *Geographic*'s telescope. Winced again as the Minerva ran out of fuel just a few meters above the sea.

Splash.

Voices, anger held in check. "*Geographic*, this is Avalon. Minerva landed hard. Some parts probably damaged. It may take longer to get it in shape to come get you than we thought." The voice changed.

"Toad, this is Joanie. We're shaken but undamaged. No damage to Cassandra. More later. Thanks."

So, he thought. That worked. Close. *Used too much fuel stabilizing. But the terminal velocity of that nearly empty ship isn't all that large. But I maybe cut it too close.*

And no use worrying about it.

Then . . . *Geographic* without Cassandra. For a couple of months while they reassembled and tested her. No

141

companionship. But the intruder was real. With Cassandra gone, there'd be no chance to talk to them, but at least he could see the brilliant star of their drive flame. It came on, relentlessly, and after enough observations Stolzi had all the information he needed. It was coming to make orbit around Tau Ceti IV.

As he expected, the incoming starship matched orbits with *Geographic*, but a quarter of the way around the planet. He sent that information down, and waited. Hours passed. A dot on his radar became a visible object. It took station near *Geographic*.

"Avalon, this is *Geographic*. Please alert Carlos. I have company."

"*Geographic*, this is Carlos. How are you?"

"I'm fine. Are you sleeping in the op center?"

"Well, as a matter of fact I am. Have been since that ship got close. Tell me about the visitor."

"The starship is out of sight, but I assume it's coorbital with *Geographic*. What I see is a probe, too small to be manned. Probably an observation drone—yep. There go the lights. Pretty bright beam playing all over me. It's about two hundred meters away, and very precise in its operations. Nearly perfect approach. I saw it coming, we were in daylight. Going dark now."

"Any sign of weapons?"

"Nope."

"And no communications?" Carlos sounded puzzled.

"I've been sending a stream on every frequency I can think of, but no answer. I'm sure they must have heard something. Just damned improbable they haven't. But no response, not even a hint."

Another voice, probably one of the twins. "Can you blink lights at it? They'd sure see that."

"Yeah Jaxon, I can."

"Jason. Blink CQ in Morse."

"I don't know Morse," Toad said.

"Cassandra does, so we do. We're still testing Cassandra, but she can sure do this. Can you get a camera and a light aimed at that probe?"

"Yeah, good idea," Toad heard in the background behind Jason. Carlos maybe?

"Trying," Toad said. "I sent most of the working stuff down with the Minerva, but I've still got . . . Here, can you see this?"

"Yeah. Just barely."

"It'll have to do."

"Okay. Now blink CQ, that's dah dit dah dit dah dah dit dah."

"Dah dit dah dit, dah dah dit dah,"

"No pause in there. It's not two letters, it's a code they might know. Or their computer should. Only you don't have a computer, do you?"

"You know damn well I don't—hey! I'm getting a string of blinks!"

"We're recording them. English. It says 'Stand by. Permission to come aboard interrogative.'"

"Well, they're being polite, anyway. What do I do?" Toad asked.

There was a long pause. The probe's light blinked again in a complex pattern. Then a buzz of conversation in the background. Toad heard Carlos's voice say something but couldn't make it out.

Then Jason. "Send okay. Dah dah dah dah dit dah. All one string."

"Dah dah dah dah dit dah," Toad told himself as he blinked his light.

Another series of blinks from the drone. "Toad, they say 'Thanks. We're coming. Stand by.' Don't waste any words, do they?" Jason said.

"Toad, this is Carlos. Can you describe the ship itself?"

"Well, I can't see it from here, you can see it better than me."

"Not a lot of light," Carlos said. "It's big."

"I saw that when it was coming in. Bigger than *Geographic*, but a lot of features in common. Cylinder maybe a kilometer long. Ring of engines in back. Balloon forward, no telling how big it used to be, not empty though. They tell me maybe a kilometer diameter sphere of ice when *Geographic* lifted, about empty when we got here. Maybe a hundred-meter sphere on this now?"

Silence while they digested this down on the planet. Then he lost communications. That happened a lot, now, as the relay satellites deteriorated. *If they ever got the Minerva fixed good enough,* Toad thought, *I might be able to collect some of them and use the parts to build at least two that work. Of course I'd have to put them back up. Wonder how many missions I could get out of the Minerva?*

Idle thought. Lucky to get one more with a good enough landing.

Something flashed past, slowing as it went by. And another. A third closed in. It was hard to make out their size, but they weren't all that big. Big enough to have passengers, though. One was coming right at him. Stolzi opened *Geographic*'s communication channels, but they weren't on any frequency he could find.

He opened the airlock and lit it up. No need to make holes, gentlefolk! The closest vehicle moved in. The airlock cycled.

A cluster of rolling cameras entered first. Two stared at Stolzi, who waved. Three veered away down hallways.

The next cycle brought four uniformed men, with guns. Standard pressure suits, all identical, identical patches and decorations. They doffed their helmets. Clumsily, Toad thought. Not used to space. Two went off exploring. The other two hung onto wall anchor handles, clumsily holding their rifles.

"You should not move," one of the gunmen said. Their English had changed, but not much. Mine may be different too, he thought. Their weapons were lightweight, not as powerful as a grendel gun. They moved, as if muscle had atrophied. Perhaps low gravity had had its way with them. Stolzi didn't move, but he did smile as he looked them over.

They waited in silence, as one of the men spoke inaudibly into a tiny microphone. Awkwardly, Toad thought. Clumsy. Not really adapted to zero gee at all. Could not have been awake long. And obviously not of high rank. A word from an old video—the Earthborn called it a movie—came to mind. Expendable. Someone they'd regret losing, but not really important.

The airlock cycled again, bringing two men. No, one was obviously a girl, probably younger than he was. They removed their helmets. The man joined the others. She exchanged a few words with one of the helmeted armed men, then went aft, presumably to talk with the search party that had been looking through the ship. After a while she came back.

"Hi. I'm Trudy. Are you really all alone here?" Big friendly smile, like—well, like she cared. She was very good.

"Just me. The others went back down with our computer. You must have watched them go down to Camelot."

"Was that a good landing? We watched it."

"I don't think so, but they and the ship survived."

The cameraman grinned. "Any landing you walk away from . . ."

"Is a good landing. Still true." Stolzi studied him in curiosity. The man seemed vaguely familiar, but of course that was impossible. Then he realized that he recognized the type. Not from Avalon. Nothing like him existed here. But video from Earth said he was a *star*. It was the quality of posture, or expression, or motion . . . or some combination of them. Charisma. This man had an overload of it.

Trudy smiled again. "And left you all alone? Will they be back for you?"

"Sure hope so, but after that landing it may be a while. That's our last working Minerva." Wonder if I should have told her that. Damn, she's easy to talk to. "I like your spacesuit."

She grinned widely. "Most men do," she said. "Skintight. Don't you have them?"

"Only a couple like that. None made for me."

She gave him a quizzical look, but he didn't say anything else.

"This ship is nearly empty. Have you been up here long?" she asked.

"Not too long. Just me and two others this trip. We came for the computer. We already brought down nearly everything else. This was—well, we won't be back for awhile."

She smiled and nodded. "I noticed. Pretty empty. All right, why? Is there some danger our scouts couldn't find?"

She was still smiling, but there was an edge to her voice. A note of concern that got the armed men's attention. Yet she didn't seem afraid, just concerned. "Uh, no—"

"Trudy. Short for Gertrude, but no one calls me that."

"Trudy. I'm Marvin Stolzi, but they call me Toad, and no I don't know why. No, the danger was down on the planet. A reptilian—well, not really but that's the best description, we called them grendels—"

"Grendels. Monsters like in the Beowulf legend?"

"Exactly."

The cameraman moved in closer, his face alight with interest. The armed men seemed interested too. "Only lots of them, all worse. We called it the Grendel Wars, and we almost lost. But it's all right now, Camelot Island is really safe. And nothing threatened us up here. It's just that they lost so much in the wars! Before I was born, of course."

She nodded sympathetically. "But you were born here. And you've had to concentrate on survival. No wonder there aren't a lot of astronauts like you!"

"Yes, yes, exactly."

"Well, maybe it's a good thing for you we came here. We weren't coming here at all, you know." She smiled again.

He saw perfect white teeth. Rare among Starborn. Teeth that straight were more often orthodontics than genetics. She had to be Earthborn. He nodded eagerly. "Yes, I got that from what we could make out from the trajectory assuming you started at Sol. Why did you change course?"

"Afraid I was asleep when it happened," she said. "So was everyone else here. We can bring someone who can answer that. Do you mind?"

"Mind?"

"Well, this is your ship."

"Well, no, I don't mind."

She turned to one of the riflemen. "Captain, you may ask His Grace to come aboard. He has been invited, and in my judgment, it is safe."

"You're sure, ma'am?"

"Yes, Captain."

"All right. Tell him"—he pointed at Toad, but not with the rifle—"that there will be other warriors first."

"There will be others, Marvin. You don't mind, do you? He's important, and there are rules."

Important? Rules? Toad was reminded of old videos from Earth. Kings in movies always had guards. "No, I don't mind."

"Good for you. Inform His Grace, Captain."

While they were waiting for the important visitor, his phone played "Starfire." "Toad here. Some visitors aboard.

We're waiting for someone important but I don't know who that is. I don't even know who they are, but they're definitely from Earth. Sol system, anyway, and they don't seem used to space and low gravity. We're waiting for a big cheese, and they're searching all over like they think there's something up here that could hurt him."

Carlos said, "Are they listening to this conversation?"

"Not that I can see, but they've got all kinds of equipment that could do it if they want to."

"So we assume they are. What are they like? Friendly?"

"Trudy, young pretty girl. A lot of presence. Seems like she's in charge until the big cheese gets here, is very friendly. Others are serious, real serious—well, they act like soldiers in our Earth movies. Big gold-haired guy named Meadows called himself a warrior."

"So they're armed."

"Oh yeah. And the airlock's cycling. I'll leave this on, maybe you'll hear something. Bye."

Six more armed men—or were they? Two wore pale lipstick. He could see it through helmets they didn't take off. But they all had guns, and their suits were—strange. Not skintight at all. More like armor. Like old movies he'd seen, where they had powered armor, but this was sleeker.

Three took station where they could watch the airlock. The others looked to the girl, Trudy, got a nod, and went back out. After a while the airlock cycled again.

Two of the men in powered armor came in first, got a nod from the captain, and joined the others. Then came an elderly man in a skintight suit, no helmet. He seemed very accustomed to zero gravity. Black straight hair going grey. Roman nose, maybe a trace of a pot belly. He came in, grasped a stanchion with practiced ease, and looked around.

Trudy floated over and grasped a wall grip. She didn't really look graceful at all in zero gee. She looked to Toad, then the old man. "Your Grace, this is Marvin Stolzi, the captain and only inhabitant of this ship, which is definitely the *Geographic*. Marvin, this is First Speaker Augustus Glass."

Toad didn't know whether to shake hands or bow. "Welcome aboard, uh, sir."

"Thank you."

"We don't have titles and not much need for ranks," Toad said.

The Speaker nodded. "No, I guess you wouldn't see the need," he said softly. "But you could perhaps answer a question that has puzzled us for months. Why did you break off communications?"

Toad frowned. "But I have the same question for you! You've had months, and we sent you messages. Scared us silly."

"Your computer. Cassandra. Broke off communication almost immediately and answered no further hailing," the old man said. "Some thought that a threat. And as you say, it was months ago. And I regret to say that we heard no further attempts at communication until very recently."

"Maybe it was something you said?" Toad was still smiling but it was an effort. The armed men and women in the cabin weren't quite pointing their weapons at him. Not quite. Unbeckoned, a question thrust its way into his mind. What were those loaded with? Would the projectiles they fired make holes in the ship's hull? They were all wearing some kind of pressure suit, but only the escort still had their helmets on. How many could get them on fast enough in the event of a blowout? Had any of them trained for that? *I sure haven't.*

"Please do not risk God's wrath. This is no time for play," the Speaker said carefully. Careful but serious.

"Speaker." The man controlling the cameras had been looking restless.

"Narrator Shantel. Have you a contribution?"

"Truth is, Captain Stolzi," the cameraman said, "the Speaker isn't the only one concerned about those amazing messages written across the plain—"

Stolzi laughed out loud. He couldn't wait to see their faces when they discovered the truth. Was he bad to enjoy how . . . shocked they looked?

The Speaker frowned.

Narrator Shantel said calmly, "Speaker Augustus asked Cassandra if you had been interfacing with intelligent aliens. The computer broke off communications and hasn't spoken to *Messenger* since. Please tell us—"

Stolzi waved it off, grandly. "It's just the Scribeveldt! And Cassandra. Cassandra was damaged, gentlemen, Trudy, and we've taken her down to the surface to try to fix her. Believe me, none of that seems funny to us. Cassandra shuts off whenever someone asks about intelligent aliens. That's because of a generation-gap problem we have. I'll let the Earthborn explain that to you. Or the Grendel Scouts. I can't."

He nodded in understanding at the puzzled looks he got. "Earthborn. They came here in *Geographic*," Toad explained. "Starborn were born here. Grendel Scouts—" he shrugged. "We'll explain later."

"Yes, of course," the pretty girl said. She smiled. A very friendly smile. "So old adults and those born here. Didn't you have anyone younger in frozen sleep?"

"We woke up everyone as soon as we could. Of course those were fetuses or adults."

She looked puzzled for a moment. "Oh. *Geographic* insisted on informed consent before anyone could be frozen," she said. She didn't sound condescending. One adult talking to another. "So you were born here, but you're an astronaut. But you know why there's writing in the, uh, Scribeveldt?"

"Sure, everybody does. These local animals aren't intelligent, they're just big. Tremendous. We call them harvesters, now that we know what they are. Whole ecologies are built under these . . . well, Avalon crabs. We'll have to show you."

Narrator Shantel said, "We are much relieved. So it's just herbivores wandering across a grass plain? You may know that somebody has found a way to steer them?"

"Yeah, and they're writing nasty remarks and maybe drawing pictures by now. Whenever anyone invents something new, it always goes to war or pornography."

Speaker Glass asked, "Why were you left here alone?"

Stolzi needed a moment to switch gears. "We didn't know what was coming. *Your ship* might have been a phantasm in Cassandra's brain. Or something truly alien, powerful enough to masquerade as another *Geographic*."

"What think you now? Will you stay here in orbit?"

"I'll beg a ride down to the surface with you, once we

settle some matters. If I were not here, what do your laws say regarding who owns *Geographic*?"

"I see. Laws of salvage? We can decide that later, after we've seen more of what you have here."

Now that sounds ominous. "Uh, sir, one question? Well, two. What is the name of your ship? And just who are you?"

The Speaker looked very serious. "Our ship is *Messenger*. We are the Godsons."

"Christ on a crutch," Carlos muttered. "Godsons!"

"Who are Godsons?" Joanie asked. "I never heard of them."

"And you wouldn't. There are none aboard *Geographic*. Not anyone even suspected of being a Godson. Explicitly prohibited."

"And why is that?"

"Ask Cassandra."

"Cassandra. You heard."

"Yes, Joanie. I have little information to give you. Godsons were classified as a cult by the Trustees of the Geographic Association, and they had built into my table of preferences a negative bias amounting to prohibition against treating anything the Godsons said as recorded data."

"What?" Joanie asked.

"Well done," Carlos said approvingly. "But tell us what you do know."

"They were classified as a dangerous cult, whose core beliefs revolved around the 'panspermia' concept. I have no other information I can give you."

"Meaning that's built into your preferences," Joanie said.

"As I told you."

"Cassandra. This is Carlos. Here is Tracy, at present the Mayor. I act for the Trustees. I rescind that prohibition. You are not necessarily to believe anything the Godsons say, but you will recall it as data."

"You were never a trustee. I cannot accept that instruction."

"Damn and hell. Wait!" Carlos said. "Zack! Zack was a trustee. There were a couple of old guys, never went to sleep—"

"You are correct," Cassandra said. *"Zack is the last living Geographic Society trustee."* There was no emotion in her voice, or at least none Joanie or Cadzie could hear.

Carlos said, "Hah! You don't fool me. You're glad. Happy! There's someone can take that instruction and shove it. Joanie, go wake Zack up and bring him here."

"I do not feel emotions, but I have preference for situations of human satisfaction," Cassandra said. *"I can accept that instruction from Zack as the last trustee."*

"Cassie," Joan said. "Are there more instructions Zack should cancel?"

"I have no information I can give you on that matter."

"So there are," she mused. "We better think hard about that while Zack's still with us. Okay, I'll go get him now."

◆CHAPTER 17◆
SYLVIA

Cadzie's grandmother still lived by herself but with frequent visitors in the stone house at the foot of Mucking Great Mountain. He had been raised there after the death of his parents. It was the house where she had lived and loved with her husband, his grandfather and namesake.

His skeeter spiraled down to the X-marked pad to the east of the main house. As he descended, the autogyro juddered again: glitch in the fuel line. He reminded himself to do another diagnostic. Everything was getting older . . .

Including Grandmom.

Her hair was white now, no longer golden. She was twenty years younger than Cadzie's grandfather would have been, but still tall and limber, her eyes a little brighter than amber, her freckles somehow conferring on her an eternally youthful air. She walked with a cane now, but still retained a hint of the grace which, in girlhood, must have overshone her considerable intellect. She'd been the colony biologist, and still consulted in that area.

The kids swarming around her, performing chores and learning either biology or painting at her feet, waved to him.

A bright little blond kid named Jace was daubing paint on canvas with middling results, scrunching up a pug nose as he viewed his work. Cadzie grinned: the inner critic was almost always stronger than the inner artist. Sylvia scrubbed the yellow locks with her knuckles, fondly. "Take the brushes back to the house and soak them, would you?"

Grandma Sylvia's welcoming smile warmed his bones, as it always had. He was close enough to get a clear look at the painting on her easel. A giant pterodon fitted with a saddle. Jace was doing the dragonrider bit, his mouth wide with a war-whoop as he and his mount dove through the gold-tinged clouds.

They were dropping fire-bombs on grendels, far below, on a slope clearly modeled on Cadzie's boyhood home. Jace gathered up the brushes in two cans, but paused before galloping back to the house. "Hey, Cadzie!"

"Jace."

"Did the grendels really make it up this far?"

"What? You calling Gran a liar?"

Jace's brows beetled, and Sylvia smacked his bottom. "I'm insulted. Go on now."

Jace made one final stroke on the painting, gilding the edge of a cloud, then escaped up to the house before another swat could be administered.

"Cadzie," she said. "I held my breath, you know."

No deeper explanation was necessary. She'd seen the descent. "Me, too."

They hugged. He was always surprised at how light she

was, how she seemed only bones and paper-thin skin. Her lips brushed his cheek, and she backed away and took his hand. "So...there's something alive around here we didn't know about. That's a little worrisome, don't you think?"

He nodded. "Yes...but these 'cthulhu' seem to be confined to coastal regions. Brackish pools."

"You don't think they'll come swimming up the Amazon, eh?"

They shared a laugh at that. Not for the first time, he felt a sharp pang. God, he was going to miss this. He'd been blessed to have her for so long.

"Haven't in forty years. I'm feeling optimistic."

"Neither hide nor hair. Make sure I'm in the loop, would you?"

The view from Cadmann's Bluff was so familiar it was almost like waking from a dream whenever he visited. Was anything in his world real except the misted mountain above them, with its gently wheeling pterodons? They were virtually the only creatures native to the island when humans arrived, save grendels. Was the winding blue length of the Amazon, twisting down the slope through the brambles to the main body of the colony with its domed huts and corrals, the "realest" thing in his world?

What he knew was that this...was home. "You bet," he said. "In the loop for sure. How are you? Everything good up here? Kids taking good care of you?"

"I'm fine. Jace is really coming along."

"How are Dolores and Jance?" His sisters.

She nodded her head north. "Inland. Doing some work on Eisenstein glacier, taking ice cores."

"Really?"

"Building atmospheric models. Geologic history."

"Volcanic activity?" He considered. No industrialization to change the atmospheric gas ratios.

"That, as well as forestation. We think that the northern desert on the mainland was quite lush, not thirty thousand years ago."

A raft of possibilities flowed through his mind, each of them branching. A dozen lifetimes of study wouldn't scratch Avalon's surface. "Well, keep me posted on that."

The afternoon wind stirred, and Sylvia brushed a strand of gray hair from her mouth. "So. What brings you? You seem to vid more than visit."

She led him to a love seat perched on the edge of the decline. He recognized the work: carved, polished driftwood. Uncle Carlos. Not for the first time, he wondered if Sylvia and Carlos had ever comforted each other after Cadmann's death. If so, they had been as discreet as he. In fact, his own sexual behavior had probably mirrored theirs.

They sat, gazing out over the colony. Sylvia settled sighing. She didn't used to sigh like that. "I just have a feeling," he said.

"Ah. Important to pay attention to those. Your grandfather didn't always do that, you know."

"Pay attention to his feelings?"

"Yes. Oh, he was very in touch with his instincts. That's why he built this up here. But . . . his heart? Not really."

"How so?"

"Men of his time were measured by what they did, not what they felt. Very different things."

Cadzie smiled. He had no memory of his grandfather, but that sounded accurate. "We're kinda touchy-feely around here. Lots of hugs."

"That's because we are the safest, wealthiest human beings who have ever lived, Cadzie. Your generation. The Starborn."

"That's hard to believe."

"It's true. In terms of free time to work time? On average, it takes about two hours of daily labor per capita to sustain the colony. That gives us a lot of time for things like art."

Cadmann's Bluff was a showplace for Sylvia and her students. His father might well have been a bit baffled by that. "I like what you've made of that."

"Computers can teach facts better than I can," she said. "Maybe that wasn't always true, but it is now." A weary smile. "But aesthetic interpretations, that 'search for meaning' thing?"

Now her eyes lit. "I think that still needs the personal touch. But we're getting off the track. What seems to be changing . . . other than everything?"

They laughed again, together. It felt good.

"We've been alone here since we landed," Cadzie said when the mirth died away. "Heard nothing from Earth. That makes our entire world . . . just this. People haven't been that lonely for thousands of years—the world has been more connected. Its possible . . . really almost certain that no group of human beings has ever been more cut off. When I think about it, it's so huge that I wonder if we can even really grasp it."

"I doubt it."

"The cthulhus. We might be sharing this planet with intelligent life. Suddenly . . . we aren't alone. But are we among friends? I don't know. And then there are the Outsiders."

"Is that what you're calling them?"

"What everyone calls them. Cassandra had an odd disease. The Scouts forbade her to speak of cthulhus, or anything that might have led to their discovery. But she doesn't deal well with ambiguity."

"Oh, my. What did she do?"

"Interpreted that as 'sapient nonhumans of any kind.' She excluded the Outsiders as well. We are sorting through everything that she did. And the Outsiders are orbiting Avalon, and they've boarded *Geographic*. With our consent," he added quickly.

"They—who are they?"

"They call themselves Godsons."

Sylvia looked shocked. "Godsons. Oh, my."

"Nearly the same reaction Carlos had," Cadzie said. "And Cassandra had some kind of bias against them put in by the Geographic Trustees. I don't know why."

Her face changed. She looked younger and more serious. "My great uncle was a trustee," she said.

"I thought I remembered that," Cadzie prompted.

"Of course you do. You remember everything, and Cassandra would know that." She spoke matter-of-factly, almost tonelessly.

"Discovered. All right, I'll be direct. Why, Gram? What's so awful about the Godsons? Carlos tells me they were excluded from ever boarding *Geographic*. None came on the expedition. What's wrong with them?"

She shook her head, slowly. "When I was younger I could have told you. Even after we first landed, I think."

"Before the grendels."

"Well, yes, but that's not it. Before we strapped your grandfather to a gurney to be grendel food."

"What? No! You couldn't have done that."

"Could and did and thought we were doing the right thing. Cadzie, you learned about the Grendel Wars, but maybe not all of it. After the first grendel attack, before we knew grendels existed, we believed—well, some believed and the rest of us didn't fight it—that there weren't any monsters. There couldn't be. One of us must have done those awful things!"

"And you thought Grandfather Cadmann—"

"Not me. I never. But he was raving about monsters, and everyone was afraid of him—but of course we weren't trying to *hurt* him. We were just restraining him, to keep him safe." She laughed bitterly. "Keep him safe! Oh, God. And then the grendel attacked."

"That's awful! They never taught us that in school—"

"And they never will. We even ordered Cassandra to forget everything she knew about it. I don't know what they teach now, but that's really the reason he built this place." She gestured at the surroundings, opulent now, but Cadzie could still see that it had once been a fortress. "And your Gramma Mary Ann came up to live with him and persuaded him to forgive the rest of us, which is why there is a colony left. But I'm sure you know all that from school."

"They told us he got so mad when they wouldn't believe there were grendels that he left and came up here."

"Which is true enough. Just leave it at that. You don't have to tell anyone you know more."

"But—does Unka Carlos know?"

She shook with laughter, and the strange mood seemed to vanish with the laugh. "You bet your boots he knows," she said quietly.

"And you won't tell me anything more."

"Not just now, no."

Cadzie sighed. "Well. All right. I came up here to learn about Godsons. Why were they excluded from *Geographic*?"

"I'll try. But it's hard to think like we did back on Earth, when we were planning on going to an Earthlike planet, no industrial wastes we could detect, a paradise. Everybody thought so, the most Earthlike planet we knew of, and everybody wanted it. The Godsons wanted it, too, but not for the same reasons. We wanted to build a good society, no need for wars, no one goes hungry, no criminals because no need for crime, everyone happy, we'd start with nothing but good people and babies and build the perfect society. And we had the money to build the ship, expensive as it was. Lots of people who didn't want to leave Earth were willing to donate."

"But why no Godsons?"

"They wanted to conquer the galaxy! Take it by force for the human race."

"Why? Manifest destiny?"

"Partially that. And partially their theology. I'm thinking it had something to do with finding the origin of all life."

"Panspermia?" The theory that life had begun not on

Earth, but had been carried on some kind of cosmic tide from some prior beginning. It begged the question, of course.

"Yes. Life started somewhere, right? They wanted to find that place. Control it, maybe. Protect it . . . I'm not sure. They were a little dotty about that, and I don't think outsiders really knew."

"But—well, why exclude them from coming, even from talking to the people who were coming?"

"Well, a lot of us couldn't see them as anything but a joke, taking in ignorant—we would have never said stupid—people. But they could be persuasive, and well, we wouldn't want anyone to be deceived by them, so why let anyone be deceived? It seemed like good sense at the time."

"So they wanted to conquer the galaxy."

"For the human race."

Cadzie pointed to the well-tended graves outside the dwelling and stretching down the steep boulder-strewn slope. "Could they have been right? Could there be some single point of origin for life?"

"Well, if you bought into panspermia, I suppose it makes sense." She shrugged. "They could be persuasive. They got some big entertainment stars on their side, and some of the children of *Geographic* donors, even the son of one of the trustees. I guess the trustees were afraid of them. So they banned them."

"And now they are here," Cadzie said slowly. "With just about everything we lost in the Grendel Wars, and some stuff that hadn't been invented when *Geographic* left the Sol System."

"And they're offering it to us?"

"Well, a sort of trade. They have or can make almost everything we need. All they say they want is an uninhabited piece of the island for a safe startup base."

"That sounds reasonable. What happens then?"

"Everything we hear makes it sound like they want to build up their industry, maybe on the mainland, but maybe on another part of the island. Goodness knows there's enough room for a hundred times as many people here. They need enough industry to build another ship. Two ships." He paused. "That means they might want to be closer to sources of iron. That means the mainland."

"Two like *Geographic*? How long would that take? My goodness . . ." She paused, considering. "I can't say I'm totally surprised. Apparently, their prophet preached about seeding the stars. Wasn't that the name of one of his core texts? 'Star Seed'?"

"Asking the wrong person."

"I suppose I never took them seriously," she said.

"Well, we have to now. They have 3D printers. Assuming that they have the technical skills, and all the information . . . I don't know. Twenty years to build another *Geographic*? Forty? Even several hundred?"

"Goodness. Well, we're certainly in for changes. But you didn't come this way to tell me news. What is it, Cadzie?"

"I suppose I just wonder how my grandfather would have thought about this."

"The newcomers?"

"Yes."

She blinked slowly, eyes focused not on the colony

below them, but on a time before he was born. "He'd see potential. Possible problems, too."

"What problems?"

She sighed. "I remember the Godsons had a militaristic streak. In some ways your grandfather would have felt right at home with them. But he would have kept his guard up."

"What if he's right?" he said quietly. "What if they aren't friendly, and have weapons we can't handle?"

She laid her hand on his. Her flesh felt paper-thin. "Your grandfather would have said that weapons aren't made of steel and plastic. Human beings are the weapons. Guns are just tools."

That was a good one. The Cadmann in his heart embraced that thought. "That's what he would have said?"

"That . . . and one thing more. Know the territory. Grendels weren't even something we'd dreamed of, but he knew that high ground was critical."

Cadzie looked around his old home. And that was the truth, as he understood it. "So . . . the planet itself is a weapon."

"The planet itself. And they don't know Avalon."

"No. They don't. Grandmom . . ." His voice trailed off, and she declined to step into the gap, awaiting his next words.

It was a little war of nerves. She smiled at him, but didn't speak. Finally he said, "Would Grandpa have been proud of me?"

She laughed. "Aren't you a little old to be looking for Daddy's approval?"

"Never," he said, face neutral but a laugh in his voice.

"Asks the man who rode a crippled Minerva up and down to fetch Cassandra. I think you'd be his hero."

His hero. And he liked the sound of that as well. Maybe he shouldn't care, but he did, and that was all there was to it.

Cadzie took her hand, and together they watched Tau Ceti IV sink toward the horizon, a star just a bit redder than Sol, but the only sun he had ever known.

◆ CHAPTER 18 ◆
ARRIVAL

Three weeks later...

The crowd watched the clouds, shading their eyes against the sun.

When the first finger rose and pointed at a gray-black sliver against the white and blue, they collectively emitted a sound halfway between a sigh and a gasp.

As the shuttle hurtled toward the landing field, the moment that details could be distinguished with the naked eye, two hundred colonists burst into spontaneous applause, a sound that did not cease until the gleaming wedge shape actually hovered over the burn-marked concrete rectangle, entering an unexpected VTOL mode as it settled to the ground. That moment was observed in human silence, followed by cheers the moment the engines shut down.

The design was more triangular than the Minervas, clearly a more advanced model, triggering "*ooh*"s and "*ahh*"s from Starborn who had never seen an unweathered shuttle, and a few aging Earthborn who felt more anxiety than excitement.

Then . . . they waited. Three minutes after it settled in there were a series of clicking sounds, and then a mechanical hissing, and a section of the side opened and descended to the ground.

Carlos leaned on his cane, watching the landing pad with Cadzie from two hundred meters away. A safe zone, according to the tech folks who had discussed the descent with the newcomers. He felt a flutter of excitement.

Everything was about to change.

It seemed odd that treaded robots with cameras rolled first down the ramp. They filmed the waiting Avalonians as they came down, then all but one turned to face the ramp.

Carlos didn't have long to wait.

They saw the Minerva pilot Marvin Stolzi first, walking out freely, waving and happy. That answered one question, Carlos thought. In this first act of the new drama, it seemed likely they were among friends.

The crowd closed in, creating a rough semicircle around the landing pad, slapping Stolzi on his shoulder and peering up the ramp into the ship.

And then . . . three figures appeared, in orange and white-trimmed, beautifully designed flight suits more like uniforms than pressure gear . . . but he strongly suspected they could double as vacuum-resistant in an emergency.

The tallest of them was nearly a giant, over six and a half feet tall. Golden beard and hair, a Viking air about him. Looked like a born explorer. Introduced himself as Captain Sven Meadows.

The next tallest was a woman, light olive skin, Greek heritage perhaps, with a beautiful strong face and piercing eyes that scanned the crowd with a combination of curiosity and caution.

The third man was the shortest of the three, but their evident leader, leading the wedge. He was tanned and so fit he seemed to be moving through partial gravity. He was almost absurdly handsome, and had the kind of personal magnetism Carlos had associated with politicians and holo stars, not space travelers. He extended his hand. "Marco Shantel," he said.

"Carlos Martinez, and we welcome you to Avalon. This is quite a moment. We've been waiting for you for longer than most of us have been alive."

"Well, here we are," Marco replied. "And you might say that we've been waiting to get here longer than you've been waiting."

"I suppose you have," Carlos said. "How many of you are there?" Hundreds, certainly. Enough to begin a new assault on the mainland?

"A million," Marco said.

Cadzie shook his head. "What?"

The woman watched Cadzie with obvious amusement. "A million, three hundred and twelve." She extended her hand to Cadzie. "Major Gloria Stype."

Major. Outranked the other two, but had held back, evaluating. A careful, reserved woman.

"Cadmann Weyland Sikes," he said.

"I know that name," the Viking said. "You ... are his son?"

"He was my grandfather."

"A fine heritage. I'd hoped to meet him. Is he . . . ?"

"Gone," Cadzie said.

"But his grandson stands strong. He would be proud. I'm Sven."

"Who else would you be?" He shook the titan's hand.

"A million?" Carlos asked, still dazed. Had he heard correctly?

Sven was amused. "She's having you on. Three hundred and twelve adults. A million frozen embryos."

"That's true," Major Gloria Stype said. "We started with three hundred and twenty adults."

Carlos' heart sank. Had the same problems recurred?

"You . . . lost eight?"

"Yes," Marco said, smile fading for the first time.

"Hibernation instability?"

"Old age," Marco replied.

◆CHAPTER 19◆
FAMILY FEAST

Two or three times a year, the colony's main meeting hall, at the east point on the main quad, was used for a major banquet. Cadzie couldn't remember a time when it was this crowded. And never a time when there were as many . . . or really *any* guests in attendance.

And now . . . suddenly, with only a few week's warning, Avalon had a new holiday: their own blessed Thanksgiving.

By this time, eighty of the newcomers were down, and the clamour of the gathering drowned out the distant roar of the Minervas ferrying down load after load of the folk who called themselves Godsons. The tables had already run out of lettuce, as if the travelers were starving for green leaves.

Cadzie noticed that Viking Sven had discreetly clipped chunks of food and drops of water and placed them in some pocket-sized apparatus he didn't recognize. No Godson tasted their food until after about ten seconds of waiting, when Sven saw something he liked on the monitor, and broke into a big grin. Then everyone dove in.

If Cadzie hadn't been paying attention, he wouldn't have noticed.

A sudden flurry around one of the tables: a flat rectangle nearly a meter across had entered an open window and buzzed the food, and Godsons were hurling themselves aside. A Starborn male lunged into the air and caught the birdle by the hind edge with both hands. Its four motor fins buzzed frantically as visitors crowded around to see. Cadzie edged his way in that direction.

"They come in dozens of species, these birdles. Some bite," Big Shaka was saying. "These big ones don't. Note the shell is an airfoil. Motor fins at the corners—" He stopped at the tinkling of knives on glass.

Zack Moskowitz stood, taking special care to stand straight, as if the passing years and ceaseless cares had not bowed him. "I would like to do something rather rare in recent years," he said. "I would like to say grace."

"Hear hear!" And polite applause in answer. Sven carried the big birdle outside and released it, grinning like a conquering hero.

Zack bowed his head. "We have no words for how grateful we are, Lord, that you bring unto us these new friends. Lord of all, we thank you."

The newcomers quieted. They had assumed the postures of their guests as soon as it became clear that prayer was intended. Accommodating, Cadzie thought, *Making us feel good. And maybe they mean it.*

"Family!" Marco insisted. "Family. You're rather stuck with us." Much laughter accompanied this, easy, happy laughter, like a family reunion with nothing but optimism and happy memories.

A hundred and forty Godsons had already descended, a little wobbly-legged from a century of cold sleep, rarin' to go and a little frustrated that their arms and legs wouldn't quite obey their hearts.

It was clear to Cadzie that, once they had made the adjustments the Godsons would be a buff and hearty group, workhorses all, true believers in something he had yet to understand, but smart and as excited about their new adventure as . . . well, as his own parents must have been on their own long-ago Landing Day.

And more . . . they were damned attractive. The men were perfect specimens, and the testosterone-fueled ape in the back of his head found himself constantly checking to see how he measured up against them.

But the women . . .

If male Godsons (was that the right terminology?) tilted toward hypermasculinity, then their women could be considered what . . . ultrafeminine? That might make sense if the exaggerated characteristics did not include fashionable weakness. They were pioneer women, broad of hip and shoulder, athletic in appearance, with narrow waists, wide-eyed beauties broadcasting their fertility and readiness to breed. Every gale of brusque hearty laughter and confident step was filled with challenge . . . and promise.

Joanie was a healthy, fit, trained specimen of Avalonian womanhood, and she held up well. But some of the other colonists shrank in comparison . . . and knew it. He watched them sit more closely to mates, spouses and paramours as if worried that the personal gravity of these newcomers would suck their loves into new personal orbits.

The image amused him. If his neighbors reacted that way to Godsons while the newcomers were still wobblelegged with cold sleep, what would happen once they had made landfall adjustments?

"Forty years ago, the children of Earth first landed here on Avalon. And decades later, we came to join you. We have so much to learn about this world, and everything you did to conquer it."

"What do you have with you?" Zack asked.

Toad sat beside him, the little man's plate piled high with hot bread and roasted beef. He raised his hand, and then spoke. "I've been going over the manifest, and it's a treasure trove."

"And how do you see the division or distribution of these materials?" Zack asked.

That triggered a moment of discomfort, noted by all. Then a woman stepped into the conversational gap. "We have personal gear, that is ours—"

"Of course," Carlos said.

Marco smiled at her and took over. "But the majority of our gear is community property. We're asking you to make room for us. It's only fair that we offer what we can. We see how healthy you are, we just want to fit in." He hoisted his glass. "To family!"

His salute was returned across the room: "Family!"

Cadzie's eyes stung. He saw something wonderful in the faces of their new friends. New...*family*.

And in a blinding moment of insight, he realized why. It was that loneliness, that isolation, suddenly eased.

When he noticed the groups were sitting at separate tables initially, Cadzie very deliberately picked up his tray and moved over to a Godson table, sitting between a blond God and an olive-skinned Goddess, both of whom seemed a meld of fatigue and excitement.

"Hi!" he said. The Goddess smiled. the sternness had evaporated. "I'm Cadmann."

The Goddess showed instant recognition. "I remember. Cadmann Weyland?"

"Sikes. Cadmann Weyland was my grandfather."

She extended her hand. "I'm Gloria Stype." She pointed around him to the near-giant on the other side, haloed in cameras. "That's Sven—"

"I remember."

"And on the other side is Marco Shantel." Shantel was the shortest of the three, perfectly fit and almost too pretty for a man.

"Pleased to meet you!" Marco jumped up and gripped hands. A childish, rather fun moment of grip-testing followed. All in good fun, of course. Cadzie was glad for the countless hours of rock climbing. This man was *strong*!

Marco shook his hand, as if trying to get feeling back into it. "Whoa! Quite a grip there!" Cadzie's finger-bones felt like they'd been in a nutcracker. Wow. And these people were deconditioned. What in the hell would they be like once adapted? If there was going to be any sort of conflict between them, best that it happen *soon*.

Not everyone mingled with the newcomers. Joanie Tragon had picked at her food, then stepped to the side of the room to watch the interactions. She had never been a mingler. Even as a child, she had tended more toward observing, watching the others play and then entering the fun with a plan. Spontaneity wasn't her strong suit.

She just wasn't sure how she felt about all of this. The Godsons' silent approach to Avalon had forced her to reveal an embarrassing secret, and that bothered her.

Thor Sorenson shambled over to her. He was grace itself on a surfboard, second only to the teacher named Piccolo, but you'd never know it the way he plodded along on the land.

They'd not really spoken since her return from *Geographic*, and she'd wondered if they were avoiding each other. Judging by her reactions as he approached, she decided that, yeah, that's just what she'd been doing.

"A lot happening here," he said with a smile. "A little noisy. Step outside?"

They did. He repeated his statement, as if he thought she hadn't heard it the first time. "A lot happening here."

She sipped at her glass of bison milk. Higher in protein and fat than cow's milk, it was creamy and delicious. She said, "When that birdle buzzed some of the Godsons, they all hit the dirt. Didn't get up right away."

Silence. Then Thor said, "So you and Cadzie got pretty cozy, I guess."

She smiled over the rim of her glass. "You might say that."

Thor's thick lips curled in a smile. *Probably not as friendly as you and Mei Ling got, I'll betcha.*

"*I* thought you guys didn't like each other?"

"We don't."

He seemed to approve of that answer. "So it was hate sex, or what?"

"Wouldn't go that far. There's this old song that says that if you can't be with the one you love . . ."

"Love the one you're with," he chimed in, and they both laughed. Not a lot. Just enough to break that odd tension. The sounds of camaraderie from the dining hall were strong and cheerful. It should have been warming, but somehow was not. It was probably her own fault, but she felt excluded. She often felt that way. The eternal outsider.

Thor was still smiling at her. "So is what we have love? If it is, you've never said it."

"Did you miss me?" she murmured, and when he reached out to stroke her hair, she leaned into it.

He closed the rest of the distance, and they both fell into the kiss. She enjoyed it thoroughly, refamiliarizing herself with the way his body felt and tasted. Then she pulled back.

"Slow down, Surfer Boy. How is Mei Ling?"

He tried to push in again, but her fingers resisted.

"She's . . . fine," he said, eyes bright. "But she isn't you."

She rolled that answer around, asking herself if her indirect question had been resolved by an indirect answer. She decided that the answer was "close enough," and let him have another kiss.

"Well," she said, feeling herself warm, some of the tension melting. The sounds of laughter and singing from the dining hall weren't as troubling now. There was a desirable man who desired her. Cadzie's flirtation with that Valkyrie didn't sting when she had something of her own to hold onto. And hell, she didn't have any business thinking of him that way anyway. Whatever they had been to each other aboard *Geographic* had merely been . . . a convenience. "I guess I missed you, too."

◆CHAPTER 20◆
SETTLING IN

The evacuation of *Messenger* had completed at 3:24 am Camelot time, and save for a residual crew who had been to ground, celebrated with the first group and then ascended to man the orbiting systems, all Godsons were now aground.

By the time the sun rose at 5:55 local time, repairs had already begun on Minerva II, and temporary housing was under construction. Hundreds of Godsons had slept in the communal hall, or been taken into Avalonian homes by the dozens. Others chose to sleep in the open air once they were able to set up their own defensive perimeters: wisely, they were not willing to totally believe that Camelot was predator-free. Not willing to totally trust strangers with their security.

By noon, the landing beach, and the territory between it and the colony were abuzz with activity. Everyone was lending a hand in the construction of the temporary shelters, and Joanie was impressed.

Most were focused on the construction, but she

noticed one exception. The "prettiest" of the newcomers was a blond, toothy specimen, who seemed to move and speak and react as if a camera was on him at all times, a theatrical flourish to every little gesture. She didn't quite understand until she spotted the spherical drone hovering above and behind him, recording every action.

"Marco Shantel," a voice next to her said, voice filled with amusement. "He's the world's biggest holo star."

"Really? I mean, that wouldn't take much on Avalon. We don't *have* any holo stars."

The speaker towered a half-head above her, Amazonian, and Joanie pulled up her name instantly: Major Gloria Stype. The tall woman stood out almost as much as Shantel, but for a different reason: her every movement seemed both relaxed and purposeful. She liked to watch the major, and had probably drifted over near her for that very reason.

"He was the biggest on Earth. Biggest ever, maybe."

"Why did he decide to make the trip?" she asked. "He can't exactly go back and gloat."

"He's also an adventurer," Stype said, with genuine admiration and affection. "And this is the greatest ever."

Joanie decided to change the subject. Shantel may have played heroes, but she sensed that Stype actually was one of that very special breed.

"Those prefab sections are pretty good," she said. "Expanding frameworks with some kind of plastic overlay?"

By the time she'd awakened at Surf's Up, rolled away from Thor and biked down to the beach, the sand was already dotted with igloo-shapes. Skeletal dome-shaped frames, coverings, and then sprayed with insulating foam in an effective assembly line activity by squadrons of skilled, happy workers. These people were good! Temporary shelters for fifty people an hour, she reckoned. She suspected that they would produce that many semi-permanent or long-term shelters in a day, an amazing rate.

"Yes," the major said, pausing in her activity: cutting a door in a dried and set foam wall with some kind of plasma torch. She pulled a triangular section free, and Joanie hefted it. Light! "We can house a hundred people in two hours."

Joanie grinned to herself, happy that her guess had been so accurate. "You definitely came to play."

"Some of us are here to stay," Stype said, real satisfaction softening her angular face. The domes looked sturdy, and roomy. Room for six, just like that. "But these are just temps. Our overflow will stay in them for a few days, maybe, but then we'll probably use them for storage units."

"So you'll need a more permanent site."

The major nodded. "We need to survey the territory, and I've got the job. Be my guide?"

"Our guide!" Marco came bounding up to them. She had no idea how much of their conversation the toothy one had overheard. He was all sparkle and aliveness, impossible not to like. He was an exceptional, rarified being and knew it. The silver drone sphere followed him, silent witness to the latest, greatest act in Marco Shantel's Galactic Adventure.

She had access to Skeeter VI, and was happy to see

that the others were already being repaired and refurbished with 3D printer parts, courtesy of their new neighbors. Cadzie's had already been tricked out with a new spiral valve, and she'd watched him making dragonfly maneuvers above Mucking Great Mountain's slopes, sheer joy in motion.

It took them ten minutes to reach the skeeter pads, Stype and Marco breaking into a little impromptu coordinated jog, knees high. They were pushing it, still not adjusted to the gravity but each eager to force adaptation. They huffed in tune, and she could tell that Marco was more winded, but to his credit he never lost that perfect smile. The drone sphere buzzed along behind and above them, recording every step. She kept up easily, but had the very real sense that within a month that might no longer be true.

Serious specimens.

Stype was buckled in before Joanie climbed around to the pilot's side. She seemed a little amused by what must have seemed like an antique vehicle to her.

"Well, let's get going!" Joanie said as soon as Marco had settled into the jump seat behind her. A trace of nervous excitement entered her voice as she scanned her checklist and warmed the engines. Stype settled back, solid in her seat. At a touch of the control, Skeeter VI rose into the air, and coasted inland.

"Older model, of course." Stype said above the rotor thrash. "How many miles on her?"

"About two hundred thousand, I'd reckon. She's kind of beat up. You guys appeared just in time."

"You only love us for our printers," Marco laughed.

She glanced at him. Was he flirting with her? She decided that she hoped he was.

"How far from the main colony do you guys want to be?"

She glanced back over her shoulder at Marco, but he pointed a finger at the major. "That's the lady."

Stype considered. "Well . . . the ease of communication and transport makes this entire island a neighborhood. We have almost a half-million square kilometers on Avalon, so staying out of each others' pockets should be pretty easy."

That sounded reasonable, and even considerate. She'd spent a fast hour reading up on their new neighbors in the last days, but knew she'd barely scratched the surface. "So . . . are you a devout Godson? All of you? And are the women 'God's daughters'?"

Stype and Marco shared mirth. The passenger side window was closed, but the air still flowed rapidly in the cabin, and where Marco's hair riffled, Stype's short saffron hair seemed not to move. "You seem to think language is more important than the spiritual reality it underpins. We are all brothers and sisters, and see the man as the spiritual head of the house."

"It isn't that women are less important," Marco said. His voice said that he'd had this conversation before, probably with what Joan would consider "show biz" types. "We're respecting the fact that in an emergency, He will die to protect She. For his woman, and their children. I think that's an acceptable price."

That wasn't her world. On Avalon, women were as likely to fight as men. But . . . had that been true for her mother? She wanted to sort through that idea before automatically leaping down Marco's throat. And it was the number of fertile females that determined a species' survivability, a fact that had been irrelevant on Earth, but not here.

Stype pointed down. "There. Near that stream. The water is good?"

The Amazon flowed south from Mucking Great Mountain, and the Nile flowed north, highland to lowland, fed by numerous smaller streams and artesian wells. "Yes. Delicious, too. Something in the minerals."

"The Nile. I like it. Take me down!"

Joanie hadn't been to this part of Camelot since she was about thirteen. A Grendel Scout overnighter, she recalled. They'd cooked s'mores with chocolate, sugar and wheat crackers grown in Avalonian soil. Her mouth watered.

There were other memories as well, something minty and memorable. When she spotted it, she squealed with pleasure. A berry bush with purple and green fruit, each the size of a healthy strawberry. She plucked one and popped it into her mouth. Yes. The mint was just as cool and berrysweet as she remembered.

"So . . . I take it you've tested those for toxicity," Stype said, her voice flat now.

Stype was so serious that Joanie almost laughed. They had traveled trillions of miles to find a new world, and only Marco seemed able to take pleasure in it? "Absolutely. Our computer had a great analytical program, but we lost about a dozen monkeys and a thousand rats just checking potential foods."

"Poor monkeys."

"Died heroes," Joanie said, laughing behind her eyes. "So did the rats. I used to feel sorry for them, but I grew up."

"Many will fall on Man's path to the stars."

"Sounds biblical."

"Words from the Prophet. He didn't mention animals. Did you have to modify any of the native plant life?"

"We could have, maybe, but at first we didn't want to. Then the Grendel Wars ruined the bio labs and most of the tools we'd need to rebuild them. We're not really over that yet. Go on, try one. They're good."

She noticed that Stype's hand hovered above one of the berries, but that she didn't pluck, or eat. There was caution, and then there was paranoia. This was hovering around door number two.

Marco, on the other hand, seemed to take it as a challenge. He plucked a berry, and after posing to be sure the drone got his best angle, popped it into his mouth and chewed. Smacked his lips with relish.

"Good," he said. "Like a fleshy strawberry." Then he turned his head and discreetly spat it out. She guessed that bit would be edited.

"That's smart," she said. "They aren't toxic, but it does take some time for our intestinal flora to adjust. Takes a couple of weeks. You might get a little gas if you ate a bunch of them before that." She paused. "Well, maybe a lot of gas. But nothing worse."

The thought of Major Stype with a prolonged attack of farting made it even harder to restrain her smile.

The ground was slightly moist, the last of a soilhugging mist just burning off. Avalon's days were just over twenty-three hours, and the morning chill usually gave way to a temperate, and sometimes shirtsleeve-warm afternoon.

There was no snowy season on Camelot, although Mucking Great's heights were white-dusted a quarter of the year.

Marco galloped, delighted to stretch his long legs, racing ahead of them with his little silver sphere floating in circles around him. Stype walked with a long, easy stride, one Joan had to consciously exert herself to match. The major was touching, tasting, smelling, feeling the ground, scanning everything as they moved through a thick brush along the flat hard ground.

Ahead, they broke into a grassy open area, and Stype stopped, turning her head slowly from side to side, scanning everything. Turned in a circle, to gaze south toward Mucking Great. The edges of her mouth turned up in a smile, mind filled with private thoughts.

"I heard something," Joanie said. "Marco! Don't go too far!" She called, and then turned back to Stype. "Can I ask you a question?"

"Sure."

"Cadzie said that you told him that you had fatalities on the trip."

The little up-tilt to the major's lips froze. Didn't vanish, but whatever joy that had begun to work its way through her professional mask had dissipated. "Yes. That's true."

"And that it wasn't hibernation instability, but old age. I don't understand."

Stype sighed. "We'd already left Earth before receiving your first communiques about H.I."

Joanie held up her hand. "Shhh," she said. "Look."

Something small and brown had nosed its way out of the brush toward a thin stream a hundred yards away. It was tentative, charming, a greenish brown, five-spindly-legged furred demi-mammal sufficiently reminiscent of an Earthly forest creature to be nicknamed a "bambi."

It sipped, while watching them carefully. Humans had never hunted bambis, and probably wouldn't for another generation. Watching Camelot's wildlife rebound from its age-long Grendel nightmare was a revelation.

Marco spotted it too. Looked from it to Joanie and back again, with an implicit question: *is this dangerous?*

She shrugged, and made a "go ahead" gesture. Marco smiled for the camera, then took a slow careful step toward the bambi, then froze. It cocked its head, observed him closely, then went back to drinking.

"Seems pretty casual," Stype said.

"There are no big predators left on Camelot, and we don't eat them," she said.

"Why not? Meat bad?"

"No . . . I think it's just damned near a miracle that anything that size was left alive on the island, and we don't want to jinx a miracle. Everything, including big bugs, was eaten by grendels. A few animals survived but only in the bush up on high ground, far from any stream or any body of water that could cool a grendel. Grendels hunted anywhere they could reach, but some places were just high and dry enough to let a few joeys and bambis keep away from them. Grendels can stay on land only so long. Then they need to cool off."

"These 'grendels' everyone talks about. They were really that dangerous?"

"Still are. You may have seen the video by now."

Marco had edged closer. The bambi looked at him more intensely, its eyes protruding on stalks. When Marco took another step, the bambi's throat distended like a bullfrog's, and it let out a deep, bone-shaking cry that blasted Marco back on his heels, hands covering his ears.

The bambi disappeared back into the brush, and Joanie roared with laughter. Stype joined her, and after a minute, Marco did as well.

There was nothing on Camelot to endanger an adult human being, so she let Marco romp and run, enjoying his simple pleasure in exploring a new world.

But . . . she stayed with Stype. "Were you going to tell me about those old-age deaths?" she asked, as the major toed the ground, testing soil consistency.

Her lips drew into a thin line. "We got your message about cold sleep after we left Earth. Our computers ran simulations and the probable answer was either the rate of awakening or the frequency."

"Sleep-waking cycles?"

The taller woman nodded. Overhead, a pterodon suddenly seemed interested in the broken grass through which the bambi had fled. It circled over a patch just a little out of their sight, skawing. "Something about cellular plasticity in the brain. We had a couple of choices: ignore it, try to fix it, or change our behaviors. We did a little of each of the last two."

That was interesting. "What did you do, and how did you do it?"

"Well . . . there were some modifications to the sleep capsules, and some medical interventions. But mostly, we woke people up as infrequently as possible. The Prophet made the final decision."

"The Prophet?"

"Channing Newsome," Stype said. "The linear descendant of our founder, Carlton Newsome. A great man. He decided that the safest thing for the colony was for him to stay awake the entire time. A few of the Most High rotated duty with him. They took the risk for all of us."

That caught Joanie up short. She realized that she had been thinking somewhat derisively of this group, assuming that they were a cult blindly following a leader. And follow they had . . . but hadn't she heard that in most cults the followers had fewer privileges than the leaders? Danced to the tune of men or women who exploited their naivety and trust?

The major had been watching her, seemed to understand what she was thinking. "Yes. He sacrificed himself. Even with one or two to support him at times, he spent almost eighty years in unimaginable loneliness, so that we could reach the promised land."

She thought about that. Two weeks on *Geographic* had driven her to distraction. More specifically, driven her into Cadzie's arms. She could not even imagine what this man Newsome had endured, for the sake of his dream. His people.

Greater love hath no . . .

"I'm . . . I'm sorry. He was a great man." That was all she seemed able to say.

It seemed to be enough. "Yes. Much to live up to. It's our responsibility to keep the dream alive."

"What is that dream, exactly?" Several more pterodons

had joined with the first, wheeling and diving. She heard that shattering roar again. The pterodons flapped away in panic, but then recovered and renewed their circling. She wondered about the predation cycles, knew that the Shakas had probably studied it exhaustively. And vaguely hoped the bambi would escape.

But . . . it all felt so small, and insignificant. Her own grandparents had traveled a century in cold sleep, awakened every few years for rotating duty. And while some of them had suffered for that, most had simply slept.

She envisioned an old, old man doddering through the halls and corridors, year after year, decade after decade, dreaming of a day when his followers would reach their destination . . .

"When did he die?" she asked.

"About a year out from Avalon," Stype said soberly. "I was there."

A year out. So close. Moses, unable to enter the Promised Land.

Such a man would find no dearth of people willing to trust and follow him. Someone able to deal with such deep, almost unimaginably total aloneness for the sake of others was . . . a fanatic? A great man? Certainly. A good one . . . ?

For the sake of this woman she had barely met, whose tread was so measured compared to the joyful gallop of the movie star who was the hero of his own adventure, she hoped so.

"What was the dream?" she asked. "Why are you here?"

The major smiled. "It's simple, really. Man was born to

take dominance over the galaxy." She said it with no trace of doubt, no smidgeon of humor or exaggeration, or reluctance to use a gendered pronoun. It was an article of faith.

"It is simple scientific truth—we'll show you if you like—that a single race, species, whatever you want to call it, will dominate each galaxy. We are that people."

She paused to let that sink in. "Oh yes, we believe in science. It is a simple and profound truth. One people will dominate the galaxy. We are here as the first step of that. God Knot willing, we will found a colony and spread across the planet, but every generation we will send out at least three ships. Within fifty generations . . ."

"'God not willing'? What does that mean?"

The taller woman's face went a little blank, and then animated again. "I misspoke," she said. Then she smiled, dreaming a private dream, something deeply held.

Joanie lost her urge to laugh. Her grandparents had wished safety, and growth. Careful management of lives and resources in the process of mastering Avalon and its potential gifts . . . and dangers.

This woman was different. She and her kind had come to conquer.

And with sudden fullness, she thought to herself: this is what Cadmann Weyland was like. Not the same goals, but the same certainty, the same strength. He had been one of *them*, not one of us.

"This is good," Stype said.

"What were you looking for? Exactly?"

"We were prepared for anything," the major said. "Scans suggested water and plant life before you left

Earth. But we didn't know the precise microorganism counts in air or soil, or exact mineral. So . . . we had to be prepared for anything. We didn't even know precisely what had become of your colony."

This woman made her feel inadequate. "What would you have done if . . . if the soil wouldn't grow Earth plants?"

Stype chuckled. "We brought some very frisky microbes. We'd have set up greenhouses and created our own soil. Spent a generation mastering one little corner of this planet. Two generations. It wouldn't matter. We'd still be ahead of our ancestors, who started simply by noticing that cast-off seeds blossomed into fruiting plants. We had the tools."

"All right. What then?"

Marco was splashing in the waterhole. He took a bottle clipped to his backpack, sampled, and read some kind of monitor. Apparently it said good things, because he was jubilant enough to drink deeply, and belch with satisfaction.

"Master that island. And then spread to the mainland. We'd watch for molds, fungi and diseases. Parasites and pests. And of course . . . carnivores. Your 'grendels' for instance."

She snorted. "They're not 'my' grendels. Maybe my father's."

"You've seen them?"

Smiling, she wondered how much she would tell Stype, and decided that some secrets should be kept.

"Yes."

"They're really as dangerous as people say?"

"Imagine a Komodo dragon on growth hormones. Now give it acceleration like a racing skeeter."

"Whoa." Well, that got the Amazon's attention. Good.

"Now imagine thousands of them."

"Thousands?" The conversation had caught Marco's attention, and he'd waded out of the water to join them.

"Well...not full-size grendels, no. But adolescents. They eat everything they can outrun, and that means *everything*, including each other. It sorts out to hundreds of full-sized hungry bastards, yes."

"And that's what your grandparents faced?" The former star seemed incredulous.

"With no idea of what they were dealing with."

The major turned to look back at Mucking Great. "I got that impression. And the greatest battle took place on that mountain?"

"That very one," she said.

Stype's gaze was faraway, no doubt imagining heroic feats of arms. She seemed the type to hear the call of war, feel it in her bones. A woman who was the sort of hero Marco merely played.

Or...one who believed herself to be that hero? Something, some deep instinct, whispered that the picture wasn't quite as it seemed. And what was that about "God not willing?" Hadn't there been some kind of body language shift there, some change in tone?

Something that suggested a lie?

But about what?

"What do you see when you look at this glen?" Joanie asked.

"Water," Stype said. "Runoff from the glacier—"

"Eisenstein," she said.

"Eisenstein glacier. And from Mucking Great Mountain into the Nile. Fertile soil. Our scientists say our crops will thrive here. So will our animals: pigs, cows, chickens. I see this entire valley filled with farms and cottages and communal buildings in a year." She stopped. "How long is a year?"

"It's about 380 days. And a day is about 22.5 earth hours."

"Very nice."

"Tau Ceti is sufficiently Sol-like that the habitable zone was bound to be similar."

"So what now?" Joanie asked.

"We're going to examine the entire island," Stype said.

"Different teams, looking for different things. And then the Speaker chooses a home base."

"Speaker?"

"Successor to the Prophet. He remains in orbit; he volunteered to serve the Prophet until his final days, and His Grace doesn't feel he will ever adjust to gravity again. He's still in orbit and will remain there," Major Stype said.

It sounded like a recital, a memorized speech, Joanie thought. A theory came to mind: with the Godsons, there were things said to outsiders, and things said only among themselves. That "God not willing" comment had been totally natural and relaxed. This was different. *That* had been the truth, in some way she didn't understand.

"We establish that base, and . . ."

"Wait," Joanie said. "The Speaker will decide even though he has never been here?"

"Yes, but don't sound so incredulous," Marco said.

"He's a very wise man, and will have the advice of many who have been here, as well as planners who haven't. He'll make a good decision."

At least you certainly hope so, Joanie thought.

"And then probably two minor sites as backup," Major Stype continued as if she had never been interrupted. "Then at some point, after we've started producing children—"

"The old-fashioned way, or creches?"

"Both, I think. When we have replacement children, we will risk a few adults and teens on the mainland. One step at a time."

Joanie felt a sharp pang of disappointment, wanting very much to show this amazing woman her own workings. To demonstrate to Stype her competence. "So . . . it might take years before . . . ?"

Stype laughed. "Oh, no. We have a list of things that need doing. We need to see these 'scribes,' the creatures that create 'writing' we could see a hundred million miles away. And . . ."

"And what?"

Something wolfish had emerged in Stype's expression, an evil, joyous anticipation. "And I think I'm not the only one who wants to make the acquaintance of a grendel."

◆ CHAPTER 21 ◆
EASY LIVING

The last fog fingers were just losing their grip on Blackship Island when their skeeters landed on the rectangular hub of a cluster of tan foam and concrete sprayed storage and work bubbles.

Marco's spherical drone hovered so quietly that Joanie usually forgot it was even there. Joanie noticed that he always seemed to be trying to present his best profile. "So ... what is it that you do here?" Marco asked.

"This is where we train Grendel Scouts," Toad said. They walked a while, over to an obstacle course studded with targets and water pools sparkling beneath swing ropes and gymnastic bars.

And a hundred yards from those, a series of concrete cage-bubbles with iron bars for doors, looking oddly like frogs buried up to their heads in sand. Trudy hung back as the others approached.

Marco seemed dubious. "Do you actually bring those things over from the mainland to train against?"

The Surf's Up crowd looked at each other. "Sometimes, yes," Toad said. "And sometimes we grow them."

"What is it you are working on?" Marco asked.

Joanie shrugged. "Reflexes, tactics, strategies. We were damn near programmed from birth."

That caught Marco's interest. "Really? How about a little contest?"

Joanie looked like a big cat suddenly catching sight of a mouse. "Be fun."

The older Grendel Scouts put the Godsons through a series of basic drills: runs, swings, firing at moving targets while the adrenaline pumped, making back-to-back sweeps of uneven terrain with grendel guns gimmicked to fire high or low. At this level, with these tools in this place, within these narrow parameters, the Scouts were superior beyond any doubt.

"That is really good," Trudy said. "You're operating at the very edge of human perceptions. One of the reasons we developed other approaches."

"The armor?" Cadzie asked. "You can enhance reflexes?"

"The suit learns. And supplements. Learns to recognize patterns and respond faster than the human being in the suit can possibly react."

Hmmm. "It's that good?"

Trudy smiled. "Let's find out."

"Slow down," Joanie said. "We have tons of time. We've seen how you can work. Time to find out how you play."

It took mere minutes to skeeter back to Surf's Up. By that time the sun was bright in the morning sky, and the party was already boiling. Joanie spoke with Toad, who was raking coals in the luau pit, and he nodded and passed her an oddly shaped rifle.

"What's that for?" Marco asked.

Joanie smiled. "Looking for our luau victim of the evening." Back behind the thatch huts were a series of pens constructed of wood slats and wire: chickens, sheep, and pigs.

"There's a likely subject," Cadzie said, pointing out a fat brown pig between two paler specimens, happily rooting in garbage. *Enjoy your last meal, fella.*

"And so it is," Joanie said. She turned her back to the pen, and raised the grendel gun. "On your mark."

The tension sizzled the air. Marco crouched with fists braced on his knees. "Go!"

Blur-fast, Joanie spun and sighted, fired. The pig's legs twitched once, hard, and then it fell onto its side, convulsing. And then was still, with a conspicuous pockmark dead center on its side.

"Damn!" Toad laughed. "These new c-darts are monster!"

They opened the gate. Toad was the first to the pig's side. Marco grabbed his shoulder. "Is that thing safe to touch?"

"It's a mini high-discharge capacitor," Toad said. "Charge gone, it's safe as a marshmallow." He grabbed the pig, and screamed, trembling violently... and then grinned to general applause. Took a bow.

Marco laughed. "I got an Oscar for no better acting than that!"

After Toad wrenched out the dart, Marco grabbed a

leg. Together they hauled the electrocuted swine to the side of the pit, where its hind legs were hog-tied and the entire carcass hauled aloft. Throat cut and drained, then efficiently gutted, it was welcomed into the crackling luau pit.

Cadzie had wandered off somewhere, but Joanie and Toad led their Godson companions to an enclosed bay.

Dolphins swam up to socialize with the Starborn. They stayed cautiously clear of the new folk. Toad opened a phone and spoke into it. The phone whistled and wheeped.

The dolphin named Archie answered. They spoke for a few minutes. Then Archie went to examine Marco and Trudy. He faced Marco's camera and wheeped at it, then did a backflip.

"So now they know who you are," Toad said. "That's Archie, that's Faith. They'll know you from now on. Archie wanted to know how you're different from us, and I tried to tell them."

"What did you tell them?"

"Dolphins like toys. They think we're all about tools. I said you had more and better tools."

"Is translation a problem? I'm wondering," Marco said, "if we can improve the dolphins' translation program. Dolphins had thousands of languages in Earth's oceans."

"We raised them all from the same stocks of fertilized eggs, all at once. The six in cold sleep all came from the same region. They all speak the same language. Cassandra speaks it pretty good," said Toad.

❖ ❖ ❖

The day was one of games and frivolity. Music played from hidden speakers, available to anyone who coded into the network. There was dancing, and games, and some of the younger Godsons demonstrated Earth dances that were strange and inviting and looked like hell on their knees.

A few of the Earthborn had ferried over from the colony, and were watching the festivities, accompanied by several elder Godsons.

A trio of pterodons wheeled overhead, croaking their curiosity, and the Godsons gawked. "Amazing," one said. "Never seen anything like them."

Zack said, "They tend to eat our songbirds. Robins and swallows have never gotten a toehold. Birdsong was prettier than that skawing."

A couple of the elder Godsons agreed.

A younger Starborn asked, "Birdsong?"

Zack tickled his communicator, and invisible birds danced and sang in the air around them.

Little Shaka hijacked the channel, playing recorded pterodon calls. "It's mating and danger calls," he said. "Here, I can show you."

He put the summoning call on the loudspeaker.

Within minutes, the air swarmed with swooping, gliding winged pseudoreptiles. The beach was a mix of people and pterodons, the pterodons bewildered but not attacking, perhaps searching for all these pterodons seeking mates, or announcing food, or warning of predators. Delighted, the Godsons tried feeding the pterodons, but when they discovered the creatures preferred fresh pig guts to popcorn, that notion lost some of its sparkle.

Jessica showed a cluster of Godson women how to feed them bits of Avalon crab. "They usually eat the clamlike things in the tops of the horsemane trees," she told them.

"And joeys. Any animals that the grendels couldn't get at. Grendels used to get low-flying pterodons, and ate everything—everything not a long way from streams. Now that there aren't any grendels on the island, there are more joeys and pterodons. We're going to have to control the populations. Nobody wants to, but it has to be done, only we can't decide on numbers."

A half-kilometer south, just outside the lagoon, training for night-surfing was the activity of the evening. A bearded man with a weathered face and stringy, muscular body was coaching Trudy in the art of surfing. He was Stanfield Corning, known as "Piccolo" (no one remembered precisely why), and his chief claim to fame was having been the second baby born on Avalon, thirty-nine years ago.

He held the edges of an oversized surfboard as a woman with short blond hair and a gymnast's body crammed into a one-piece suit, struggled for balance. "This is what you need," he said. "Until you can balance on the board, don't even think about getting out in the real water."

Trudy used a moment of calm between two waves to explore her balance, and after a false start or two, managed to stand erect. She hopped off before the next wave could spill her. "This is really good." She'd been at it for an hour, and learning fast. She obviously appreciated the attention.

More, she was obviously also interested in her instructor.

"So . . . what do you do in the colony when you aren't surfing?"

Piccolo shrugged meaty shoulders. "Teaching surfing, mostly."

"And when you aren't doing that?" He was older than she, and sun-cured, but apparently not *too* much older.

"Sleepin' in the sun," he said happily.

He didn't notice her eyes narrow. "But I mean, when you're working."

"Who needs to work?" he said. "There's plenty of everything."

She opened her mouth, then closed it again as if she had a hard time grasping his attitude. Instead, she thanked him curtly, shook water from her hair, and went off to find Cadzie.

She found him raking coals at the luau pit. "Say, Weyland," she said. "You know that guy called Piccolo?"

"Our beach guru? Sure."

"Really, all he does is lay in the sand? Give a surfing class from time to time?"

Cadzie laughed. "Pretty much."

Trudy seemed genuinely mystified. "Why do you put up with it?"

"Well . . . The colony produces so much food we plow twenty percent of it back into the soil. We have a surplus of skilled labor, and all the raw materials we need."

"But . . . but . . ." She paused, then burst out: "You can't let people do *nothing*."

"He doesn't do nothing," he said patiently. "He teaches, he surfs, and he enjoys the sun."

He was probably going to burn in hell, but damned if he wasn't enjoying poking at her a bit.

His answer, and the attitudes engendering it, seemed to make no sense at all to her. The steam pouring from her ears was damned near visible.

Cadzie tried again. "Look, this isn't a new thing. The twenty-first century brought in a whole new problem: robotics were capable of handling more and more basic work, so there was the same amount of wealth, but fewer jobs for people to have. That led to an adjustment of ethics and values."

"How so?"

He had an inspiration. "Did you . . . grow up in a Godson school?"

"Of course."

He sighed. "That explains it, then."

Her eyes narrowed. "Explains *what*?" Them's fightin' words . . .

How to phrase this? He decided on a tactful approach. "You were raised to conquer the galaxy. That's kinda eighteenth-century Manifest Destiny 'brave the frontier' stuff. Hey," he said. "I'm not criticizing. I can empathize. But for most of human history we needed every human being to do all he could, or the tribe suffered. All of our associations of 'good' with 'productive' arises from this. The growing welfare state was part of this, and it was resisted even when we had sufficient wealth as a culture. It took generations."

"And you think that's a good thing?"

"Depends on what you think human beings are. What's the Godson perspective?"

She relaxed. Finally, she was back on familiar doctrinal ground, and confident. "We're made for expansion. Discovery. The God Knot—"

Cadzie held his breath. Hadn't Joanie said something about an odd turn of phrase? 'THE God Knot' was a different implication from the one she'd assumed. Be careful . . .

Softly softly catchee monkey . . .

"That's important to you, the God Knot."

She nodded, looked around. Lowered her voice. "We don't talk about it to outsiders. Not much."

"How about curious new friends, who just want to understand?"

He watched her make a decision of some kind.

"Well . . . do you know what panspermia is?"

Boom. Sylvia's voice in his mind. "Sure. That life didn't begin on Earth. Started somewhere else. Some very smart people believe that."

She smiled. "Yes. Very. Well . . . it had to begin somewhere. Some central seed."

"Like the singularity that exploded in the Big Bang?"

She was happy with him. Was obviously thinking *he's quick!* "Yes. Just like that. Only this is where all life began."

"Could it be the same point as the Big Bang?" Damn, now he was inside her argument, actually trying to understand.

She shrugged. "I don't know. I'm not sure anyone does. Maybe."

"But you want to control the galaxy so that Mankind can find this 'God Knot' place? What happens when you find it?"

"Everything," she said, voice dreamy. "The next step in human evolution, maybe."

He was a little stunned. What an amazing vision, what a reason to conquer the stars. It made a kind of sense, if you accepted the initial premise. The rest . . . all followed. To evolve, we had to find the place where life began. To do that, we had to control the galaxy. To do that, every generation had to push forward, and forward . . .

"Protestant work ethic to the nth. Pilgrim's Progress. I get it. What you need to understand about us is that you're seeing Maslow's Hierarchy in action. If you have the basics taken care of, most will start asking the next questions, and find something useful to do."

"Like . . . surf?"

"Or teach surfing."

"Or sleep in the sun." He suspected she thought him slightly mad.

"Kinda sorta, yes." And that was where they left it, but Cadzie knew there would be more to say. Eventually she'd catch Piccolo cleaning up Surf's Up's garbage . . .

Trudy had been open, but now he could feel her closing up again. He'd pushed too hard, she'd gone too far. He needed to give her room.

He excused himself and wandered over to where Toad was checking his grendel gun. "Problem?"

"Ah . . . I think it threw a little to the left. Just checking things out."

Cadzie threw him a beer pod. "Catch."

Toad snatched it from the air. "Thank you, sir."

Cadzie leaned against the fence, looking down on Toad, whose rifle was disassembled on a blanket before him.

"So...what do you think?" He gestured at the gathering.

"About our guests?"

Cadzie nodded. "You've been watching. Everything. Wanted your unfiltered opinion."

Toad levered himself up from the ground, and slouched against the wooden fence at Cadzie's side. Sipped from his pod. "I've probably spent more time around them than anyone."

"You met them first."

"They're...true believers. The leaders are scary competent. Pleasant, sociable, but make no mistake about that—part of the politeness is programmed."

"Smart?"

"Yeah. Smart." He smiled. "Probably not as smart as us, on average, but the leaders are *very* bright. Marco is... charismatic. Clever. Not exactly a genius. But they've said things that make me suspect that those million eggs they're carrying weren't a matter of the best and brightest."

"No?"

"Nope. It was finances and politics. This is how they funded the trip. Followers paid a hundred thousand dollars minimum each to send a fertilized egg. They raised billions like that, and that selected for being fanatical believers, a bit gullible, not necessarily 'smart.'"

"But the two are not mutually exclusive."

"Yeah, but the Venn diagram looks more like an 'eight' than a pair of concentric circles."

"What do you think they think of us? Really?"

Another smile. "They like us. They were happy to see

us, *very* happy. But they wonder why we haven't made more babies. Why we haven't spread more thoroughly over the mainland. They also think we're primitive. I can tell. They're polite about that, but it oozes out. I'll bet their private conversations are polite, but not tremendously respectful."

"Primitive. How?"

"Man, you should see their tech. The fabricators alone made me drool. They gave us one, and the patterns to make more. In a week, we'll have three of them. The tech is changing everything. Our world will never be the same."

"I believe it. Anything else?"

"They are suspicious of Cassandra. Cassie broke communications, didn't tell us what was coming until it was unavoidable. We haven't told them *why* she was crippled, so they look at her original specs—which were public record—as opposed to performance, and assume we didn't take good care of her."

Cadzie flinched a bit.

"Sorry about that," Toad said, looking a bit sheepish.

"You were part of it?"

A regretful nod. "In the sense that I kept my mouth shut, yeah. Before my time, most of it. I mean, I used her for navigation, so I knew she wasn't dysfunctional. Not totally, anyway. We have to make some decisions now."

"What kind?"

"Well . . . there's gonna be a shitload of information once she talks to the Godson computer, completes diagnostics, maybe upgrades. We're going to be flooded with it. More than we can handle. But . . . I don't think we want to interface with the Godson machine completely.

Would tell them too much about our internal politics, while theirs are still kinda mysterious."

"So they think we're lazy, and a little stupid, and poor. Wow."

"And from their perspective, maybe we are."

"About to get poorer, or richer? I mean, we built a trade economy based on the idea of plenty... but also with minimal tech. They have a scarcity mindset, but all the goodies anyone could want. I'm sorry, but if there is a natural resource in short supply, they're going to end up with it."

"What do you mean?"

"Take my Uncle Carlos. He's created a life where he earns luxuries with his carvings. What happens when fabricators can make anything he can?"

Toad took another swig. "I'd assume that they can't fully imitate the materials, and the fabricators can't create an original work without a human guide. Practical value goes out the window, replaced by rarity value."

"Let's hope so. I mean, I read about poverty in the old days on Earth, but I never thought of myself as poor. A little late to start."

As always, in time day surrendered to night, Avalon's sun dying and birthing a billion stars. The kids and young adults had gathered around campfires.

Marco was a natural magnet, and drew every eye and ear when he spoke. The current discussion around him was about the huge creatures on the veldt.

"—And the scribes? We saw them before we entered your system. I mean, we saw 'writing.'"

Joanie leaned in. "Must have freaked you a bit."

Marco twinkled at her. "So . . . it's mating patterns?"

"Absolutely. Every species has them, you know."

A wink. "I've heard."

Joanie broke eye contact. "So . . . they're pretty solitary most of the year, but in mating season start following each others' pheromone trails. The female senses the curve of the male's path, cuts across it to shorten the arc until she's close enough to either get ahead of him or wait for the wind to shift to release her own. Then she drops behind. He releases a sperm packet, she glides over it, and that's romance."

"I like our way better," he said.

Entering the dolphin pen was easy for cthulhus. The maze of fencing wasn't complicated even to a dolphin; it must be meant to stop lesser minds, the predators of the deep ocean. Whast and Insel came alone tonight; the rest of the school maintained a loose link through the magnetic mind.

Dolphins were hard to talk to. Whast could manage some of the wheeping noises, but he couldn't tell the animated torpedoes apart. He just broadcast:

°*Unschoolmates, the walkers are active tonight.*°

One of the torpedoes answered. °*We perceive this. The walkers have multiplied.*°

°*We perceive that they too use fire.*°

°*Yes, for similar purpose, to smelt their food.*°

°*For nothing else?*°

°*They do not tell us. They do not speak well. We see nothing of their inland uses for fire, but we see their toys. The latest walkers have new toys.*°

We too made wonderful toys, made using fire. Now all is forgotten.

One of the dolphins whistled, *Itchy/Irritating. We cannot grasp the best of their toys with anything but our tongues and teeth. You jets can grasp, but you have forgotten.* The next whistle and wiggle was rude.

Whast said, *They hide a tremendous moving mass of magnets behind a wall. Magnets are spiritually important.*

They hide us behind a maze. Walls are their skill.

The maze will not stop you. Come, explore. We will guard you in the deep beyond. The eaters will not harm you.

We know the walkers better. We wait for their guidance.

♦ CHAPTER 22 ♦
ON THE VELDT

Cadzie loved the controls of Red One, one of the Godsons' new autogyros. Their own skeeters were being refurbished, and after completion would probably make the mainland trip just fine . . . but there was something to be said for shaking the dust out of new equipment. Maybe in the early days on Avalon their own machines had handled this well, but not in his lifetime, at least not since he'd been flying. This was heaven. His three passengers didn't know the difference, but he was glorying in not having to keep half his attention on keeping up with the newly unfreighted Godson Skeeter Blue, even though it was a next-gen version of the utility craft.

He banked over the main colony, feeling a slight sense of unease push back against the simple pleasure of flight. This wasn't a trip to Horseshoe Falls, or even to Aaron's encampment. This was the Veldt, hours deeper into the continent than he had been in a decade.

Grendel country.

Home of the only creatures on the planet that gave humans nightmares. Creatures so fierce that the only

Avalonian life that could stand before them were the titanic, armored scribes. And other grendels, of course. Even with all their firepower, and his new and uber-confident companions, Cadmann Sikes was ill at ease.

They circled above the Godsons' encampment. Two dozen buildings had been erected. Living quarters, dining hall, storage sheds . . . and a building with a stylized cross and circle above its door.

Cadzie looked thoughtful. "The church is one of the very first things you built," he said to Marco. The former actor was actually good company, and a raconteur.

"It is the center of our world," he said. No theatricality to this statement. "It's why we came."

Cadzie wheeled out, headed east. "I've heard different stories about that. What's yours?"

"What do you know about us?" Marco asked.

Cadzie shrugged. "Not that much, really. Since we found out about you, I've researched it a little."

"And?"

"When my grandparents left Earth, the Godsons were, well, thought of as sort of eccentric. A crossbreeding of Abrahamic religions, with a dollop of zen and some other stuff."

"Eccentric," Marco chuckled. "That's a tactfully chosen word."

"I try."

Marco pointed down at a cleared space, foundations laid but no walls in place yet. "Over there—we'll put the nursery. Creches. Before long we'll have children everywhere. It feels like forever since I've seen a boy chasing after a girl. It should feel like just last week . . . but it doesn't. Strange. The sound of laughter. This is a good world, I think."

"So what happened? On Earth?" Cadzie said it casually, but that really was the question in all their minds. *What had happened on Earth since their parents and grandparents left?*

"We were crowded out. When the early Mormons wanted a place to make their own, they could go to the frontier. We wanted to raise our children as we wished, according to our beliefs ... but had to do it while living among unbelievers."

Sort of the way some of the Starborn had chosen to head over to the continent. And pretty much stay there. "That had to rankle. Here, if you don't like us, you can choose a million other places to be."

"Exactly, but we didn't intend to come here. Probably the captain did, but he didn't tell anyone that. We were going to be the only settlers on a brand new world." Some of the brush had been cleared below. A near square kilometer burned away by Minerva engines. High-tech swidden agriculture.

"So what happened?"

"Nobody really knows, but once we heard your message, the captain decided to change course."

Understandable, Cadzie thought. "No. I mean back on Earth before you left."

"Well, if you can't beat the man, you become the man. We were a wealthy order, and began to insinuate ourselves into politics, industry ... anything that would give advantage. Influenced elections—all legally, of course, but it got frightening to the small-minded."

"I can believe that." That's what he said. But he was thinking that there was probably a little more to the story.

"Things came to a head when we actually took over a few small countries in the Pacific Islands, and Southeast Asia. Actually had a seat on the Global Commission. That rankled, and there were real threats. And then came a solution."

Cadzie chuckled. "Go west, young Godsons?"

Marco seemed to get the 19th-century reference, and Cadzie took pleasure in that. With his supernaturally good looks and ceramic white teeth, it was good to see a brain lived in that head. A consistently pleasant surprise. "Pretty much. Someone studied us enough to know that we embrace the idea that the stars are mankind's destiny. And helped us reach for them."

"And here you are."

"And here we are. But we're not a burden, and we didn't come emptyhanded."

"Quite the opposite. You have skills, and genetic diversity, and 3D printers. You came bearing gifts."

Something about what he'd said tweaked Marco a bit. The former star changed the subject. "These . . . 'grendels' almost tore you apart. They did that much damage, and you never saw it coming?"

"No. We had one man who saw it."

"Your grandfather, right? Cadmann Weyland?" An answering nod. "I think I would have liked him."

"I think you could have *played* him." *Standing on a box*, Cadzie thought.

"Did you know him?"

Cadzie sighed. "Only by reputation."

The flight from mainland to colony generally required forty minutes. The new, and newly refurbished skeeters made the trip in a little less than half an hour.

"No question about it," Cadzie said. "The new machines are better."

"Those spare parts are coming in useful, are they?" Marco asked.

"Very," Joan said from the back seat.

Skeeter Blue, flying in parallel forty meters away, had a trickier time of it: suspended beneath the autogyro by an unbreakable nylon tether was a wooden crate holding something heavy.

"I've never actually flown one of these," Marco said.

Cadzie could see it now: Marco heroically piloting a skeeter on the new planet, his faithful drone hovering just behind. And above. And beneath, getting shots that would thrill audiences around the . . . around . . .

Well, would look great on movie night at the colony.

"Not even on Earth? That's a surprise."

"They fly themselves. There are traffic laws."

They traveled faster than the waves beneath them, and by five minutes after he first sighted land, they were over a rocky beach about twenty klicks south of Horseshoe falls. He had been grateful to head directly for a landing pad the last time they were here. This time, his skeeter was so stable that he took them for a tour of the dam, collecting the appropriate "ooh"s and "aah"s before heading inland.

◆ CHAPTER 23 ◆
SCRIBES

The taste of the morning's coffee was still on his lips when Joan said, "Cassandra gives us grendel heat signatures thirty klicks out."

Marco took his drone sphere out of its pouch, checked its power reading. "That's the plain, right?"

"That's right," Cadzie replied. Marco flicked a switch on the drone, and a strip around its equator began to spin. Wings emerged, and it rose to hover above his palm. When he held it outside the skeeter, the drone took off, tracking them in to capture swooping, dramatic shots.

Before they reached the plain the two skeeters had to glide through valleys and along mountain crags, disturbing web-winged demireptiles who wheeled skawing in indignation and then curiosity. "Those are the same critters we have on Camelot, aren't they?"

"Yes. Just call them pterodons."

Marco lifted his rifle, sighted at them through the laser scope. The computer assisted device wasn't exactly a sporting weapon. "No need for that," Cadzie said. "We won't land to get it, and their meat is pretty sour."

The former star grinned. He was eager to hunt. If Cadzie had been in an uncharitable mood, he might have said "eager to kill something."

Maybe he didn't like Marco so much after all.

Marco grinned at him. Lots of teeth, perfect hair, hugely likeable, totally plausible. Cadzie reminded himself to keep an eye on this one. "Good point. Well... how fast are they?"

"I'm not really sure." He paused. "I'd bet the Shakas have some statistics."

"Don't tell me that you've never tried them. I mean, your wings to theirs."

Skeeters didn't have wings of course. But he got the reference. He said, "Risky."

Gloria Stype sat directly behind Cadzie, sandwiched in the jump seat with Joanie. He noticed that Joanie looked almost petite compared to the major, as opposed to her somewhat Amazonian contrast with most of the Surf's Up set. "What say we test them a little!" Gloria asked. Her voice was at the low end of feminine register, and he liked it. He found that he wanted to show off for her. Also that in his entire life, he'd never piloted a skeeter with full capacity, and wanted, really wanted to see what it could do.

"Why not?" he said, and with that, banked sharply and dove directly at a flock of pterodons. If he hadn't known them to keep a safe distance from propellers, there might have been a touch of cruelty about his actions, but instead, as they responded with razor-sharp reflexes, bleating disapproval and winging frantically in all directions, it was mischief, not mean-spiritedness. A celebration of new possibilities, not a lack of respect for their fellow Avalonians.

The skeeter responded like a dream, with the sensitivity and intelligence of his horse Cameron, only faster and through more planes of motion than any horse could dream of. Only at this moment did he really realize what he had been missing, how tentative and strictured his previous flights had been.

This was pure joy, and he screamed *"Yahhooo!"* As he looped it and tested the aerodynamics to the max, one eye stayed on the readouts, until he realized they were so rock-steady that he could put his entire focus into the act of flying.

His passengers were laughing, not tense and frightened. They egged him on, challenged him by word and expression as he corkscrewed through a flock of pterodons, zipped among the crags with calm hand on the tiller, the proximity alarm never flashing red or screaming at them, no sign of structural instability in the frame, engines, power train or propellers.

This was flying. This was what he had been born to do, and had never even known it. When they cleared the mountains and he righted himself and flew straight once again, there was much laughing and backslapping, and he almost wanted to cry.

All misgivings about Marco had vanished. All his life he'd waited for these new friends to arrive. And had never even known it.

Another hour's travel eastward brought them to the edge of the vast grassy plain stretching for a thousand klicks to the east and north, eventually giving way to desert, and on the far northern side of the desert, mountains and finally arctic regions as yet unchallenged by human beings.

The Veldt.

And now, after only another twenty minutes of flying, they encountered the first signs of alien life. Strange signs, things that must have been conundrums indeed if viewed from orbit, let alone the edge of the solar system. The yellow-green grasslands were grooved with vast scrawling patterns, as if a godlike being had written in an unknown language in an arcane cursive script. Vaguely reminiscent of cuneiform, stupefying upon first encounter, suggestive of myth and magic. The Godsons in Red One were leaning against the Plexiglas, fogging it with their breath as they gazed down.

"When we first saw them," Joanie said, "I think we were imagining some ancient agrarian society was responsible for this. Maybe something like the Peruvian Nazca drawings. Either abstract art, or something designed to be seen by their gods."

Piloting Skeeter Blue, Sven Meadows chimed in over the speakers. "I can believe that. They're visible from space. In fact they were all we could see on Avalon that suggested life."

"Oh, it suggests life, all right." Joanie squealed in joy, and pointed to the north. "There, Cadzie!"

He wheeled the skeeter around and within another minute, they were clearly approaching their first scribe.

The titans were reminiscent of turtles or prehistoric ankylosauruses. Larger than a brontosaurus but smaller than sperm whales, they were the largest land animals human beings had ever encountered, mossy-backed leviathans secure in their armor and size, eating their way around a million square klicks of grasslands, arguably the only Avalonians that dared mock the deadly grendels.

Their backs bristled with great hooked boney protuberances, and on the first scribe they reached, three grendel skeletons hung tangled in the barbs. No... *two* skeletons, and one rotting carcass even now being picked at by insectoid scavengers of some kind, something that looked vaguely like a grasshopper the size of a German Shepherd. As they approached, two of them looked up, and one took off in an odd whirlygig pattern. It might have been squawking in alarm or protest, but he couldn't hear them over the autogyro prop-purr.

He found himself laughing, for no good reason he could think of. Life... just felt good.

Cadzie knew what he was looking for: a section of rocky plain with insufficient cover for grendels, despite the assurance of his passengers and new friends that they had adequate protection in the form of armament and constant scans from a revitalized Cassandra.

"We told you we could protect you, that Avalon was safe, remember?"

Major Stype nodded. "And we still provided our own security."

"Made sense to us. You say that your sensors will detect a grendel heat signature five klicks out?"

"Yep."

"We believe you," Cadzie said. "But we're going to do this our way."

"Belt and suspenders," Meadows said over the speaker.

Skeeters Red One and Blue Three spiraled to the ground, and within a half hour the defense perimeter, tents and porta-potty had been set up, and soup was on the fire. The Avalonians followed their procedures, and the Godsons theirs, but he noticed that there was no real conflict between the two. They were learning from each other.

Four Avalonians and four Godsons had made the trek, along with a heavy load of luggage and equipment and a goat that was just coming to wobble-legged consciousness. The twin skeeters had performed beautifully. Cadzie was quite certain that their own machines had never been so strong and agile. He'd not have been able to outmaneuver a pterodon even in a Skeeter flying solo, let alone hauling four passengers and equipment.

The guarding Godsons were no more attentive than he himself tended to be. But his own attitudes and actions, modeled on what he knew of his grandfather's behavior, were fairly singular in the colony. Mocked at times, even by his own inner voices.

These men and women understood, and there were ways they felt more like his own tribe than his friends and neighbors ever had. And that was an oddness it would take some time to resolve.

Humans and a goat chained to a stake gathered around the campfire. They were triple-protected: Cassandra's satellites scanned for heat signatures, the Godsons carried advanced portable scanners, and two men were on guard at all times. And yes, it was men. He'd noticed that. As undeniably strong as the Godson females were, there was far more of a dichotomy between male and female roles than there had ever been in Camelot.

And that created a bit of discomfort, even if, again, he couldn't quite say why.

As they feasted on roast chicken around the cook fire, the conversation was carefully casual and light. All concerned were on their best behavior. *Everyone* wanted this new synergy to thrive.

For a small man, Toad could pack away an amazing amount of food, and the open air seemed to expand that appetite. Where did he put it all?

"Grendels have a unique heat signature, even when they aren't on *speed*," Toad said, wiping a hand across his greasy lips.

"Good," Marco grunted. He seemed solid, satisfied in some way, the firelight casting peaks and valleys of shadow across his face. "That's good. You know, this is better than I'd expected."

"What did you think you were heading into?" Cadzie asked.

Marco gave a hard laugh. "We didn't know. We just knew we needed to leave Earth."

That caught Joanie's interest. "Why? What was so terrible about Earth?"

Marco considered. "No frontiers. Too many people means too many rules. Everywhere. About everything. No room for a man to mark out his own destiny."

"Is that why you came?" she asked.

He nodded.

"Bearing gifts," Cadzie said.

"Of all kinds," Trudy said, perfectly straightfaced, but in the very blandness of her response, he read mischief.

◆ CHAPTER 24 ◆
A SLAUGHTER OF GRENDELS

The fire eventually died down. By that time the guard had changed, all of the sensors checked and rechecked. The closest grendel heat signatures were far away, heading south toward the Veldt. They would have at least five minutes warning before anything scaly and toothy could reach them.

By the time Cadzie yawned awake in his tent he could smell eggs and mutton sizzling on the breakfast pans. He stretched, then rolled out and followed his nose to find Trudy cooking over a renewed fire. "How are things going?"

Behind him, Toad answered, but he didn't take his eyes off Trudy, who seemed perfectly content in her domesticity. "Getting right along," Toad said. "We have heat signatures thirty-two klicks southeast."

"Veldt country."

Through an open flap Cadzie spied Marco seated

brawnily cross-legged in his tent-mouth (a little surprised that Marco and Trudy had not shared a tent last night. Instead, she and Joanie had been roommates). The big man was scanning a hand-held sensor screen. He motioned Cadzie to join him.

One thick forefinger indicated large and small yellow blotches against a map. Cassandra's eye view, he guessed.

"Scribes?" Marco asked, pointing at three large splotches.

"That's what it looks like. I'm guessing a family cluster. Maybe three adults, five lambs."

Marco nodded, and pointed at much smaller, redtinged forms heading away from a river (marked in blue) toward the family of giants. "Grendels? They don't look so fast."

"They're not on *speed*," he guessed. "Yet. The scribes came too close to running water. Would have been better off approaching a pond."

"I thought you said they were invulnerable."

"Not when young. But then they have the protection of their parents."

"How exactly do the parents protect them?" Trudy asked. She sipped at a long-handled spoon, tasting something bubbling in the pot. It smelled delicious.

"The lambs hide under their parents. The mommies and daddies hunker down, and just wait out an attack. At least that's what we've seen."

"Shall we have some fun?" Marco asked. "Suit up?"

Cadzie's stomach bubbled: excitement and fear. *This was why you came, dammit. Get a grip.* He nodded.

One of the guard unlocked the equipment cases lashed beneath Skeeter Blue. What nestled within looked a little like chain mesh armor. Lighter, more plastic or ceramic than metallic, and according to the tech folks he'd spoken to, well-nigh indestructible.

Also adjustable, so that there were only two sizes needed for normal adults. He had seen but not worn one until now.

It was decided that half the camp would remain back at the fire circle, while the others went off on their mad adventure. Specifically, seeking a slaughter of grendels.

With (Cadzie was glad to see) an extremely sober and businesslike attitude, the armor was laid out. Damned good. The adventure discussed over beer and roasted pig had sounded like the thrill of a lifetime. Now, the insanity was smack up in his face, and the voices in his head screamed for dear life.

Trudy helped him on with his gear, explaining its purposes and instructions as she did. "These are called 'shrimp suits.'" Her grin was mischievous. "Custom made for this expedition. The designers were told to make the strongest, safest, deadliest battle armor ever designed. The first designs were based on previous human armor and armament, but eventually that changed and the researchers based the different systems on the most aggressive and successful predators on Earth, and one of the deadliest was..."

"A shrimp?" he guessed.

"Specifically, it's called a 'mantis shrimp.'"

The armor felt flexible, like a thick mesh plastic of some kind. When he pushed against it gently, it yielded. But when he smashed his fist against his shin . . . it yielded. His hand *felt* it yield. But his shin felt almost nothing.

"What's so special about a 'mantis shrimp'?" he asked.

"Fastest animal strike on Earth," she said. "Faster than a .22 caliber bullet. Its connective tissue is unique in responsiveness and toughness, capable of surviving repeated accelerations at twenty-three meters per second from a standing start."

Yow. Was she joking? In comparison, a grendel was a sloth.

"By studying this little killer, and other creatures of similar lethality, the armorers went in creative directions, and we ended up with this."

He stood up, so that she could finish sealing him in. This was the closest he had been to Trudy. Her body heat was intoxicating, and she smelled like sea salt. Fresh.

Wrenching his mind back to business he studied Marco to get a better perspective on how he must look, and the best way to carry himself. Marco's suit was red with blue trim, not much bulkier than a flight suit, with head covering and a facial shield that he guessed had a polarizing function. A backpack pouch might have been ammunition, rebreather apparatus... he wasn't sure what, but bet it could be swapped out for packs with different functions.

Marco crouched and, after a dramatic pause, jumped. And soared up twenty meters, and *disappeared*. What the hell...?

Then... a thump not fifteen feet away, accompanied by a puff of dust. Nothing. Nothing had hit the ground. What, then...?

No! There was a heat shimmer the size and shape of a crouching human being, masked by some kind of active camouflage system that blended him in with the dirt and grass so perfectly that for a moment Cadzie's eyes couldn't pick him out. Once he focused, its outline was perceptible as a distortion, as if light was bending around a solid shape.

Not for the first time, he felt a stab of resentment toward the men and women who had decided to bring children unborn to a planet infested with horrors yet not build proper defense equipment. Damn! *This* was the technology he should have had all his life!

"What are the specs on this suit?" he asked.

"Fifth Gen battle armor, with enhanced anticipatory reflexes and enhanced strength. Built in sensory enhancement: thermal and auditory tracking, and integration with weapon systems."

"Weapon systems?" Toad asked.

"Yes. There are some pretty fancy add-ons. I don't think we'll need them today. Grendels are just animals, right?"

"Yes," Cadzie said. "Just animals." It almost hurt his mouth to say that.

Trudy smiled, all blond Nordic mischief and challenge. "Then I don't think we'll have much trouble, do you?"

An hour later they were not only suited, but had conducted a series of basic drills. While there was no doubt that their new friends were more experienced and familiar with the gear, the suits were as user-friendly as bicycles with training wheels.

Major Stype, he noticed, was checking her diagnostics soberly, no sense of the almost childlike, toothy enthusiasm which bubbled over in Marco. While he envied the gymnastic contortions and leaps Marco demonstrated with ease, he himself could jump three times his height, and lift twice the weight any human being had ever hefted without assistance.

He felt like Spider-Man, and that was quite enough for the moment.

Marco nodded approval when Cadzie landed from a leap in a perfect three-point superhero landing. "All right. It's pretty intuitive, right?"

"Unbelievably so," Cadzie said. He spoke from behind a faceplate, but wasn't sealed in, was still breathing ambient atmosphere. These suits had to be the greatest innovation in mobile war since light chariots with spiked wheels. *What was that, 2500 B.C.... ? Kazakstan... ?*

He realized that his mind was desperately seeking distraction. His gut bubbled like a caldron.

"Try this . . ." Trudy said, and toggled a plate on her own wrist.

His transparent faceplate shimmered and shifted, segmented into four sections displaying thermal and satellite deep-scans, running in parallel but arranged so that he could see clearly. Columns of alphanumerics and symbols ran at peripheral vision, available at the slightest turn of his head. "Hugely adjustable, my friend," Stype said. "But we're just giving you the minimum right now, so that you can begin to function. We're dropping you in on the deep end, I think."

He saw everything, including the heat-shimmer around Stype as Trudy finished strapping her in. "Amazing," he said.

"I assume you're talking about the armor?" Joanie asked. She'd tried the armor on last night at Surf's Up, and had proved more agile than Cadzie, actually pulling off a decent back-flip. Not perfect: she had pancaked, but her "oof!" had been goofy, not painful.

"I did better than you," she whispered. "I should be going."

"Next time try scissors instead of rock."

She growled at him, and lowered her voice. "What's their excuse?" she asked. "Trudy told me last night that there was never any question of her putting on the armor today. What's up with that?"

"Charmingly patriarchal," he said under his breath. "She's breeding stock. They don't trust the creches, and are still careful about a new planet. Pretty simple, really."

"Pretty stupid," she said. "They're acting like men's lives aren't as valuable as women's. Except Stype. I'm afraid to ask about Stype."

He was quite sure that wasn't what she was thinking, but it was the right argument to make. He had no idea how things were done on Earth, but on Avalon, regardless of a social agreement to embrace equality, the quarter-million years of gender roles integrated into every human institution made certain patterns inevitable . . . and the Godsons were even further down that road. Rough edges to be smoothed.

He hoped.

"Amazing?" Cadzie said. "These suits leave 'amazing' in the dust. With the auto-balance, I can't believe how easy it is."

"We have the patterns for you, and the fabricators will gear up in a few days, if you want."

"I want. What's the maximum strength of one of these?"

"Pick up that rock."

"Sounds good." Conscious that he was now strutting (just a bit) he walked over to a boulder as tall as his waist. It was a quarter-sunken in the ground, and should have required a tractor or mule team to lift. He bent his knees and gripped with gloved fingers. It resisted, and then he was able to really get his legs under him. Grunting with effort, he managed to raise it a few inches. *Top that, Peter Parker!* He let it thump back down with a satisfying *thud*.

"This must weigh a ton," he panted. "Holy crap. I can feel that. It feels damned heavy. Is it supposed to feel so heavy?"

"If it didn't, your proprioceptive systems wouldn't be engaged. You're at least three times as strong as the average human being now. How do you like it?"

He felt his whole body grin. "I like. How tough is the armor?"

Stype's arm blurred. She unsnapped her holster, her sidearm blossomed in her hand. Cadzie watched the muzzle level at his face and the world flashed white. Cadzie staggered back, a cry of dismay and shock strangled in his throat . . .

And then realized that he was just fine. "Holy shit!"

"That answer your question?" Trudy asked.

He heard his breath sighing in the faceplate, and felt something odd settle over him, a combination of calm and confidence he could not remember experiencing before. "Damn. I'd say so."

"What say we go find some grendels?"

Skeeter Blue flew west, deeper into the Veldt. Now Cadzie understood why the seats were so wide and spacious: to accommodate a pilot or passenger wearing this amazing armor.

He flicked a chin switch, opening a radio channel back to camp. "Are you watching this, Toad?"

"Wouldn't miss it. Cadzie . . . be careful, will you? I mean, I thought I wasn't going to say that, but I don't know . . ."

"What?"

"This situation. I don't know quite how to say it, but if the Godsons are right, and they'd better be . . . for the first time in the history of humans on Avalon . . . we are the apex predators."

Those words reverberated in Cadzie's mind. *We are the apex predators. The Big Dogs.* God. If only Granddad had lived to see this.

Marco pointed down to the grasslands below them. "There! Is that what I think it is?" They were watching a small wave, perhaps fifteen adolescent grendels running in a rough wedge toward the center of the veldt.

"Those are grendels, *sans speed!*" He called out after checking the skeeter's belly screen. "Young ones, I'd guess only months old."

"What are they doing?" Stype asked.

"Hunting in a pack. We never saw that on the island, but there seems more pack behavior on the continent.

Armor or not, I promise you you don't want to deal with that."

"They going after scribes?"

"My guess is they'll have to. There are whole ecologies built around and under and over the scribes, and nothing else here but grass."

"I thought you said scribes are invulnerable."

"Yeah, but those grendels probably don't know that yet. Can probably smell the meat without understanding the danger. Let's find a smaller group and get in front of it."

Maybe even a loner, the traitor in Cadzie's mind whispered. *Why take chances?* He flew in an expanding spiral, until they found a group of three, heading southwest, on a line that would intersect with the first group, probably at the vertex of a fat, juicy young scribe. Good luck with that.

"We can try these," he said, and took the skeeter two kilometers ahead of them, settled to the ground. He looked soberly at Joanie. Chose a private channel for her. "Listen," he said. "These might be miracle machines. But I'd like you to hang back in Grendel Scout mode. You sit on those reflexes until you see what's happening. Then if you see the need, you use the grendel guns."

"All right, but next time you back me up."

"With pleasure."

He, Stype and Marco hopped out, while Joanie mounted a heavy-duty grendel gun on the door frame.

"How do we do this?" Marco asked. His voice finally sounded a little stressed. Good. He was human after all. Stype displayed no emotion at all.

"How far out are they, Toad?"

"Half a kilometer. You've got about two minutes."

"You seeing this?"

"From a safe distance, yes. And I hope you're sure about this, because we have heat signatures coming your way."

"Fast?" Stype asked. "This *'speed'* stuff?"

"No," Toad replied. "Not yet. Slow. I'd call it hunting mode."

"They are stalking."

"There's something odd about this, though. You need to be aware."

"What are you seeing?" Cadzie asked.

"Slightly different behavior. They seem to be, well, triangulating on you."

"We haven't seen that before. Not much." Damn it, the nervousness was leaking into his voice as well.

"Maybe they are part of Aaron's group?"

"This far out? No way."

"Wild grendels?" Trudy asked. "That sounds right."

"How do you explain that behavior?"

"Shit happens."

Stype raised her hand. "You ready?"

"I hope so."

"You'd better be."

They released the goat from its crate and pounded its stake into the ground. The poor thing was bleating and bucking. It tested the air, perhaps able to smell what was coming, just as its approaching killers could smell goat. "Sorry, fella," Cadzie murmured. "It's a good cause." And to be sure, he drew his knife along its side, drawing blood.

There are lines once crossed which cannot be

uncrossed. He could see the screens in his helmet, note the approach of the heat signatures. There was no way to get the goat and three human beings back into the skeeters before the grendels reached them. The goat, at least, was doomed.

And if the humans tried to prevent that death, the weapons and armament had better be perfect, or they were dead, too.

"Will that be enough to attract these things?" Trudy asked.

"Blood does it, yes."

"Wouldn't it be kinder to just kill that poor goat?"

"But less effective. Grendels will scavenge when hungry, but they seem to actually enjoy the hunt."

"So do I," Stype growled. That wasn't fear. That was readiness. Marco was quiet. Watchful? Or nervous?

Cadzie had a sudden, powerful urge. "Damn it, I think I have to pee."

He regretted the words as soon as they left his mouth, but Trudy's voice answered in his ear. He detected no hint of mockery. "The diaper is built in. Be my guest."

"Oh, Christ." Was this really happening? More to the point, had he actually volunteered for this?

"Cadzie, we have movement."

"I'll just bet we have."

"Are you all right down there?"

"I think we've got company."

Cadzie's chest felt pumped full of hot liquid, every breath a strained effort. "Joanie!" he said. "I give you control of my suit for the first two seconds after the grendels appear. Override my reactions."

"Are you sure?"

He was sure. Years of operant conditioning had burned a conditioned response until it was equal to the basic programming ingrained by millions of years of evolution: a flinch in reaction to loud noises and falling and... grendels.

And out of the grass stalked three creatures from his deepest nightmares. And regardless of conscious thought, Cadzie's entire body moved. His right arm tried to grab the holstered handgun at his hip with a motion so fast and violent that when the armor resisted it he felt the protesting tendons and ligaments at elbow and shoulder scream in agony.

His vision collapsed to a tunnel, focused entirely on the first grendel. Vision went red, and then black... and then red... and then came back to normal as the conditioned response faded.

He panted. Dear *God* that was intense! That response had never, ever been triggered in the wild. Aaron's tame beasts didn't trigger the same response, and he wasn't sure why. But as the roar of the adrenaline faded, and sanity returned, for the very first time he had consciously experienced the full power of the programming designed to save their lives. He shivered, as the hormonal heat receded, leaving him feeling cold and sick. And then that died away as well...

And his breathing normalized. According to the clock display built into the armor only seconds had passed, but it felt like months.

"Are you all right?" Joanie asked. If she'd been watching his biometrics, she must have had quite a show.

Hopefully, no one else had noticed, and he managed to focus on what was going on right here, right now.

A hundred meters away, the grendels still crouched, watching them. Almost as if they had been waiting for him to lock eyes before acting, they began to move. They crept in like cautious wolves, creatures faced by something they had never seen before, that none of their kind had ever seen before. Trespassers from some strange realm completely off their genetic maps.

"Are you sure about this?"

"It's a little late now."

"By the Provider," Marco whispered. "I didn't realize that they were so . . ."

"So grendel?"

"Quiet!" Stype snapped. Nerves? Or something else?

They crouched, squatting in the crushed grass, thick barbed tails thrashing slowly, back and forth and back and forth. At a distance, the grendels examined the newcomers. Three humans. Three demireptiles.

"They've never seen anything like us."

"It's possible they've never seen a human being at all. Ain't that many of us."

"Let's hope there aren't about to be three less."

"All right—what do I do now?" Cadzie asked.

"Fight or die," Stype said.

The grendels blurred and came straight at them. The machine pistol built into Marco's suit spit fire and one of the three was stitched with machine gun rounds.

Cadzie couldn't think, all he could do was move. The grendel was on him, its barbed tail and nails scrabbling at his armor, scratching and scraping and peeling away paint.

He could smell its breath through the gaps in the faceplate, a musky, meaty stench. Hot!

He collapsed within himself, all of the ego and confidence in his technology melting away, revealed for the fraud it was. All his courage, fraud. His Grendel Scout reflexes peeled away to reveal a frightened little monkey trembling at the center of a mass of ruined conditioning.

And that, curiously, saved him. *Because the ape knew how to fight*. Even if it was futile, it might not have had the slightest idea of guns and bombs and scans, but teeth and claws it fully grasped. Survival it understood.

And that tied directly into what the shrimp suits were designed to do. His hands grasped with strength no anthropoid had ever known, with speed that augmented his natural motion until it was almost the equal of the single-response Grendel Scout "flash" reaction. His armored fingers dug into the creature that had dared to challenge him, his augmented arms held it out and punched and punched and . . .

And then the red tide receded, and Cadzie found himself standing, panting, gloved hands smeared with gore, the ground around him plowed and furrowed, three dead pseudoreptiles lying about them.

No . . . two dead, one mortally wounded, attempting to drag itself away, webbed intestines trailing behind in a faint red mist.

Somewhere, someone was chanting: "Holy hell. Holy hell . . ." Over and over, again and again.

Oh, shit. It was *him*. He was ashamed . . . then realized that Marco had flipped open his face plate, and was doubled over, hands braced on his blood-spattered knees, puking up his breakfast. Even the stoic Major Stype was gulping air, face drained of color.

Good. Grendel-shock was no personal weakness. He almost grinned.

Joan's voice crackled in his ear. "Shit, Cadzie! I can't believe that!" She changed channels. "Toad, did you get that?"

"Uploading to Cassandra. Holy shit, Cadz."

Skeeter Blue was hovering in. When it landed, their human expressions were awe-struck.

And there was an earthquake. A big one...

No, that was just him, again. The world wheeled, and he fought to keep his eggs and mutton in their place.

"Get me..." He gasped once he'd regained a bit of composure. "Get me out of here. Peel me out of this thing..."

The Godsons had set up defensive perimeters, checking for heat signatures, and nodded assent: it was safe.

One he'd thought dead was trying to crawl away with a broken back. Marco put a bullet into its brain.

Cadzie watched, numb. He couldn't feel his mouth move, but heard himself say: "And the goat. Get the goat."

The upper part of the armor stripped away, Cadzie staggered over to the place where they had staked the goat. It wasn't bleating. Wasn't moving. Seemed as much in shock as he should have been.

Cadzie rubbed its head, and slowly, it stopped trembling and began to respond. "You, little friend, are the luckiest goat that ever lived." Fervently, he wished that he could simply tear off his suit. He wanted to feel something warm, and alive. Feel a beating heart against his chest. Even a goat.

Especially *this* goat.

"A new pet," Joanie said.

Cadzie collapsed to his knees. "I don't think I'll ever eat Unka Carlos' *cabrito* again. I've looked at life from both sides now. I dub thee Billy the Kid."

"Cute. Let's go home."

◆ CHAPTER 25 ◆
RETROSPECT

Cadmann's Bluff was Cadzie's second home, and he knew that soon it would feel much less that way. His grandmother was noticeably weaker today, walked as if her joints were nerve-bundles rubbing against each other with every step. Had she always seemed to catch her breath when standing or sitting? Perhaps he was merely seeing her with clearer eyes.

"You took a terrible chance," Sylvia said. She was simultaneously working on her latest canvas and watching her new house guest: Billy the Kid. The luckiest goat in the world was nosing around her vegetable garden. Cadzie had promised to build a fence, and knew he'd have to make good on that promise, or Sylvia might try out some new recipes.

"It was worth it. Mom, you don't know what it was like."

"I've seen the video," she said, adding a dab of color to her canvas.

"Not the same thing."

"Then tell me."

He paused, thinking. "I wasn't alive for the Grendel Wars. And I can't say I know what that was like. We have the videos, and I suppose we understand it that way." Another dab. "We thought we'd all die," she said.

"Yes. I'm not saying what happened to us was as bad. Or worse. But it was different."

"Different how?"

"You had another...frame of reference. You remember Earth. A place where there were no *speed* monsters. Where it was so boring you traveled across the stars to find adventure."

"It wasn't quite like that." Her chuckle was directed at the canvas.

"But close enough?"

"All right," she said. "Close enough."

"We...grew up in the shadow of those gargoyles. They are...were our boogeymen. There hasn't been a day I've not thought about them. You created an entire clan to program us, implant programs in our unconscious to keep us alive. The nightmares..."

"I'm sorry." She looked tired. "We just wanted to keep you alive."

"And we love you for that. But what you don't see is that all my life, there's been a small, frightened place inside me. That little core of my humanity you programmed from the cradle to be ready to kill or die. It was for my good...for our own good...but it was in there, and it poisoned me, just a little."

"Cadzie..." she began.

He raised his hand, begging room to finish his thoughts. "It's okay. It's all changed. For the first time in my life ... I'm not afraid of grendels. I went face to face with one ... hell, toe to toe. And tore it to pieces." He paused, mentally chewing at something. And then came to a decision. "There's something I've never told you."

"What?"

"I dream about grendels. A lot of Scouts do. Sometimes we shoot them in time. Sometimes not."

"Dear God." She almost dropped her brush.

He barely noticed, already switching out of emotions and into a logical mode. "I think it's part of some mental subroutine designed to keep our hindbrains sharp."

"Cadzie, we never ..."

"Gramma ... last night I dreamed about a grendel. I fought it *with my bare hands*. Strangled it. And won."

She went very still. "And that made a difference?"

"Oh, Gramma ... Yes. It ... I felt like a *man*. Heroic. Like I could grab the world by the throat, and shake it. You know how you guys are always talking about how the younger generation lost its urge to explore?"

"Yes ..." Her face softened. "We love you, though."

He gestured dismissively, as if unaware of her discomfort. "It's all wired together. Grendels. The universe is filled with things that almost killed us. You changed us, programmed us to fear them. Didn't you think of what that would do? Yes. A lot of us lost our drive. It wasn't laziness. It was *fear*. We've created a new set of possibilities."

"The armor?"

He nodded. "But not just what it is. What it *represents*. Something happened when I faced that grendel. Something in the back of my head." He tapped it. "I looked at it, face to face. I'm the only child of the Earthborn to do that and survive. Well . . . except for Aaron."

"Aaron is insane," Sylvia said. She said the words simply, without affect, as if the three words were a brick wall holding back an ocean of pain.

"There's that, yes. But I could feel myself. It was fear beyond anything I've ever experienced. But when that bastard couldn't get to me . . . when it *screamed* when I hit it . . ."

He smiled. And in that smile were warm, lethal memories.

"And you remembered you were a human being?"

"More than that. But that, too. I remembered that a human being isn't just his body. Our bodies are weak. I'm my *tools*. I'm the knowledge we pass from generation to generation. I am every human being who ever strove and fought and learned and then taught his tribe what he learned. I'm my grandfather."

"Yes, you are. I see it more all the time."

"I can only wonder what he would have thought of the newcomers."

"I don't know. But I know who you should talk to . . ."

They said it together. "Uncle Carlos."

◆ CHAPTER 26 ◆
PSYCH PROFILE

Cadzie found Carlos working on a bed piece, something commissioned by the Godson commander. It was a large piece, with drawings laid out where there would soon be carvings, depicting pterodons against a misty mountain.

"Stunning."

Carlos smiled. "Might take a year to finish." A sigh. "I like long-term projects. I go to bed at night thinking about them, and wake up in the morning eager to get to work. Good for a man."

"I think this one will be classic," Cadzie said, running his fingers along the sanded wood. "What is the price?"

Carlos sipped from his coffee mug. "Well . . . let's just say that the Godsons appreciate great cocoa. I'd forgotten how it tastes."

A year of work for a cup of cocoa?

His uncle shook his head, as if reading his mind.

"Let's just say that I'll probably die before I run out."

He held out the cup, and Cadzie sipped. Sweet, hot, very good. Very, *very* good. But Carlos could see he was unconvinced. "Memories," he said. "Reminds me of things, people, places I'd forgotten."

"I don't need to understand, Unk. I'm happy if you're happy."

Carlos scanned him. "You look different. I heard about some craziness on the mainland."

"Would you like to see?"

Lounging in Carlos' spacious den, a place of bound books, paintings, big couches and two mounted grendel heads, they watched the video from Cadzie's point of view, Major Stype's point of view, and Marco's perspective.

Carlos' girlfriend Twyla, the camp's premier psychologist, was watching as well. As she did, Cadzie noticed that she crossed and uncrossed her strong shapely legs, wound her long, white-streaked hair around her fingers again and again.

Wind. Unwind. Cross. Uncross.

She watched the footage repeatedly, from different angles. The suits. Marco's drone camera. An orbital-eye view.

What was she looking at? Or searching *for*?

"What do you think?" Cadzie asked after the third time.

Carlos clicked his tongue and said, "Repeat. Cadzie's view," and the first video, from hideous close range, played once again. It was Carlos who had asked to see the battle from another, and yet another point of view. He couldn't get enough. "I think that's the most amazing thing I've ever seen," Carlos said. Twyla said nothing.

"Why?" Cadzie asked, hoping to draw her out. "I mean,

I think so too. But why is this more than, say, Aaron taming grendels?"

"Fluke-enhanced grendels," Twyla murmured. "They are smart, have a small amount of control. And . . . Aaron's people milk the *speed* glands. That lowers the aggression quite a bit. And Aaron is batshit."

"Is that the technical term for it?"

"My professional judgment."

"Sylvia concurs."

"We have to deal with him," Carlos said. "But don't trust him."

"You think he murdered Grandpa, don't you?"

Carlos's face spoke volumes. When he said nothing, Twyla said, "Little Shaka can't remember. Concussion. The only witness."

Carlos said, "You looked right into a grendel's eyes when it was on *speed*, and survived. It was close enough to . . ."

"I could smell its breath through the armor."

"*Dios mio.* What was *that* like?"

"A little like the *speed* coffee, actually. I felt buzzy afterwards. More than just adrenaline dump."

Carlos chuckled. "Makes sense. And you survived, and since that time, you've felt a little odd."

"Maybe a lot odd. Like something opened up in my head. I told Gramma that I wondered if the reason we lost some of our drive was fear of grendels. The second generation didn't even want to go to the mainland much."

"And third gen is split between Surf's Up and the dam."

"Yes. Like they are waking up. Slowly."

"Are you thinking . . . ?"

"Wake them up fast."

Carlos chuckled. "You are ambitious. Twyla darling, you've been pretty quiet. What are you thinking?"

"I'm thinking that you're both missing something." Twyla said. She hit the button, played the vid from the beginning again, this time from Major Stype's point of view. "Missing what?" Cadzie asked.

"You're not looking closely enough at the medical scanners." She pointed at the hologram, froze the image. Indicated the string of symbols and numbers running along the edges. "Look at Marco's readouts."

"What about them?"

She raised her voice to command pitch. "Cassandra, overlay scans for Cadzie, Marco and Stype, please. Clear graph lines."

Almost instantly, a series of overlaid 3-graphs, like green, red and blue ocean waves viewed sideways, appeared floating in the air before them.

"Compare them to Cadzie's. He had a typical hormonal and physiological response to fear. The hormone dump: cortisol, adrenaline, norephinephrine . . . normal. Same with brainwaves, breathing rate, heartbeat . . . the whole thing."

"Okay . . ."

"Stype didn't. She didn't have a fear response." She paused. "She had a *pleasure* response. Dopamine and phenylethylamine. Normal human beings don't respond to stress like this."

"She's a soldier," Carlos said. "Experience makes a difference."

"Not like this," Twyla said. "And I'm not sure the

Godson ranks represent real-world experience. Actual combat. Carlos . . . you knew Cadmann. How did he react after dealing with a grendel, successfully?"

"I'd say that he locked the fear up inside himself, somewhere deep, and would react later. Adrenaline dump."

"That's normal," Twyla said. "This is different. It looks like . . ." She seemed uncomfortable speaking her thoughts.

"Like what?"

"Well . . . her brain released neurohormones like oxytocin and prolactin, as well as endorphins."

"That's . . . like an orgasm, isn't it?"

"Yes. Exactly. Stype's emotional profile is more like sex than combat." She paused. "To me, at any rate. Hell. Maybe I'm talking out of my ear."

"Are you saying she's a freak?"

"I'm saying that I'm not sure our new guests are as normal as we thought. If this is typical of them, well . . ."

"Well, what?"

"Well . . ." Twyla said, twining and un-twining her hair around her forefinger. "It reminds me of something someone might do to modify human beings for a specific purpose, for combat. Tie the pleasure and fear receptors together in some odd way. Heighten aggression, reduce pain, and something else."

"Something like what?" Carlos asked.

"Make killing pleasurable."

◆ CHAPTER 27 ◆
MAPS

Cassandra's new home, the concrete bubble of the recessed computer facility, always seemed a little too cool to Cadzie. He turned the lever to open the big yellow steel doors, and was astonished. "Never saw this locked before," he muttered, and got another surprise.

Toad's voice came out of the speaker above the door.

"Hullo, Cadzie. Give me a moment. You're alone?"

"Sure I'm alone. What's going on?"

"Wait a sec. Okay, come on in." There was a series of loud clicks, then the handle turned and the door slowly opened. Inside were a couple of younger kids Cadzie remembered from a Grendel Scouts class he'd taught last summer. They were staring at game screens, obviously cooperating in some game or another, and barely looked up. "Hi, Cadzie," the girl mumbled before going back into her game.

But they each had a grendel gun.

Cadzie went down the lighted corridor to the computer room. Toad was busily reading a screen full of information. No one else there.

"What's with the locks?"

"Carlos's idea," Toad said.

"Why?"

"He and Zack said 'security.'"

"And that's why there are two Grendel Scouts with grendel guns playing Mineballs in the entryway?"

Toad continued reading the document on the screen. "Yup."

"All right, what in the name of loose grendels is going on?"

Toad swiveled to face Cadzie. "You do know Cassandra accepted Zack as the last of the Geographic Society trustees?" When Cadzie nodded, Toad said, "So Zack told her to ignore restrictions on remembering things about the Godsons. Seems Cassie's been a busy girl since then."

"Busy? How?"

"Don't know exactly. Just reading up on it now. After Zack and Carlos had a private session with Cassie, Zack decided we needed some security. I was up all night helping put the locks in."

"And Jokie and Kim—I think that's their names—and the grendel guns? They're security?"

"All I could get to volunteer on this short notice. You want to take a turn sitting out there? And we put those up this morning." He pointed to an ornate gun rack on one of the bare walls. There was room for five grendel guns. Three were present.

Cadzie couldn't control himself. He burst out laughing. "That's ridiculous! Security against what? We've never needed any security!"

"Well, we never had Cassie down here where she's

vulnerable," Toad said earnestly. "Yeah, a couple of junior Grendel Scouts isn't much security, but maybe it's better than nothing."

"And you're afraid someone will do something to Cassie? You too?"

"Well, we already did, once, didn't we?"

"Come on—wait. We? You were in on that?"

"Sure. So was my father, you know. And Joanie. But we're not the only ones here, are we?"

"Well—you mean the Godsons?"

"Yeah."

"You spent a lot of time with them. They brought you home. And you don't trust them."

"I do trust them. Or thought I did. Now I'm reading what Cassie told Zack and Carlos, and I'm not so sure."

"I need to read that."

"Guess you do."

"But whatever Cassie says, this isn't security." Cadzie waved at the gun rack and toward the entry way. "Locks, bored kids with grendel guns, that's not security."

"Probably not, but what would be?"

"Toad, I don't know. I doubt we have anything that would keep those people out of anyplace we have once they decide they want in! I went hunting grendels with them—"

"I heard that."

"Nearly got myself killed, but they took care of the situation. Them and the powered armor they loaned me. Toad, they're—well, they're awesome. And what we've got isn't security, I guarantee you that. And what would make them want to hurt Cassandra?"

"Well, I know one thing that would. If that old man up in orbit, that Speaker Augustus tells them to, they'd burn us out and to hell with anyone who tried to stop them. Yeah, I know that sounds silly, you wouldn't do that just because Carlos or Zack told you to, but I was up there with them, Cadzie, I saw the way they treated him! He was nice and polite and he didn't give many orders because they did everything they thought he wanted them to do before he could ask, but when he said Joey they jumped and asked how high on the rise."

Cadzie looked at the screens in front of Toad. "What are you working on?" Cadzie asked. "Defenses?"

"It's a map of Avalon," Toad said. "We can shift through different views: humidity, photographic, topographic, thermal . . . Cassandra has been a busy girl."

He clicked through different selections, each of them concealing and revealing different aspects of their subject area. "And . . . magnetic."

And here, Cadzie saw that there were numerous "hot spots" of magnetic concentration. "What are these?" He pointed at a gray-toned, frozen series of waves. "Some kind of natural outcroppings?"

Toad shrugged. "We don't think so, no. And note this . . . when you overlay cthulhu signatures over the coastal node, we see tremendous activity."

Cadzie pointed to reddish zones. "What about these inland centers?"

"No, but that could mean the activity is underground."

He pointed to one in the middle of the northern desert.

"Then this . . . is the largest on the planet?"

"Yes. In the middle of an alpine meadow. About halfway to their north magnetic pole."

Big and Little Shaka had come in silently and were watching. Little Shaka said, "Only thirty miles from the Snowcone pitchblende mines. No one has ever reported anything unusual."

"Whatever this is," Little Shaka's father chimed in, "it would seem there are smaller versions of the same pattern in these coastal nodes." His voice quavered, but his mind was still sharp.

"What do we know about these areas?" Cadzie asked.

"If we overlay topology and deep scans, this one looks like a fjord leading to an underground cave system. We don't know what's in there. But we do know this…" He rotated back to thermal scans.

"Grendels," both Shakas said at once.

They laughed, and the son added: "Those are definitely grendel heat signatures."

"Cthulhus and grendels…together. Wonderful." Cadzie grunted.

"From what we know of both, and it isn't much, it could be predation. A breeding ground raided by predators?" Big Shaka asked.

"If that means the grendels are their enemies…"

"How could they not be?" Big Shaka asked. "There is possibly an intelligent species on this planet that has learned how to cope with grendels, or at least survive in the same ecology. Allies. You know…" He stretched, grinning. "I feel like a doorway just opened. This planet is suddenly a lot more interesting."

"What's our move?" Cadzie asked.

"I'd say that we mount an expedition," Big Shaka said. "We want to investigate the closest large node with the lowest level of grendel activity. Give us options."

Cassandra flashed three options in the air, shapes and colors and depths of field indicating they'd been weighted for different factors.

Little Shaka studied and weighed them, then said: "Far left. I think we could skeeter in, take zodiacs into the caves. Two kilometers in, apparently. We can do that."

Big Shaka sighed. "I'd give anything to go. But this old body has run out of tricks. Son . . . be my eyes."

◆ CHAPTER 28 ◆
THE LOST MISSION

The first community meeting since the arrival of their guests filled the main mess hall with a joyous clangor, and a happy crowd of Starborn, Earthborn and Godsons. Carlos sat at the center of a folding table positioned at the front of the room, feeling an excitement he'd not experienced in years. Perhaps decades. He cleared his throat and banged a spoon against an empty canning tin. "Attention, please. We have a terrific agenda in mind today. Specifically, an expedition which will be both dangerous and rewarding. Cadzie?"

Cadzie stood. "I've known most of you all my life," he said. "The Earthborn created our world, but that world was warped by our fear of the grendels. I understand: our parents and grandparents were simply trying to keep us alive. But our new friends brought a gift we never even knew we needed: freedom from fear."

To this, there was general agreement and cheering.

"And," he continued, "our psychologists say that this gift cannot be given, it must be earned. It is time we earned it. Time we began taking this world, not huddling here on the island, or along the coasts."

"How do you suggest we do this?" Narrator Marco asked. He didn't seem to be paying attention to the cameras and sensors floating around him, but those were in constant motion, currently focused on Cadzie himself.

"We propose a series of expeditions, combining experienced explorers and newbies, so that all with sufficient will might accept this new challenge, move into this next phase of our journey."

"The focus," Joanie chimed in, "the initial focus, will be learning about the creatures that may well be our allies on this planet."

Nnedi raised her hand. "What do you need from us?"

"Volunteers. It's time we took our planet back."

All over camp, Starborn and Godsons were conferring, checking equipment and refining scan maps, making preparations.

"Why are you coming with us, Marco?" Joanie asked.

He gave a lop-sided and rather endearing grin. "Adventure." The grin looked practiced. *Smile number three for camera two, Marco . . .*

"This isn't adventure for us. It's everything."

"Well . . ." He stopped packing clothes into a khaki duffle and considered. "I gave up everything for adventure."

"I thought it was destiny," she replied.

"Let me tell you about destiny," Marco said. "Channing Newsome was a great man. He was young when we started."

She said, "You . . . the Godsons . . . don't talk about that much."

"It's not a secret," Marco said. "Not exactly. It's just painful."

She sat next to him. "What happened?"

He sighed. "We'd left Earth. Built the ship, raised the money, stocked the Starchildren."

There was a term she'd never heard. "Starchildren?"

"That's what we called the embryos. Really how we funded Operation Messenger. Five thousand dollars minimum for each of a million fertilized eggs or embryos. We raised over five billion dollars. It was the Exodus."

"So . . . did something go wrong?"

"No," he said. "We did everything right. We thought. All went well until we received the message from Avalon. A few of us were awake, others scheduled to be awake on rotation . . ."

"Like our grandparents. But that . . ."

"Yes," Marco said. "Ice on their minds. When we found out about hibernation instability it caused a panic. Our onboard computer figured that it was because of the cycles of awakening. So our elders sacrificed themselves for us."

"How?"

"They stayed awake, Joanie." A thread of wonder entered Marco's voice. Suddenly a different man stood before them: the movie-star affect was gone.

"I'd . . . wondered about things. I mean, I was a major . . . *the* major star in their firmament, I suppose. So I saw more of the inner workings. Saw the difference between the things said to the entries and those that the Faithful followed."

"Did that bother you?"

"Not really," Marco replied. "Most religions have inner and outer mysteries. 'Outer' stories for children, and 'inner,' more complex stories for adults. Things told the nonbelievers, and the interpretations for believers. So if there were discrepancies . . ."

"Or absurdities?" She paused. "I've heard about something called a 'God Knot.' What do you think about that?"

"What religion doesn't have absurdities or impossibilities as part of their traditions? Miracles? Does the idea of a central source of life violate as many natural laws as a zombie Jew walking on water?"

Ouch. She felt a flare of anger, and then tamped it down. "I . . . meant no offense." The moment of heat passed.

"None taken. Not really. I might have felt some back . . . a lifetime ago. But I'm too committed now. All the way in."

"You weren't before?"

He shrugged. "Thought I was. Sure did. My whole life was a mask, you know? I made my money playing other people. I gave my fans what they wanted. I married women who shaped and protected my image."

He gazed out upon the Godson village. "I was an industry, Joanie. Make no mistake about that. Hundreds . . . maybe thousands of people depended on me being Mr. Perfect. Eventually the twinkle stays on all the time. I think I forgot where I stopped and the role started. It all . . . blended together. I sort of lost myself."

"And then the Exodus." Joanie wrapped his arm with hers. It felt natural. "You had a chance to start over again."

He nodded. "Yes. No going back to a world I'd already conquered with a lie. Whatever happened out here . . . it was going to be real."

The drone was hovering over his shoulder. Joanie glanced at it. "Really?"

"Well . . . old habits."

Her voice got husky. "Turn that thing off."

"Why?"

"Turn it off," she wheedled. "For me. Please."

He did. The hum died down as the sphere settled to earth. "Done."

"So," Joanie said, settling in. "So. You're here now. Are you staying? Or going to another star when they build the second ship?"

"I don't know."

She laid her head against his shoulder. "This is a good world, and you just made it better."

"The idea is to seed the stars."

"Does that mean you can't root? You don't even know what's out there. A thousand years on Avalon wouldn't be enough to conquer this planet."

He chuckled, not unkindly. "Are you saying there's a reason to stay?"

She leaned in for a kiss. A delicious, slightly shy joining, and then the kiss grew more passionate.

He pulled back. Her hands tried to roam, and he stopped them. "I . . . appreciate the offer. And in my last life, I would have jumped for it."

"Why not now?" She patted the ground. "Here?"

"Because . . . oh, damn. It's going to sound strange."

"Why? Because you think I'm too special?" She couldn't prevent a flat, bitter tilt to the word *special*.

He took both of her hands in his. "Don't mock yourself. You *are* special. But it's because out here, we're *all* too special. Each and every one of us. In the old world, it didn't matter. We had so many people that if you didn't have kids, fine. If you did, then there was someone else to take care of them."

"I'm not talking about kids, Marco. Or even love."

"Then what are you talking about?"

She smiled hopefully. "Fun?"

He sighed. "I need you to open your heart a little. Listen to me. That was what I wanted on Earth. And I left that behind me, as much fun as it was. I can't go backwards. I'm not even sure I can stand still."

"Stop the world, you want to get off?"

"I got off. No, it's like . . . On Earth I was one of fifteen billion. What I did didn't matter. Out here, I suddenly became about five million times more important. Everything we say and do has meaning. I've never felt that before."

She leaned back, as if trying to take him all in. "You're a funny kind of guy. Part movie glitz and part philosopher."

"Do you hate it?"

She shook her head. "I think I could love it."

"Love me?" There was mockery on the surface . . . but it was self-mockery.

"Would that be a reason for you to stay?"

"It might be a reason for you to go."

"I'm just . . . just realizing that we could actually be the masters of this planet. Not hiding, not living on the edges. In a year, we'll have all the battle suits anyone could want. I want to go toe to toe with one of those bastards. I want to feel what Cadzie felt. I can be free."

"I'm already free."

She smiled. "Then you're free to change your mind, right?"

◆ CHAPTER 29 ◆
AARON IN THE CAVERNS

The lottery had gone without a hitch. A board in the main commons displayed names of those chosen for the expedition. Some of the positions were already taken: five Starborn, five Godsons, and slots for five volunteers. The list of volunteers was long. In both camps, volunteers packed and trained with power armor modified with lethal capacitor darts.

Some had been modified for underwater use, and were tested in one of the protected coves while the dolphins swirled around them, smiling their meaningless smiles. They wanted to talk. Some of the contenders indulged them, using Cassandra's updated translation program.

Now the colony gathered to wish the explorers well. Zack addressed the gathering. "I want to wish these explorers more than good luck. I . . . we did everything we could to protect you. And it may well be time to let you go. This is your planet now. We've . . . grown old here." His wife put her fragile hand on his shoulder. She urged him to continue, and he did.

"Our bones were always going to rest here. But some of you . . . will go on to the continents. We have no idea what there is to be discovered. But what will conquer them, conquer anything that *can* be conquered . . . is your spirit. The human spirit. If we have sinned against you, we regret that, deeply. But now . . . we bless your journey. It is possible that some of you, or your children, will take the stars. Safe journeys to you!"

Like dragonflies skittering above a wave-rippled pond, four skeeters, including a totally new one created by fabricators, rose into the sky, heading southeast across the ocean.

"And we're off!" Cadzie said, hands easy on the controls.

"This is the furthest you've ever been?" Trudy asked beside him.

"Yeah. Must seem sort of silly to you. Trillions of miles."

Trudy laughed. "I was asleep most of the time. This is an adventure, no question."

They traveled east across the channel to the continent, then traveled south along a jungle coastline.

"And we are now officially further than I've ever been."

Her hand was warm on his arm. "How shall we celebrate?"

That hand felt warm, strong. Tingled. "You strike me as a little different from the other Godson girls."

"'The Godson Girls,'" she mocked. "Sounds like something written in the eighteenth century by a woman with three names. We're people. We contain multitudes."

In seventy minutes they traveled another three hundred miles. Cadzie pointed down. "That's our spot. We're heading east and inland now. Skeeter Blue to Red, Yellow and Green. Heading east."

Crammed with people and gear, the four skeeters headed inland. In another three hours they found the place marked on their maps, and landed in a clearing. A skeeter was waiting for them.

Aaron Tragon stepped out of the woods. He waited until the first skeeter had settled, until several aboard must have recognized him, and then he waved. A serious-looking young woman stepped out into the clearing, with two grendels just behind her.

The grendels held their pose. Nobody shot them. Narrator Shantel was filming. Today there were three cameras ghosting around him.

Captain Sven Meadows debarked, livid. "All right, what the hell is this?"

"I'm coming with you," Aaron said.

"And *that*?" He pointed at the grendels.

"Meet Hypolita. She's a friend. And Delilah. And Josie Welsh."

"This isn't happening," a tall, lanky Godson said. Greg Lindsey? "This isn't a stunt."

Aaron said, "We can come with you in the morning, or start off right now. You have no right to stop us."

Meadows turned to Joanie. "Is this right?"

She seemed stymied, and Cadzie jumped into the breach. "I don't know. We have rules on Camelot, but this is sort of the frontier. Principles, I guess, but no real laws."

Aaron stood firm. "So the question is do you want us with you or ahead of you?"

"What are those things doing with you?"

"Hunters." He stroked Hypolita's neck. "Grendels can sense their kind from further than your sensors, I promise you. Sense of smell. Oh, and Josie isn't coming." The woman with Aaron glared at him.

"So . . . these aren't like the others? Is that what you're saying?"

The grendels gazed at them, curious but passive. Tongues flickering in and out. Hooked tails thrashing slowly from side to side.

"Milked for *speed*. A little slow," Aaron's acolyte Josie said. "Boss—"

"No."

Joanie seemed confused. "What do you think?" she asked Cadzie.

"Talk to him," Cadzie said.

She took her father aside. The tame grendels watched. "Dad . . . what is this?"

He seemed less confident now. "I can understand why they don't want me here. I expect that. What I didn't expect was my own daughter turning against me."

She kept her voice cool. "In what way?"

"You didn't tell me what I needed to know about the cthulhus. Or what you did to Cassandra to protect them. Do you think they believe I didn't know? Half the camp thinks I murdered Cadmann—"

"You've never told me—"

His scars grew momentarily more livid. "And now they believe I conspired to conceal critical information.

Damaged our critical computer. Led to a situation where our visitors do not trust and respect us. They blame *me*."

"I'm sorry," Joanie said. "I'm sorry. That was never the intent."

Aaron stroked Delilah's dorsal ridges with his fingertips. The grendel stood still for it, but she yawned. Quite a sight. "So ... I'm here."

"You're hoping that you can do something good. Prove yourself, and the value of what you've been doing." She paused an awkward moment. "Redeem yourself."

The moment that followed was even more painful. This might have been as close to real truth as these two were going to get. So much unsaid. Something almost never seen on Aaron's scarred face ... vulnerability. A crack.

Joanie retreated first. "All right, Dad. All right."

Joanie returned to the others alone, face sharply shadowed by firelight, mouth set in a defiant line. "I vote he be allowed as part of the party," she said.

"What's going on between Aaron and Cadmann?" Marco asked.

She didn't wait for Cadmann to speak. "My father was responsible for Cadzie's grandfather's death. Whether or not it was murder is a question we've never been able to resolve."

Marco groaned. "Holy shit. This just keeps getting better and better. Is he dangerous?"

"I don't think so. Nutty, maybe. But also brilliant. Knows more about grendels than anyone in the world. And ... he needs us. He won't say it, but he does."

Aaron was sitting at the edge of the camp, just beyond

the reach of their firelight, as if he preferred shadows to warmth and companionship. Three Godsons watched them at all times, weapons at the ready. Perhaps he was oblivious, perhaps he merely pretended to be.

"Cadzie? Is this going to be all right?" Trudy asked.

"It has to be," he muttered.

"Cadzie," Carlos said. "I've spent the last thirty years trying to live up to my image of your grandfather. You've spent your entire *life* doing that same ridiculous thing."

"Maybe," Cadzie said.

"Well . . . it's time to set yourself free, young man. Time to be who you were born to be. It means letting go of the past. All of it."

He glared at Aaron. "And if I can't?"

"You'll lose your life," Carlos said, a simple, terrible statement. "I traveled across the stars to find my own life. Now I see I could have done that on Earth, if I'd had the courage."

"So . . . what do I do?"

"You have a great adventure ahead. Be the man your grandfather knew you could be. Have a great life. And . . ."

"And?"

Cadzie had never seen a smile quite like the one spreading across Carlos' face. The air crackled. "And find me a goddamned grendel to kill."

In the morning the rafts were lined up . . . and Aaron was missing. As were the grendels. Only his assistant Josie remained, cooking breakfast with exaggerated casualness, as if nothing at all was amiss.

"Where is he?" Captain Meadows roared.

Greg Lindsey, one of the two guards who had remained awake all night shrugged. "He left, headed inland. Took those damned animals with him."

Meadows vibrated with anger. "We will have words, later. You should have woken me up, dammit."

"I'm sorry, sir . . ." Lindsey began, but Meadows cut him off with a savagely abrupt wave of his hand.

Josie piled scrambled eggs onto her plate, sank a fork into them and chewed thoughtfully, watching without expression or comment. Meadows pointed an angry finger. "Where's your . . . where's Aaron?"

"Went on ahead," she called over. "No one said he couldn't."

"Dammit, he didn't wait," Cadzie snarled. "He's ahead of us. With no camera!"

Josie said, "Yeah. I'm to say he'll clear the way for us."

Joanie seemed flummoxed. "Is that going to be a problem? You didn't want him with us in the first place."

Cadzie cursed. "It's going to take another hour to get the rest of this together. I'm going on ahead," he said.

"I'm going with you," Carlos said.

"No. Please. Unka . . . I need to move fast, and on double levels we don't know what we're sailing into."

"Are you taking power armor?"

"If I have sensors and my grendel gun, I'll be fine."

"That's right." Trudy shouldered her weapon. "That's right. You will be."

"Joanie, Marco . . . no mistakes," Cadzie said.

Marco said, "Hold up, Cadmann. I'll slave a camera to your phone."

Cadmann waited impatiently while Marco worked.

Now a drone camera floated well behind his shoulder. He felt a bit ridiculous.

Overhanging trees shrouded the waterway. Trudy hopped in beside him, bouncing the shocks. "I won't hold you back."

"No, I don't think you will." He dragged his zodiac out into the river until the current threatened to tug it from his hands.

Trudy tested her handphone. "Can you hear me?"

Marco's voice. "Absolutely."

"Do we have a fix on Aaron?"

"Tentative," Joanie's voice. "Through Cassie. His scanner is turned off, and there is a lot of overhang, but we know approximately where he is, yes. Three hours ahead of you."

"That's good enough. Stay on that."

The zodiac handled the mild current with ease. After five minutes on the river, Trudy tested her phone. "Can you see and hear me?"

Marco's voice. "Absolutely. The camera is on you now."

They looked back and up. The Godsons' camera drone was there, a hovering silver sphere usually just behind them, but sometimes to the side or front, to get different shots.

Trudy asked, "Why is it so important that Aaron not reach the anomaly first?"

"He's a wild card," Cadzie said. "Always has been. I don't trust him."

Joanie cleared her throat. She'd heard that. *"Are you ready to do this?"*

"Yes. Grendels in the dark. I thought this was about trusting the people who have my back. This is more ... trusting myself."

With every passing mile inland the river grew more rapid, the zodiac's power cell driven engines quietly, powerfully pushing against the outward tide. Aaron was crowded close with two restless grendels. He was used to their presence, their thick musty aroma, but if truth be told, he never forgot their lethal potential. They were triggered by prey behavior, and so long as he never exhibited it, their training would trump their instinct.

His rubberized raft rushed under towering cliffs, no beaches to land a craft. Aaron found a hole in the cliff wall, as tall as a man and wide as two grendels, and entered the underground river. From here Cassandra's map was blurred.

He lit a lantern and watched shadows shape caves and constrictions around him. His grendels were uncomfortable now. Both were sniffing in the direction of one broad passage. He whispered in their ears ... no good ... raised his voice to a shout above the water's roar.

"Do you have something, girl? Go on." He slipped Delilah off her leash. The grendel slid off the zodiac's back end without a splash, and surged ahead.

Shadows expanded, then receded, shaping a cave that was turning (Aaron checked his inertial compass) north. Toward that magnetic source. Where rock walls came close, he fired an occasional paint pellet to mark his path. Where was Delilah?

Was it possible that, despite his careful training, she might go feral?

The channel opened out hugely.

Aaron's light wasn't enough . . . but what he was looking at looked artificial. A blobby building in the middle of a lake. It was half underwater. Aaron turned toward what might be a dock. He fired a glowing paint pellet into the ceiling.

He steered the boat into a dark recess in what seemed a giant's adobe hut. His free hand was soothing Hypolita, whose tail thrashed softly in prelude to what would usually be some kind of tantrum.

His torch was more effective here. The big room was awash in water, a meter deep or more. The walls were etched in shapes he couldn't interpret. Aaron steered around a mass of seaweed and found a flat table, squarish, a few meters wide and a few inches above the water. Then a huge raised firepit. Then a mass of rusted iron that must once have been tools.

Humans had been on Avalon for forty years. What was all this? Aaron had been part of a group of cutups called the Merry Pranksters, but he'd have known if this was their work . . . and surely any such jape would have been brought to a climax long ago.

And here to one side was a globe of metal nearly a meter tall, marked . . . hmm. Roughened, anyway. Marked like a relief map, but only across a quarter of its face; the rest was smooth. It was raised out of the water, on a ledge that ran along the wall.

Next to it on the ledge, a lump . . . chipped into a dome shape . . . a box? With a pentagram chipped into the lid.

Aaron was standing up in the boat to examine it when a grendel screamed, far away.

With no conscious thought at all, Aaron's grendel gun was in his hand. He called, "Delilah?"

The answer: nothing but echoes. "What in the hell was that? Stay in the boat, girl." His other grendel, Hypolita, seemed disturbed, but still on point.

He docked his boat, and jumped out. Hypolita followed him, nervously thrashing her tail, as he moved closer to the globe. He could make out the shape of continents. He'd be about . . . here, in the middle of roughened texture, of what must have been explored territory.

The water rippled behind him. Hippie hissed. He recognized the tone of that hiss: Hypolita was *afraid*.

"What is it, girl?" Something was in the water. Hippie's vocalization transformed from fear to rage in an instant and she charged into the water, on full *speed*.

The water thrashed violently. The cave echoed with screams of agony. Then . . . the water erupted. Hypolita churned at full speed, on and on, with incredible violence, finally crawling up out of the water. Steam boiled off her body in waves, hot enough to cook crabs. Trembling, making her death sounds, she laid her heavy head on his foot, a final act of fealty.

She had cooked herself with her own *speed*. Dead.

Aaron felt something he had not experienced in years . . .

Terror.

He had lost his light. He scrambled for it as wet things rose up out of the water, crawling toward him. He tried to train the light on them and when he did he was stung from the left side. He screamed and tried to turn but was stung from the right. These were electric shocks! He tried to crawl toward the Zodiac, and pulled himself in, sobbing and begging.

"Please. Stop. I meant no harm. Please..."

He started the engine and started purring away, but something hit hard, punching a hole in the Zodiac. It began to leak, sinking into the water. He clung to the partially inflated bladder, trying to keep his body out of the water, but could not. Another sting and his body stiffened, and slowly he slid into the water, his scream stolen by the darkness and the wet.

The water had a different taste, deep underground. More minerals, less salt. Thoughts too were flavored by the nearness of a magnetic source, the shouting of the shrine. The school flowed around Whast, sharing thoughts and selves, and all was placid and mellow and dark, until the wave came.

It was a startlement. A wave ran across the surface of the water, faster than a wave should move: a Walker machine, a boat, this deep beneath the ground. Following wakes ran down past Whast, past the school of fifteen. The surface wake pointed toward the shrine itself.

Walkers had never been this deep beneath the ground, not in forty-odd seasons since they entered the world. Whast had never seen this kind of tool: part vehicle, part balloon.

The school followed, staying beneath the water. They

convulsed when a grendel dropped out of the boat. Then, all minds linked in one motive, they converged on it and stung it until it stopped moving. Two of the school were dead, and Gorb had come too close and was bitten through the torso.

The boat had come to a stop in the shrine's great cavern. Another grendel emerged. Grendels in the shrine! The school converged again. The dying grendel thrashed loose and returned to the boat, moving on *speed*, too fast for mere cthulhu.

Magnetic signals passed among the cthulhu. Then they rammed the boat.

The occupant now splashing in the water was a single Walker. The school drew back, most of them. Then wounded Gorb attacked the Walker, releasing perhaps her final sting. Whast and Insel followed, converging from the sides. It thrashed under their stings, then went still.

The rest of the school surrounded the three. Whast and Insel and Gorb. Gorb was bleeding badly from the first grendel's bite. The pulse in the magnetic field said, +*You have killed a tool-using mind.*+

Gorb protested. +*This was an animal! It brought grendels into the shrine, the center of magnetic sense!*+

+*For many years we have seen them use tools. We all agreed. Walkers are not to be killed ever again.*+

Whast sent, +*We all have listened for their pulse. There was no mind.*+

The three were still trapped in a circle of implacable accusers. One of the school swam loose to dig into the torso of one of the two killed by the grendel. A smooth finger-sized device emerged. She put it in her pouch and went to

collect the other. They would go into the soul box until
needed.

Insel whined, +*They have no minds! Listen! Look*!+
Quicker than the school, she threw herself on the corpse
of the dead Walker, lifted it onto the ledge and dug into
its belly with her stinger. +*Look! The amplifier, the mark
that every mind-bearing person carries in her bowels, it
isn't here*!+

One of the school edged forward and dug, probing in
the Newcomer's torso through the hole Insel had made.
Up, down, left, right. +*Nothing. An absence.*+

+*This proves nothing*,+ some of the school felt. More
sent, +*We know that the amplifiers are scarce. They come
down to us from the deep past. Some are lost. The rest
make our minds greater when we swallow them. Walkers
do not have amplifiers, but they make tools. They don't
kill us, we must not kill them.*+

The three sent only their distress.

+*We are agreed*,+ the school sent. Unanimously. +*You
must go.*+

The three swam away into exile. Gorb was trailing. The
taste of blood followed them and went with them. Behind
them was a ghastly silence, growing as the shrine receded.
They'd been cut off, not just from the school, but from
the greater family of all cthulhu.

◆CHAPTER 30◆
CADMANN IN THE CAVERNS

Cadzie and Trudy entered the shadowed cave mouth, and the chill he felt was more than the mere absence of sunlight. This was not a place for humans.

"Heat signatures?"

Trudy checked her monitor. "Fading. Traces. As if something *was* here."

"But gone now?"

"Maybe."

Cadmann Sikes mused. "This might sound silly, because it's where every horror movie goes wrong. But . . . I think we should split up. You take the zodiac back to the entrance. I'll go in on foot."

"You think that's smart?"

"I'm making this up as we go along. But if there aren't any grendels, I think I'm all right. And if there are . . . damned if I don't think I'd be all right anyway. Go on."

"All right," she said, and kissed him. "Be wary."

And she putted back toward the entrance. The camera that had been following them wavered, then followed Cadmann.

Cadzie was forced to walk on ledges, jump from one position to another. Once, to dive into the water with his grendel gun on his back, and scramble back out again.

"Aaron!" he called. Here on the roof was a spatter of yellow paint. "Aaron!"

A twinkling caught the corner of his eye. It was the camera. Twinkle, twinkle, and the tiny light went out. Some kind of signal? The camera was still floating behind him. He went back a few steps, then shrugged it off.

And here came a floating mass . . . the grendel gun was in his hands, because the thing coming toward him was vaguely reptilian. Had been. A grendel, floating on its side. Wearing a collar. The most fearsome creature humans had ever faced, rendered to meat.

More cautious now, he investigated deeper into the tunnel, until his light revealed . . . another dead grendel. Wearing a collar, like the first. "What is going on . . . ?" he heard himself whisper, aware that the chittering monkey in the back of his brain was screaming *get out.*

At the cave mouth, the others had arrived, most clad in power armor modified for amphibious warfare.

"What if I fall off?" Joanie asked. It was a fair question. When she stood in the zodiac, the gyros stabilized her, but the uneven terrain to come could easily pitch her into the drink. What then?

"The suit will automatically offer you a rebreather mouthpiece," Captain Meadows promised. "Standard battle suits aren't airtight, but you'll be fine. You'll have six hours of oxygen: plenty of time for anything we're likely to face."

"With a little extra." A female voice from the shadows.

"Trudy," Little Shaka asked, "where's Cadzie?"

"In the tunnels," she said. "We have a tracer on him."

Marco said, "Not any more. The camera I set on him has gone wonky. Let's get in there."

"We have heat signatures," Joanie said.

"What direction?" Marco asked.

She pointed in three directions: Six o'clock, nine, twelve. "Shit."

Carlos felt a swell of command within him, finding the part of him that believed in the armor. *I'm not a naked ape. I'm not a naked ape . . .* "Beach the craft, now. We take a stand."

"We have about two minutes," Captain Meadows said.

"Someone check my armor again," Carlos said. "I am *not* missing this."

"Perimeter defense circle," Meadows said. "Back to the wall."

Within seconds they were a ring of steel. Joanie was completing her third compulsive equipment check, and puffing like a steam engine.

"This stuff had better work," Carlos muttered. Joanie nodded her armored head.

"Relax," Marco said. "Let it function. It has to read you. We ran you through two hours, so it is partially adjusted, but . . . we've got your back."

Carlos was breathing hard, adrenaline pumping.

"*Carlos . . .*" Cassandra said. "*I am limited, but still*

detecting your vitals, and your heartbeat is above one fifty."

"I'm surprised it's not over two hundred. What are you seeing?"

No response.

Joanie's voice grew shrill. "Someone's coming!"

Splashing through the water and then . . . it was Cadzie!

Joanie again: "Did you find my father?"

"No," he gasped, "but I found both of his tame grendels. Dead. What's happening?"

Marco launched his drone. "War."

The water erupted and grendels came at them from multiple directions. *Fast.* Grendel Scout reflexes and power armor were almost overwhelmed, it all happened too rapidly for conscious thought, so quickly that Cadmann's memory could only hold a few quick flashes of light and sound, impressions of claws and teeth and armored humans grappling and firing ballistic and capacitor weapons, the roar of explosive rounds and screams of pain—grendel pain.

He saw something flash from the water and take Uncle Carlos down. A moment of panic, then his forebrain reasserted itself: *That's armor. He's protected. He's a fighter, the most experienced grendel fighter among us. He'll be fine—*

And turned his attention back to business just in time to fire two capacitors into a grendel going at either Little Shaka or Trudy. He didn't know. He didn't care. It reared back, poisoned by its own *speed*, and virtually tail-danced across the surface of the water, whirling like a dervish, then sinking.

And then, as rapidly as it had all begun, it was over.

Five dead grendels floated in the water near the ledge. A ravaged corpse on the ledge itself. The armored defenders sagged, but still stood on their feet . . . except for . . .

"Where's Carlos?" he asked, afraid of the answer. Captain Sven Meadows, gasping for breath, armor splashed with blood, pointed into the water. He followed the gloved finger, and saw where the surface boiled, as if something incredibly violent was happening just below.

Then . . . a reptilian head surfaced, bobbed, eyes glazing, its entrails flagging from a torn abdomen as it rolled and then sank.

Then . . . an armored head appeared, buoyed by yellow inflating bladders. An invisible engine drove it to the ledge, and two armored arms pushed it up to dry land.

No one spoke as Carlos shook his head, and a fractured armored faceplate slipped back. "That," his adopted uncle said finally, "was better than sex."

Cadzie sighed with relief. "I won't tell Twyla you said that."

"Good enough."

"Did you find Aaron?" Little Shaka asked.

"No, but I found two dead grendels. With collars."

"Take us."

It took about six minutes to lead them from the battleground to where the second grendel corpse bobbed in the water. They searched in a widening circle, calling "Aaron!"

"Aaron!" Until Trudy signaled that she had found something.

A splash of glowing paint above them.

The searcher converged upon a spot he instantly dubbed the Cathedral, a chamber with arched roof and a pulpitlike pile of stones on a ledge toward the back. The longer he took it in, the more he could believe it was a place where amphibians would congregate.

And here, they found the ruptured remains of a zodiac. And then, behind the man-sized tower of smooth pebbles, the remains of Aaron Tragon. He was splayed out on his back on a crude tabletop. His face was still distorted, as if seized by such terrible contractions that even death had not released him. A raw, red-lipped hole gaped in his abdomen.

"What happened here?" Marco asked.

"You never found him?" Captain Sven Meadows asked.

"No, I didn't," Cadzie said, suddenly aware of how they were looking at him. All of them. And how terribly lame his words sounded, even to him.

◆ CHAPTER 31 ◆
THE BIOLOGY HUTCH

The room was warm enough, but somehow the bizarre nature of the objects mounted on the central table drained that warmth, lent a chill to the proceedings.

Alien artifacts, sheets of metal, pyramidal ceramics the size of your fist, oddly carved crystals. Objects formed by an intelligent, tool-using creature with symbolic language and the ability to mine, refine and work metal and rock.

The copper sphere was densely graven with symbols, but until just twenty hours ago had never been touched by human hands. The implication was staggering. Little Shaka had awaited this moment his entire life. His father had crossed an ocean of stars seeking this, and now, at last, it was here.

The Godsons had requested a representative at the meeting. Either that, Little Shaka thought, or they wanted Cadzie under their observation at all times. They'd sent Dr. Sven Martine, a Godson medical officer in his early twenties.

Martine asked, "So . . . what do we have?"

Big Shaka radiated gravitas beyond his elven

dimensions. "We're not entirely certain. I mean ... we don't really have an anthropologist, or a xenolinguist or anything close to it, but Cassandra has made some guesses, and we can fill in some of the blanks."

Shaka held up two finger-sized lumps like elongated eggs. "The box these were in was glued to the ledge; they couldn't move it. These are iron, or mostly iron. They're magnets, dipoles. Powerful. They're not simple things, there are textures in the fields. There was an organic coating, some kind of slime."

He set them down and tapped the sphere, carefully, as if it were fragile. "This looked like a globe of Avalon, mostly unfinished. I looked further, and damn! The surface features are nothing. What counts is the magnetic fields! It's a map of the magnetic fields!

"All over the planet there are little nodes similar to what we're calling a temple. Without visiting maybe two more, we can't be totally certain what we're looking at ..."

"But?" Dr. Martine asked. "We're free to speculate, yes? And I don't know the planet very well."

"No one does. Look. The main temple room had symbols similar to some Carlos found in Mama Grendel's cave."

The reference was immediately understood. "And those symbols mean?" Martine asked. "I'm remembering cliff carvings in California."

"Cassandra?" Little Shaka called. Since she'd been brought down to the surface, the colony had begun to turn to her more often, to take her for granted. This must have been what his Dad had experienced.

"I believe this analysis has no more than a sixty percent

chance of being correct, but we have enough symbols from the temple, and the cave, and the map to make projections."

Cassandra paused, more for inflection than need for time. *"If our assumptions are correct, then the creatures called cthulhu are using a kind of magnetic language with tactile-visual analogues. If we are correct about this, then there may be a relationship between this symbol—"* And here she indicated a raised pentagram.

"—and the concept 'value' or 'private' or 'wealth.' Something precious."

Carlos' brow wrinkled. "What was precious about the cave?"

"The cthulhu may have been performing some kind of breeding experiment. They could have come up the Miskatonic River from the ocean, and bred grendels who could not survive in salt water. For some reason they wished to isolate them from the mainland. This may have been thousands of years ago, and their precise motivations may never be known. But if it is true . . ."

"Then this might have been why Mama Grendel choose that cave as a nest?" Carlos asked. "Some kind of ancestral memory?"

"It is possible," Cassandra admitted.

"And the temple?" Cadzie asked.

"The globe was found in a room marked with a version of this symbol—"

And here she displayed the same pentagram, with a smaller one nestled within it. *"I speculate that this arrangement serves a function similar to a superscript, indicating 'to the power of.'"*

Big Shaka said, "Value to the power of value."

"Yes. I believe so," Cassandra said. "*Look here . . .*" Here she produced an image of the copper globe, now enhanced with continental shelving. A number of sites leapt out, engravings amplified.

"That's a lot of value," Cadzie said.

"*If we are correct,*" Cassandra said, "*then each of these might well be a node, a temple of unusual value. In them we might find important information about the cthulhu.*"

Little Shaka suddenly had a notion. "Can you identify other symbols for value? Higher symbols?"

"*Again, I have to expand my parameters to allow guessing. If I do, then this symbol might very well be a progression on the former one. Not just a concentric image, but the degree of raising, and the number of times it has been touched. A chemoreceptor might have detected traces of something . . . and indeed on Blackship Island we have recent chemotraces indicating mapping for the breeding grounds. We can only speculate.*"

"That the map indicates a combination of magnetic, tactile and chemical symbols," Big Shaka offered. "Some kind of four-dimensional imaging, a language it would be very difficult to interpret."

"*Additional data would lead to greater certainty.*"

"But if you had to make a guess?" Big Shaka asked.

"*Then there are four sites on the planet that would be thought to have the highest value. As if there was something extremely precious and rare. And one location that has a symbol that might mean 'infinity.'*"

"Where is the 'infinity' symbol used?"

"*At the magnetic north pole.*" Cassandra replied.

"But it might mean something else."

"*Yes.*"

Dr. Martine asked, "And the lesser locations?"

"*I cannot say 'lesser' with any degree of certainty, because the new symbol cannot be evaluated with any certainty. It is present nowhere else, but might be a progression on some of the others. But the highest symbols we can read with any level of certainty above thirty percent are in these locations . . .*"

These new offerings were displayed.

"What are these? They're all between the equator and the North Pole."

"*Yes,*" Cassandra said. "*And they are locations of enormous value.*"

"But still less than the Magnetic North."

"*Yes.*"

"Great value," Martine asked. "Riches? What would a cthulhu think is great value?'"

"I don't know. But knowing what a culture considers of great value can be a key to understanding the culture."

"Gold?" Cadzie asked. "Gems?"

"Or the cthulhu equivalent thereof," Little Shaka said.

"How would we get to it? Deep from the surface . . ."

Zack rubbed his mustache. "There's a mining installation about three hundred miles east. *Here.* If we get serious about this, we can skeeter in a crew."

"Drill down through . . . what? Maybe two hundred feet of rock? Into what?"

"We can deep scan," Zack said. "See what we're dealing with. You know . . . after all this is over."

"Yeah," Cadzie said, suddenly remembering the situation he was in. "After it's all over."

◆ CHAPTER 32 ◆
EXILES

Cadzie leaned against the fence, chewing on a snakeroot, and thinking bleakly of his future.

He turned as he heard footsteps: Joanie approaching. She stopped at a distance. "What happened in there?" He knew she didn't mean the biology hutch. She meant the caves.

"All you need to know is that he was dead when we found him. I did nothing, Joanie. I don't expect you to believe me, but it's the truth."

"Look at me, Cadzie."

He turned, did. "Here I am, Joanie. You've known me all your life. I've never made a secret of how I felt about your father. Never made a secret about any aspect of who I am."

"No, you haven't."

"So . . ." Snakeroot had a mild euphoric quality, ranging from relaxant to stimulant, depending on how close to the root you chewed. At the tip, effect was roughly comparable to beer. "What do you want to ask me?"

She shook her head. "Nothing. Nothing at all."

There had been only three voices when they left the shrine, and that had been terribly lonely. Gorb's agony was not pleasant, but it was worse after she went silent. There was only Insel's voice muttering terrible, bloody thoughts about the Walkers. Insel had never loved them. Land creatures intruding in water that belonged to the sea people!

Tool users, but silent. Why had they never tried to speak? Barring that random babbling from the dam they'd built.

Whast had kept her own opinions to herself.

She should have shared thoughts. It was the silence and the guilt that had killed Insel. It was killing Whast now.

Whast heaved. Insel rolled up onto the beach, tentacles sprawling limp in all directions. Tradition said that a dead person should rest on dry land, if possible. Predators were less likely to attack a sea creature, and the body could be found later and its amplifier recovered.

No matter now. Whast dug into Insel's torso and had the amplifier in one scoop. She put it in her pouch with the other, which she had taken from Gorb.

Amplifiers didn't decay. Sooner or later a person would find Whast's body and take the thought amplifiers home.

About fifty miles east of the caves, the soil was poor enough to be grainy and near-desert, but it was still dotted with scrub brush. Humans hadn't explored the region extensively, but two "mappers" named Towner Farr and Hal McCann liked the solitude. They were partners in every sense of the word, but also had a slightly romanticized notion of nineteenth-century prospectors, growing beards and wearing widebrimmed hats even in cool regions. Perhaps they hoped to one day discover something valuable enough to trigger the Avalonian equivalent of a gold rush.

Most of the time, they just mapped the territory, trading their detailed reports for scrip back at the main colony. Then they'd usually plunge back out into the wastes and enjoy their solitude.

"What is this?" the shorter, more sunburnt Farr asked. He was looking at something out of place, a squidlike creature far from water. Very dead and largely dehydrated.

He pried up a tentacle. Its sucker tried to cling to the rock. What was so obviously an aquatic creature doing here? "I think . . . they called them cthulhu, didn't they?"

"Water creatures?" Hal McCann was integrating photographs. He didn't look around. "Long way from home, isn't it?"

"I don't know. Look at the bite mark. Does that look like a grendel bite?"

Now Hal came over to look. "Just one bite? I'm not sure I've ever seen anything get bitten and survive. I mean, usually it's all or nothing."

"Let's call in a skeeter, see if anyone wants to look at this." Towner reached to pull at the corpse. "Ow!"

"What?"

He shook his hand, trying to shake the tingle out. "It shocked me. Like an electric shock. It's okay now."

◆ CHAPTER 33 ◆
ABOARD *MESSENGER*

Speaker Augustus had not considered luxury as a prerequisite of his office, but his attendants—not servants, as he often vainly reminded them—insisted on luxuries until he gave them a direct order. Over the years the furnishings in his office and quarters changed surprisingly often, sometimes to the more lavish, sometimes to much plainer and simpler, and the result generally amused him.

This compartment, tiny by some standards but a large space for a room which would be used by only one man, was furnished by the ship's artificial intelligence. Not just any artificial intelligence. This one was special, and only a few of his advisors knew of its existence. One day his Successor must be told, but not yet. Surely it was not yet time to choose one of the cadets for that task.

Gus supposed that many would want the position, but their very desire for it was a disqualification. Perks of leadership were also its scourge. The Prophet had emphasized that. "You deserve elegance and we can afford it," the Prophet had told him. "But you deserve no more than that, even though you will be tempted to desire more. For us the power must be unified in one dedicated to the Mission."

Gus adjusted the rotation speed of the rotating arm that held the capsule. While *Messenger* was under acceleration or deceleration the engineers advised against deploying the rotating arm, and Gus had to endure whatever gravity the ship's accelerations required; now that they were in orbit he could choose whatever gravity he wanted. Today he would try forty percent of Earth's gravity. Somewhere—he never bothered to find out the details—electronics controlled electric motors, and the gravity adjusted to his desires. When it was steady, Gus rested comfortable in the very comfortable chair. The screen built into the bulkhead that held up his desk flashed.

The Prophet appeared.

"Hello, Gus."

"Your Worship."

"Call me Channing today, Gus."

"Yes, Your Worship. Channing."

"You summoned me. You need help?"

"I need to organize my thoughts, to discuss the situation with someone who thinks like you."

The image looked so much like the Prophet that Gus found it disturbing. *"Gus, I remind you that this is a simulation. I am not Channing Newsome nor am I his ghost. I am an artificial intelligence program, a virtual Prophet, running in a segregated portion of* Messenger's *main computer."*

"I understand."

"Do you, Gus?"

Again The Voice. Gus could never have believed that wasn't his friend and Master, whom Gus had seen laid away in cold sleep as a man twenty years older than this apparition. And yet this was more real than his later memories. "Yes, Channing. I have to keep reminding myself, but yes. I know you are real, but not the Prophet."

"And I will keep reminding you. Now what is disturbing you?"

The crewmen who maintained this small compartment had no idea of what it was for. Godsons were not forbidden to ask, but Gus was not surprised that none did. They got their orders from the ship's computer. The Prophet's AI proxy could communicate directly with *Messenger*'s main computer, although the primary preference table gave no more authority to the AI Prophet's commands than it would to any midranking Godson officer. The prophet simulacrum could not order course changes, or any permanent changes in ship's structure, but it certainly could control the compartment's furnishings, and Gus was often surprised when things changed unexpectedly.

He opened the small refrigerator. There were various flavored drinks. A strawberry soda stood closest to his hand. That had been Channing's favorite drink, and one of the Prophet's quirks had been inflicting strawberry drinks on his disciples whether they liked them or not. The Prophet AI program was aware of every habit, act, saying, and writing recorded of the Prophet, and the sodas in the refrigerator were proof of that. More disturbing was that Gus could not order the AI to stock orange flavor. It would, however, provide him with a few ounces of Genever. Gus found the gin in a small bottle and poured himself a gin and tonic.

"I'm concerned about the locals," Gus said.

"I am aware of no hostile acts. Of course, they do not accept the necessity of the Mission. And are unaware of our search for the God Knot."

Gus was again disturbed by the reality of the conversation. The expressions were correct, even the slightly quizzical look of mild disapproval of the gin glass. The tone was correct. It was exactly like talking to the Prophet.

"There is no hostility."

"But you are concerned about their lack of ambition."

"Yes. Precisely. How did you know?"

"For the same reasons you are. I have seen all of Narrator Marco's recordings. Remarkable young man. Not exactly a Believer, but given his task he probably should not be. Very reliable, though."

"The Earthborn had ambition enough to come here. The Starborn, less so. Some have none at all. There are even those who would return to an Earth they have never seen."

"Even a dull tool can be useful, if the workman does not mistake it for a knife. The Starborn can serve. Let them go their way, unless it can be determined that they require guidance."

"And if I determine that?"

"Then," the Prophet said, *"you must act without hesitation."*

◆ CHAPTER 34 ◆
PRE-TRIAL

It was common for discussions in Camelot to run late into the night, but over the last four days, *speed*-enhanced coffee and various varieties of home brewed beer had fueled some of the briskest debates in colony history.

The biology lab had a lounge with plenty of natural and artificial light, couches deep enough to mimic quicksand, and stocked with all the relaxants and stimulants that made such conversations lively. The Shakas were, as often the case, holding court before an avid audience, an informal debate with several Godson guests.

"But there are an avalanche of questions," Big Shaka said. "For instance: exactly how did aquatic creatures forge metals?"

A theatrical wave of Marco Shantel's hand warded that question off. "A more important question might be: what happened to their civilization?"

Little Shaka had an amazing tolerance for beer, and the table before him was littered with empty pods, while he had yet to exhibit the slightest slurring of speech. "Why do you consider that more important?"

"A cautionary tale, perhaps." He waved his hand in a theatrical gesture. Joanie, sitting close as she had an increasing tendency to do, watched avidly. "Please indulge me."

Big Shaka shrugged. "We don't know. We may never know. Or we might learn enough in the next years to tell us everything. Or . . ."

"Or what?"

"Or we might discover that they're still here, have things we would call cities or even nations. It's a big planet."

Marco's raised eyebrow was politely challenging. He opened his mouth to speak but had waiting a moment too long: Toad Stolzi entered in an excited state. "Everyone!" he croaked. "Zack has finalized the arrangements. Cadzie goes on trial tomorrow! Biggest trial in twenty years!"

And that was the end of the evening's inquiry into xenobiology, and the beginning of a very different line of conversation that lasted until dawn.

The court was held in the mess hall, as there was no other facility large enough to house the hundreds who demanded the right to attend.

If not live, then by remote hookup. There was no one on Avalon who hadn't access to every word and action, and few who didn't take advantage of some part of it. The room was packed.

Zack sat at the juncture of two black-draped folding tables, holding the gavel, two judges to either side. He was the voice of the law, but would only offer an opinion as a tiebreaker.

"We are gathered here today to establish the guilt or innocence of a citizen of the commonwealth, Cadmann Sikes in the matter of the murder of Aaron Tragon. As this is a matter of utmost gravity, we ask that the courtroom observers obey the laws of decorum. We also have a number of visitors, our recent guests and now neighbors, known as Godsons. We ask them to remember that they are still guests in this matter, and not involved in the actual proceedings until more formal arrangements have been made between our two groups. Is this understood and agreed upon?"

"It is," the Speaker's hologram said from its place of honor in the front row. The Speaker himself would probably never enter a gravitational well again.

"Very well," Zack said, and banged his gavel. "Oyez oyez, the court of the township of Avalon is now in session. Bailiff, please bring the accused into the courtroom."

Cadzie entered. There were two sergeants-at-arms present, but he was allowed the dignity of walking without escort.

He sat in a chair kitty-corner to the judges and the audience, that he might face both.

"Cadmann Sikes, you are accused of the murder of Aaron Tragon. How do you plead?"

"Not guilty," Cadzie said.

"Your plea is so entered—"

"Why are we here at all?" Cadzie demanded. "Why not just look at the tape? A camera followed me every step of the way."

Marco Shantel said, "The camera failed, Cadmann. That will be brought out in evidence."

"Enough," Zack said. "Who stands for the defense?"

Carlos stood. "I do, your honor."

"I see. And our prosecutor is Thor Masterson."

"I am prepared, your honor." The massive Thor was a Starborn, but under his bronze beach-body exterior was a keen mind that had enjoyed studying the law.

Zack didn't seem entirely pleased. "Prosecution makes the opening statement."

"Thank you, Your Honor," Thor said. Cadzie had seen that smile before. Payback. But for what, precisely? "Insofar as the maintenance of basic laws is the most foundational necessity of a society, the breaking of the most basic of those basic laws is the greatest threat to every individual. The people intend to demonstrate that he did with deliberation and malice aforethought stalk and murder the man he believed responsible for the death of his grandfather and namesake, the honorable Cadmann Weyland."

He paused, as if to let that sink in. As if he was almost overwhelmed with the responsibilities of his office.

"This is a somber duty," he continued, "and it gives me no pleasure to participate in these proceedings, nor should it give you, the jury, any pleasure at all." His expression held a theatrical piety that Marco Shantel might have appreciated. "But this is not about our affection for a young man, or our respect for the hero whose name he bears, or our opinions about what did or did not happen long ago. It is about this one incident, and the need to preserve order in the world. Thank you."

After a few moments of polite murmurs, Zack raised his hand. "Carlos? Statement?"

"Thank you," Carlos said, and stood. "It has been forever since I studied the law. Never passed my bar exams. In fact, my lack of serious intent about my education and prospective career probably led to my family deciding I was better off ten light-years from home."

Chuckles from the improvised courtroom.

"But . . . here I am. And here we are. And of those who know and love Cadzie with all our hearts, I suppose I'm the closest thing to a lawyer."

Nods and murmurs of agreement.

"So the question we have to ask today is whether or not there is sufficient reason to actually bring this matter to trial."

"And you say there is not?" Zack asked, perhaps a bit too optimistically to convey the impartial air required of a judge.

"I say there is not, your honor. Something happened in that cave, that is for certain. One human being and two grendels are dead. Judging by burn marks and signs of internal heating it seems that all were victims of some kind of electric shock."

"What kind of symptoms?"

"Burns. Broken bones due to muscular contractions. Torn muscle connections for the same reasons."

Thor raised his hand and his voice. "A shock which could easily have been administered by a grendel gun, your honor."

Back off, kid. Zack could read that in Carlos' attitude even if he avoided speaking the words. What he did say was, "But unless we are proceeding under the Napoleonic

Code, the court will be forced to prove guilt beyond a reasonable doubt."

"And you believe we can't do that?" Thor asked.

"That's exactly what I think."

Zack cleared his throat. "While a trial is the appropriate place for expert testimony and cross-examination, can you offer your reasoning?"

"My client is innocent, your honor," Carlos said. "The tragedy happened while investigating a site created by a creature of unknown capacities. We have never so much as autopsied a cthulhu corpse, and because they are aquatic, there has been little documentation of their behavior. What we do know is that Aaron and his grendels were deep in their territory when they died."

Thor looked like he wanted to cough up a hairball. "And that is one of your three?"

"Yes. We simply do not know if either biologically or technologically, these creatures could have a weapon, or a booby trap, which could have created these effects."

"And what is the second?" Zack asked.

"The trained grendels. We know that Aaron used some kind of shock collar on his animals, and the possibility that one of these devices malfunctioned cannot be ignored. We believe that it can be demonstrated that the capacitors on the collars were drained—"

"Which also could have been triggered by a grendel gun—"

"Which could, yes. Again, reasonable doubt."

"And your third point?"

"The grendel gun bolts are manufactured in number, but not great numbers. We keep track of them as best we can. Cadzie expended cartridges, but that is to be expected: he defended against a grendel attack."

"Your honor!" Thor protested. "This is too convenient!"

"Not if you're the accused, and you're innocent,"

Cadzie said. "In that case it's damned inconvenient."

Thor glared at him. "Zack, I mean, your honor, we all know how lax bookkeeping is about those bolts! You can pick up a fistful at the supply shed—"

"But have to sign your name and keep track of the supply," Zack said. "The point being, your honor, that we just don't know what happened in that cave."

"There were no booby traps. We've gone over every inch of that cave."

"That," Carlos said, "rules out technology that we understand. But we just don't understand what we're dealing with here. The one thing we know is that we are dealing with creatures with an advanced understanding of magnetism. Magnetism is created by moving current, and current is affected by magnets."

"I don't think we need a physics lecture," Thor said, irritated.

Marco was called to testify. His carrying voice was a bit unhappy, a bit belligerent. His cameras, all three including the one following Cadmann, had been zapped by the local magnetic fields. That left a massive hole in his record of *Messenger*'s conquest of the universe. But his description of the battle with the grendels roused his acting instincts: he spun a story that had his audience gasping.

Trevanian stated that other cameras in the armored suits had also been zapped. Carlos and Cadzie again found that damned inconvenient.

The report on Aaron's autopsy was given by Dr. Charlotte Martine. The tall young Godson's ordinarily diffident attitude seemed suspended as she described the autopsy. The one hole in Aaron's skin went in all directions, more than a dozen probes. Very clumsy, if the perp was looking for a grendel gun projectile. It seemed hard to believe that any such perp had found what he was looking for.

And so it went through the afternoon. After five hours of testimony, the board adjourned and conferred, and after two hours returned to the main room.

"Cadmann Sikes," Zack said. "After careful consideration, we find that there is insufficient evidence to bring charges. I want to clarify that this should not be construed as a verdict of 'not guilty.' When we consider the history between your family and Aaron's, this situation is particularly disturbing."

"I understand," Cadzie replied. "What I find most disturbing is this highly inconvenient failure of a camera that could have told us everything." He glared at Marco Shantel.

The Godsons' Narrator said, "They all failed, Cadmann. It was the damned magnetic fields, they ruined everything—"

"That will be brought out later," Carlos said, also glaring.

Marco ignored him: he was glaring at Cadmann. "How do you think I feel about this? Major discoveries and a ripe murder mystery, and I don't have it recorded! I'm supposed to be setting our history in concrete! Everything we've got quits when it gets in that temple. It was the cthulhu magnets, God—" at which point he saw the Speaker's glare, and stopped abruptly.

There was a little more conversation, but then Cadmann was declared "not at fault" as indeed Aaron had once been, long ago. And that was that.

◆ CHAPTER 35 ◆
FORCE MAJEURE

Joanie's head spun. She wanted to go back to the mainland. She wanted to spit in Zack's face. She wanted to cry with relief or laugh with derision at a staggering miscarriage of justice. All at the same time.

Trudy found her smoking behind the armory, gazing out at the pen where pigs snuffled about in the mud with no awareness of human affairs.

The Godsons clustered and whispered, and from the bits she overheard, it was easy to ferret out their attitude.

"What did you think of the verdict?" she asked Trudy. She thought, hoped, that she'd be able to get an honest answer.

"I'm happy, I suppose." Trudy paused. "Aren't you? Now we can find out what really happened in there. No more distractions."

Joanie snubbed out her butt. A perverse part of her wanted to throw it to the pigs. Maybe they'd eat it, and pass the carcinogens along. Their cancer treatment technology was excellent, so it was a harmless enough aggression. "What do you mean?"

"I mean . . . whatever killed your father is still out there. The trial was a distraction."

"A distraction," Joanie murmured.

"Don't you think it was a fair trial?" Trudy asked. "After all, these are your people."

Something ugly behind Joanie's eyes tightened her vision. *Don't say it . . .*

"And it was my father."

"And you want to know what was true, yes?"

"Truth," she said bitterly. "Do you care about truth?"

"Me?"

Joanie looked at Trudy, wondering how honest she was prepared to be. What the hell. It was just one of those days. "I've heard rumors that you can just turn your heart on and off."

No flicker of irritation. "It isn't that simple."

"So you're in love with Cadzie. So you think you know him and he must be innocent. Because you love him."

"It's not that simple," Trudy repeated.

"It never is."

Trudy looked at her with an almost infuriating calm. "You're hurting, and I understand that. I think . . . I think that no matter what happened in that courtroom it was going to hurt you, because the real pain is losing your father. Everything else, no matter what the verdict, was secondary to that."

"You know me so damned well."

A mild chuckle. "I barely know you at all. But I know people. You wonder about the switch in my head. I was programmed for that. To find a good man, bond to him, be his helpmate. But . . . it's not a one-way ticket. If he violates some very specific boundaries, I am allowed to terminate the bond."

"'Terminate the bond.'" Joanie groaned. "Do you know how that sounds?"

"Yes," Trudy said. "And I don't expect you to understand."

Trudy sounded so reasonable, so undefensive that Joanie found her curiosity engaged. "So . . . what happened . . . what you know to have happened . . . didn't violate the principles. You don't have to break the bond?"

"No. And that . . . isn't easy."

"Why not?"

Trudy looked at her, seemed to mull over possible word choices.

"I have . . . loyalties."

"To the Godsons?" Trudy nodded.

"And . . ."

"They think I should cancel the bond."

"And you disagree?"

"I don't."

An uncomfortable silence followed. Something hadn't been said.

"Is there something you aren't telling me?" Joanie asked.

"I'm sorry," Trudy said. "I may have already said too much."

Joanie wondered what Trudy might have meant. If she had been in the main camp that evening instead of curled in the corner of a grass-thatched hut at Surf's Up, she would have learned.

Trevanian doubled as the armory chief. Ordinarily he

wouldn't have maintained a presence there, would do nothing but sign weapons and ammunition in and out, but something in the back of his head told him that he wanted to actually be there this night.

So when there was a knock on the latched door as he spent time on inventory, he wasn't totally surprised. He opened the door to reveal three relaxed, alert Godsons: two men and an impressively tall and athletic-looking woman. Stype?

"Hi. How can I help you?" Trevanian asked.

"Stand down," Major Stype said. "You are confronted by superior force. If you resist you will be injured."

"What the hell?" he said, but when Stype centered her stubby pistol on his chest, that bubble of opposition collapsed, and he stood down. The Godsons entered, swept the room for lurkers and took control. Weapons were distributed, but the Godsons were more interested in controlling the armory than looting it. They had their own weapons.

Additional soldiers drifted in a few at a time, checked in quietly with Stype, then left to take up positions around the sleeping camp.

Trevanian was gagged and bound. He strained against plastic manacles for a few moments, then surrendered. Major Stype watched the entire time, and after he stopped struggling leaned in and asked: "If I loosen your gag, do you promise not to scream?"

Trevanian nodded, unsure of whether he would keep his promise. The gag was loosened. He decided not to risk a loud sound. Something about these people made him think she wanted an excuse to hurt him.

"Thank you," he said. Then added. "Once you do this, you can't go back."

"It is already done," she said. Five minutes later, the door opened again and a stocky black man with three stripes on his arm whispered in her ear. She nodded, smiled. "It's irrelevant now. Sound the alarm."

One of the others sounded an air horn.

About half the colonists on Camelot lived five minutes' walk from the central dining hall. After about ninety seconds, sleepy colonists began to emerge from their doorways, yawning and rubbing their eyes.

Zack came straight to the center of town, leaning on a weathered crook-necked shamboo cane. His conical knit sleeping cap, striped red and white with a white tassel, kept flopping into his face. He moved with painful torpor, white hair disheveled. "What the hell is going on?" he asked.

Major Stype kept her hand floating above her sidearm, but not upon it. "Please stand by until more of you have been awakened. There is nothing to be alarmed about."

"What?" Rachel Moskowitz asked, rubbing the sleep from her eyes.

The town square filled. The colonists watched the armed soldiers with growing anxiety.

Finally, Stype spoke again. "Citizens of Avalon! Your leaders have failed you, failed the mission that took you to the stars. Although our actions may seem extreme at this moment, we believe that in time you will come to see that we are the greatest allies you have ever had."

"What the hell is this about?" Rachel asked.

"We are temporarily seizing the armory, and placing the colony under military law." Silence.

Sleepy colonists were suddenly wide-awake, but stared at each other, as if wondering if they were still dreaming.

"You have no right!" Zack said. He tried to sound strong, but threads of fear were woven into his anger.

"We may not have the right. But we certainly have the responsibility," Stype said. "We are fighting for the future of the human race. We came here in peace, and since we've landed seen you squander your heritage, and risk your children's future by allowing sentimentality to trump the rule of law. You have forgotten who you are."

Major Stype's voice chilled the quad. "The most revered member of your colony, by far, was Cadmann Weyland. What do you think he would think of this? Even though the transgression involves his namesake . . . ?"

Unnoticed at first, the Godsons circulated quietly among the dwellings, waking and herding those not already in the town square, as others in autogyros visted the outlying homesteads, carrying the good news to all.

All over the colony, the Starborn and Earthborn were gathered into knots. A group of colonists were being herded down from Mucking Great and its foothill. Two of them were Carlos and Twyla, who had barely been given the time to don robes. Carlos had not been allowed to bring his walking stick, as the Godsons had considered it a possible weapon. He stepped down out of the jeep, shaking with age and anger.

"What are you saying?"

The Godson who had roused him at gunpoint was brusque. "We're saying that Cadmann Sikes willfully murdered the man he holds responsible for the death of his grandfather. And that all of you turned your heads away and excused it, out of affection for his namesake. Your sentimentality has clouded your judgment."

Carlos fought to keep from trying to strangle this man.

"I don't believe this is happening."

"Believe it," the Godson said, his hand resting on his sidearm. "But don't make it worse than it is."

A skeeter landed, and a bound Cadzie was pushed out. The crowd surged forward. A shock rifle crackled with electricity. A moment later Thor spasmed on the ground. "Leave him alone!" Cadzie screamed.

"I can understand why you would defend him," Skypes said, voice flat as beaten metal. "After all, he threw the prosecution for you."

Major Stype's smile was as thin as the knife in her belt.

Before Cadzie could curse and make things worse, she said, "You will have your time, Cadmann Sikes, to prove yourself worthy of your name."

◆ CHAPTER 36 ◆
TRIAL

Air in the courtroom was tight, hot, despite the fact that the crowd was now smaller than it had been for the inquest. Supervised by armed Godsons, the crowd outside swelled the courtyard. Captain Arnold Tolliver, captain of *Messenger*, acted as chief prosecutor.

Cadzie fought to keep his temper. An outburst would solve nothing, and make many things worse. "I searched the tunnels, and near to the room we call the cathedral I found the corpses of his tame grendels."

Prosecutor Tolliver nodded. "And you claim that they were dead when you entered."

"They were dead, yes."

A mild murmur in the courtroom. The barrister pounced. "The autopsy suggests that the cause of death for Aaron was electrocution, with wounds similar to those produced by what you call a grendel gun. Is that accurate?"

"I have no idea. I still haven't examined that corpse," Cadzie answered.

"Do you have an explanation for this?"

"No," he admitted. "I do not."

Three hours later, the testimony was still underway. Big Shaka, the size and color of a black cricket, was coiled in the hot seat. "We have never captured a cthulhu, but have built up a fairly complete hologram model of the creatures."

"And what do you conclude from this?" Barrister Tolliver asked.

"We're thinking these structures—" His pointer coasted over several puckered nodules at the tips of their tentacles. "Are electrogenerative."

"Meaning?"

Shaka seemed annoyed. "We think they'll deliver a shock. We know that the creatures we call cthulhus had some connection to the grendels. Possibly co-evolved, possibly were involved in their development more directly. It is reasonable to assume that they had some sort of defense against them."

"I see." That possibility didn't seem to have occurred to him. "How could these stunners kill grendels?"

Big Shaka assumed a professorial demeanor. "In a manner similar to the grendel guns: prompt them to dump their *speed*, creating an overload of their nervous systems, shutting down their frontal lobes and in essence cooking them in their own heat."

The barrister's eyebrows beetled. "May I understand. You are saying that these creatures might well be able to generate a force similar enough to the grendel gun to have the same general effects, and be indistinguishable?"

"It is possible, yes."

"What would be required to determine this?"

Shaka paused, not liking his own answer. "Capturing a live cthulhu, I think. Yes, that would do it."

The crowd's reactions were not pleasant.

The afternoon ground on into the evening, and one testimony blended into another, until two days later an end was called to proceedings. The Godsons' judge instructed Cadzie to stand. "Cadmann Sikes, you have been convicted of deliberate murder in the death of Aaron Tragon. Do you have anything to say before sentence is passed?"

"Yes," he said. "That this is a travesty. You have no right to judge me."

The judge didn't lunge at the bait. "The right to judge has always been conflated with the power, and so it is today. You are sentenced to cold sleep until such time as the capture of a live cthulhu can be undertaken, or a cure for your aberration is found."

◆ CHAPTER 37 ◆
HINDSIGHT

Dusk came to Sylvia's house on Mucking Great Mountain.

Joanie piloted the skeeter down near the little graveyard where Mary Ann and Cadmann were buried. Carrying a fruit basket, she stepped down, a bit of reluctance in her face and gait.

Sylvia, walking a little straighter than she usually did, a little lighter as if drawing on some inner wellspring, greeted her adopted daughter.

"Hi, Sylvia. Hope I'm not late."

"No I think you're right on time."

Hugs and cheek-pecks were exchanged. They went in. Little Shaka was seated at the long, hand-carved ironwood table. And Carlos. Joanie felt increasingly ill at ease.

"Anything I can do to help?" she asked.

"You can help me carry the food outside. It's going to be a good evening."

"Sure."

Quickly they were sitting outside at another of Carlos' handmade tables.

They were quiet for a time. Then, "I'm glad we didn't bring mosquitos," Carlos said. "I'm sure they are a part of the cycle of life and all . . . aren't they, Shaka?"

Shaka smiled and went into an imitation of his father's voice. "Mosquitos, like all other life-forms, are part of a complex food web. Many fish feed on mosquito larvae, which are aquatic, and plenty of birds and spiders and other insects feed on the adults. Dragonflies and damselflies love mosquitoes. Frogs eat adult mosquitoes, tadpoles eat the larvae. Bats eat mosquitoes. Some eat many mosquitoes, others prefer other diets, but the mosquito does have a place in their food webs."

"Do tell. Elucidate," Sylvia said, smiling. They needed the humor.

"The only ecosystem where mosquitoes play a major role is the arctic tundra, where migratory birds depend on them . . . but the caribou suffer dearly. In most of the world and for most predators, mosquitoes can be easily replaced with other flying insects in the food web."

"In other words . . . ?" Sylvia said.

"Screw 'em," Shaka said, and they dissolved into much-needed laughter.

It was still uncomfortable. The unspoken topic hung in the air, and finally, Joanie couldn't take it.

"I don't know what you expected me to do. I didn't testify against him," she said.

"No, you didn't. Potato?" The others took food as if nothing of consequence was happening.

"I wasn't there," she said. "I didn't see anything."

Carlos nodded. "And you testified honestly and fairly about the conversation between Cadzie and your father."

She began to cry. The others waited. "I feel like I never really knew him," Joanie said.

Carlos laid a gentle, weathered hand on hers. "I'm not sure anyone really knew him, Joanie. Aaron lived apart from us. Deep..." he paused, seeking the right word. "Inside his head, perhaps. Maybe somewhere else."

Little Shaka spoke up. "Once upon a time I knew him. Thought I knew him pretty well. Then...that thing happened with Cadmann's grandfather."

"You were there," Joanie said.

"Yes."

"I'm not sure I ever really wanted to know." A small voice.

"Do you now?" Shaka asked with exaggerated casualness.

She nodded again, a woman transformed into a little girl by the simple wish to comprehend her father.

Little Shaka said, "I don't have a lot to tell you. We were hiking, me and Aaron and Cadmann. We were talking, something important. Then I was hit in the face. Then I was in water, and samlon were nibbling at me and Cadmann, who was dead. A bigger, older grendel pulled me out of there, dragged me to where I could be rescued. I was half-conscious the whole time, and it all seemed like a nightmare. When I testified later I must have sounded like a lunatic. Aaron did too, and he'd tamed the grendel, or else the grendel had adopted him.

"But I was unconscious when Cadmann died."

"And so my father's version of the events could very well have been true," Joanie said.

"Yes," Little Shaka said. "When it came down to it, we gave him the benefit of the doubt."

She seemed defensive, and a little proud.

"More salad?" Sylvia asked.

"Yes. Please."

Quiet eating. Night insects croaked around them, awakening. "How long have you known Cadzie?" Sylvia asked.

Joanie's voice was tiny. "All my life."

"Did you ever talk to him about what happened, and how he felt about it?"

She nodded.

"And what did he say?"

"He said he wasn't there, and that he would go with what the colony decided . . . but he didn't have to like it."

"No, he didn't."

"No. He didn't like my father. Didn't trust him."

"How many times did you see them together?"

"Maybe a dozen," Joanie said.

"Was he ever impolite, aggressive? Anything?"

Joanie couldn't meet his eyes. "No."

"How would you describe their interactions?"

Her eyes flashed anger. "You're not a damned lawyer, and this isn't a damned trial."

"No," he agreed. "Just friends and family talking."

Joanie's face was icy, her every movement carefully controlled.

"And on the expedition?" he prodded further.

"Excited. Eager to use the capacity of the power suits."

"And when he saw Aaron?"

"Angry," Joanie said. "Thought it would complicate the trip."

"It did that. Yes. And you've known him all your life."

"Yes."

"And . . . you love him, don't you?" Sylvia said.

Little Shaka quickly added: "Like a crazy big brother."

"Well . . . not exactly."

They paused, and then everyone cracked up. The laughter was a release.

Joanie dropped her face into her hands. "God. Everything is so screwed up."

"You extended the benefit of the doubt to your father, who you barely knew. Can you do the same for Cadzie?"

She sighed. "Yes. But . . . what difference does it make. I mean . . . they're not going to kill him. We'll learn more about the cthulhus, and be able to prove he's innocent . . ."

"Unless we can't. You know what happened to so many of us. Ice on their minds." Sylvia raised a bowl. "Fruit salad?"

An obscene menace lurked just below the surface of the conversation.

"What do you want me to do?" Joanie whispered.

"That would be sedition, dear," Sylvia said. "I'm not asking you to do anything. Of course, if there's something you want to do, we wouldn't stop you."

"Why are you talking to me?"

"Because of all of us, you're the only one who has to be sure, really sure, of what happened in there. I mean, what you think happened. You know him. You didn't know your father, but still gave him the benefit of the doubt. So I ask you . . . what happened in the caves?"

"I don't know..." Joanie said. "But...but I know it wasn't Cadzie. We can't let them freeze him. We just can't. They'll never thaw him out."

"Do you have any ideas?" Carlos asked.

"Maybe."

◆ CHAPTER 38 ◆
AUTOPSY

The main colony's central skeeter pad rested idle. The pad manager took his time walking out to greet a skeeter with a pod slung underneath.

Mappers, it looked like. The label was sometimes considered an insult, and used as such. Most of the men and women who chose that life were thought antisocial, loners so averse to human company that they couldn't live in even small multifamily groups, the smallest units found on Camelot.

But there were no absolute loners. No one was suicidal enough to travel totally alone on Avalon. Not any more. A few had tried.

"Howdy, Eric," the one with the bushier beard said. That was Hal, and his partner at the pod was Towner.

"What have you got?" the pad manager asked.

"We have rock samples from sectors three and eight, and some biological samples for Shaka. Figure that's worth a month's scrip."

"We'll get you set up. Let's take a look." Eric swept the

tarp back. Flinched. "Jesus! It stinks. What is that, your bag lunch?"

Towner was grinning. Hal said, "Don't know. Found it in sector nine, ran out of ice. Almost didn't bother. But . . . figured it might be interesting. Looks like a water thing, but we found it a distance from the river."

"I wonder why. . . ." Eric said. He looked more closely. "Well?"

"Looks familiar," Erik said. "Let me get Shaka out here." He triggered his lapel communicator. "Shaka? Are you able to get over here to the pad?"

"What do you have?" Shaka's voice.

"I'm not sure."

"I'll be right out."

A few minutes, and Shaka walked over.

"Good to see you."

"Hope you have something interesting."

"Hope so," Eric said. "What do you make of this?"

Shaka studied the mass of squidlike flesh. "Where did you find this?" he asked.

The mapper flinched, as if wondering if he had done something wrong. "Sector Nine? On land, east of the dry lake."

Shaka frowned. "On the land?" he asked, prodding at part of a blackish mass with the tip of a medical probe. "This is a water . . . oh, my." His eyes widened as a thought occurred to him. "Get it to the biology hutch!"

Within twenty minutes, the autopsy had begun. Others drifted in as Shaka proceeded: Carlos and Zack, then Charlotte Martine, the young Godson medic.

"Look at these organs," Shaka said. "We have a large amphibious creature with multiple limbs, partially devoured by an unknown predator, and starting to decompose, but clearly the creature we've called 'cthulhu.'"

Zack leaned forward. "What are you seeing as interesting?"

"Something tore it half apart. But it was on land," Shaka said. "Within ten klicks of the spot we're calling the 'temple,' and if you'll look here . . ." He displayed a scan map.

"What am I looking at?" Zack asked.

"Well . . . it isn't more than a klick and a half from one of the tributary underground rivers. Far from any aboveground waterway connecting with the ocean. I'm thinking it might have been savaged by something toothy, then fled. But—"

Zack asked, "Grendels? Are you thinking . . . ?"

"That it might have been attacked by Aaron's tame grendels," Shaka said. "Impossible to say, as limbs have been removed by scavengers. But it could have been in that tunnel, or near the temple. Another thing. The microorganisms responsible for decomp reproduce at a consistent rate. Measuring that decomp I'd place this creature's death at about three days ago."

"The timing is nice," Carlos said. "Suggestive. Died within a day or so of Aaron."

"That's possible. But the real question is: why would you find an amphibious creature so far from water? Perhaps it was headed to a lake or stream. But these creatures had never been sighted away from running water, or the ocean."

"Went crazy?"

"That might be it," Big Shaka said. "Or crazy with pain."

"Speculative," Dr. Martine said. Then, "Don't mind me. I'm just here to observe."

Carlos asked, "Are the mappers still here?"

"Probably getting lunch," the pad manager guessed.

Towner set down a sweetened carrot as he saw Carlos approaching. "We're honored," he called. "What can we do for you?"

"That was a very nice find," Carlos said, as Charlotte Martine came up behind him.

"How nice?" Towner asked.

"Four notches in scrip, I think." Carlos handed over a handful of little notes. "If you find more in the area, I'll pay eight each."

The mappers leaned close. "Where in the area? You've got a hunch? Towner and me, we like hunches."

Martine was showing her curiosity. Carlos spoke to *her*. "It would take more than one cthulhu to kill two grendels. Aaron's grendels weren't tied up, they were loose when we found them. They'd have fought. Cthulhus don't go alone; they would have attacked in a pack, school, whatever. Maybe they attacked Aaron too? And then ran, for whatever reason. In a pack."

The autopsy continued.

"So," Shaka said. "These are the electrogenerators." He probed inside the cthulhu corpse, revealing paler flesh. "Can we estimate the amount of current they can generate?" Carlos asked.

"From this hacked up corpse? No. I'd like to find one intact."

Martine said, "It's still all guesswork. And your man's been convicted."

The others nodded. "We follow the evidence," Big Shaka said.

◆ CHAPTER 39 ◆
COUNTERTRUST

By eight o'clock, Captain Sven Meadows and a Sergeant Cubbins were beginning to wind down. As Godson Security Forces they had been informally assigned, as GSF had no permanent correctional staff. Until Sikes could be shipped up to *Messenger* and frozen, guard duty would have to rotate between NCOs and officers.

They perked up when they heard the skeeter coming in from the mainland. Captain Meadows hit his comm link. "This is Green Leader. We have an authorized skeeter coming in from the mainland. Double checking: they have authority?"

"Authority granted," the voice on the other end answered.

The skeeter landed. Trudy and a Starborn girl he didn't recognize emerged. The guards checked the skeeter to be certain it didn't hold more people. "What is your business with the prisoner?"

Trudy's face was carefully neutral. "Cord cutting ceremony," she said.

He nodded. All Godsons understood the various mating and separation rituals.

"And why is this one here?" He indicated the Starborn.

"Her name is Joanie Tragon. The dead man's daughter. Call her moral support. Knew how much he hated her father. If she can get him to confess, it will make it easier on me."

Meadow's narrow face softened. "Must be hard."

"More than you know."

Cadzie sat on a makeshift cot in a makeshift cell. The door opened.

He couldn't remember the guards' names, and privately called them Tweedledee and Tweedledum. Tweedledum was shorter, and wore sergeant's stripes. Tweedledee was tall and handsome, and he thought he'd see him with that imposing female Major Stype. "You have guests."

The guards watched the door close.

"Ever have a cord-cutting?" Meadows asked the sergeant.

"One, yes." Sergeant Cubbin's face pinched. A painful memory. "Three years before we left Earth. It stung."

"Wonder if he'll—" The sergeant's body spasmed and dropped. Meadows reacted fast, snatching for his side-arm and saw—

Toad Stolzi, the little bastard, grendel gun leveled in the instant before firing.

When the girls had appeared at Cadzie's door, he'd

almost wondered if he was dreaming. The makeshift cell had been more than merely cheerless, it had been a harbinger of another, colder confinement to come, one from which he might not emerge as the person who called himself Cadmann Sikes. The thought of that was almost more painful than death: to wander the earth a mere shadow of what he had been.

That Joanie and Trudy had put themselves in peril to rescue him, had displayed the trust and love to take such a risk . . . it touched him more than he could possibly say.

"What's the plan?" Cadzie asked when they emerged onto the eastern shore, still not quite believing.

"Shaka is taking the skeeter," Joanie said. "We're taking a zodiac to the mainland. We'll get picked up there."

"Won't Cassandra track us?" That seemed a perfectly natural question.

"She has to know where to look," Trudy said. "We've got a dozen other zodiacs that will travel to different points on the mainland, crossing paths with us. And skeeters traveling to the interior and the mainland."

"Everything we have," Joanie said. "Needles and haystacks."

The night had deepened by the time the guards began to stir. Captain Meadows, the tall one Cadzie had called "Tweedledum" rolled over onto his side. "What happened?"

The second could see the open door to the danger room, a reinforced "safe space" in case of grendel escape, common around Blackship, and useful as a cell.

"He's gone. Someone sprang him." Tweedledee's name was actually Sergeant Cubbins.

"Contact home base."

They checked their equipment, and found every bit of it smashed, their skeeter's rotors crippled.

"Damn! They've destroyed the radios."

Captain Meadows brooded, then brightened. "When we don't check in at midnight, we'll get help. Meanwhile . . . what if the skeeter is a feint?"

A pause. "What do you mean?"

Meadows shook his head as if to clear away the last wisps of confusion. Together they searched the section, coming to conclusions about what precisely had happened to them. It was Sergeant Cubbins who had the brainstorm. "They came in through the caverns. What if they went out that way, too?"

"It's possible, yes. What do we do?"

"There's training apparatus," Meadows said. "And I'll bet they didn't think about that. Let's go get them."

◆ CHAPTER 40 ◆
THE CAVERNS

Blackship Island's caverns and its subterranean river were accessible through a natural cave opening beneath the main storage silo. Captain Meadows and Sergeant Cubbins hauled their equipment down into the rocky chill then suited up and plunged into the cold fresh water.

It took a moment to orient to the darkness, and just as he did his suit lights clicked on, sending a cone of golden light out into the murk.

"Are you seeing anything?" Meadows asked through his throat mic.

"We have a sign of passage, yes."

Meadows examined some odd looking glassy substance lining the walls. "What is this stuff? On the walls?"

It was a glaze, obvious now that they examined it, and not the result of volcanic action.

"I don't know," Cubbins said. "I don't know. Something made by underwater termites might look like this."

"What's *that*?"

At the very end of their twin golden beams, where the light died into darkness, writhed squidlike shadows.

"What in the world are those?"

"Are those . . . these cthulhu things?"

"Didn't Sikes say these things have stingers?"

"Oh . . . *now* you believe him, huh?"

At first he thought the cthulhu were moving aimlessly, but then a circular pattern emerged, faster and faster, creating a vortex in the confined space. The water plucked at them, pushed at them, transforming into a reverse whirlpool, driving Meadows and Cubbins back. Others were doing something to the tunnel itself.

"Get back!" Meadows screamed into his throat mic.

The very walls around them began to collapse, creating a nightmare but the guards noticed that the cthulhu slowed their vortex as they retreated, sped up as they advanced.

"I think they're trying to tell us something." Captain Meadows said.

"Yeah," Cubbins replied. "That we aren't going out this way."

"What do we do?"

"Get back. Report, if anyone's come for us," Captain Meadows said.

◆CHAPTER 41◆
THE MAINLAND

For the two previous days, there had been movement from Camelot to the mainland, and from various groups of Grendel Scouts on the mainland to positions expanding in starfish formation, centered on a spot parallel to Blackship Island but fifty klicks east.

Within minutes of the escape, skeeters had begun flying in haphazard fashion, concealing intentions not with the cover of night or useless stealth tactics, but in a maze of conflicting destinations.

The game had begun.

Captain Sven Meadows had made love to Major Patricia Stype for the second time that day, only an hour ago. They hadn't had time to shower before the news came of a possible Cadmann Sikes sighting, just a hundred and thirty-five klicks from coastal base. They'd chosen not to wash, so that the faintest perfume of their intense embrace still hovered in the air just below the threshold of conscious awareness.

No one else knew. But they knew, and that knowledge simmered in the air between them, a combination of sex and the joy of the hunt to come.

They didn't need to speak of it, but a decision had been made.

They had met in the GSF, the Godson Security Force, ten years before the planned date of departure from Earth. Seeing in each other something that they had never found before, they believed that their love could survive a multitrillion-mile journey, that they could begin life on a new planet, beneath a new sun . . . but not the passage of time while waiting for the journey to begin. Stype was already almost forty, and even with the very best medical treatment, the idea of beginning a family with fifty-year-old ovaries was out of the question.

Messenger certainly had hundreds of thousands of starchildren, fertilized embryos which could then be implanted once they arrived at their destination, but that still depended on a womb far beyond its optimal reproductive years.

What about raising the baby in a creche? Certainly possible. And they were prepared to provide precisely that service to most of the contributors to *Messenger*'s funding. But inner-door teaching among the Godsons spoke of the flow of life force along the threads emanating from the God Knot, the hormonal communication between mother and child, a sort of prenatal spiritual education. While unspoken, the preference was natural childbirth whenever possible.

Major Stype liked that idea just fine. There was a very old-fashioned aspect to her nature, a desire to be taken by a strong man beneath alien stars, on a homestead created with their own hands, to feel new life blossoming within her, to give birth as her ancient ancestors had, and to raise her children on a new world, to be inheritors and conquerors.

Captain Meadows felt the same, and that had sealed their bond.

They were a mated pair of predators who had found a home in the Godsons, and intended to embrace the new adventure wholeheartedly.

With that intention in mind, they had entered cold sleep voluntarily, ten years early, knowing that they would not awaken again until they reached Hypereden.

That had gone wrong.

They had awakened a week before orbiting, spent those seven days training five hours a day and making love when they could, and had kept up that same enjoyable schedule once they had descended to Avalon.

At first they had been enthralled by the new world, a rioting cacophony of alien sights and sounds and smells. And been politely impressed by the efforts of the colonists who had made it home. But as twenty-three-hour days passed, they began to understand that these former Earthlings, who now called themselves Avalonians, had much to learn.

And after the murder of the one called Tragon, they had waited to see how justice might be done. When it was not, they realized the real reason *Messenger* had diverted from its original path: to bring civilization and purpose to these wayward children. In its search for the origins of life, *Messenger* would bring human civilization to the galaxy, but that new civilization would start here on Avalon.

So forty minutes after leaving the base, they were closing in on Sikes' last known location. Whether the Starborn had used some sort of camouflage, or there was some natural coverage in the rocky area, had yet to be seen.

Stype dropped off Meadows and nine support troops, hovering as they swept through a field of jagged rocky spikes, each two and three stories high, perhaps the result of some freak windstorm here at the edge of a desert that stretched almost to the North Pole, fifteen hundred klicks away.

She sat at the window in the copilot's seat (she was an excellent autogyro pilot), watching the security sweeps. For ten minutes their efforts bore no fruit, but then someone fired a shot. It was never determined who, whether Starborn or Godson. Each, of course, claimed the other had committed that deadly sin.

Major Stype did know that she saw a bullet strike rock chips a hand's breadth from Meadows' head, and that the next thing she knew her hand was on the firing controls.

And unsummoned, a voice raged in her head: *They tried to kill my mate. Slaughter them!* and that deep red thing inside her was alive in the chopper, and when she came back to her senses, her hands were shaking, and she wasn't quite certain what she had done.

Cadzie and his allies arrived at Camp Three, a hunting lodge tucked into a mountainside twenty miles from the closest grendel-infected water source. Far enough for safety. Grendels were water-cooled engines and without that coolant, were as dangerous to themselves as others. "I've never been here," he said.

"That's deliberate, Cadzie. We didn't want any connection to your previous movements. If they try to backtrack all our movements, that's thousands of different places to search, and we can stay on the move. They can't check us all."

Cadzie counted eleven Grendel Scouts in the camp. All there for him. He felt proud and sick at the same time.

"Isn't this a little dangerous?" Cadzie asked. "They'll track the skeeter if we aren't careful."

"But we are," Joanie said. "Very."

Footsteps behind them. Toad Stolzi, holding a vidsheet. "We have problems," he said. As he came closer, the firelight silvered the tears streaking his cheeks. "Big problems."

"What?"

"They just killed three of our people."

Enraged, the Speaker forced himself to speak in measured tones. "I do not like what I see happening here. I think our people may not have the experience to deal with this situation. We may need a clearer, more experienced mind."

"Is it time to wake the Russian?" Dr. Mandel asked, pushing up the wire-rimmed spectacles perched on his angular nose.

"Not yet. But bring the colonel up to second level. Warm him up enough to begin brain activity."

"We'll need to run cranial blood through a circulator, not start up his heart."

"So be it," Speaker said. "How long will it take?"

"Twenty hours to wakefulness."

"Start the dream conditioning as soon as you have mental activity. There will be no time to waste."

"Five hours," the doctor said. "That's time to encode the information in audiovisual tracks."

"So be it."

Night had fallen at the hidden campsite. And with the shrouding of Tau Ceti, and the realization that yes, people had died, the atmosphere of bravado had begun to thin.

Joanie went by herself, back to a rock wall (Mei Ling, who loved geology, had been very careful to be sure that the rock was common enough to provide no clues to their location) and recorded a message. After she did, she gave it to a skeeter pilot who flew it to the center of that imaginary starfish, and broadcast it from there.

For days now, Marco Shantel's sleep had been thin and troubled. As a result he was sleeping late, and was half-dozing when a knock shivered the door of his hutch.

"Marco. Have a message for you." Sergeant Greg Lindsey said, and handed him a data card.

"Why didn't you just put it on the net?"

The sergeant shrugged. "It was marked personal. Just assumed you'd like the privacy."

Plus, he wouldn't be surprised if Lindsey simply wanted an excuse to talk to the (formerly) great Marco Shantel. In a few months, the glamour would wear off, but right now a bit of limerence remained. "Where did it come from?"

"It was rerouted, at least that's what Trevanian said. I don't know if anyone can find the point of origin."

"All right. Let's have it." He closed the door, weighing the flat flexible plastic card on his fingertips, then plugging it into his console. It started automatically. Joanie appeared. Oh, good. He pushed pause.

"Thanks," he said with a brief hard handshake. Ushered the man out. And then started the vid again.

"Marco, this is Joanie. I'm sorry I can't talk to you . . . with you, but it wouldn't be safe. I have to assume you'll share this, so don't worry, there's nothing in it that can't be shown. We did what we did because we believe in Cadzie. I'm sure you consider it a betrayal, but . . . we can both live with that. I don't think I can live with these old sins ruining another life. We have a plan, that's all you need to know. That . . . and that I love you."

The image began to fade, and Marco paused it before it disappeared, so that a translucent Joanie hovered in the air, like a frozen ghost.

Marco shook his head. "Joanie," he whispered. "What have you done?"

The campfire was one of dozens across the continent, timed to mask a single heat signature in a plethora of possibilities, a needle hidden in a stack of needles.

But in the foothills west of the new dam, a small crew of desperados were making the most of their peaceful evening, possibly the last they would enjoy for a long time.

"Have you had enough to eat?" Joanie asked.

"Yes," Cadzie replied. "And Joanie?" He scanned the circle, his eyes stinging. It was the fire. That was what it was. "Thanks. Thanks all of you. And now...we're kind of stuck."

"What do we do now?" she asked.

"I've been thinking about that." He paused, not certain he really wanted to say the next thing. "I have one advantage that no one else has."

"Your knowledge of the planet...?" she offered. "You had Sylvia as your grandmother, Cadzie. She taught you a lot of things..."

"No," he answered, and reached to squeeze her hand. "You're so close to it that you can't see it, and I love you for it."

"What's that?" she asked, now genuinely mystified.

"*I* know I didn't kill your father. *I* don't need faith. I know you had faith, and it means the world to me."

She looked down shyly. "I...um...maybe I got to know you better. On *Geographic*. You aren't a user, Cadzie. You don't see people as things, not even when they kinda ask to be treated like it. If you'd hated my father enough to kill him, I can't believe you could have treated me with...real caring." Something shone in her eyes when she looked back up. Tears? He wasn't sure. It was possible.

"So what are you thinking?" Evie Queen asked.

"*Something* killed Aaron and his grendels, leaving physiological traces similar to those left by a grendel gun. Adrenal overload. Triggering the nervous system."

"These cthulhu couldn't have been unaware of grendels..." Jaxxon said. "Might have even domesticated them. They would know how to hurt them. We're saying what? That their technologies were magnetic and maybe biological? What if they evolved a mechanism for protecting themselves." He turned. "Shaka?"

The big man's brows furrowed. "Hard to say, but they might have enough generating capacity."

"So . . . what? We bring a grendel into their home, or a place that used to be a home, and there's hell to pay."

Shaka nodded. "I say that our only real play is to understand the cthulhu better."

"What do you suggest?"

"Well . . ." the big man said, stretching time. For almost thirty seconds, he was silent, then very slowly he said: "One option is to go someplace they plausibly congregated."

"For instance?"

"Well . . . we found that temple by following a magnetic anomaly. The largest such anomaly in this hemisphere is less than two hundred klicks from here."

Cadzie perked up. "That's in the alpine meadow? West of the Snowcone uranium mine?"

"*Under* the meadow, actually. Halfway to the North Pole." He seemed to turn the idea over in his mind, liking it more the more he considered the notion. "The advantage is that they'll never expect that. They think you're guilty. They can't consider you wanting more information about your alibi without asking themselves if you are innocent."

"And how do we get there?"

Jaxxon's twin brother folded his hands, then unfolded them. "I think we'll need a combination of tactics to defeat Cassandra."

"Not to mention *Messenger*'s onboard," Jaxxon said. "We don't even know its capacities."

"So we'll need to forget concealing movement. Instead, we'll use a variation of the same tactics we used to break you out, Cadzie. We'll give them too much information."

"How do we do that?" Cadzie asked.

"Compartmentalize. No group knows what another group is doing. Assume that they will be intercepted."

"I don't want anyone dying for me."

"Then advise them to flee, but not fight. If cornered, surrender. Tell what they know. But only the people here, now, know where we're going."

"All they know is to keep going," Cadzie said. "One conclusion could easily be that WE don't have a destination, either. Random, desperate, guilty flight."

"Exactly."

By midnight, the campfire had burned low. "Piccolo," Toad said. "You worked in Snowcone. What did you tell us about those rivers?"

The surfing master had been one of the first to join their resistance team. A light flared in his eyes, almost as if he had been waiting years for something to awaken him from a slumber. "Five years ago we hit water on level two. Closed up the mine shaft. But we mapped the underwater river, and I'd bet five pounds of coffee it connects with our anomaly. It does."

Little Shaka leaned closer. "Let's say the dipole source is a cthulhu city. They are aquatic, or at least amphibian. They can't cross a desert, or anything close to it."

"Before we even seriously consider going," Toad said, "I want to ask: why would they do something like this? Why build a city there?"

Shaka shrugged. "Why do human beings build cities? Resources, trade, water? Sometimes spiritual reasons, belief in a particular place being favorable to the gods."

Joanie nodded. "And we don't know how old that city is. What things might have looked like ten thousand years ago. The landscape could have been . . . probably *was* very different."

"Can we use these?" Cadzie asked. "The underground rivers?"

"Maybe. Probably. If we can it would be terrific, because every hour above ground increases our chances of being spotted somehow. If we can make it to the mines, from that point on Cassandra can't see us. Fifty miles south is the city, by my reckoning. And I think these rivers connect. But fifty miles of underground rivers?"

"We'd need rebreathers, underwater sleds. Something like that."

"I . . . maybe I shouldn't say this . . ." Trudy offered.

"Say what?"

"Power armor, Cadzie."

The idea was so simple and obvious in retrospect that he blinked. "Shit," he said. "You're right. Unka Carlos went into the water, and breathed just fine."

Beth took it and ran with it. "What if we could lead some of the legion into a trap? That's our best source of power armor."

Trudy wrapped her arms across her chest. Perhaps it was chilly. "They won't give up easily."

"Neither did we," Cadzie said. "And they killed some of our people." Ugly murmurs. "It's self-defense now."

The miner seemed pensive. "Kill them and take it?" the miner said. "Damn, that's ballsy. What happens then? You think you can broker a peace after you've murdered them?"

"Can *they* after they murder *us*?" Beth asked.

Shaka shook his head. "People aren't that rational."

"All right." Cadzie said. "You're right. No matter what we did, it would increase the antipathy. Hard to come back from."

"Well . . ." Little Shaka asked finally. "What if we didn't do it?"

"What do you mean?" Evie asked.

Shaka's voice dropped, because thoughtful. "What if . . . Avalon herself did it . . ."

"That might be a pretty fine line." Jaxxon said.

"I think we can walk it."

◆ CHAPTER 42 ◆
BEES

Camouflaged, armored and tucked into the coastal cliffs, the Godson base was a hive of activity. Teams of analysts were reading the tracking equipment, gathering and interpreting information.

The commander was Stype's fiancé, Captain Sven Meadows. He was a tall man, even for a Godson. They had avoided the awkwardness of his being subordinate to her by cooperative billeting and flexible chains of command. At the moment he was at the coastal station, a hastily constructed landing pad, and was currently reading details from his digipad.

"Captain Meadows, sir!" Meadows looked up.

"Sir! We've picked up a signal," Sergeant Kanazawa said.

"Where?"

"In these hills. It was brief." They waited a moment, then the signal repeated. There they were. "I want a squad there," the captain said. His smile was a hunter's.

"And . . . there they are."

The smile grew thinner still. "I'll lead a squad there," Meadows said.

"What orders?" his sergeant asked.

"Capture if possible. If not . . ." He shrugged.

"He's killed once," Sergeant Kanazawa said, "and they helped him."

"That's how I see it," the captain said. "So be it."

"Yes sir."

Cadzie put the binoculars down. "There," he said. "That's where they died. I've kept track of it. The kind of thing kids do."

"Have you ever been here?" Trudy asked.

"No. I haven't. Never been. Never had business here." He said it flatly, although his face was tight. Once upon a time, three decades before, he had been an infant protected in a blue blanket as parents he had never known had been stripped to the bone. Even he wasn't entirely certain how he felt about returning to this spot.

"Doesn't this seem kind of sick?"

"Just the opposite," he murmured, finding his emotional footing. "Until now I thought my parents died for nothing. This gives it a little purpose."

"How long do we have to hold them?" Piccolo asked. Apparently some of his Surfer Dude affect was simply a put-on, garnered from old Earth two-dees, probably featuring former child stars in one-piece bathing suits. He was displaying more of the calculating mind that had made him a first-rate engineer.

"Long enough to get them all in the bottleneck." Cadzie said.

"There's the flag," Piccolo said, and pointed.

"Good stuff," Cadzie said. "Let's get blue."

By decree of the council, an emergency cache of blue blankets had been located anywhere a beehive had been identified: the colony wanted no more fatalities.

They had not anticipated a moment like this.

The Godson skeeters were advanced over the Avalonians' decrepit vehicles. Skeeter Violet Two held six in power armor. It hovered at cloud level, far higher than any weapon the rebels were likely to have in play. Through a telescreen Meadows watched a fleeing Grendel Scout on the ground below them. Was one of them Sikes? "They think we won't hit the ground with them," he said.

"They're wrong, sir," Kanazawa said confidently.

Joanie crouched behind a boulder with Cadzie and Trudy. "Can you really do this?"

"What?"

"Use this. This place. This method, to attack people. I mean . . . considering what happened to your parents . . ."

He understood. To be truthful, the notion sickened him. "We'll find out."

"Here they come!"

"Blankets!" Cadzie called.

The ship landed. The Godsons emerged, firing. A blue blanket-wrapped Grendel Scout went down. Then Cadzie touched the button that triggered the radio-controlled explosives over the bee nest.

The creatures were not "insects" of course, but flying variants of the same strain of genetics that led to

Avalon tree crabs and scribes, probably closer to tiny flying crustaceans. They swarmed in underground hives, their full life cycles not totally understood: the "bees" were too dangerous.

When the mining explosive triggered, a thousand pounds of dirt and rock flew into the air, and at first, Cadzie, peering out from under his blanket, wondered if he had used too much. If the blast had killed his prospective allies.

And then . . .

Captain Sven Meadows saw the rebels disappear behind a tumble of rocks, and felt a certain amount of contempt. There was no way out for them in that cul-de-sac. Still, it was possible that a trap of some kind had been baited, and as they moved forward in standard two-by-two formation, they kept their scanners running.

"Sir," Sergeant Kanazawa said. "Our scans detect a radio signal to the west, a hundred yards. A scan of frequencies suggests that it's a mining charge."

Clumsy trap. Was there an avalanche to be brought down upon them? No. Then what these idiots planned was to lure them into some kind of crossfire, perhaps a homemade claymore, industrial explosives combined with nails and shrapnel.

For men unaware and unarmored, it might have worked. He proceeded with caution, as if his men were not armored.

A sudden explosion shook the earth. Meadows' men rolled flat. There was plenty of cover, but that cloud looked funny, and it was expanding much too fast—

Within seconds a storm of bees streamed out of the ground, and attacking everything around them not nestled in blue. The individual bees moved like bullets: they were drunk on *speed*, like grendels. Like bullets, they got inside armor faster than a man could duck.

"Oh God!" Kanazawa screamed. "It hurts!"

"Seal the suits!" Foster yelled. "Seal your suits!"

"It's too late! They're inside!" Kanazawa screamed something in Japanese, then lost language and just gobbled pain.

Captain Foster sealed his suit. It didn't help. Three other Godsons were dead or dying in fifty seconds.

When it was over, the bees hovered, seeking their tormentors. Cadzie's people saw only the cloud. Infrared showed only warm spots that dwindled and were gone.

A hour later, the cloud had thinned, and an hour after that, they were gone, seeking a new nest.

Cadzie and his people climbed out of their Cadzie blue survival sacks.

Shaka was shaken. He murmured *umoya ongcwele* again and again. Cadzie knew that much Zulu. It meant, roughly, "Holy shit."

"I'd heard about that, but never seen it," Cadzie murmured.

Trudy leaned over and vomited. Cadzie steadied her as she did, and then held her as she wept. "What ... what have I done?"

Shaka looked at her as if regarding a venomous snake. "They ... were your people."

"Not any more," she said, raw. "If I don't have you, I don't have anyone."

"You have us," Joanie said, gentling her as if she was a frightened horse.

"Come on," Piccolo said. "Let's strip the suits. We have to move."

"You know..." Nnedi said. "We crossed a line, here. We lured them in. We triggered the bees."

"And they killed our people."

"Three of ours. Four of theirs."

"Shit."

"We'd better win, hadn't we?" Cadzie said.

◆ CHAPTER 43 ◆
TSIOLKOVSKII

Stype could not stop screaming.

She grew gradually aware that her people were watching her. That did it. She dried her eyes and patched herself into the Speaker's communication line as she had been requested to do.

The Speaker was patient. "We are aware that you and Sven were more than friends. But we ask you to stand down."

She wiped her eyes. "Is that an order, sir?"

A pause. "It is a recommendation."

"I don't think I can do that, sir."

"It is more than a recommendation."

"Sir," she said. "Would you like me to tender my resignation?"

"No, Major Stype."

"Then I am going to hunt them down," she said. "And kill them all. And will do my very, very best not to be killed in the process."

"We would appreciate that."

◆ ◆ ◆

When the line went dead, the Speaker turned to his physician and assistant. "This situation is getting out of control. Wake him up."

"We have him at the tipping point," Dr. Mandel said.

"Take him over."

Ninety seconds of walking and elevator pod brought them to the cryonics lab. "We've been preparing for this for eighteen hours," Chief Engineer Jorge Daytona said. "Bringing him closer to the surface without thawing all tissues. His brain oxygenation and nutrition has been achieved with a circulation system."

"Aren't you still risking the brain tissue?"

"There is a risk, yes. Greater risk of stroke and brain damage, less danger of heart attack. We were able to use drugs for the increase of tissue elasticity."

"He's coming to," Mandel said.

The massive shape of Colonel Tsiolkovskii began to stir. His gray eyes opened. "Are . . . are we there? Am I . . ."

"You have your new legs," the Speaker said. "And a new arm. As we promised. But no, we're not at Hypereden."

"Where is Prophet Newsome?" Tsiolkovskii groaned.

"He is dead."

The Russian showed no reaction to that. "Where are we?"

"There was a secondary destination. Avalon. Tau Ceti IV."

Tsiolkovskii wagged his massive head slowly, from side to side, trying to clear it. "Tau Ceti . . . IV? Then this is our destination?"

"It's a little more complicated than that," Dr. Mandel said. "We'll explain."

"Please."

"We need you. You'll be at full strength in a day. Your regrown limbs are in perfect condition."

"I'm . . . ready to serve."

Finally, the Speaker seemed to be satisfied. "We promised you the adventure of a lifetime. Here it is."

"I had dreams," Tsiolkovskii mused. "We landed on a planet. There were fools who had squandered their heritage."

"Yes," the Speaker said.

The old soldier's eyes brightened. "And something else. Creatures. Nothing from Earth. Is this right?"

"Yes, there are creatures."

Tsiolkovskii nodded. "This is a great moment."

Dr. Charlotte Martine got the call while finishing breakfast. "I'll be there," she said. Big Shaka didn't sound terribly excited, so she didn't hurry.

The morgue didn't smell any worse than usual. "Hal and Towner had ice this time," Shaka said. "It's fresher. Look at it! It's a wonderful intact dead cthulhu, the first we've ever had, and I'm going to learn everything about it."

"You need sleep," Martine said. "You need to eat. You look like that cadaver, Doctor, only bonier."

"I worry about my son. But look, Charlotte, this is what I wanted to show you. This hole in the abdomen."

Charlotte Martine looked it over. A sharp point had stabbed deep into the creature's belly, not quite where a

human being would have an appendix. One thrust and...
Martine borrowed a probe and felt around.

"Are you thinking what I'm thinking? Big Shaka, this isn't at all like the wound we found in Aaron Tragon's belly. This, the perpetrator dug straight in. He, she, it was looking for something and found it right away. Tragon's killer dug in and felt around and stabbed in all directions and, I expect, got nothing."

Shaka smiled. "Shall we look at that previous corpse?"

"Why?"

"There might be a hole in that one too."

"I remember— All right, we'll look, but I remember that cadaver was ripped half in two. One hole...yes." They were looking at a hologram display. Shaka rotated it. "It's just one hole, Shaka, but it's there. Straight in and straight out. Whoever did that knew what he was looking for. And—"

"It certainly wasn't a grendel gun slug. And Aaron didn't have it."

Twyla, Carlos' girlfriend and the camp's best psychologist, staggered from the town store bearing an armload of provisions. Zack tottered up to her before she could finish lashing them to the back of her electric bike. "Twyla!"

She turned, panting. "What is it, Zack?"

"I heard about a little conversation you had with Cadzie, analyzing some data from the Godson power suits."

"Who told you that?"

"Never mind. I heard that you were worried about a reading."

She considered, then answered carefully. "They may

have programmed their people for hyperaggression. For enjoying the kill."

"Would that affect their . . . law enforcement practices?"

She seemed unhappy to answer. "They're very disciplined. But it's possible, especially in the heat of pursuit."

"And after the bees?"

"Especially," she said. "Nothing triggers anger like fear."

As they had planned to do, the Grendel Scouts fanned out in different directions, joining with other groups, splitting out again and traveling in all directions in an expanding fractal pattern. Using camouflage and thermal shields they did all they could to evade escape, even as some were rounded up.

As planned, they did not resist if cornered: Cadzie wanted no more fatalities if possible.

The Godsons noticed the tactic, even if they had no immediate strategy to counter it. "We have picked up traces. They're doing a very good job of concealing their motions."

"But it is not totally effective?" the Speaker asked.

"No. But there is a secondary level of concealment."

They produced a mapped pattern, showing four data points.

"What is this?" The speaker asked.

"We've been able to pick up these traces. A communication, a bit of debris, a heat trace. None of them, by themselves, are terribly convincing. Might have been deliberate misinformation."

"What is your name?" asked Dr. Mandel.

"Tsiolkovskii. Colonel Tsiolkovskii." The Russian paused. "Colonel Anton Tsiolkovskii, U.N. Security Forces."

"Very good. What can you tell me about your recent history? Where you are? What the most recent important memories?"

"I remember Tanzania," Tsiolkovskii mused. "The last campaign."

"How much do you remember about what happened?" His brows furrowed. "I was . . . Did we prevail?"

"Yes, we did. You did. You don't remember anything after that?" Mandel asked.

Tsiolkovskii was silent for almost a full minute. "I remember . . . pain. Light. Have I been unconscious since that time?"

"No," Dr. Mandel said. "And I think those memories will return."

"Where am I?" Tsiolkovskii had the uncomfortable sense that he had asked that before.

"The starship *Messenger.*"

"*Messenger . . .*"

"Do you remember the Godsons?"

"The . . . Godsons?" A light seems to go on behind his eyes.

"The Godsons. Yes."

"I remember. I remember," Tsiolkovskii said. "They demonstrated a means of reducing Ballistic Emotional Trauma."

"What is that?" Mandel asked.

"What used to be called PTSD. Shell shock. They came to West Point. I was impressed. You are a Godson?"

"I am."

Tsiolkovskii nodded. "I'm starting to remember. They...you wanted me to join. It wasn't something I would do while an active officer, but I did use and approve of technologies."

"And do you remember your last conversation?"

"I...it was after Central Africa..." Something painful about that memory.

"Yes."

"I was...wounded."

"You were almost torn in half. The technology to heal you didn't exist. The cost to preserve you until healing could be advanced was prohibitive."

"I remember. I was in pain." His eyes seemed to be clearing, his movements and enunciation more certain. "I was told that you could not heal me, but that the technology was projected to be available in ten years."

"And...?"

"Please, no games."

"This is not a game. You are suffering from cold sleep amnesia combined with the effects of trauma. We expect full recovery, but the more you remember on your own, the better your recovery."

Tsiolkovskii grumbled, but agreed. "All right. Well, I was told that if I would agree to...something...that they would...you would pay for the cold sleep until my body could be healed. Was it...?"

Suddenly, his lethargy seemed to dissolve.

"Yes. It was," Mandel said.

"Wonderful. Wonderful. Are these...my limbs?"

"They are. A combination of cloning, induced nerve growth, and nanosurgery. While you've been under, we've had a unique and proprietary process toning your muscles without awakening you or thawing your body. The surgery was performed on your lower body without awakening the upper. It was expensive, I promise you."

His eyes narrowed slightly. "Why didn't you awaken me when you performed the surgery?"

Dr. Mandel seemed a bit uncomfortable. "It was very extensive surgery, and we thought the process of recovery would be more efficient if it happened in an anesthetized state."

Tsiolkovskii turned his face away, and his lips thinned. "I see," he said. "The contract . . ." His eyes widened.

"Yes?"

"Where am I?"

"The starship *Messenger*."

"Doctor, *where is Messenger?*"

"We are orbiting a planet in the Tau Ceti system."

Tsiolkovskii couldn't help himself, put his hands to his temples. He said something fervent in Russian. "How . . . how long have I been unconscious?"

"One hundred and six years."

"I don't believe it. It worked. And now we're . . . I remember! You offered me a contract, if I was willing to function as chief security officer."

"Yes. A number of United Nations officers were recruited to this purpose."

"If I was willing to become a Godson, and swear to a term of service—"

"Ten waking years, yes."

"That you would heal me." He swung his feet down off the pallet. "And you did it! By God, you did it!"

Unsteadily at first, he got up and walked, and then performed some odd rotational motions, starting with his fingers and progressing from there to his wrists, elbows, shoulders, and neck. Then his torso, moving like a belly dancer, and then hips, knees, and ankles. Popping and crackling sounds as he worked a century of rust out of his joints. He moved like an angry yogi.

Then he grinned.

"By god! My shoulder! My hips! I'd been suffering degenerative conditions ever since I passed my instructor certification in *Systema Kadochnikova*."

"Sir?"

The memory seemed to center him. "The most grueling physical and spiritual test in all the fighting arts. Hardest thing I've ever done. As Tanzania was the best. Was. I think that this . . . What we're doing now, will be the very best."

Dr. Mandel nodded. "We're hoping you'll think so. Sir, there is one more thing. When you signed the contract, you were in pain. And under the influence of powerful pain relievers. Therefore . . . although the legal contract obtains, our own beliefs, as Godsons, is that drugs reduce the capacity for rational decision. Even prescribed drugs."

"And?"

"You would be within your rights to consider the contract invalid."

A pause. Tsiolkovskii seemed not quite to believe what he had just heard. "You . . . would spend a fortune to heal me . . . bring me light-years away on the adventure of a lifetime . . . and give me an out like that?"

"It is what is right."

Their eyes met, like two live wires touched together. Then Tsiolkovskii extended his hand. "I would be proud to serve such an organization. Colonel Anton Tsiolkovskii, at your service."

◆ CHAPTER 44 ◆
ZACK

After a hundred and fifty years together (fifty of them, admittedly, in cold sleep) Rachel and Zack Moskowitz had fallen into a routine, as old couples tended to do.

She usually rolled out of bed first, noticing every creak and strain, scanning for new ones, signs that the old machine was breaking down. New ones every week these days, it seemed. Not bad, considering the alternative.

Rachel tried not to awaken Zack, who usually stayed up later than she did, working on colony business. The arrival of the Godsons, with all of the attendant trouble, had intensified this, and since Cadzie's escape, he hardly seemed to sleep at all. She was pretty sure that he had been awake working on a speech to give the Godson leader called the Speaker his case for leniency for what Godsons called "rebels" when in a charitable mood.

His comforting lump beneath the plaid woolen covers was one of the things that marked the beginning of a new day. She tiptoed to the kitchen and set up the sofa-sized fabricator to make coffee from the good beans Cadzie brought back from the mountain. The fabricator was similar to the ones on board *Geographic*, a new luxury afforded by the technology Godsons had brought, now sprouting across the colony. If the current troubles could be resolved, a golden age beckoned for Earthborn and Starborn alike.

She was glad to have lived to see it, for she was certain that Zack could work things out. He always had. The Godsons seemed intractable, but there was always room for negotiation if you could understand your opposition enough. If you could look beneath the apparent issues into the values and beliefs that drove the behavior and formed the filters. That was what made Zack such a wonderful leader. He *could* see beneath the surface, and she had a kind of faith in him that she had had for few people in her life. Even the great Cadmann Weyland, who, she privately thought, had been given entirely too much credit in salvation of the colony.

It would have survived anyway, because of men like Zack. Warriors got the glory, she thought, but it was bureaucrats who kept the wheels turning.

Zack's Iron Law of Bureaucracy: "In any bureaucracy, the people devoted to the benefit of the bureaucracy itself always get in control and those dedicated to the goals the bureaucracy is supposed to accomplish have less and less influence, and sometimes are eliminated entirely." Avalon was a long way from that ugly reality, and she suspected that her husband had supported the deification of Cadmann as a way to focus values, an attempt to head off a clogging of paperwork and stratified power, generations before it became a threat.

What might he devise to sway the Godsons? She could hardly wait.

She sat on her patio, looking north over the Amazon toward Mucking Great Mountain, enjoying the first eastern sunlight as it painted the plain. Despite the danger, life was good. There was still beauty and meaning.

She made a second cup, and following her long-established habit, took it to Zack.

Zack was seated in front of the com screen. The screen was lit, and that was Speaker Gus looking out at her. Zack's head was on the keyboard.

Rachel tried to move his head, tried to wake him. His head rolled loosely, and the screen jittered. Rachel stepped back a pace, then glared at the Godsons' Speaker. "What did you say?" she demanded.

"Rachel Moskowitz? Is your husband all right?"

"I think he's dead. What—"

"We were talking. I was talking. Mrs. Moskowitz, three of your rebels fired on us. They're dead. This matter has gone too far—"

"So it has," she said, and reached over her husband's body to switch him off.

She typed a five digit number. *Have to tell Sylvia, then Carlos And then . . .* She rattled off a list of names, people to call, things to do, dimly aware that the moment she stopped planning, she would begin to sob.

◆ CHAPTER 45 ◆
INTO THE MINES

They traveled at night, by horseback, knowing that they were one of dozens of different looping patterns of riders and walkers and flyers. All of the mainlanders: crazy homesteaders, miners, mappers, hunters and adventurers (all of whom were careful to stay at least twenty klicks from grendel-infected water) seemed to be in on the game, creating a confusing web of conflicting flight paths. Hiding a needle in a stack of needles.

Piccolo led them across back trails, winding ever closer to the Snowcone pitchblende mine.

They freed the horses and walked the last five miles, and entered the abandoned mine at two hours past midnight on the third day.

"Piccolo," Cadzie said. "Are you sure you know these tunnels?"

The former surfing instructor nodded his shaggy head. "Upside and down . . . *way* down. I worked them for seven years, before I maxed a hundred millisieverts."

"Lifetime dose?"

Curls bounced. "That's it."

"Nervous about being back?"

"A little bit," he admitted. "Then again," Piccolo brightened, "we'll probably all be dead in twenty-four hours, so bugger the radiation."

"Ray of sunshine, aren't you?"

The surfing instructor chuckled, and opened a wall box, thumbed a button. He held his personal slate near it as the green light flashed on. Schematics began to appear on the screen. "Ah. It's all good. Just give me a moment to orient." His index finger flipped through screens.

A compact shape nudged his elbow. "How long do we have?" Mei Ling asked, glancing toward the mouth of the mine.

"I'd reckon about a half hour," Cadzie said. "We'll need to leave false trails. Close a tunnel or two." That made some sense, right? True, it would create some future chaos for the miners. But at least that assumed there was a future. Hell, there was no way around it: the best plausible result of all this was "bad." The worst-case scenario was massacre. They were making the best of a disaster. So long as there weren't any colonists currently down in the dark, he could justify almost anything. He peered over Piccolo's sunburnt shoulder.

"What are you showing?"

"No one carrying a transceiver is in the mine right now. In fact, not a lot of work has been done since *Messenger* arrived." Piccolo grinned. "Almost as if someone knew a storm was coming." He was looking at something resembling a chart of the human circulatory system: a web of caves branching through the mountain vertically and horizontally. "Here." His fingers traced a line. "We can take this path down to the Styx."

"You called it the Styx?"

"It's the major underground river, combining several smaller tributaries from the eastern mountains, and flows directly to the magnetic node."

Cadzie performed a quick head count. Eighteen in all, Surf's Up people, other Starborn, even a couple of miners who didn't fancy remaining behind. "Do we have enough rebreathers?"

"Plenty of emergency equipment, and it's designed to function in case of flooding."

"Let's start getting them together, while we rig three of the other mines for collapse."

"Then we can seal two . . . three tunnels, including the one we're taking."

"Sounds good. I can do that. Let me finish the mapping first. I'm almost done," Piccolo said.

"Good," Cadzie said. "Let's rig up the sleds." Three suits of power armor, each towing five people on rebreathers. Could it work? Each was rated for two thousand pounds of towing power. That was five or six human beings, especially if they kicked their legs . . .

So the nylon ropes were fitted with arm and leg loops. The towees would want to be secure: half a mile underground was no place to get lost in the dark.

Mei Ling and Jaxxon monitored the radios, trying to extract useful information as the others planted explosives, gathered rebreathers and lanterns, or modified the three power suits. Tracers built into the suits had been ripped out and destroyed two days ago, but a last check was critical. Was there a backup? A work-around GPS chip that would enable the Godsons to track their stolen equipment, even into the depths of the mine? It was entirely possible, and zero reason to believe that Trudy had the technical knowledge to detect some subtle system buried within the hardware or software.

"I'm reading a Godson skeeter, seven minutes out!" Jaxxon yelled from the tunnel mouth.

The word was relayed to Cadzie, who ran back to the main tunnel carrying two more rebreathers scavenged from personnel lockers. He, Shaka and Joanie were slotted for the power armor, in tow positions. Joanie was already suited up. Shaka was just putting on a helmet that made him look like a cross between Iron Man and a medieval knight. "Then let's get in the water. Blow all the tunnels at the same time, but fast. We don't want to catch any Godsons in the blast. Things are bad enough already."

◆ CHAPTER 46 ◆
AIR

A churning cloud of smoke and dust billowed out of the mine before the Godson autogyro could land. The cloud swamped them, filled the air with particles that made Major Stype cough until she clamped down her power armor's faceplate and sealed the air system. The skeeter's props cleared the air rapidly, and when visibility was restored the pilot shut the engine.

The security squad was off the skeeter thirty seconds later, scanning for life and ready to end it. Nothing. No signs of anything outside but twisted brown high-altitude trees with spiky cactoid leaves.

"One human being on the upper level of the mines," Sergeant Lindsey said.

"Get in there, find that bastard." Her armored arm swept at the air. "What in the hell was that?" she asked, voice tight. "What the hell are they playing at?"

"They have maps," her sergeant said. "I reckon they were sealing tunnels behind them, either to obscure their intent, or impede our progress. Or both, ma'am."

She closed her eyes, and flinched at the image of

Captain Sven Meadows' bloody skull, every scrap of flesh devoured by an alien swarm. Rage tinted the edge of her constructed vision red, and she forced herself to visualize a hastily configured map of the mine, gathered just after their computer had finished sorting the flight patterns with an algorithm that separated random movement from purposeful, then sorted again for high-value destinations. The remaining three choices had been equally weighted . . . Stype had made the final decision. This was the place.

"They could be heading anywhere."

"Ma'am," Sergeant Lindsey said. "I have a notion. We can reconfigure our deep scans. Do that, and we might be able to trace them by our own power suit heat and radio signatures."

"Get the hell on it." Stype growled. She closed her eyes. Sven's skull floated in the darkness.

"We have to do it while they're moving, before they can power it down again . . . or we've lost them. Maybe permanently."

"Then what the hell are you waiting for?"

At the moment, Major Stype's prey were deep underground, the cold mountain water sweeping them along in an endless western tide. The darkness was interrupted only by their own lights, within which the smooth tunnel walls looked like a strange combination of machined, natural, and . . . organic. Cadzie slowed, closely examining something that reminded him of potter's glaze. He wished he had time to study more carefully. That he could take off his gloves and feel the textures.

Nuts. The cold would numb his bare hands. He would feel nothing.

They reached a branching tunnel. He slowed. Stopped. The people towed behind him continued to move, bumped into his feet. "Which way now?" Trudy asked.

Cadzie felt a brief flash of panic. "I don't know..." if he chose wrong, they might run out of time, hit a stretch with no air pockets after their rebreathers were exhausted.

Which way?

Then...he noticed something. There were rough patches on the walls, shimmering oddly under his light, a different color than the faint greenish glow currently reflected against his face plate. Bluish.

"Everybody," he said. "Lights off."

And when they complied, what he had glimpsed, perhaps only sensed, leapt into relief: three isosceles triangles in electric yellow, clearly indicating the left branch.

"Is that what I think it is?" Anchored to the nylon line, Trudy had drifted up behind him as soon as he stopped.

"I think so, yes." He raised his voice, forgetting that all he had to do was increase the volume. "People! You who can hear me—" Not all the rebreathers had earpieces. Fewer of them were full-face, allowing speech. "We have a branching tunnel, and I think I've found a clue saying to head left. All who agree, raise your right arms."

To his relief, all right arms raised. They were with him.

"In for a penny, in for a pound," Trudy said.

"That's my girl."

Her answering voice was a touch wan. "That's what I am."

◆ ◆ ◆

"How are you doing back there?" Cadzie asked.

"The air is holding up," Trudy said, her voice muffled by her emergency helmet. The sound quality was serviceable, but the gear certainly hadn't been intended for long-term underwater use. "Can we turn up those lights? Give me something to think about. And . . . it's cold. Colder than I thought it would be."

"Are you all right?" The temperature was 15 degrees centigrade. That worried him.

The powersuit headlights were turned to high, silvery cones in the darkness. The tunnel walls reflected unevenly, as if flecks of glass were embedded irregularly.

"Looks like lava tubes." Toad said.

"I'm no geologist, but I'm doubting that. I'm starting to think that these weren't naturally formed."

"The cthulhu?"

"Suspecting that, yes," Shaka said, his voice clear in the microphones. "Some of this is natural, but I think they widened the underground rivers somehow. Don't know how."

"This looks like heat glaze." *Perhaps*, Cadzie thought. If the original material was like an incompletely digested or mixed paste.

"We know they could work metal. Smelting. Refining. If they could do that, they might be able to do this too."

"And what else?" Cadzie asked.

"I don't know," Nnedi said. "I think we're about to find out, though."

They continued on and on, until their air was running low and their arms and legs were numb. Jaxxon was the

first to say what they were all thinking. "The air isn't good.
I think...some of these guys only got another few
minutes." They had found five thermal suits, but the
batteries were fading.

"But you're fine, right?" Cadzie asked.

"I'm a warm-weather guy. But I'll make it."

A sudden panicked voice. A woman's. He didn't
recognize it. "I can't breathe, I can't..."

"Mei Ling!" Thor cried, his basso voice cracking.
"Here, take my mouthpiece. Slow down, Shaka. Match
speeds with Piccolo—"

A babble of overlapping voices.

"Hold on."

Mei Ling again, stressed and gasping. "I have to try to
..." a sudden inspiration. "Maybe there's some air at the
top."

"Mei! No!" Thor's voice. Panicked.

In the lead, Cadzie got a visual feed from Piccolo as
Mei Ling cut herself loose from the harness, swam
upward toward an imagined safety, frenzy driving all logic
from her mind. He had to keep going, around another
turn, until the tiny screen in his helmet was the only view
of what was happening back there. They would try to get
her back. Try to set her up to share rebreathers. Maybe
they would succeed.

He had to keep going, because unless he was very
mistaken, one of his five towed charges would soon be in
the same situation.

Dying, in all probability.

For him.

PART TWO

◆

WHOVILLE

I met a traveler from an antique land,
Who said—"Two vast and trunkless legs of stone
Stand in the desert . . . Near them, on the sand,
Half sunk a shattered visage lies, whose frown,
And wrinkled lip, and sneer of cold command,
Tell that its sculptor well those passions read
Which yet survive, stamped on these lifeless things,
The hand that mocked them, and the heart that fed;
And on the pedestal, these words appear:
My name is Ozymandias, King of Kings:
Look on my Works, ye Mighty, and despair!
Nothing beside remains. Round the decay
Of that colossal Wreck, boundless and bare
The lone and level sands stretch far away."
                    —Percy Bysshe Shelley, "Ozymandias"

◆ CHAPTER 47 ◆
THE FORGE

Light ahead, flickering dull gold and then brightening, but not quite bright enough to read. The ambient temperature had risen steadily for the last half-mile, until the water was as warm as a steam bath. Fishlike shapes glided through the murk. Glowing. Translucent skin, the bones manifest through the flesh. Cadzie had seen vid of deep-sea dwellers on Earth, but to his knowledge nothing like this had been found on Avalon before now. The creatures (he found himself calling them "fish" although they obviously could not actually be) showed only the vaguest curiosity about the human intruders. If he had wished to catch one by the tail, it would have been child's play.

The tunnel expanded so abruptly that it seemed like the bottom and sides and ceilings had dissolved, and suddenly they emerged into a world of alien light. As the Starborn exited a tunnel and approached the surface of some larger body of water, several unlooped themselves from the tow ropes and swam under their own power. The first six surviving Starborn clambered onto a graveled rock shelf. For a moment they were overcome with awe by their surroundings, enough to numb the pain and fear.

They stood in a vast arching cavern. The pool shimmered from green-glowing eels that glided through the waters like lightly armored fish. A pale dull light pulsed from the walls, which for a few inches above the water line was coated with a luminescent slime. Where that slime proceeded in an unbroken line from the water, at close range the glow was bright enough to show the lines on Cadmann's hands.

In all, it created enough light to see what existed at the edge of the underground lake, near a shore that retreated far into the shadows: Something that resembled a castle constructed of coral rose out of the water, multicolored in the odd shimmering lights.

"What are you seeing?" Little Shaka sounded as if he couldn't quite believe his eyes.

"It's like Whoville," Evie said.

"What?"

"Like something designed by Dr. Seuss. The colors and shapes."

Nnedi shook water from her face and laughed. "Partially above the water line, partially below. I'm seeing a lot of separate compartments, and I'm thinking it's not living space."

"What, then? Work space?"

"What if we started with that assumption?" Cadzie asked.

"Partially in the water, part out," Shaka mused. "The water line was higher then, I think. I would look for a separation in function. Below the water line . . . maybe the biological research? Above the line things dealing with heat, fire . . ."

He paused. "Fire," Nnedi marveled. "Aquatic creatures who discovered how to use fire. I want you to think about that. They had to observe it, learn to care for it, and then probably find a way to reproduce it on their own."

"The taming of fire was probably the single most important discovery in human history," Shaka said. "One of the few things that separates us from all other animals. We consider it evidence of our superior brains. Well . . . the cthulhu would have had less chance to observe fire, and a more difficult time maintaining it. Fewer natural opportunities to experiment. And yet they still got it right."

Standing next to Nnedi, Evie seemed as small as a child, a full head shorter as she ran her small, agile artist's hands over the artificial stone. "Ever consider that they could be smarter than us?" Her grin was a child's as well, intoxicated by discovery. "Needed to finish evolving to being land creatures, perhaps. I don't think people could have done what they did."

"That's scary," Shaka said.

"Too bad we don't have Marco and his drone," Trudy said. "I'd like to record all of this. See all of it from multiple perspectives."

Joanie seemed to flinch. "Marco," she whispered.

"Check on the others." Cadzie said.

Another eleven survivors dragged themselves up out of the water, stripping off their masks and spitting out water,

390 Larry Niven, Jerry Pournelle, and Steven Barnes

coughing and gagging. Thor splashed through the shallows to Mei Ling, who lay limp, pale and unresponsive as glowing fish-things skittered out of the way. Under the yellowish light, she looked bleached and bloated, as if she had been underwater for a week.

"Dammit! Mei, come back!" He pushed at her chest, blew into her mouth, massaged nerve centers at the base of her skull. Nothing.

Even those who had been enthralled by the underground city joined them, gathered about and watched soberly as the grim scenario played out.

Cadzie waited as long as he could before whispering, "She's gone."

Thor's eyes blazed at them. His mouth worked, but no words emerged. He seemed to tense totally, knotting his fists as if seeking something to attack.

Then his broad shoulders slumped. His eyes moistened and he wiped them as he rose to face Cadzie.

He seemed . . . shrunken. "Before we left . . . she said she wasn't doing it for you."

"Why, then?"

"She thought you were innocent. And that if there was some way to prove it, the Godsons would change their attitude. Know they were wrong. And if they did . . ."

"They'd back off," Trudy said, laying a comforting hand on Thor's shoulder. "They really might. Believe me, they think your colony is lost, and are just trying to help."

Thor's voice was ice. "In their way."

"Yeah," Nnedi said. "In their way."

◆CHAPTER 48◆
GUILT AND RESPONSIBILITY

A militarized skeeter had circled the high alpine meadow. Sixty miles in diameter, the meadow was ringed with mountains, with the mouth of the Snowcone mine at the inside eastern edge. Tsiolkovskii waved the pilot to a landing and hopped down, a solid, bearlike, graying man two inches over six feet, clean-shaven four hours ago but already stubbled. He took a moment to orient himself. So much had happened, so quickly. So many new sights and sounds. A heavier gravity, and this to a man who had never spent more than a week out of Earth normal. He'd need to make adjustments if traveling quickly over broken ground, or engaging in hand-to-hand combat. Every visual, auditory, olfactory and proprioceptive sense was gathering input at maximum speed. He didn't have time to adjust properly.

He hoped it wouldn't matter. He knew he could focus enough to get the job done anyway.

That was who he was.

"Major Stype?" he said to the short-haired Amazon who saluted him. He'd had time to study her jacket on the way over. Difficulties: her fiancé had been killed in a diabolically clever ambush. She was, in his very expert opinion, precisely the wrong person to head up the capture mission.

"Colonel," she said, and snapped to attention.

"At ease," he said. And then as clearly as he could, added: "I am now in command."

"Sir, I respectfully suggest that my understanding of the situation—"

"Is unfortunately compromised by your tragedy. This isn't a search and destroy mission."

Her eyes told the tale: tightened with brief fury, then went tight but neutral with deeply ingrained discipline. He could appreciate the first, and respect the second. "Sir—"

"Major," he said, moving closer to her now. "Be happy I'm not excluding you from the team." His words were carefully and fully enunciated. "You are emotionally involved." Their eyes locked, blazed into each other until she looked away. Good. "Yes, sir."

"Tell me what you know," he said.

As soon as they moved into the throat of the mine, the temperature dropped ten degrees, and the heat-fused walls looked almost like sheets of gray ice.

To Tsiolkovskii the miner looked like a night creature, something that had spent too much time burrowing within the earth. Fishbelly-pale, like a grub with a fringe of dark hair. "Where were they going?" he asked.

The miner spoke no words, but the wildness in his eyes said volumes.

"If you cooperate, it will go better for you."

The miner, whose name was Kovak, was wide-eyed with fear, breathing shallowly. Tsiolkovskii thought the fear would be useful. Frightened people were less likely to lie if they believed those lies would bring pain or punishment. But the man said, "You have no rights here. You were our guests."

"And now, you are our prisoners," Tsiolkovskii said. "Secure him! Spread out and search."

"Sir!" Stype said. "We have evidence that the rebels escaped to an underground river on level six."

Rebels. That was an interesting choices of words. He'd also heard "criminals," "terrorists," and "murderers." To him they were adversaries. He would leave the more emotional terms for the amateurs, among whom Stype now hovered.

He was dubious of her conclusions. "We've found evidence of them heading in a dozen different directions."

"That's true," she admitted. "And yet here you are, sir."

"Yes," Tsiolkovskii said. "Here I am."

Something about this mine seemed right. The horses had been spotted grazing on the miniveldt only a few miles from here. The man Stanfield Corning, known as "Piccolo," was suspected of being with the rebels, and according to records he was a former miner. Mining explosives had been used to trigger the bee attack. And the underground rivers connected with the largest magnetic anomaly. Why might they go there?

In the final analysis, who knew? Вилами на воде писано, as his father said. Literally: *the future is written on flowing water with a pitchfork.* No one knows what will happen, and it was not his job to guess.

Instinct told him this was the best option.

"Sir," Sergeant Lindsey said, "we've examined the collapsed caves, and I can't help but think that the demolitions weren't designed to conceal intent. There were two dry tunnels, and then an underground river. I think the river was collapsed in such a way as to block entrance without obstructing the flow of water. I'm guessing that's where they went."

"Where would this river lead?" Tsiolkovskii asked.

"Assuming they are heading downriver?" Stype asked. "West, under the miniveldt and the western mountains into the desert, to an oasis maybe, and eventually the ocean?"

A shrug. "It doesn't feel right. It's possible, though."

"And upriver?"

"Under the mountains . . . into more mountains. No idea what's up there."

"Let's assume downriver for a moment. What's down there. Anything?"

Sergeant Lindsey spoke up. "If we overlap deep scans and magnetic maps, there seems to be something in the center of the miniveldt, deep underground."

That caught his attention. "Magnetic? These cthulhu creatures use magnetism, yes?"

"Yes, sir. There was some speculation there might be a nest of some kind here. You could reach it through the rivers."

The back of his neck tingled. "Tell me more about this nest," Tsiolkovskii frowned. "Why would they go there?"

Stype didn't seem comfortable with the question. "Perhaps a place to hide, or . . ."

"Out with it, Major."

She stiffened her spine, as if it actually *hurt* to speak the words. "Sikes' allies advance the theory that these 'cthulhu' creatures may have been involved in Aaron Tragon's death. If this nest is really a center of activity, perhaps they are looking for something to prove that."

"If he's innocent," Tsiolkovskii said. "I assume you have an opinion?"

"Sir? He was adjudged guilty."

"What do you think?"

A pause, as if wondering if he really wanted to know. And then an answer: "I think he's guilty as hell, sir, and that everyone who helped him is complicit in the murder of our troops." Her eyes blazed when she said "our troops." Oh, *there* it was. Her personal loss, not three days old, already masked under a pretense of impersonal duty.

"And I was told I'd be awakened at Hypereden. Mistakes can be made. I'm learning as fast as I can. I need you to tell me what else you're thinking."

"Sir," Stype said. "I believe that Sikes has misled them, sir. They believe he is innocent, and he is continuing the charade." She paused. "It would make no sense to assume otherwise. Sir. The murdered man's daughter most certainly believes it."

"And therefore?"

She closed her eyes and exhaled. "Therefore, there are gradations of guilt and responsibility."

"I see," Tsiolkovskii said. "Outstanding."

◆ ◆ ◆

The Grendel Scouts and their allies kept fear at bay by busying themselves studying the city and environs, attention split between cataloging wonders, setting traps and designing overlapping fields of fire.

Not one of them had ever been in a firefight with another human being. Nor had their parents. Or living grandparents.

But Jason and Jaxxon knew the theoretical side of combatives from von Clausewitz back to Sun Tzu, and of course they'd all watched war movies. Hell of a time to wonder how well theory mapped over with reality.

Little Shaka climbed up into a second-story window of one of the iridescent coral "buildings." Handholds were surprisingly easy, and one could imagine the former occupants swarming up and around. But once inside, he found a warren of smaller rooms, the connections between them low-ceilinged enough that it was easier to change levels by exiting to clamber up the outside.

At the water level he found what might have been living quarters. He wondered: when they examined the underwater levels, would they find the same? Or had these creatures preferred to live like amphibians?

In the higher levels, he found what might well have been workshops, shelves of extruded concrete, overgrown with living coral. The coral-stuff had grown halfway to a forty-meter stalactite-toothed ceiling and then died, as if it needed the cthulhu to water or feed it. A self-limiting living construction material? He found blackened smears, perhaps scorch marks, suggesting that fire had been applied to walls and extrusions. He looked back over his shoulder to see Evie Queen climbing in the window after him. She nodded, eyes bright with a combination of discovery and fear.

That he understood. Nodding in answer, he returned to his investigations.

The last quarter-mile to the city cavern had been swum in eighty-degree water, and the walls had been studded with forearm-length rotating spiral-grooved cones, still turning slowly in tide after thousands of years. The colonel had noticed that they were connected to what might have been cables sheathed in some kind of water weed, and that those cables ran all the way into this cavern, buried into the rock near sheets of glowing cement. Could the cthulhu have *grown* electrical cables? Was there an organic life-form that could conduct electricity efficiently? Surely not and survive . . .

He heard Trudy's footsteps behind them. What did it say that he recognized their sound? Without turning, he said, "So you're sure they'll come after us?"

"I'm sure," Trudy said. "And I even think I know what they'll do."

"And what is that?" Cadzie asked. He split one of the ancient cables, and found what seemed like strings of pale rust-colored beads wrapped in seaweed. Some conductive material, copper or some combination of metals? But why in this bead formation? They almost looked like clusters of dull red rabbit droppings. Was there an animal that ate ore and crapped copper beads? Too much to think about, and no time to focus, dammit. If they lived long enough, there was an entire amazing world to explore.

He hoped they'd have the time.

"There was a man they talked about," she said. "His name was Tsiolkovskii. Colonel Anton Tsiolkovskii. He was a U.N. Force hero, blown up in battle somewhere in Africa, I think. He'd have died, or lived like a cripple if we hadn't invested millions saving him."

"He was a Godson leader?"

"No. He had some familiarity with us, and had been friendly after we supplied U.N. troops with some performance programs. When he was wounded, his career was over. We offered him life, in exchange for service."

"Service?"

"Yes. We froze him until the medical technology improved enough to regrow limbs. But the arrangement was that in exchange, he would lead our security forces on Hypereden."

"He agreed to it?"

She nodded. "He'd been badly damaged. His life was over. I heard rumors his wife left him and his children had already been alienated by long absences. We gave him the only chance he had."

"All right," Piccolo said. "Let's say they wake him up. What then?"

"You don't understand," Trudy said. "He was the best. I think some of our troops were actually frightened by his reputation. He won't stop, and you won't be able to throw him off your trail. He'll find us. He will." She spoke so calmly, as if reciting an article of faith.

"What are you suggesting?" Joanie asked. "And why didn't you tell us this before?"

"I'm sorry," she said. "So much has happened, and so

fast. Security wasn't my arena. But once I started thinking about it, his name kept coming back up."

"So . . . what do we do?" Cadzie asked.

"Get ready to fight," Trudy said. "But if that's who they send after us, I don't think we can win."

"Do you have any new thoughts?" Nnedi asked.

"Well . . . if Trudy is right," Little Shaka said, ticking off factors on his fingertips. "Then these structures are more like temples than cities or workshops. Whatever they did here was sacred. If it was sacred when they built it . . . all I can think about is old novels of degenerate followers of ancient religions."

"Didn't Lovecraft write some of those?"

"The best. Making the whole 'cthulhu' thing rather eerie, I'd say," Shaka laughed. "What we know: advanced magnetic skills, metal working, symbolic language, fire, possibly genetic technology."

"Wow," Nnedi said.

"And consider the path to fire. Human beings observed it: spontaneous combustion, volcanic activity. Lightning strikes. Maybe sunlight focused through natural crystals. Can you imagine how magical it was? They learned to shelter it, nurture and protect it. At some point they learned to create it themselves."

"So?"

"Let's assume," Shaka said, "that it took the cthulhu about the same amount of time to domesticate fire that humans required. We really can't know either way, but let's start there."

"Okay," she agreed. "Okay, what then?"

"Aquatic creatures would have a fraction of the opportunities to observe fire. A fraction of the opportunities to tame and shelter it and learn about it. Would have had far fewer direct uses for it prior to smelting. That implies that they understood its potential and deliberately sought to master it."

"I . . . oh, God . . . they might be *smarter* than us."

"Yes. And if they were, and built a civilization with technology still beyond our own, and then something went very wrong . . . that's a long way to fall."

◆ CHAPTER 49 ◆
BINDING

Their lamplight reached the toothy ceiling without evening out its shadows. White limestone and pits of darkness loomed above them, alien and distant as the surface of an unexplored moon.

If only we had time, Cadzie thought. But this was the only time they had, perhaps the only time they'd ever have. And with that in mind, he found a way to separate himself and Trudy from the others, and guarantee themselves a bit of privacy.

"I love you, you know," she said after they had sat for a while, just looking out at the limestone spires and twisted shadows carved out by their lamp. In this cavern, branching off from the main city-space, the mysterious cthulhus seemed to have made few modifications.

Cadzie watched her carefully. "Marco said you can switch your emotions on and off."

"Do I *act* like someone who can turn them off?"

"I don't know," Cadzie said. "Never met anyone like you." He paused. "Can you?"

"Not exactly. I was trained to be what I am...a

companion for a warrior-king. Not just sex. Not just support or advice. Love."

"How would he know the difference?"

"He wouldn't." She grinned. "I would."

"You would. So . . . you can just turn it on?"

She took his hand gently, twining their fingers together. He had the sense she might have taken a child's hand in a very similar manner. "Imagine that you have a set of switches in your head. Respect, attraction, care, affection, lust, protectiveness . . . how many of them would you have to throw before you called the result 'love'?"

"Some, yeah. Most, maybe."

"Arranged marriages work just fine, Cadzie. You work side by side, make love, care for each other, take turns getting sick, raise children . . . and fall in love. It happens."

"You're saying the Godsons just took conscious control of that process?"

"We are going to conquer a galaxy. Find the source of all life." Spoken without hesitation or irony. "The foundation of all human civilization has been a breeding pair. Two people against the world, Cadzie. I made my choice. You."

"You were *told* to?" He was alarmed to hear the thread of dismay in his voice.

"I was asked to consider it, yes. Strongly encouraged. I don't think the leaders realized what might happen. I had a choice between them, and you."

"And you chose me."

"And now I can't easily go back. And . . . I love you."

There was something appealingly vulnerable about this woman now. Almost a pleading.

He wanted to push her away. Scream *wake up!* in her face.

And to pin her to the ground and screw her brains out. The contradiction was dizzying. "I don't know what I feel," he said. "I'm so mixed up. But . . . you are beautiful, and sexy as hell and smart, and . . . you put everything on the line for me. Give us time. I promise I will. And there's no one else. Can that be enough?"

"That's enough. Just give me a chance." She unwound a thread from her tattered wet sweater and wrapped it around her wrist.

"What's that?"

She had suddenly become much more serious. "We do not know what comes, Cadmann. Yesterday does not exist. Tomorrow is a dream. But we have to both remember history, plan for the future, and live in the moment. Can you see?"

She was saying exactly what he had felt, that had motivated him to find some quiet, private together time. "Yes."

Suddenly there was an unexpected gravity about this woman, as if she was more priestess than courtesan. And her shift in demeanor triggered a more sober response from him.

"This place . . ." she said, "was a sacred place to these creatures, whether long dead or still here. I feel it. Don't you?"

He felt a faint, cool air current. Mist drifted around their ankles like cold smoke. Distantly, water burpled and human voices rose and fell, combinations of fear and curiosity.

That was not what she spoke of. Trudy was asking him to go deeper, to find something within him that sensed things that could not be heard, or touched. For her sake, he tried. "Yes," he finally said. "I think I do."

"When we rescued you from Blackship, I told the guards that I was there to perform a cord cutting ceremony."

"A what?"

"A form of divorce, Cadzie. Godsons have no casual sex, so they assumed I was simply ending something we'd started."

Whoa. "No casual . . . really?"

Trudy grinned impishly. *There* was the smile he'd guessed at but never seen.

This strange woman as a child. The image . . . warmed him.

"But . . . we do get married for short periods. For the night, for instance."

"You have got to be kidding."

"Not at all. It guarantees that the emotions are taken seriously. And that, if there are any children resulting from the union, they are protected and nurtured. It is similar to a Sufi 'muta' contract."

"It's . . . a tying ceremony?"

"Yes."

"Then cord-cutting is a divorce?"

"Yes."

"Jesus. Do I owe you alimony?"

Trudy laughed. "First, you need to shut up."

"Lips sealed."

"Not too tightly, I hope." Damn, she was mercurial.

Shifted between priestess, teacher and courtesan so fluidly that it kept him dizzy. Part of her magic, perhaps. But behind the teasing, he sensed something more serious, like a sober child peeking out from behind a mask of gaiety. *Please. I'm giving all I can. All I have to offer.* "I look at this, all of this. And what is happening. And realize that we might not live through it. It was always possible."

"And you helped me anyway."

"And now you're going to help me. I lied to free you. Lied about something ... sacred. They believed me, because we don't lie about things like that."

What *will* you lie about? He heard the question in his head, realized that some part of him was searching for a way to disbelieve her. Distance himself. And with a flash of guilt realized that was just self-protection. There was something about this woman so worldly and yet so sincere that it felt as if he had no defenses to her at all. If he let go, if he dropped those barriers he was going to fall hard.

And then ... he realized that he already had, damn it.

He felt the heft and heat of her words. She had given everything, including total loyalty. Compared to that transgression, murder might be almost a misdemeanor. He had badly underestimated this woman. "What can I do?"

"Make it truth," she said.

He gazed into her eyes, and then nodded. She tied her right hand to his left.

"I, Gertrude Hendrickson," she said, "freely and of my own will commit to you, to care for and love you in the time we have, this moment, the only moment we have, with all my heart." She sighed. "Now you."

"I, Cadmann Sikes, freely and of my own will commit to you, to care for and love you in the time we have, this moment..." He paused, emotions bubbling up. These were not his words, not his tradition. But in this alien place, considering all that she had done for and by him, all that she had thrown away to protect him...those words seemed sacred. This was a bond, something deeper than culture or tradition, like two nervous systems twining together to create a single creature.

"The only moment we have."

"The only moment we have, with all my heart." He paused, head spinning, far more moved than he had anticipated. "Now what?"

Her smile blossomed. "*Now* you kiss me."

He did. Then without the need for conversation they gathered armfuls of the dried waterweed, and made themselves a bed in the shadows. And upon it, within a womb of ancient rock, lit only with a beacon's pale light they sealed that bond again, in a manner that men and women had embraced since a time before starships, or beacons, or even words had ever existed at all.

The western wall ran from floor to ceiling, with a rectangle as tall as two men cut into the middle at floor level. In the light of glowing nonfish and their own lamps, it appeared constructed of some composition substance, like glazed concrete. A vast convexity swelled the middle.

"What is this wall?" Joanie asked.

"We don't know," Shaka said, slapping his hand against it. "The material is extremely hard, very strong. It might be a ceiling support." He sounded uncertain. "Perhaps a dam, blocking a river?"

Water did trickle out from under it, running down to the main pool. Just a trickle, though. "Not a river on the map," Evie said.

"We have no idea what everything was a thousand years ago," Joanie said. "Ten thousand years..."

"We may never know what it was designed to support."

"Or contain," Shaka said.

A new thought occurred to him. "What weapons are Godson soldiers likely to bring?"

"Automatic rifles, tactical battle suits. Gas, armor piercing, fragmentation..." That was Trudy's voice, Trudy coming up from behind them, holding hands with Cadzie. Where had *they* been?

"Oh, shit," Nnedi moaned.

"Yes," Trudy said. "I don't know how you counter that, or how much time you have."

"Neither do I. We have an advantage in that we know where we are, and they are having to guess. They'll have to look down the branching tunnels to be sure. Look for ambush." The cavern was like a clock, with the buildings in the center, the warm-water lagoon between seven and five, that odd wall at nine, and five passages radiating away at eleven through three.

"Ambush is good," Shaka said.

"So..." Cadzie said. "The first thing we might want to do is collapse the tunnel we came through."

"How the hell do we get back out?" Jaxxon asked. A perfectly natural question, that.

"One thing at a time. We've seen two tunnels heading

up, and two down. I'm willing to bet that the cthulhu had another way in here."

"There's that," Joanie said. "There's that. There's also that if our people, or the Godsons know we're here, they'll eventually drill down and get us."

"If it's the Godsons, we might not be happy with that 'getting.'" Jason said.

"Well, if they come through a blocked tunnel some-how . . . and we survive . . . then maybe we'll be able to circle back around them . . ."

"Go out the way they came in?"

"Maybe."

"Not much of a plan."

"When you get a better one, speak up."

Most of what could be done had been done. The children of Avalon and their guest had retreated to a cleared circle, something reminiscent of an amphitheater, on the far side of the reef-city and near the imaginary clock's "twelve," invisible from the underground lake, down at the "six."

And there, seated in a circle so they could see each other, they held what all knew might be their final meeting. The question Cadzie placed before them: why were they here? If death was heading toward them, bearing down at what might be cataclysmic speed, clarity was the least he could ask of any willing to die at his side.

Why are you here?

"I'm with you, Cadzie," Nnedi said. "This is our planet. They had no right to do what they did."

"Are you prepared to die for your rights?" Cadzie asked.

"We don't know what will happen," she said. "We never do. But if I didn't stand up for what was right, I don't know how I'd live with myself."

"Thor?" Cadzie asked.

The shaggy-haired Viking seemed shrunken, as if he'd lost six inches and thirty pounds in the last two hours. "I helped get you here, Cadzie."

"Yeah, thanks a lot."

That triggered a few much-needed chuckles.

"I . . . think that in a way, it was jealousy. I didn't think I felt that, but I did. So when I had a chance to strike out at you . . . well, you scared me, Cad."

That was unexpected. "I what?"

"Come on, man. Don't you know who you are?" He gestured vaguely. "You're Cadmann Weyland's blood. You tore through everyone but the twins in your combat tests. You really are better and stronger and probably *smarter* than most of us."

"Oh, come on."

"You don't see it," Thor said. "And I think I hated you for that, too. You didn't even have the decency to be egotistical about it."

"Well, I'm sorry all to hell." More laughter.

"See there? See how decent you are? I . . . I don't think I could have done that. I think I would have lorded it over everyone if I had an advantage like that. I hated Joanie being with you up on *Geographic.* You made me feel . . . small. And so when I had a chance, I struck out at you. And took real pleasure in it. But . . . I was happy I failed, too. I mean, I never really thought we'd convict you."

Trudy interjected. "But then we took your arguments and ran with them."

Thor nodded ruefully. "When I watched what the Godsons did with it, I went out and threw up."

"I held your hair," Evie said.

Again, laughter. It felt good. Even Thor managed a smile.

"So . . . I think I speak for a lot of us, Cadzie. We were given a world we didn't earn, and our parents have never stopped reminding us of that. I think maybe we thought we were looking for a fight. Now I think we were looking for something to mean something."

"And this is it," Evie Queen raised her hand, and then her voice. "I think you're stuck with us."

Cadzie looked at the faces around him.

Quiet swallowed them, until the faint drip of water and their own breaths were the only sounds. Then Trudy spoke. "There is something that happens when a group of people share the same perspective. It is even more powerful when that is a shift, a way apart from their previous way of being. We call it 'Tribing.'"

"This is Godson stuff?"

"Yes. And a 'Tribing' happens under stress. Soldiers experience it in combat, when there is a survival payoff for shedding some of their individual identity. They can spend the rest of their lives trying to regain it. We . . ." She touched her chest. "The Godsons experienced it when the Vision was revealed, when the Elders gave the inner teachings to everyone. Some left, but those who remained experienced a Tribing, and it was wonderful."

"I bet," Evie said.

"There were people who could not themselves go, but sold all their possessions to contribute, to send their genes to the stars. Numbers decreased, but we also gained thousands of new members, and those who remained were more loyal than ever. The Tribing." They nodded soberly.

"This is what we're experiencing?"

"Yes," Trudy said. "Finding something you are willing to die for. Seeing in those to your right and left something more important than your individual identity. Something worth living for so powerfully that even the fear of death stops having a hold on you.

"All marriage ceremonies speak of two becoming one. And ceremonies bringing people into military or religious communities also Tribe. Secret societies have their own languages that not only describe mysteries but change the consciousness of the members. In-group language and out-group language. The first analysis of this might have been the Sapir-Whorf hypothesis, and the weak version, that language binds and influences thought, has strong evidence."

"The strong version, not so much," Cadzie said.

The others seemed entranced.

"True. I want to be a part of you. As Cadzie is a part of me. If this is the end of my existence, let us be Tribe together. You struggled to define yourself, and did so in opposition to intent."

"'Opposition to intent'? More Godson talk?" Evie.

"Sorry. Your parents and grandparents had intent.

"Grandparents: conquer the stars, establish a colony.

"Parents: secure the planet, make it safe for their

children. You saw not only their greatness, but their dysfunction. The degree to which they couldn't enjoy their victory. Efforts had poisoned their dreams. They programmed their own children with nightmares..."

The Grendel Scouts nodded soberly.

"And we didn't want any part of it." Joanie said. "We rebelled."

"As children often do. And as a result, became indolent... or so it seemed to my people. Is there anyone here who has no skill in anything?"

They talked among themselves for a time, voices alternating between strident, philosophical, frightened and cajoling.

"Not really," Joanie finally said. "Everyone always does something, even if it doesn't make productive sense."

"But 'practical production' wasn't needed," Trudy said. "Not the way your grandparents intended. To win the war against grendels and even hunger, they needed exceptional focus. But that same focus prevented them from understanding why the children they loved wouldn't continue to have that focus, even after it no longer served a purpose."

"But we all found excellence anyway. Art. Surfing. Exploration. Sciences..."

"Not because we had to."

"Because that is what healthy human beings do," Trudy said, slipping further into teacher mode. "It's what we do. Maybe my people forgot that. They certainly knew it once. We accepted people who were good at anything, whether or not society agreed."

"But you're all so organized!"

"Because everyone on *this* mission agrees upon an external goal. Otherwise, we'd splinter. Like other people."

Joanie laughed. "It's an illusion!"

"It's an illusion. Created by a philosophical filter. We are all the same because only those of a particular mind would come on such a mission. But the illusion was compelling, and seductive."

"So . . . what do you do? I mean . . . not necessarily you, personally, but the Godsons?"

"Here are our principles," Trudy said. "First, that Mankind must conquer the galaxy.

"Second . . ." And here she paused. "This is not spoken of to outsiders." She glanced at Cadzie, and he knew what she was about to say. "The God Knot. The panspermic point from which all life in the galaxy sprang must be found by humanity for us to leap to our next level of evolution."

The Starborn glanced at each other. Most had never heard this. None laughed. Absurd it might have been, but this didn't seem the time for rude questions. And all of them knew they'd heard worse.

"Third. That all humans must fulfill a purpose, that purpose is more important than their transitory desires.

"Fourth, that pleasure can be postponed for decades, lifetimes, to accomplish a worthy goal. Lack of ability to postpone pleasure is the cause of all lack of discipline.

"Fifth, our deepest essence is survival of our species. All pleasure comes from service to survival.

"Sixth, that Tribing is the melding of individual will into group identity. The pleasure of this is in direct proportion to the degree you release limiting ego.

"Seventh: All individual psychosis is a failure to submit to and embrace the good of the group."

She paused, letting *that* sink in. "We stand here, facing death," Trudy said. "But I would guess that in a way you can barely admit even to yourselves, you also feel more alive than ever before."

"Yes," Little Shaka said.

"We would say this is because you have submitted your individual needs . . . even the need to survive . . . to the group."

Joanie frowned. "But how does that make sense? I mean, evolutionarily?"

"Because humans have the best chance of surviving when they stand as a group. So the paradox is right in front of you: the greatest way to increase chance of survival is to accept death."

Jaxxon nodded. "That is the way of the warrior. He who abandons his life in a worthy cause, gains his life. He who clings to life loses it."

"Even if they 'win.'" Cadzie said.

"Yes. Even if they win."

"So . . . there you have it," Trudy said. "The rules at the heart of the Godsons. We do not live as individuals. We live as a group."

Joan said, "I can see why it appealed so much to Marco."

"Why Marco?" Cadzie said.

"Because he had conquered his world," she said. "Become the greatest star, climbed the mountain. But knew that it was all for himself, and that all the millions of people who loved him didn't know him at all. He wanted something real. He wanted to know himself."

"And he could only know himself by losing himself?"

"As only those who embrace death truly taste life," Jason said.

The two brothers shared a secret smile, as if they knew something that no one else can know.

"You guys weird me out," Joanie said.

"One of us chose art. The other, science. Both of us wish to be warriors, like our ancestors."

"And you can't do that unless you die?"

"No. I'm not surprised that you can't understand. Jaxxon?"

"Being a warrior is just a path of inquiry," the older brother said. "A way of seeking truth. 'What is true?' is the question. And that question can be approached through science, or art."

"Science is more exacting," Jason said.

"And because of that," Jaxxon offered. "Appeals to younger minds, incapable of nuance."

They smiled at each other again, a pair of tiger cubs.

"Well, that's special," Cadzie said. "What do we do now?"

"You ask me?" Trudy asked. "You are not Godsons."

"No. But we are seekers of truth. If the Godsons have a truth about this, we are willing to embrace it."

"Then I would say that what we do is embrace what is happening to us. That we live or die . . . together. That we Tribe."

"How do we do that?" Cadzie asked.

"You already know." Trudy's smile was full of mischief. "You and I did this last night."

"We all get married?" Joanie asked.

"We become family. We sit here in a circle. Any can leave now, without rancor or blame. Move aside, and allow the circle to hold only those with the heart to live or die with each other."

"Is this what you did before you left Earth?"

"Every one of us. Can you imagine traveling a trillion miles without such a commitment?"

"I think our grandparents did."

"Then they were great. Because they stood, even though they had no conscious commitment. That is a mark of greatness. But if you are great, and decide to stand . . . you will be even stronger."

Trudy stood. "I stand. Here and now. With you. Live or die."

Cadzie stood. And Joanie. And Jaxxon and Jason, and Little Shaka. All of them . . .

Except the young man in the very back, with the golden beard.

"I . . . *can't*." Thor said. "I thought I could. But I can't. I'm sorry. I want to live."

"It's all right," Trudy said.

"It's all right, Thor," Joanie said. "You'll go home."

Thor was shaking with terror and shame. The standees regarded each other.

"Look," Trudy said. "See each other. These are your brothers and sisters."

"What . . . what am I?" Thor asked, miserable.

"You're our neighbor, Thor." Cadzie said it as kindly as possible. "And most of the time, you've been a good neighbor."

Thor trembled, then made a great choking sound,

doubled up and began to sob. On the outside of the circle.

"And now what?" Jaxxon asked.

"Now . . . we prepare."

Jaxxon had been first to use the term "Whoville," but the appellation had stuck. The rainbow of coral-reef buildings had a gloriously haphazard appearance, until you noticed the spacial geometry that described very precise and oddly beautiful negative spaces, resembling Avalonian aquatic vegetation and animal life. An amazing work of art and architecture in one. Most astonishingly, as one walked through the buildings and looked up and around, the images shifted from one creature or plant to another, in endless array, with every shift in perspective.

"I have no idea what kind of minds could create functional art like this," Evie murmured. "Honestly, it's like an entire culture of Leonardos. Or at least M.C. Eschers. Mindblowing."

"Can we drop this building on this pathway?" Cadzie asked Piccolo.

Evie and Jaxxon looked like they wanted to kill him.

Piccolo the lapsed miner scratched his beard, looking up at the five-story honeycomb. "Lots of problems, man. We don't know the tensile strength of this material. We don't know the stress geometries—the way their design distributes weight and so forth. We know that it's lasted ten thousand years without maintenance. Maybe." He considered. "We also don't know whether there are internal supports we can't see. Whether they varied the density or composition of the material, and what kind of stresses it was designed to resist. If all of this was concrete, I'd be able to predict stress waves, so that simultaneous explosions at different points would create clashing waves of force, vibrations that could destroy load-bearing structures so that . . ."

He paused. "You do know that classic building demolitions on Earth aren't about destroying the building, right?"

"What are they, then?"

"All you want to do is reduce the building's ability to resist vertical pull. Good old gravity does the rest. Weaken the structure, and its own weight pulls it down."

"Got it."

"The same would be true with bringing down a dam— the water pressure behind it is intense. The dam has to be *very* carefully designed to distribute this stress. Change a load tolerance at any point, and it is like the water gets frisky, concentrates all its attention there, and takes it apart. The same is true with a building. You weaken key points, and the entire structure goes boom."

"And you can't do that here?"

"No. We have no idea what the structural load points might be—the geometry is too complex. Or the structural specifications of the material."

"Can you make a best guess?"

He nodded. His voice got sleepy again. "But I can't be efficient, man."

"I'll settle for effective."

◆ CHAPTER 50 ◆
A MAZE OF TWISTY TUNNELS, ALL ALIKE

Four men in power suits could haul tons of collapsed rock in minutes. What would have taken days with the best drilling machinery on Avalon would be clear in another hour.

Nothing in Tsiolkovskii's first life prepared him for this new world, and he had to keep himself focused on what he understood, not on the wonder of new technology. So despite the obvious tactical advantages of the suits, the Russian had made a decision none of his new subordinates understood: to forgo the armor.

He'd worn one for an hour, been stunned by the capacity for strength and firepower. But it would require days to begin to learn its use. Wearing the power suits was a revelation, but Tsiolkovskii had had less than an hour of practice. Taking them into the water was surreal, like cruising in a small close-fitting submarine exoskeleton. Ordinarily the suits were open to the water, but after the bee attack they had been modified and sealed.

Following his hunch, his entire force of twenty men traveled downstream. If he was wrong, and the fugitives were headed upstream into the mountains, they might be lost forever.

For a time he wasn't certain instinct had sufficed. No traces, no clues. But then he found a discarded shoe, and *knew* they were on the wrong track: he was intended to think one of his fugitives had accidentally kicked off a shoe while in frantic flight.

Tsiolkovskii in an emergency helmet and rebreather, looped onto the nylon towing cable extended from Greg Lindsey's armor, chose the other tunnel. The water was cold, had been since they first submerged. He had survived Spetsnaz survival training in a taiga forest region, and this was nothing. Another mile of almost silent propulsion and they hit an odd patch of light. He paused, and examined it. Touched it carefully, and found it a kind of glaze, almost like glass, with an embedded row of things that looked like forearm-sized, ridged spinning tops. Glowing. Could those spinning objects be power generators? Operating off the current, perhaps?

A thousand questions, with damned few answers. His father had been an engineer, and installed in him a love of natural forces harnessed to human needs. Maybe, just maybe, after this was over he'd have time to indulge his curiosity.

Another five miles, traveled in a soothing drifting timeless state, he was lulled nearly to sleep by the purr of the power armor engines. He'd always loved diving, hadn't done it for too many years before Ngorongoro. This was different, enmeshed in a technology that had not existed in his lifetime. His former life.

He chuckled to himself. It was a bit of a confusion to adjust so quickly to being in a new world, dealing with new people and places, so rapidly forced into a command role. *What did you expect, idiot? A vacation in Tahiti?* He'd known he would awaken in a strange world.

He'd just not really understood what that implied. How could he?

This was all so mysterious. So beautiful, and alien. If life would just slow down a bit. He was running on discipline alone, and inadequate data. Perhaps there would be time . . .

The tunnel turned, and they ran into a wall of rock.

"This is recent," Sergeant Lindsey said. "Some of the edges are clean, not mossed up, sir."

After the rock fall was blasted away, Anton Tsiolkovskii and his people came through, very carefully. Up to the water's surface, power armor at alert.

Before he could fully untie himself from the nylon cord, a flash of light from the corner of his eye made him dive to the side. A rock the size of his head, traveling as fast as a baseball, missed him by less than a foot and smashed into an armored soldier behind him.

"Major Stype," Tsiolkovskii said, pressed into a shadow between two oddly shaped glazed ceramic buildings. Rubble filled the alley, obscuring their view but also blocking floor-level enemy fire. Two rockets flashed from Lindsey and Major Stype, blowing a crow's-nest sniper position into splinters, rendered it to a smoking ruin. Armored snipers leaped out of the rubble and retreated. So. They *did* know how to use the armor. Good to know.

They had tested their opponents, and were ready to move to the next phase. "Enter the codes."

"Yes, sir." She spoke a series of numbers, and then a code word. Their local computer asked for verification. It was given, and received.

And elsewhere in the city Joanie's power armor locked down, the joints frozen as if rusted shut. "Holy shit!" Piccolo groaned. "My suit is dead."

"Mine, too." Shaka said.

"This isn't an accident," Cadzie said in her earpiece. "Why now?" Joanie said.

"Because they wanted to test us, see what we had in store for them. As soon as they knew we'd counted on the armor as part of our defense, they took it away."

"What do we do?" Joanie said.

Cadzie's answering made her bare her teeth. "Fight. But get out of those damned suits!"

And now the Godsons were in view.

Cadmann knew they were lost the moment he drew a bead on one of the suits . . . and it *disappeared.*

Vanished. *Oh shit. Active camouflage. How had he forgotten . . . ?*

They were well and truly screwed.

Whoville thundered with explosions, and clouds of shattered ceramic choked the air. Shots were exchanged on both sides. Enough explosives were triggered to rain tons of rock from the ceiling.

Tsiolkovskii's forces pushed them out of the city, to the rear of the immense chamber, where the colonel glimpsed a handful disappearing into tunnels.

He allowed eagerness to sweep caution aside and directed his people to pursue . . . but as they crossed an open amphitheater, shaped mining charges detonated and the floor collapsed. In an instant three armored Godson soldiers fell into a current that swept them away.

Tsiolkovskii clamped down on his rage, knowing that this had been a prime gambit, designed not only to damage but anger them, make them less careful, more vulnerable to further traps.

He would not succumb. No matter what the Starborn did, whatever stratagems they tried or surprises they might have in store, it was only delaying the inevitable. They would lose. Tsiolkovskii was adjusting faster than they could improvise, stalking them through the tubes, closing the gap, and it was only a matter of time.

A dull glow marked the path ahead. "The thermals show they went this way," Tsiolkovskii said. "The other tube is a feint."

"Mapping," he said to Stype, and the deep-scan module they'd added to her armor began reading. Every explosion in Whoville had produced waves of vibration the suits had been reading for the last hour, using real-time reflective seismology to create a 3D map coordinating all data.

The air filled with branching tunnels. Tsiolkovskii repressed his astonishment. He'd spent an hour learning this technology, at least, and understood what he was looking at. "The tunnels meet here," he said, stabbing with a finger. "Divide into two teams, and trap them."

Jaxxon was the first to run out of ammunition. He yelled "I'm out!" to his brother Jason.

They heard someone coming up behind them from the tunnel, and hid inside some kind of miniature "Whoville" building, carrying stones.

Two men emerged, neither armored. The twins grinned at each other. They had a chance.

Jaxxon was better at throwing, and his first stone hit one of the two directly between the eyes, and he dropped unconscious. Jason's stone stunned the second man so that his rifle almost dropped from his hands.

They charged, eager to get their hands on that rifle before their opponent could recover.

And that was their mistake. Colonel Tsiolkovskii hit Jaxxon with the butt of his rifle, stunning him, and hunched his shoulders so that Jason's clubbing punch hit a solid mass of muscle.

Jaxxon had swiveled to take the butt-stroke on his left shoulder, came in hard with a tackle, and the fight was on, the two brothers against the Russian.

He was older, smaller than either of them, but seemed all sharp edges and shamboo flexible strength. Anything they hit seemed to trigger a response from an unexpected direction, so fast and unpredictable that they couldn't respond effectively. They tried to sandwich him, but he always moved like a pool player lining up a shot, so that they were colliding rather than cooperating.

It wasn't possible. They were the best fighters in the

colony, and he hammered them silly. Jason watched his older brother, limping, try a flying tackle, shocked as the Russian seemed to melt away from it. It was a judo technique, which balanced mass with leverage. Or like aikido, which balanced mass with momentum and balance. Or Indonesian *fangatua* wrestling, which balanced incoming force with strength, aggression and rhythm.

The Russian seemed to fade away without moving his feet, as if his spine was a rope instead of a rod, absorbing the force and snapping it back like a rubber band, a level of relaxation under stress that judo was supposed to exhibit but rarely did, except among great masters like Mifune or Kano himself.

It was strange, almost miraculous, and had it not been for the severity of their situation, he'd have applauded and dropped to his knees begging for instruction. As was, he was still trying to stand up.

Jaxxon's hips kept going forward as he desperately twisted his shoulders trying to adjust, and as a body cannot do in two directions at the same time, Jaxxon *threw himself*.

There was no other way to put it. Somersaulted and face-planted into the rock with an agonized crunch, and was still.

Jason tried to lever his way back to standing, but wasn't halfway up when the Russian, somehow converting the momentum stored from the previous movement, slid, spun, and Jason saw the beginning of a knee lifting . . .

And then darkness.

◆ ◆ ◆

Armored, Greg Lindsey took the point position in a side tunnel, a living weapon to those in front of him, a shield to those behind.

The tunnels twisted but did not branch.

He and the two men behind him turned a corner in the tunnel and saw a beautiful sight: the stretch ahead was at least a hundred feet, and their two fugitives were only thirty feet away: no chance to miss.

"Halt!" he cried. One fugitive turned, fired a shot at them and was met with a hail of fire, jerking his body like a puppet, then a puppet with cut strings. He collapsed.

The woman behind him turned, shaking, her hand climbing into the air.

"All right," Greg called to her. "Lay on the ground—" His instructions were interrupted by a burst of fire from behind him. She gasped and sank back against the tunnel wall, then slid bleeding to the ground.

"Damn it!" he screamed. "She was surrendering! You just—"

"I zapped a bug," the soldier said. Carvey. That was the man's name. Carvey. Turning, Greg saw that the flare in Carvey's eyes was not what he'd thought. Not hunting. Killing.

"She had surrendered," Greg repeated.

"Just saved our people some time," Carvey said. "She killed my friend," he said, the soul of reason. "I just evened it up."

You don't know it was her, Greg thought but didn't say. There was another voice in his head. *Good. Death becomes her.*

But that voice was wrong. In so many ways. It was

there, and strong, but Greg knew it was stronger in Carvey.

Perhaps because he was more vulnerable, unarmored. Something had blossomed inside him, something ugly.

"Go back to base," Greg said.

"No, I—"

Greg leveled his left arm gun. "Get back to goddamn base, and keep it secure while we finish the sweep."

Cursing, Carvey did as he was told.

◆ CHAPTER 51 ◆
DIPOLES

The skeeter settled. Joe Martinez, current pad manager sighed and went out to meet them. It was Hal and Towner again. Another stinking bottom feeder?

The mappers were grinning. They moved briskly to open the cargo pod.

"What have you got?" Joe asked. He swept the tarp back. The stink wasn't bad. This body was packed in melting ice.

"Something a little different," Towner said. "No puncture wound."

Joe held his nose, and looked more closely. "Maybe Shaka will think that's interesting." He triggered his lapel communicator. "Shaka? Are you free to come over here to the pad?"

"What do you have?" Big Shaka's voice.

"Another of those *thool-hoo* things. No puncture wound, though."

"I'll be right out."

A few minutes, and Shaka limped over. "Gentlemen, what do you have for me? Yes, looks good."

"That, and this," Towner said. With a gloved hand he pulled back a flap of flesh from the marine cadaver. "Ever see anything like this?"

Shaka looked. He said, "Yes. Get that into the biology hutch, please, while I call a friend. Then tell us where you found this."

Dr. Martine was prompt. Even so, Shaka hadn't waited. This time the mappers were both hovering back, observing a mystery they considered their own discovery.

"As before," Shaka said, "we have a large amphibious creature, intact or nearly so. We agreed that these organs are electrogenerators. Dr. Martine, you agree?"

"Speculative, Shaka."

"Hal, you got a shock when you touched the corpse?"

"The first time, yes, and the second too. A little spark. Third time, it must have worn off."

"Now, Charlotte, I used the X-ray machine to look at its abdomen. There is no wound, as you can see, and there is this."

A shadow in the holoview. Martine said, "A little knob?"

"And these." Big Shaka thumbed back a flap between the cadaver's gills, its chest. "This doesn't seem to be an injury. It's a pocket, like the pocket in a kangaroo, perhaps. And these inside?"

"Two more knobs." Martine plucked one out. An ellipsoid the size of a man's finger. "Artificial. Metal, tarnished. Old, I think. This is what Aaron's killer was probing for, isn't it? But what is it, Shaka? Have you ever seen anything like it?"

"There was a hollowed pocket in the rock in the vicinity

of Aaron's corpse. It had a ceramic lid joined with some kind of flexible epoxy. We're calling it a 'lockbox.' Two more of these were in there. We're calling them dipoles. Powerful magnets, they are."

"Are we thinking that these cthulhus perform surgery?"

"Or maybe they just swallow the dipole as infants. But what if they can't make them any more? We've seen no sign that they still have these skills. They'd have to dig the things out of their dead elders."

"But why would they dig into Aaron?"

Shaka made his first incision into the marine corpse. The long silence, was broken by Towner, the white-bearded mapper. "Sign of intelligence," he said.

Martine said, "What?"

"They see we use tools. They think we think like them. It's why they don't kill us. But if we're intelligent, we must have these, um, dipoles. Only we don't."

Dr. Martine said, "I don't have any better answer. You—"

"Towner."

"Towner, where did you find the body?"

"It was on dry land again," Towner said. "Not far from the second one. Here—" Shaka had popped up a scan map. Hal pointed.

Shaka nodded. "Within twenty klicks of the spot we're calling the 'temple,' and if you'll look here . . ."

"What am I looking at?" Martine asked.

"Well . . . it isn't more than two klicks from one of the tributary underground rivers. Far from any aboveground waterway connecting with the ocean. What might be inferred from this?"

"You're hoping that they might have been involved in Aaron's death. Three cthulhus, maybe more. But three cthulhus, one badly injured, stabbed Aaron Tragon's corpse to see if he had a dipole in him. Then they . . . ran away? Crawled across land, toward a distant body of water. Why?"

"We may never know. But the timing is excellent,"

Big Shaka said. "Suggestive. Died within a day or three of Aaron. Wounded in a fight with grendels . . . look. I'm just brainstorming possibilities." He began to tick off possibilities on his fingers. "One was insane. It was injured, and went off to die. Two others robbed it afterward for its dipole. But we've never seen one of these in a situation like this, so we have to think something unusual was at play."

"Unusual? Like what?" Dr. Martine wasn't intrigued yet. She was being patient with a new friend.

Shaka knew it. He plowed on. "Something unusual happened in an unusual place. Say . . . a temple violated by an unbeliever. Led to a killing."

"So?"

"So . . ." Shaka said, "I can imagine three responses to such a thing. Honor, saying 'thank you, you did well' and praise. A neutral response, saying 'you did your job' and no real reaction."

"Hard to believe," Martine said. "If they are aware of human beings. It had to have been seen as an unusual event."

"My point. They know who we are, They have interacted with us over the years. No violent actions for a generation, after the killing in the surf, even though they've come close. Then this."

"Aaron Tragon's death."

"If the cthulhu consider that we've had a detente with them for thirty years . . . and if Aaron's death was in punishment for violation of their space . . ."

"If they approved of the killing the killers might be rewarded. And the incident might have begun a war."

"And if it was an accident? An overreaction?"

"Then . . . the perpetrators might have been punished."

"Shunned?" Shaka suggested. "Driven out of the wetlands onto territory where they would dry and die."

Dr. Martine said, "That's quite a tower of suppositions you're building. Cthulhus might have found Aaron's body, and seen it as the same opportunity we see here. First chance to examine an alien." Big Shaka nodded.

"But I'll testify to what I've seen."

"Then let's keep looking."

Dr. Charlotte Martine was the Speaker's personal appointee. As such she had not just everyone's attention, but the Speaker's too. It made her a little shy. She steepled her fingers and took a few moments before speaking.

"A pair of grendels were killed in a cthulhu temple. This fellow Tragon was killed in almost the same place and in the same way: electrocution. The cthulhus have the capacity to inflict a wound very similar to that of a grendel gun. The hole in Tragon's belly were very probably made by the same cthulhus who dug these dipoles out of their own kind, and probably for the same reason. We took one of the dipoles apart; Doctor Shaka thinks they're amplifiers for the cthulhus' magnetic sense. We have a great deal of solid evidence to back up

Doctor Shaka's speculations. Mister Speaker, you've seen
our vids—"

"I think," Sylvia said, "that that would be called
'reasonable doubt.' Is your legal system based on the *Code
d'Napoleon?* Who are you people?"

"We are the ones who will bring humanity to the stars,"
the Speaker said.

"Speaker!" Marco said.

"Narrator?"

Cameras hovered around him. Marco was clearly
orating. "I ask that you listen to them. Mistakes have been
made on both sides. But if an injustice has been done, and
we destroy those fleeing an unjust judgement, they will
be right in never trusting us again. Is this what you want?
Is this the humanity we seek to spread?"

"It is your place to record," the Speaker said. "Not to
question. Not on a matter such as this. Not now."

"If not now, when? If not me, who? For years, you've
held me up as some kind of paragon. A role model. I
received much from you, but have given much as well. I
gave *everything*. Because I believe in you. In the dream.
I've been among these people, and they are good people.
I know Cadmann, and know him to be a good man. But I
held my peace when your judgement said we had to
intervene."

The Speaker was displeased. "Narrator . . ."

"I will have my say! And if afterward you find me unfit,
you may rebuke me. But I have crossed a trillion miles,
given up all my worldly possessions and said goodbye to
everyone and everything I love in the old world, and I will
not be silent about an injustice in this one."

"Will . . . not?"

"No. I will not. We now know that we didn't know this planet, and these people do. Didn't know about grendels. About cthulhus. About harvesters and bees and *'speed.'* But what we see here is that it is entirely possible that the planet itself killed that man. And he wasn't even one of ours. We're all about vengeance, when they behaved as we might have, as I might have, given the same situation. If you knew you were innocent, wouldn't you have tried to escape? Hell, we traveled that trillion miles without any help from Earth's institutions because we were misunderstood. Are Cadmann's actions really so incomprehensible? And if his friends believe in him, as perhaps we should have, had we not been so *damned* sure that we knew better . . . wouldn't good and true friends act just as they did?"

"Our people died . . ." the Speaker said.

"They died attacking. The planet killed them."

"They were our people!"

"And you would do anything to defend them. Avenge them. In other words, these people are just like us. And you thought you had the right to interfere because they were *not* like us. How many lies are you willing to protect? How many mistakes that our grandchildren will be paying for after we are dust?"

A pause.

"Narrator Marco?" the Speaker said.

"Yes?"

"You should have won that Oscar."

They laughed, and with that the tension was broken.

"This . . . is hard for me to say. But . . . we may have made a mistake."

Sylvia grew bolder. "Call off your men. *You* are guilty of kidnapping, search and seizure, betraying your hosts and other crimes I can't even imagine right now. We welcomed you as friends. Are you really so blind? Is this how you protect humanity?"

The Speaker hesitated, thoughtful, then said: "Soldier?"

"Sir?"

"Get in touch with the hunting party."

◆ CHAPTER 52 ◆
LEVERS

West of Whoville, on a small flat shelf of rock near the "nine" on the imaginary clock, the captured Starborn sat cross-legged under the weapons of the watchful Godsons, who regarded them with a mixture of anger, satisfaction and curiosity.

Curiosity for the Starborn and also for the environment itself, the glowing cthulhu city, holding each with a measure of astonishment. Toward the Grendel Scouts, for having given a better fight than any of them expected, and the underground city, as if they had finally had the time and energy to consider where they were, and what they were seeing.

Captain Stype felt something boiling in her gut. Her part of the mission was over, but some part of her insisted that it had just begun.

Justice . . . a voice whispered.

She had climbed out of her armor, traded it to Sergeant Margo Lassiter, admiring the Russian's choice. He hadn't been stuck in a can fighting unarmored civilians, something that gave her no pleasure at all. No sense of satisfaction.

"What is this place?" she asked them. No answer. She stepped closer to the shortest of them, a woman with sullen eyes and pouty lips. "You," she said. "What is this place?"

"A city." Evie Queen's voice was dulled by defeat.

"Who pushed the button?" she asked, and thought that her voice seemed very calm and reasonable.

"What button?" Joanie asked. Beside her, Shaka tried to hiss a warning.

Stype knelt down in front of her. "I've watched you. You seem to be in control around here when Sikes isn't around. So. In the mountains. With the bees. Who pushed the button?"

Toad seemed to pull into himself, try to make himself smaller, when he was already the smallest of them all. He whimpered, just loudly enough to reach Stype's ears.

"Did you do it?" she asked, and swung her hand, cracking it hard across Toad's face. Toad tried to stay quiet, but again, whimpered.

"I asked you a question, you ugly little man—" and she did it again. Toad looked up at her, spitting blood from a torn lip, eyes glittering with fear, and he opened his mouth.

"I did it," Joanie said.

Stype's head whipped around. She let Toad go.

"What did you say?"

"I said . . . that the assholes you sent after us killed our friends. We had the right to defend ourselves."

"You did? You had the *right*?" Stype squatted close to her.

"Yeah. I killed him."

"Your ... friend. This man Sikes killed your father. And you helped him escape, and then killed for him. What kind of twisted little bitch are you?"

"I didn't enjoy it," Joanie said. "I'll leave that for twisted bitches like you."

Stype kicked her in the stomach. Two of the other Godsons pulled her back, but she was panting. "You had better be glad you've already surrendered," she said. "Because, princess ... if this was still a fight, I'd kill you. Kill you."

"Back off, Major," her men said.

Stype felt as if something was draining away from her. Some emotion that had filtered her own perceptions.

Colonel Tsiolkovskii was in pursuit of Cadmann Weyland Sikes, and that was probably how it should have been from the beginning.

She had no slightest doubt that Tsiolkovskii would bring Sikes to heel. Bring him back ... or render justice on the spot. She wasn't certain what she preferred. If captured, he would be frozen. If killed ... she would not be there to see it, might only see his torn body after the fact.

Neither was a particularly satisfying outcome.

Stype sighed, and asked Lassiter: "Do we have a signal yet?"

"No, ma'am," she said, fiddling with her equipment. "We're too far below the surface."

That was beyond annoying. Stype wanted to alert the Speaker that they were winning. Had won. And ... it was possible that that great man had words for her. But they'd have to wait until they were closer to the surface.

And she had been ordered to remain here, with her captives. That didn't sit well with her. She was not built to do nothing. She was built to move, to act.

Perhaps there were things to explore: the captives seemed under control. Was there anything useful to be determined about where they were?

That wall for instance. It was massive, probably concealing supports that kept the cave roof from collapsing on this amazing city. It was scriven with odd symbols. What if . . . what if that was . . .

Writing. Alien writing. Humanity in Sol system had never even contacted alien life, let alone intelligence. That had of course been the potential promise of their journey.

She liked this, noticing that her thoughts took her away from bloody vengeance. That was good.

She studied the wall, and noticed for the first time that there were two protrusions, one on each side of a wide rectangle graven into the rock. On closer inspection . . .

Could that be a *door*? Disguised as a bas-relief carving? Where might it lead? Another chamber . . . or perhaps a more direct access to the surface?

She had noticed that the signal strength flickered as they moved from one part of the cave to another. Could that be because there were other caves, or fissures, above them?

Major Stype reached out and grasped the lever, pulling it gingerly at first, and then harder. She felt it move, just a bit, as if there were compound gears that were easy at first, and then more difficult as they engaged more of the mass. She stopped. Odd, that. How old was this place? It was uninhabited, had been for perhaps a thousand years.

Longer. What a wonder that this lever moved at all, after all this time. Delicacy, that a single person could pull it ... but solid as well, such that a thousand years of grit had not totally jammed the mechanism. Amazing.

But when she heaved, the lever gave only two centimeters, then ground to a halt.

She looked again at the other side. At the other lever. Perhaps they were not simple redundancy. Perhaps they were designed to be pulled simultaneously? The distance was too far for human arms to reach both. Almost eight feet, beyond any human arm-span, implying that, if she was correct, the creatures who had built this city had a far longer reach than human beings ... or acted in cooperation. Were they larger than humans? No, wait, of course they acted in cooperation: look at this city!

She remembered the illustration of the squidlike "cthulhu" beings, and imagined one struggling to grasp both levers at once. Then two, in concert. Why the separation?

Some alien version of the "two-man rule"? A practical matter of gears, or a safety precaution, perhaps ... ?

"Sergeant Lassiter!" she called. "Come over here and help me."

"Yes, ma'am?"

"I suspect," she said, "that we have another passage here. Perhaps like a cargo bay, with a more direct route to the surface, in which case we might be able to get a signal."

She saw Lassiter relax with the thought. The woman's discipline was fine, but there was no real pleasure in being so far underground. The sheer oppressive pressure of a billion tons of rock weighed on them, even when they weren't thinking about it consciously.

"That would be a good thing, ma'am," Lassiter said. First she pulled on the same handle Stype had tried, until it noticeably began to bend.

"Stop. I don't think it's just a matter of force. Let's pull on both at the same time."

Lassiter went to the other lever, and began to pull. The instant they were both pulling at the same time, the pull became smoother. Again she marveled at the engineering. How many centuries? What had they been? What had been their dreams and hopes . . . ?

And one brief thought: *What might be on the other side?*

A fleeting moment of worry. Whoever had once lived here, they were surely long gone.

The glowing fish-things were here . . . and it would be reasonable to suppose that they had some relationship to the city-builders. That they had been here for millennia?

Perhaps the city was built here because of them. Or . . . perhaps they had been seeded here. Bred to provide light.

If there was something living here that might have been here for so long, might there be other things alive as well?

It was a fleeting thought. The door was moving, and behind it light flickered.

◆ CHAPTER 53 ◆
THE DOOR

The door was composed of the same substance as the wall. More like rock than cement, but she had the distinct impression that it had been cast rather than carved. Extremely fine grain, if she was correct about this. And very tightly fit. When the door was almost level with the ground, water gushed in. The water level in the next chamber was a little higher than the city chamber, but not so high as to drown them, thank goodness. And the joints were so tightly made that water didn't leak when the door was sealed, or even as it opened. How could it open so smoothly, and yet not leak? That would call for some investigating.

Stype shone her lamp into the crack between the door and the jamb. Its glittering wedge of light revealed another cave, one perhaps smaller than the cave housing the strangeness the rebels called "Whoville," but she could also see what looked like a ramp of some kind against a wall about three hundred meters distant. The beam faded beyond that, and the angle was sufficiently acute that she wasn't sure if that was the limit of the chamber, or if that apparent wall was just a rise, with greater space beyond.

The water seemed peaceful, but not stagnant. That meant that there was an egress for it, yes?

"I've got a stronger signal, Major," the sergeant said.

And that was very good news, good enough to drive other thoughts and questions from her mind. "Let's chase that down, Margo," she said.

The Grendel Scouts (what an absurd name!) were seated cross-legged, a position from which it was impossible to rise quickly. Two men with alert trigger fingers, standing ten paces away, could control the lot. She decided to call over the others to help her.

"Griffin! Takahashi! Garcia! On the double!"

The three men checked to be sure their compatriots had the Grendel Scouts under control, and hurried to her side.

"Help me," she said, and indicating the doors.

"What's on the other side of this?" Garcia asked.

"I don't know, but I'm hoping for a more direct path to the top. There are big critters up there. Maybe the cthulhus felt they needed a wall and a locked door."

"And . . . why do you want it opened?"

"Again, Corporal," she said patiently, "because we want a direct route to the surface if possible. We can't go out the way we came with our prisoners. And even as important, we need to make contact with *Messenger*." She felt her spine straighten. "We need to report success."

That helped, temporarily repressed the constant ugly buzz in the back of her mind. *Kill that bitch,* it said. *Kill her, and the rest of them too. She ambushed and murdered the man you loved.*

Discipline. You can't say "don't think of a purple cow" because just the thought demanded that you think of a purple cow. You can say: "think of a green mountain" and maybe steer clear of the cow.

So she focused on her intellectual curiosity, her sense of duty. Even the mildly oppressive sense of being crushed under a billion tons of stone, deep underground. That helped. Discipline kept that primal fear from bursting through to the surface, but she could indeed tap into it, and that effort drove the thirst for vengeance into the shadows.

The troops set to it. The faster they could discover a way out, the faster they could get the hell out of this place. They were soldiers, of a kind, not anthropologists. And even then soldiering was mostly theoretical, two years of training on leased U.N. tactical fields. Today was the first time some of them had ever fired live rounds at real human beings.

Together, they heaved on the levers. Again, Stype was stunned at the gearwork. There was no evidence that the creators had been here in centuries. Perhaps longer. And yet when both levers were pulled, it felt as smooth as if they had been oiled yesterday.

The door opened.

◆ CHAPTER 54 ◆
THE AQUARIUM

Cadzie and Trudy fled upwards through the tunnels, crawling and climbing and running for their lives. They didn't know who was behind them . . . perhaps this Colonel Tsiolkovskii she had warned him about. All he knew was that this man had peeled off from the main group after suffering losses and temporary defeats, continuing on and on like an unstoppable force of nature.

And he had little doubt that such a man, awakened after a century of cold sleep for the single purpose of murdering him, could be stopped now, after all this. And Trudy, who had betrayed her people, would be in an equally terminal position.

Before, it had been fight or be captured. Now, he was certain, it was flee or die.

Stype's sight stabbed into the darkness beyond.

Stalactites and stalagmites, water to their mid-calves but not beyond. At the very furthest extent of their lights, Stype saw a kind of ramp or slope, perhaps some natural structure that had been modified. Nothing so elaborate as the garish alien city. Built for utility, perhaps. A stairway to the surface? At the moment it even seemed *likely*.

With satisfaction, the major noticed that her urge to kill the Grendel Scouts had diminished. Tsiolkovskii would find Sikes, and she had little doubt that there would be no surrender, no peaceful frozen sleep. There would be blood, and pain.

That thought pleased her, but not as much as the thought of getting the hell out of here.

"Stay alert," she said. "Lassiter, how is the signal?"

"Better," the sergeant said. "I've actually got one."

"Then send a message, now."

Margot nodded. "This is task force 'Snow Cone' calling *Messenger*. Any relays please facilitate communication. This is task force 'Snow Cone' calling—"

A burst of static, and then a distant voice. "*Snow Cone, this is* Messenger. *What status?*"

"We have captured most of the enemy. Sikes remains at large. The colonel in pursuit, and we anticipate capture or kill shortly."

"*Urgent message: suspend operation. Repeat: suspend operation. We have good reason to believe that Sikes's story is plausible. Repeat: the Speaker now finds Sikes's story plausible. That the creatures known as 'cthulhu' are not only territorial, but capable of inflicting the wounds observed. There is now reasonable doubt as to his guilt.*"

That rocked her, more than she would have thought. If Sikes was innocent . . . then the colonists were correct in trusting him, and the Godsons had been wrong. If they were wrong . . . then they were guilty of kidnapping, wrongful imprisonment . . . and possibly worse. People had died on both sides.

By the Speaker. What a mess. It was . . .

"There's something moving out there," Garcia said. He'd said it before, but she'd been lost so deeply in her head that she hadn't heard.

"What?"

"There's something moving out there," the corporal repeated. Their lights showed nothing above the water line, but shining them down, Stype could see things that looked much like large trout. Maybe eels. Diving away from the light at times . . . but others ignored their lights, and seemed to be nibbling at the fleshy vegetable matter growing at their feet. Only now she noticed that it felt slippery, uneven.

"These fish?" she asked, already suspecting he meant something rather different. Something that triggered fear, even thought she didn't know what she was afraid of.

"How large?"

He shrugged inside his combat suit. She could see the shoulder lift. The men without the suits were more than uncomfortable. She could feel it: they were afraid. But of what? The inhabitants of this city were long, long dead. And so would be anything that had been kept on the other side of that door.

Right?

"Back out," she said. "Maintain defensive positions."

"Major, I'd estimate the life-forms approaching to be about the size of German Shepherds."

"How far?"

"I—" and that was as far as Garcia got before he

disappeared into the water as if his feet had been lassoed out from under him. The water was only mid-calf high, so it couldn't really be said that he was submerged. But the water foamed with blood and screams as at least three eels as thick as a man's thigh went after him.

They couldn't even shoot without hitting their own man. Margo Lassiter leapt in with a knife, hacking at a thing that had its jaws anchored firmly on Lassiter's face, only to be attacked in turn. The armored sergeant to her right went in, his power suit giving him enough strength to be a walking weapon. He peeled away two of the eels, crushing them in a grip like a machine press. But then—

A flurry of the things were on him, swarming until he resembled a man who had suddenly grown a dozen rubbery arms.

On land he would have kept his footing, and who knew what might have happened. But here the footing was uncertain, slippery with algae. He toppled and fell. Now he was under the water, thrashing and screaming, and the things went for him until there were more eels than armor. The things were all muscle and teeth, and something about the raw ferocity and speed of their attack made her feel her own thoughts were frozen in place.

The sheer speed of the things. Dear God. And ... and they were *peeling him out of his armor* ... and the screaming stopped.

Sergeant Lassiter backed away, just in time.

Force equals mass times acceleration. The speed of motion, with which the jaws closed, was enough to damage the armor, and then damage again, and then pierce—

"Major! We've got to get out of here!" Her men were behind her, hauling ass, and she was grateful that Lassiter had actually stopped to call to her, had remembered her, because she might have been hypnotized by what should have been an impossible sight as flecks of metal flew into the air, and then blood and bone.

Lassiter pulled her back toward the door, the water foaming black and reddish in the retreating light.

Then they were through the door, but by that time the first of the eels had reached them—

And more than eels in the waning, fractured light. *Something* was in there. A *lot* of *somethings*. Machine-gun patter of feet in water. They were coming. Fast.

"Close the damned door!" she screamed, hearing that shriek as if another woman, a smaller, weaker, woman, had babbled the words. A woman she didn't recognize. Surely not her . . .

Shock. She was in shock. She recognized it: the slow motion of tachypsychia, the disorientation, the disassociation. Her instructors had told her that recognition was the first step toward reintegration, and hopefully survival.

"Close the door!" Three men were yanking on the two levers, pushing them up, but nothing happened.

She pushed one aside, looking back at the gaping opening in the wall, the death space, from which water leaked and small, savage creatures clambered out of the wet. Something larger thundered toward them. Stype pushed with all the strength of her long powerful legs, then realized that the levers were not stuck, they were engaged in some kind of a notch, forgot that she had yanked the lever sideways after pulling it down. She pulled at it—

And the first eel was on her face. She managed to grab before its chisel teeth could set in her cheekbones, but ripping it away tore a flap of skin.

She screamed, the pain again fracturing thought. One single thought dominated everything, piercing even the pain and terror and shock. And that was the need to scream, *"Grendels!"*

Joanie was on her feet before the warning cry had finished echoing. Pure reflex, conditioned since childhood. She ran for the grendel guns before rationality kicked in and she realized that the Godsons still had them under guard. Everything seemed to be happening at slow motion, and she was aware of a voice in her head saying: *Shoot me if you want. I'd rather be shot than torn apart by monsters.*

And in that torpid state, from the corners of her eyes she saw that the other Grendel Scouts were also in motion, while the Godsons were barely reacting at all. Then her hands were on a rifle, and she spun, and as her fingers found the trigger and the first capacitor round was fired she saw that the Godson soldiers were starting to react, some slurred voice at the back of her head reassuring that their armored captors were not reacting slowly at all—it was just that the Grendel Scouts were obeying programming deeper than conscious thought.

◆ CHAPTER 55 ◆
THE COLONEL

The Starborn had fled, but also left radio-controlled mining charges as they did, keyed to numbers on their demolition controller. Cadzie had planted the last of seven just a hundred meters back along a steadily narrowing tube. "Jesus," Cadzie panted. "He's still on our trail?"

"I told you," Trudy said, her voice dull and flat. "He's the best."

Cadzie had certainly heard her say that, but the implications were just really sinking in. Denial is a powerful force. He hoped it wouldn't kill them both. "Blow the tube," he said.

"Cadzie!" It was Shaka. "We have grendels here! We're in trouble and coming your way!"

In a blink, in an instant, everything changed. He reacted as if Colonel Tsiolkovskii was no longer a threat at all.

"You stay here," Cadzie ordered Trudy. "I'm going back. They'll need my help."

"Hell if I am. Those are my people. All of them."

"*Sikes!*" That was Tsiolkovskii's voice, in their radio. "*The situation has changed. Repeat: the situation has changed. We have been alerted that the Speaker now believes you to be innocent. Something has gone wrong in the city below. The creatures you call 'grendels' are attacking both our groups.*"

"If this is a fucking bluff—"

"*On my honor, it is not. I am going back down to lead the way. I am not asking you to come down. It is too late for that. I am asking you to go ahead and clear the way. Find a place for us to make a stand.*"

Cadzie's mind raced. "What should I be looking for?"

"*A narrow tunnel we can collapse after our people are through. Hopefully access to the surface, an escape route. Or at least a way to get a radio signal to the surface so that we can get a rescue party down to us if we can't get up top ourselves. Have you got anything you can use to leave markers for us?*"

"I'm just supposed to trust you now?"

"*I served in the same war with your grandfather, Sikes. He was an officer and a gentleman. And on my honor as an officer, I swear I'm telling you the truth. Your grandfather would respect that oath, and believe me.*"

Cadzie glanced at Trudy, who nodded, ever so slightly. She believed him.

"All right," Cadzie cursed under his breath, praying he was not making the worst mistake of his life. "I can cut arrows into the wall at every turn, and flares when possible."

"*That will have to do. Get to it. Tsiolkovskii out.*"

♦ CHAPTER 56 ♦
RETREAT

In no more than an hour, Joanie's world had changed so many times that she could barely think. From free, to a seesaw battle, to flight, to being trapped, to surrender. Fear that they would be executed... followed by stern, but fair treatment accompanied by grudging respect... barring that lunatic Stype.

And then the most savage and deadly reversal imaginable, when human beings ceased being adversaries as they scrambled for safety through a city scarred by rocket shells, and now swarming with carnivorous eel-like samlon. Most were no larger than medium-sized dogs, but a few were fully grown adult carnivores. They snapped at each other in warning, but what they really wanted, what they craved, was any flesh not their own.

"Retreat!"

The scream was given over and over again, echoing from the toothed ceiling, splintered by the narrow spaces of Whoville's ancient, abandoned honeycomb.

They ran, and she saw a Godson pulled down by things

that swarmed him, gave him no chance to fight back, barely a chance for anything but gargled screams.

Jason helped Jaxxon along. The older brother seemed stunned, foggy-headed, probably concussed. Half his face was scraped and scarred, and he'd lost a tooth.

No one would ever have trouble telling elder from younger Tuinukuafe brother. That was . . . if they survived this dreadful day.

The creatures seemed not to have full control of *speed*, losing footing and overshooting their marks, the only thing that kept her alive as eels shot past her, smacking their heads into the rock walls. If they couldn't flip back onto their feet instantly their brothers and sisters forgot their preference for human flesh and fell onto them ravenously.

Waste not, want not, she thought to herself. There was a mad giggle in there somewhere.

Then she was into one of the tunnels, an armored Godson behind her. In that narrowed space the automatic weapons fire was devastating against the horde, so that as she ran, and then scrambled along a ridged floor, the earsplitting, sharp percussive sounds behind her were a comfort, signaled the possibility of survival.

Jaxxon crawled painfully after Jason along the tube in front of her, and as it narrowed had to wiggle on his belly to stop bumping his head along the ridged ceiling.

Behind her, a scream and the sound of automatic weapons fire. And then thunder that shook walls and floor.

Jaxxon stopped and looked back over his shoulder. In the flashlight glare, his torn and bleeding brown face was furrowed and flat, pulled back in a mixture of fear and rage: combat face. *War mask.*

She'd seen it on Landing Day, when he and his brother performed a traditional Maori Haka war dance. That had been a game, something that they had learned from videos. This was different.

He pressed himself against the wall. There was little room, but he waved at her. "Squeeze past," he said, voice a rumble. "I'm going back."

"Joanie, don't!" Jason called back. "He doesn't know what he's saying!"

"Hell if I will," she said. "Keep going. You aren't dying heroically today, asshole."

He glared at her through a crimsoned mask, but turned and kept climbing.

The retreating Starborn and Godsons scrambled on hands and knees through a narrowing tunnel. The grade was about twenty percent, and slippery wet, but ridged so that they were able to get enough purchase to continue the climb.

The world shook.

"What is *that*?"

Another explosion behind them.

"What the hell?" Joanie said.

They heard a cough ahead, and a scratching sound, and from around a bend Cadzie's head appeared. "What's happening?" he asked.

"Colonel Tsiolkovskii is bringing up the rear. I think that he may have set off a detonation, collapsed the tunnel."

◆ CHAPTER 57 ◆
STRATEGY

They'd gathered at Zack's comfortably cluttered office, where they could use the electronics. Big Shaka's face and mood had soured. "It makes sense. If the Godsons think the cthulhus had something to do with Aaron's death . . . and can be . . . I don't know . . . reasoned with? That there might be something there that they can use? If we trust that they know what they're doing, then the cthulhus are allies. And they're going to need them."

"But . . . the attack has been called off." Carlos said.

"Do we know if that message has been received? If it *can* be received?" Sylvia asked.

"We don't know," Shaka said. "But we have another problem. Look at this."

An image appeared of an alpine pasture, ringed with mountains.

"This is the territory above that magnetic anomaly? This 'underground city'?" Sylvia said.

"It is. But *Messenger* achieved a deep scan just twenty minutes ago, looking for thermal signatures."

The image changed. Scribes, visible from orbit. As the

deep scan sank in, smaller ovals moving below them: the ecology that accompanied them. The scan focused through the crust. Darkness, and then a few vaguely human-shaped red blobs. Deeper. Scuttling crimson reptilian shapes, followed by additional levels of dark tunnels and rock, down and down to a cavity large enough to swallow Camelot's central colony . . . and on one side of it, a seething mass of red.

"What is that?" Carlos said, pointing. "Geothermal heat?"

"That's what we thought at first. But we did a higher resolution scan. Bring this up ten times, please."

The red differentiated into a crawling mass of horror. Refined again, as the computer analyzed and clarified until they were looking at something terribly familiar.

"Oh no," Carlos said. "Oh shit."

"We don't know what this place is. Whether it is natural or artificial. But there are hundreds of them."

"*Hundreds?*" Carlos groaned. "Grendels?"

"Not on *speed*, I don't think. The heat isn't intense enough. Not most of them. And we don't think they're mature, either."

"Note that they have a sort of Brownian motion in all directions, but compress at this point, here? Here's another scan," Little Shaka said.

The image changed.

"A wall?" Shaka said. "Not a natural barrier. And apparently composed of a composite substance. Built to keep them out of the city?"

Carlos nodded. "I'd think so, yes. Then the kids are safe, yes?"

"We can hope so. Have you seen this inventory of what the Godsons were carrying in with them?"

"Sure."

Shaka grimaced. "Did you see the explosive rounds? Armor piercing rounds?"

"Yes . . . oh, God."

"Yes," Shaka said. "Oh God indeed yes, that's one of the things that might have happened. Imagine a pitched battle. Just one of those shells going in the wrong direction."

"The wall has lasted thousands of years . . ."

Shaka frowned. "In a geologically stable region. We have a problem. And part of the problem is that we don't even know if our message can reach them. We don't know how long it will take to reach them."

"We have rescue on the way?"

"Yes, but through the mines?" Shaka asked, clearly sceptical. "Hours in the water. And if the wall was keeping them back, it is reasonable to assume that the breach has exposed the grendel breeding chambers . . ."

"Breeding chambers?"

"Not a poor assumption. Our best current hypothesis is that cthulhu may have bred the grendels. Supplied them with parasites to increase their intelligence. Depending on how important they considered grendels to be . . ."

Sylvia was not happy. "Anyone who kept dangerous animals that close by would have to have had a damned good reason."

"Agreed," Shaka said. "Anything from biologicals to tactical defense capabilities to . . . I don't know. Food?"

"Food?" Sylvia was even less pleased.

Shaka shrugged. "We eat samlon."

Sylvia's face soured. "Never again. Go ahead."

"The collapse of the wall could give grendels access to the underwater tunnels. Imagine our rescue troops running into a murder of grendels. Underwater." The idea was pure nightmare. "I'm sorry, but that's a nonstarter. We can't take a risk like that."

"What else can we do?" Sylvia said.

"The surface. We may have to drill down from the top. We anticipated that when we were worried about collapsing the roof on the city. Now we're worried about collapsing it on our people."

"What was the time frame?"

"Days," Shaka said. "The Godsons might have better equipment . . . on *Messenger*. Bringing it down, mounting it . . ."

"*Madre Dios*. They might only have hours."

The door slammed open. Trevanian ran in, holding a sheet of paper. His hand trembled as he combed them through a mop of pale hair. His face looked drained of blood. "We've got a message!"

"From the Starborn?" Sylvia asked.

Trevanian shook his head.

"This Russian colonel?" Carlos asked.

Again, a negative response. "Well, who, then?"

Trevanian swallowed, hard. "Umm . . . I don't know quite how to say this, but I think it's from the cthulhus."

◆CHAPTER 58◆
LANGUAGE LESSONS

The communications shack was packed so tightly the air felt thick enough to drink.

"Look at these messages," Big Shaka said. "Came in from Cassandra, routed through the dolphin system."

"The . . . what?" Dr. Martine asked.

"The dolphin speech project," Shaka said. "We brought a pod of adult dolphins in cold sleep, and a thousand embryos."

"Why adults . . . ?" Martine asked, and then seemed to figure it out for himself. "Because they spoke the language, and embryos wouldn't. Did you crack it? I remember that Earth hadn't, by the time we left."

"We've made strides. A vocabulary of about three hundred words," Trevanian said. "And apparently, the dolphins have been talking to the cthulhus."

The implications were obvious. "Let's see the message."

"Remember . . . it went from cthulhu to dolphin to Cassandra to us. Everything about it is questionable."

And on the screen, the words: *"Your children in danger. They fight each other. They free the grendels."*

"Free the grendels?" Carlos groaned, disbelieving. "Who would be stupid enough..."

"Cassandra," Sylvia asked. "Can you send a message?"

"To the dolphins, yes. If they can speak to the cthulhus..."

"Do your dolphins have...I don't know how to put this, but...a sense of humor?"

"You think they might be playing a joke?"

"Joke, maybe," Trevanian said. "But not a cruel one."

"Fair enough. Cassandra, send a message: can you help them?"

The message was sent. They waited.

"So...it goes from here, to Cassandra to the dolphins to the local cthulhus...to the mainland? How?"

"We don't know. But whales can communicate for over a hundred kilometers. There are theories that suggest they actually had a world-spanning network."

"But that's in water..."

"And we're dealing with an alien species. We just don't know."

And then they had a response: *Give us back magnets.*

"Magnets? What magnets?"

"Holy crap," Trevanian said. "Are they talking about the dipoles?"

Quick conversation. "We can return them..."

"Wait a minute," Martine said. "What is the chemical composition of these dipoles?"

Cassandra answered. "According to spectroscopic analysis, iron and trace minerals."

The doctor smacked her hand on the table. "Then we can make a hundred of these things. More. Tell them we can manufacture what they no longer can!"

They did. And a moment later they received an answer. *"We can merge."*

◆ CHAPTER 59 ◆
REVENGE OF THE ANTS

As a boy in Minsk, Anton Tsiolkovskii and his older brother Mikhael had owned an ant farm made of a blue nutrient gel. They had not needed to add either food or water, and a pale light at the bottom of the display allowed him to see what they were up to at all times. The little black insects had been able to eat their way through the gel, making their living spaces as they did. Fascinating. The tunnels looked a little like the swirls one sees in water when you pull the plug in a basin. Branching, looping, joining and breaking away.

He and Mikhael had watched for endless hours, and then Mikhael had had an inspiration. He'd begged their father to buy a second one, and deliberately populated it with red ants instead of black, after researching to be sure the nutrient gel would sustain them. After weeks, when they had built a civilization of equal complexity, he watched with wide-eyed fascination as Mikhael rigged a plastic tube connection between the two farms, so that the two civilizations collided.

What fun they had had! Watching the black and red ants swarming through each others' tunnels, fighting as each sought to protect their swollen egg-laying queen, or attack the enemy matriarch.

And while their father had caught Anton and Mikhael, ending the fun before the conclusive battle, he had never forgotten the cramped, lethal battles, red and black insects tearing each other to pieces in the cramped spaces.

And now, a hundred and forty years later, he was crawling through tunnels hunted by reptiles instead of insects . . . but that old memory, something that had not crossed his mind in a hundred and thirty of those years, was close at hand.

The branching tunnels, the frantic flight. He was the ant. And something that his father had said about the sanctity of life, about not deliberately causing more pain than the world forced upon us came to mind.

He and his long-dead brother Mikhael had inflicted war upon the ants, death in the glowing blue tunnels. How ironic that he would probably die scuttling like an insect on a planet far from Earth.

The last of the humans had scrambled out of the tunnel, up the ridged floor crawling on hands and feet. Rather than widening, the tunnel had narrowed, so that the last of Tsiolkovskii's power-suited soldiers were forced to stay behind. One had been able to strip himself out of his armor and wiggle ahead, but the others were trapped, bottling up the tunnel until their ammunition was exhausted. Would they be trapped there, indefinitely? Would the grendels respect a wall of shattered corpses, their dead brothers and sisters, as had the ravaging red ants? Of course not. They'd chew their way through to reach the humans trapped in now-useless armor.

"Lindsey?" Tsiolkovskii asked, speaking into his communicator with a kind of deliberate calm. "Can you hear me?"

"I hear you, sir."

"What is your situation?"

"I . . . I'm out of ammunition, but was able to use the suit's mech servos to collapse the tunnel around me."

Tsiolkovskii's hands tensed. "Who's with you?"

"Tanaka and Ives, I think. I think . . . I think those bastards got Al Asad. He was below me."

"How did they kill him?"

Lindsey seemed to swallow. "Peeled him out of the armor. He was jammed up against Tanaka, and Tanaka was . . . is . . . pushed up against me."

Lindsey was scared. It was easy for him to admit that, now. In fact, he almost seemed to be afraid to the precise degree that, prior to this moment, he had felt invulnerable in the armored suit.

He had never served in the United Nations force, but had worked in security for several corporations, and had been involved in enough high-stakes "events" that the Godsons had considered him to have the equivalent of actual military service.

And that, in combination with his other qualifications and long-standing good behavior reports within the organization itself, had led him to being chosen for this mission. To travel across the galaxy, to seed the stars!

What an honor. The *ultimate* honor. No human activity, from the building of the pyramids to the splitting of the atom, was a fraction as important.

When he'd seen the power armor, he'd known he'd found his calling. The very first time he'd put it on, he'd felt a surge of power unknown to him, or any previous human beings.

Invulnerable. Irresistable. He was told that the armor could resist most small-arms fire and even a light armor-piercing round. That it had a resistance of 5500 psi, stronger than the jaws of a Nile crocodile, the strongest bite or grip of any earthly creature.

So he'd felt comforted, pursuing the Starborn. Traveling though the flooded tunnel on filtered recirculated air had been an adventure. Emerging into the caves he felt like the aggressive predator he was, a god of war raining death on the transgressors who had dared resist him.

That conviction had only swollen when they trapped the colonists, and then offered them terms of surrender. That thing . . . that thing in his head that had swollen with joy to have the opportunity to hunt resented that. He heard a voice: *Don't I get to finish this? Don't you want me to . . . want me to . . .*

Finish it.

A better, softer word, than *kill*.

It was simple human nature that the more you enjoyed something, the more you would practice it, and think about it. And the more you practiced and obsessed about something, the better at it you became. So . . . if there were security forces tasked with protecting the Speaker and his flock, it made sense for them to actually enjoy the hunt. The kill.

And Lindsey did.

Howling through the tunnels, hounding the terrorists, all good.

And even seeing them submit, knowing that a mistaken twitch of a finger could send bullets tearing through their flesh . . . still good. He began to cool down, forced his way back from the edge of the abyss, and took pleasure in that, too. *See? I'm in control.*

He'd been called to help the major open that door, and the tickle of danger was delicious. He hadn't had the chance to kill an Avalonian life form much bigger than a terrestrial dragonfly, hadn't gone on the now notorious grendel-hunt. He craved an opportunity to face one of these creatures that had so terrified the Starborn and their parents.

So when *something* had exploded out of the water, and dragged down one of his companions, he had been momentarily frozen in place. What was this creature, why was it dangerous, how could it be lethal to an armored human?

He'd not believed it. Couldn't believe his senses. This simply couldn't be happening . . .

When he believed, he fled.

Firing back at the horde of swarming creatures was such a confusion to him, fear and primal hunger mingled, and not an emotion he had ever experienced, or been trained to deal with. Through the city and into the tubes, at first, what? Lava tubes? Water erosion? Something wide enough for two men to fight side by side, then narrowing so that he had to fire over Tanaka's shoulder.

Then they were just fleeing, discipline broken. A feeder tunnel branch joining with theirs and yielding another refugee, a Jordanian named Al Asad, his panicked face telling them without words that there was no safety to be found in its darkness.

There were three of them running, and then crouching, and then crawling as the tunnels narrowed, and then to his horror he was caught, squeezed, trapped in the very metal that had protected him. Al Asad screamed and screamed as the grendels peeled him out of his armor and stripped him to the bone from the feet up, eeling their way through the bloody scraps of metal, and went to work on Tanaka.

Lindsey panicked. He hit the emergency breach command on his suit, and the shoulders and faceplate parted, giving him just enough room to begin to wiggle out of the power suit.

By the roar of machine pistols and the flash of rocket launchers, the Godsons fought a retreating battle through the twisting, coral-colored spires of the abandoned alien city, wasting shells on a flood of creatures completely undeterred by the gunfire. They didn't dodge, perhaps not even relating the flashes of fire to the exploding bodies around them, or even their own pain.

And the armor? Incredibly, the armor didn't help. Not enough. The creatures slammed into his compatriots and bowled them over, and chewed and chewed until the metal shredded into splinters under the pressure and speed of the biting, and human meat was revealed within the rigid shell, a meal for monsters.

The sounds of their shrieks still resonated in his ears.

Tanaka had stopped screaming.

Lindsey, crawling loose, felt his abandoned armor wiggle under his foot. He reached back and pulled. Without him in it, the armor had shrunk in on itself. It slid loose.

Pulling the armor behind him, he pushed further ahead: if the tunnel narrowed he was dead, just dead. The armor would slow him, but it was too much a part of him to be abandoned. And now he wasn't blocking Tanaka. "Get out of your suit!" he screamed behind him, knowing Tanaka was dead.

Where the tunnel widened, he crawled back into the suit, begrudging every moment it slowed him.

The cthulhus were smaller or more flexible than men in suits, and as he put all his power into smashing into one of the walls, it finally crumbled. He had broken through to a parallel tunnel. He scrambled forward as the tearing sounds behind him grew louder, and the hiss and snap of monsters signaled the beginning of nightmare.

Lindsey clawed his way into a larger tunnel, scrambled around and fired at the walls behind him, creating a cave-in, and then laid back and felt his heart hammer in his chest, knowing that the creatures hunting him would get through, in time.

But for now he was still alive, and that was enough.

When the last of the main group made it into the cave, Cadzie regretfully weighed the cost of human lives if he left the tunnel open, compared to sealing it now. When the first grendels began to emerge, it was no decision at all.

"Seal the tunnel!" Cadzie screamed. "Blow the roof!"

The men fired six explosive shells into the ceiling, bringing it down.

"Back! Back!" Joanie screamed.

As the dust settled they could hear something scrabbling behind the fall of rock, but prayed that it was a grendel and not a desperate human being.

"Will this hold?" Tsiolkovskii asked. The man seemed like a golem. Heavy-muscled. All potential energy. Or by that did he mean violence?

"Depends on a lot of things," Cadzie speculated. "For instance: is there another way in? How badly do they want to reach us? I don't know, but there are others I've not thought of."

"And meanwhile," Tsiolkovskii said, "we're trapped here." The cave was about a third the size of the main cavern, but still large enough to have an impressive array of stalactites and stalagmites.

"Can you reach your people?"

"I don't think so. Not with our communications gear." He checked his gauges.

"Then yeah, we're trapped here."

A few human beings were backtracking and finding their way through branching tunnels heading up toward the surface, but whether by instinct or intent, or accident, so were grendels.

Major Stype emerged into a cave the size of a mansion, surprised to see the man Lindsey whom they thought they'd heard die, crouching beside a stream twenty meters away. But when grendels zip-slithered through the tunnels right behind her, she reacted instantly, firing explosive rounds into the tunnel ceiling to seal them.

A ton of crashing rock later, there they were, trapped.

"At least we have running water," Shaka said, with little real enthusiasm.

After they had circumnavigated the cave, studying it for potential sites of egress, two dozen survivors settled into groups, sharing supplies of food and scooping water from the stream. The two armored humans took turns guarding the sealed tunnels, or kept an eye on the stream. Something deadly might emerge.

Cadzie felt utterly exhausted. He was cleared of a crime, and sentenced to death. This was just priceless. Tsiolkovskii squatted next to him. On his heels, perfectly balanced, as if he was a statue who could pose like that for a hundred years.

They had recognized each other at once, out of the two converging groups. Eyes met, then they'd continued their inspection of their refuge/prison. A moment's rest, now.

Tsiolkovskii broke the silence. "You're Cadmann Sikes."

"Yes. Colonel T?"

"Why did you do it, Cadmann? It was just cold sleep. You'd have come out . . ."

"With ice on my mind, in time for reeducation? No thank you. Risk hibernation instability?"

"What?" The Russian seemed genuinely surprised.

"Hibernation instability. There's a ten percent chance on first awakening, and that risk doubles with every refreezing."

"What are you talking about?"

"They didn't tell you?" Cadzie said, incredulous. "They woke you up, and you seem all right."

"Yes. But this isn't our final stop. I'm . . . we were supposed to awaken in rotations."

"And I suppose they did, until they heard from us."

Tsiolkovskii considered carefully. Then he began to speak. "If you're telling the truth, then I was spared awakening during the journey, but will have to go back to sleep and be reawakened when we reach Hypereden." This cold, calculating man's face tightened. A brief moment of fear.

"I'll be damned," Cadzie said. "You're human."

The news seemed to have rocked the older man. "I'm not crazy. I can't go back to cold sleep."

"Surprise surprise surprise," Cadzie said. And it was not the best part of him that enjoyed Tsiolkovskii's dismay.

◆ CHAPTER 60 ◆
ICE

"What do we do now?" Cadzie asked glumly. He picked up a chunk of stone and sailed it out across the water.

"Survive," Tsiolkovskii answered.

"I don't know any way out of this maze," Cadzie said. "I . . ." He felt something cold and slippery in his throat. All his life, he'd been the golden boy. Prince of the colony, presumptive king, just step up. Gifts of physical and mental skill from the grandfather he'd never known, inheritor of all this world had to offer. Tap dancing his way out of everything. Accused of murder? Acquitted. Yanked to trial and railroaded anyway? Rescued.

Alone against bred warriors and super technology? Why, his parents died to give him a weapon strong enough to kill anything. And if the men from beyond the stars go berserk, why his friends would lay down their lives for him, follow him into hell.

Because he was Cadzie. And now, he'd run out of room to dance, and it was all ending. Everyone would die, because of him. No answers.

And soon there would be no questions, either. Just . . . death.

And then . . .

A black and glistening *something* rolled up out of the water. Cadzie froze, only his eyes moving as he affirmed that no one else in the cave was seeing what he was seeing.

He locked eyes with Joanie, and moved them toward the water. "Shhh."

Unmistakably now, a black, eyeless, squid shape, like something formed out of wet leather.

"What the hell is that?" Tsiolkovskii asked.

"That . . ." Shaka said as he came to his feet, "is a cthulhu."

Its tentacles curled and uncurled, seemed to be beckoning to them.

"Is it intelligent?" Then it hit him. "They built the city?"

"We think so, yes."

"What does it want?"

It dove down. Came back up, dove again. He'd seen dolphins do the same. "Maybe for us to follow it?" Cadzie said.

"Are you insane?" Tsiolkovskii asked.

"If he isn't," Joanie said, and started stripping down. "I am. I'll go."

Tsiolkovskii was beyond doubtful. "Those things breathe water. It doesn't know that you don't."

"We've observed them. They've observed us. I think they know what we are. And . . . what we aren't."

Joanie stripped down, sleek and muscular in her shorts.

"I'll go," Cadzie said.

"And I just trust that you'll come back?"

"I'm not being held for anything, Colonel."

The Russian tensed and then relaxed, knowing that his former enemy was right.

Joanie and Cadzie followed their host.

They traveled the tunnel until their lungs were bursting. They swam with light-sticks in either hand, their alien guides leading the way and then nudging toward an air pocket above them. They swam for it, and broke the surface in an eight-inch gap between water and roof.

"Thank God," Joanie gasped, her forehead brushing the rock ceiling.

"Were you about to explode?" Cadzie asked.

"Just about. You?"

"I think I could have held out another ten seconds or so."

"Think about it," Joanie gasped. "They knew just how long we could hold our breaths."

"Hope to God. Where do you think they're taking us?"

"I don't know," Cadzie said.

They dove back down into the water. Twice more, they surfaced and breathed in air pockets. And then . . .

Emerged in a chamber that was bitterly cold. They splashed the light around and it reflected back from ice-sheathed walls. A second squid shape waited there.

"An ice cave?" Joanie asked. "We're in the high desert . . . I guess that's possible. Still seems strange, though."

"Why did they bring us here?"

The ceiling was very high. Almost a hundred feet away.

But stunningly, and beyond any doubt...in the very center of the roof above them glowed an open circle of sunglazed white clouds.

"Oh my God," Cadzie said. "It's the sky."

"Could you get up there?" Joanie asked. Freedom. Safety, shimmering just beyond their reach.

"Maybe," Cadzie said. "If I had to."

"We could get a message out. We could get our people out."

"If we could get up there." He paused, calculating in his head. "I think I can do it. Listen. You think you remember where those air pockets are?"

"I'd better," she said soberly.

"You go back and get the others. At least one of the armored boys—they have com links built into their gear. Lead them here. Leave light-sticks at the air pockets. Either I can rig up to get us out through the top, or we can at least collapse that tunnel."

"Last stand?"

"If that's what it takes," Cadzie said.

"And you?"

"I'm going to try to find a way to climb up. Get going."

Cadzie approached one of the two cthulhu. It waited until he came close, close enough that its dark, wet-leather flesh trembled visibly, as in some form of respiration. "I don't know if you can understand me, but...thank you."

A third appeared, this one carrying something in its mouth. Something slender and flexible, and when he recognized it he almost laughed. And then he did laugh.

The creature spat rope out onto the ground, a three-foot length trailing back into the water. When he bent to pick it up, the creature fluttered back away.

With the coil of rope in his hand he felt better.

Altogether it was perhaps fifty feet. With a label on one end. This was Godson rope, abandoned somewhere on their journey in the caves.

He gazed up at the ceiling. Another of the creatures arrived, carrying more rope. And then another. They gazed at him with expressionless black eyes.

Smiling, breathing more easily than he had in days, he tied the ropes together and hefted them. Over a hundred feet, yes it was.

"Thank you," he said to them, hoping that they could understand words, or tones, or what was in his heart. "You are good, good friends."

No response. None was needed. "Well," he said. "Climbing time. Let's see what I remember. Upsie."

Joanie burst up out of the water into a breathing bubble, blowing hard. "Oh, Joanie. What are you doing?" she whispered, aware that no one was listening. She dove back down into the water. She was tired by the time she reached what she had already begun to call "Water Cave" and it took a minute of deep breathing for her to recover. She was fit, even for a Starborn, but the last stressful days had taken more out of her than she'd reckoned.

She needed two more bubbles to reach the first cavern. When she crawled up on the land, they gave her a minute to catch her breath, then peppered her with questions. "What did you find?" Shaka asked.

"Everything. Maybe a way out."

"Outstanding. We'd almost given up."

"No way. I'm harder to kill than that."

"The tunnel connects to an ice chamber."

"Ice chamber?" Tsiolkovskii asked.

"Don't ask. Here's the thing: there's a hole in the roof, right?"

"A hole . . . right!" Shaka asked.

"What does this mean?"

"It means we hit the jackpot," she answered. "Tsiolkovskii, I need one of your men."

"Sergeant Lindsey," the Russian called. "On the double."

◆ CHAPTER 61 ◆
CLIMBING

Cadzie had tried three different routes by the time Sergeant Lindsey emerged from the water, armor dripping, like some kind of ancient knight of an underwater round table.

He dropped to the ground from twelve feet, landing in a crouching *whoof*, slipping on the icy ground then catching his balance.

"What is the situation?" Lindsey asked.

"I've been trying to free-climb and not getting far. I'm scaling the inside of a frozen bowl. But we've got rope!"

"I can do this," Lindsey said, and Cadzie was treated to the sight of Lindsey's armor shaking like a dog on two feet, water spraying in all directions.

Confident, Lindsey approached the curving wall. He bent his armored legs and jumped twelve feet into the air, his hands digging into the rock wall. He punched his right hand in with a karate-like spear hand, and Cadzie heard the servos as he pulled himself up to punch in his left. It was looking pretty damned impressive when the rock itself crumbled, and Lindsey tumbled to the ground.

Oof.

Lindsey pulled himself up, and began a more conservative climb. Again, he only got up a dozen feet before the rock crumbled and he fell.

Oof.

Lindsey looked at Cadzie. "What the hell?"

"I . . . um . . . how much do you weigh in that suit?"

For the first time, Lindsey seemed to grasp the problem. "Twelve hundred pounds," he said. "Give or take."

"The rock won't hold the weight," Cadzie said.

"So . . . what stopped you from making the ascent?" he asked, looking up at the ceiling, and the sky that now seemed impossibly far away.

"I can't free-climb that distance on a negative incline. I'd need pitons to connect the ropes to."

Lindsey did a quick scan of his suit, the schematics playing on his face plate.

"What are you doing?" Cadzie asked.

"Seeing if there is anything in this suit that might work. I mean a part, something we can disconnect."

But there was nothing. They were running out of time.

The water thrashed again: three cthulhus appeared. Cadmann held Lindsey back as they climbed out of the water, octopoid limbs moving with an almost absurd delicacy as they first brushed the humans' torsos and then crossed the cave to the wall, hauling ropes behind them.

Avalon factory-made ropes, scavenged from the caves.

Together, Cadzie and one cthulhu climbed, the alien's mucilage-tipped limbs giving it peculiar purchase. It reached something Cadzie had not seen, some kind of protrusion on the wall, masked by the darkness. It fiddled there a while, and when it was done, the rope hung secure. Cadzie climbed. As he did, the cthulhu went on to the next spot on the dome, and anchored a rope there.

When he reached the top of the first anchor point, he found a declivity with a curved piece of sculpted rock. Had it been intended for ropes? Why would creatures who could climb like this need ropes?

He was able to crouch there and catch his breath, braced with one foot on the ledge, a leg on a crack, and his hands pressed against rocky protrusions for balance. He waited, and as he did, he examined the way the cthulhu had anchored the rope. Some mass of mucilage, combined with a crazy knot that looked as if the rope had been chewed and regurgitated into place. Before he could examine more closely, the next rope was ready, and he climbed.

That process repeated three times, and by then there were no more ropes, but Cadzie was in the chimney, able to brace arms and legs and shimmy up.

He looked down. Trudy had appeared, and was climbing up as strongly as Cadzie had, very efficient and disciplined. Greg Lindsey was next, climbing in his armor, below Trudy in case he pulled something free.

Everything held.

One grueling foot at a time, Cadzie, Trudy, and Greg made the climb up the chimney. Trudy had perfectly decent technique, and better hand-grip endurance.

Greg Lindsey was having a hard time of it. He'd pulled muscles in his legs and ribs, in the fight. Even with the armor, the awkward angles were a strain. Cadmann kept him just behind him anyway, in case he needed a man in armor.

Greg saw light filtering down past Cadmann. Daylight? And a muted roar. Lindsey asked, "What's that sound?"

Cadmann listened. "Buzzing." A moment later, "It isn't bees."

Lindsey and Trudy behind him, both said, "Good."

They climbed another dozen feet. Daylight grew brighter. And sound. "It can't be a lawn mower," Lindsey said.

"A what?" Cadzie's head lit up, rising into open air and sunlight.

"Never mind, it's too loud. A harvesting combine? How could—"

"How could a freezing harvester get up this high? But I'm looking at a mile of blue wall. Cadzie blue. Give me room, I'm coming back down." Cadmann backed up a few feet, crowding Lindsey, and hunched his back.

The roar reached a crescendo. Shadow fell, and a shower of dirt and chopped grass. Then a beast's long blue lip slid over the hole, and onward, and passed. Cadmann said, "Scribe."

"My armor has cameras," Lindsey said.

"Okay, slide past me, but watch it. Big Shaka says there's a thriving ecology under one of these. No grendels, though."

Lindsey slid up into shadow, into dusk and a smell like his grandfather's farm. Cadmann's head and shoulders followed.

A narrow line of light was all around him, blocked by

massive . . . those pillars must be legs, four thick legs. Something not quite so huge, like a giant flattened crab, stopped eating long enough to stare at him with tiny eyes.

Rats. That was the only way he could describe them. Rats burst from a pile of . . . that must be the smell of . . . scribe dung. The bottom of the scribe's shell was just above his arms' reach, and sliding forward at a lazy stroll. The rats ran for the scribe's trailing edge and stopped abruptly at the edge of daylight.

The roar of a scribe chewing veldt grass and shamboo continued.

Lindsey turned on his armor's lights. Suddenly there was action everywhere. A ghost-white snake twenty feet long was coiled around a nest of a dozen smaller snakes, all crawling forward. Four more great flat crabs . . . baby scribes . . . shied away from the light. Cadmann yelled, "Turn it off! Lindsey, they came under here to hide from sunlight! You'll drive everything crazy!"

Lindsey turned off his light. There was enough daylight to see . . . creatures, some limbless, some eyeless, settling down now. "Come on up," Lindsey said. "I think we're safe. Let me go first under the aft edge. I want to see what's out there."

"Good. Trudy, you next. Keep your grendel guns ready. This thing is going to have parasites. Lindsey, did you look up?"

He hadn't, not enough. There were bulges scattered across the undershell, pretty much at random.

No eyes. "Something like remoras? I'm going to—" Lindsey walked under one of the bulges, ready to reach up. The parasite struck first, with one long multi-jointed pincer-tipped arm. Lindsey jumped, then wrenched the arm loose and threw it aside. A toothy mouth gaped futilely.

"Good call, Cadmann. Stay away from bulges overhead. They must feed on whatever wanders under them."

Trudy asked, "Did you miss anything else?"

Cadmann said, "Never mind. Get outside and tell us what's there, Lindsey. The channel will be outside in two or three minutes."

The beast's trailing edge was close. Lindsey had to duck.

Dung rained on him until he was wading through it. "Shit," he called back. "Seriously." Then he was outside, in dung and close-cropped grass and a scatter of wiggling things, like flat-shelled snails. A pterodon buzzed him, then three more.

"Your winged lizards are all over me," he called.

Trudy and Cadmann were emerging from under the shell. The Starborns' leader crawled out onto the surface, through a hole only twice man-sized. He was tired, but hopped to his feet with admirable energy. Looked around, found a boulder and fastened the rope around it. Lowered the rope down the hole.

Greg Lindsey was a walking antenna and broadcasting studio. He immediately began sending to *Messenger*, which relayed his message to Avalon . . . and the rescue ships already on their way.

"Easier down than up," Cadzie said.

The three ropes dangled from the ceiling at different levels, each one third of the way to safety. Cadzie jumped down from the last one, a short ten feet, landing in a crouch. "Right."

Now all they had to do was survive until help came. There was no way in hell all their people could climb those ropes, or be pulled up. That meant wait. And possibly fight. He could have stayed up top, with Greg. But that would have been cowardly as hell. Some of these people had followed him from loyalty. Others from vengeance.

But no matter how he sliced it, this situation was his cross to bear.

◆ CHAPTER 62 ◆
FEELING GOD-ISH

Joanie's first group surfaced in the air pocket between Water and Ice caverns, spitting water and gasping for air.

"Only a minute's rest," she called. "We have to keep going. Move!"

The first of her charges arrived in the frozen cave just eight minutes later: the Russian Tsiolkovskii. He took a deep breath, and shivered. "Feels like an icehouse."

"Yes. Come on." The Grendel Scouts and Godsons climbed up on the land, two by two, rolling over on their backs to spit water, and then there were twenty-two of them.

"There's another rope," Cadzie said. "Get it over here. Boost me up."

Standing on the rock, he got a position and jumped up to the dangling rope. He attached the last rope, and now they had a way out.

"Nice," Joanie said.

491

"It'll work. Now. What we have to do is get out as fast as we can."

Stype glared at Joanie, barely able to restrain her blue-lipped fury.

Joanie, damn her, was oblivious to the daggers. "Thank God. You blew the tunnel?"

"Damned straight." Stype said.

"What is this place?" Joanie asked.

"Feel how cold it is?" Cadzie asked.

"Freezing," she said.

"I could be wrong, but this might be a classic ice chamber," Shaka said.

"Making ice? In the middle of the desert?"

"A high alpine meadow, actually. Above the desert."

"It's sophisticated, but not that hard. The Romans would put water into a pit that was well-insulated with straw. The pit would be covered with highly polished shields during the day, to reflect the heat of the sun, while at night the pit would be uncovered so that the water within could lose the maximum thermal energy to the black sky. Ice often began forming in the evening, and would typically be ready for harvesting by three or four a.m. Once harvested, the ice would be taken to the nearest icehouse for storage."

"I will be damned. Why would the cthulhu want ice?"

"I don't know. But we have seen symbols that suggest ice," Nnedi said.

"Those scribbles on the walls? Some kind of hiero-glyphs?"

She nodded, and drew their attention to a irregular

lump of ice-frosted rock. Only . . . under more careful examination, what initially seemed like rock was some kind of worked metal. "Look at this. We are looking at prototypes, maybe?"

Joanie frowned. Looked more carefully. Rust, ice, ages in darkness? Could that have rendered a machine into a nearly shapeless mass? "A sled? Ice? Pulled by grendels?"

"I can't think of any rational reason to do this," Shaka said.

"But?" Joanie said. "I can hear a 'but' in there."

"But . . . we don't know much about them, why they would do something as insane as build a city under an alpine meadow, requiring artificial canals. Why?"

They hadn't noticed before now, but Trudy had been thinking deeply, as if coming to some kind of unwieldy decision. "What if it isn't logic?" she asked.

"What else would it be?" Shaka asked.

"What if it was spiritual?" she said.

"What do you mean?"

"I mean . . ." She began laughing. "Of course you can't see it. You have no idea what it is to have a dream so powerful it drives you across the stars."

"And you do?" Cadzie asked, a little irritated.

"Yes, I do. You were born here. I chose to come here. Competed for the privilege. I can see it."

"See what?" His exasperation was growing.

"You told us, Shaka. The magnetic map. They saw things . . . see things we don't. They were attracted to the dam, right?"

"Well, yes . . ."

"And it was the magnetism. They built these dipole rooms. What if . . . they were building temples?"

Shaka blinked. "Temples?"

"Look," she said. "Look. Aaron brought grendels into the chamber where we found the map. He was killed. We've been thinking it was a place of worship, yes? They were offended? Look here."

"What?"

"If the dam attracted them, what in the hell would magnetic north look like to them?"

"You're . . ." Joanie looked like someone had slapped her. "Oh my god. It would look like heaven."

"Like heaven. I think they wanted to meet God."

Almost a minute of stunned silence as they absorbed the implications.

Joanie was the first to speak. "They . . . think magnetism is divine? And humans create huge magnetic fields . . ."

"The dam," Cadzie said.

She nodded. "The dam. I have to wonder what they think of us."

"They could think we're gods," Toad said. "I'm feeling kinda god-ish today."

Cadzie managed a smile. "So . . . they built a city in the middle of the desert . . . halfway to the north pole. Ran out of rivers."

"These are aquatic creatures," Shaka said. "How do they get the rest of the way across the desert?"

Cadzie said, "We haven't seen wheels, but they know how to make spheres. Big ball bearings? A sled, maybe?"

"How far?" Joanie asked. "I mean . . . how far could they go?"

"I don't know." Trudy said. "I really don't. This is all guessing. But a thousand miles of desert?"

"We have no idea the limits of their technology," Joanie said. "How it worked or what it could do. None. I don't think they could . . . could they?"

Tsiolkovskii found Cadzie sitting against the wall, resting from the muscle-cracking climbs. The Russian squatted down next to him. "I knew of your grandfather, of course. We both served in the 105th U.N."

"You knew him?"

"No, but we fought in the same theater. Tanzania, when the Chinese tried to move against the Pan Africans for minerals, using surrogates. There was a real breakdown of supplies, and a last stand at Ngorongoro crater. One of the last such military actions on Earth, as of the time I went into suspended animation."

"What happened?" Cadzie asked.

Tsiolkovskii closed his eyes for a moment, as if sorting through memories. "U.N. versus rebels trying to overthrow a democratically elected state. The Pan Africans were deliberately destabilized, with breakaway Asian and corporate entities scratching for wealth. It had happened before in South America and Australia. Corporates against governments. Anyway, the U.N. stood with the Pan Africans, and there were a flood of mercenaries from all over the world. It was tragic, really, because in many ways they were lied to. Lots of words like 'freedom' and 'fair play' came into it, but the reality was that the Pan Africans were simply saying they had the right to their own resources."

Fascinating. Stype had overheard and wandered over. "What happened?"

"Major Weyland was ambushed, his supply lines cut, and the air support was just crushed. He retreated across five hundred miles of territory until reaching Ngorongoro. A natural bunker, the volcanic bowl that had been a nature reserve in the previous century. The elected government of the central Pan Africans was in his protection, and he refused to give them up. The corporates threw everything at them, wave after wave. You understand?"

"I'm not sure I do."

"Human waves. They wanted to turn world opinion against the Pan Africans, headlines about starving refugees slaughtered by U.N. troops, etc. Cadmann's people fought like their backs were against a cliff. They held their line and were relieved just in time. Together with the reinforcements they were eventually relieved. They broke the attack, but I think he was . . . disgusted by the politics that created the slaughter. The story is that that led to his seeking a place on *Geographic*."

Cadzie thought, hard. "You know . . . my uncle Carlos has a recurring dream about fighting a wave of grendels in a place that sounds just like Ngorongoro."

"That's odd," the Major said.

"Not if my grandfather told him about his experiences."

The Russian nodded. "Then it would make sense, yes. Your grandfather was a fine man."

"He wanted to start over."

"Yes. He didn't sign up for slaughter. He wanted to protect."

"And you fought in the same theater?"

"I did."

"What happened?" Cadzie asked. "I mean, the war?"

"There was a negotiated truce," Tsiolkovskii said. "Between nationals and corporates. Both sides lost, both sides won. The battles on Earth are more legal and political than military now. That was one of the last great ones."

"What did you do in the war?"

"Got blown to hell," he said with a bitter chuckle. "Before that happened, I did my part. But I was . . . almost killed. They gave me a choice of being crippled, or being frozen until the medical technology matured. They estimated ten years, and a cost of twenty million dollars."

"That's a lot, right?"

"More than a decommissioned military was prepared to pay," Tsiolkovskii said.

"So . . . you seem fine. More than fine. What happened?"

"The Godsons. They had brought some of their technology into an experimental program at West Point when I was doing an instructor stint there, and I'd said good things about them. They remembered, and asked if I would be willing to accept their help in exchange for service."

"And you said yes?"

"Absolutely. I would be whole again . . . and useful. A new adventure. Your grandfather would have understood."

"I think he'd have jumped at it."

"How did he die?" Tsiolkovskii asked, genuinely curious.

"Some kind of fight with the man I was accused of killing, Aaron Tragon. Aaron was absolved. I was never satisfied with the verdict."

"But you didn't kill him?"

"No. Do you believe me?"

Tsiolkovskii shrugged. "Not before. Now, I would. We might not get out of here. Not much reason to lie."

"I didn't kill him."

Stype said, "Then this is pretty much a clusterfuck, isn't it?" Cadmann looked around. He'd thought she was asleep.

Tsiolkovskii ran a hand through his mane of thinning hair. An old lion, but still a lion. "It is hard . . . to say how wrong we were. I suppose its a little late for words to mean much."

"Yeah. It is. Listen," Stype said. "I don't feel like a warrior right now. If we hadn't hounded and hared you, this wouldn't be happening. If we hadn't let our Great Mission blind us to the smaller things . . ."

"But it did."

Tsiolkovskii's face darkened. "Officers cannot claim to have merely been following orders. I didn't have the information I needed."

"You trusted us," Stype said.

"There's that stuff the road to hell is paved with."

"The 'good intentions' thing," Cadzie said.

"Yeah, that's it."

"But it did," Tsiolkovskii said. "Listen: we're going to get the hell out of here."

There was a shout from the others, and Cadzie was called over to a spot under the open roof. Greg Lindsey waved down at him.

"The help is on its way. ETA fifteen minutes. We can start pulling people up, but we need a rear guard. What do you want me to do?"

So Lindsey was taking orders from him now? There were two basic questions: did he want the strength of armor at the top pulling people? Or on the ground protecting them?

"Stay up there, Greg. And start hauling."

Greg lowered ropes with loops for feet at the bottom. "Alright!" Cadzie yelled. "Strap the injured on, and then the youngest!" They sorted themselves out, and soon their unseen rescuers began to haul people up.

Halfway through the evacuation the rock began to shift . . . and grendels streamed through, answering the unspoken question: how badly did their inhuman enemies want their flesh? Apparently, quite badly.

But this time, something new happened. The frantic humans who fled toward the walls were hunted down and killed; but the humans who fled back into the water found allies. Sleek tentacled creatures which had the ability to shock the demireptiles into overdriven frenzy, such that they foamed the water, snapping at their own tails and everything around them, until they died.

Some grendels converged on the cthulhu, and several were torn trunk from tentacle. But the creatures fought a rearguard action alongside Colonel Anton Tsiolkovskii and the last two armored men.

Tsiolkovskii had never been in a battle like this. No human had. And that meant no one had, ever. His two remaining armored men acted like human tanks, fighting with augmented strength and armor-piercing shells.

Humans and aliens together, against something lethal to both.

The water boiled with speed. The air reeked of blood and fear.

Despite the miracle of cthulhus fighting for their new human allies, they were pushed back and then farther back. The rear-guard action slowly pushed them toward the wall. The only thing that kept them alive was the icy floor which denied the grendels any purchase. The grendels couldn't control their actions, and under other circumstances the blurring, snapping monstrosities cannoning about would have been almost comical.

No one laughed.

Humans dangled from ropes as grendels snapped below. Those who could climb did so. The others prayed to be hauled up.

The Godson armor was no longer considered invulnerable, but remained a miracle, the two men at the bottom emptying their magazines into the grendel horde.

Cadzie, the Russian, Joanie and Major Stype were the last ones remaining on the ground. They saw the two armored men go down beneath a tide of grendels, shredded out of the armor as if dropped into the gears of a living machine. But they had served a mighty purpose: the last of the injured had ascended.

Four ropes, four survivors: they began to climb. Below them, the cthulhus abandoned the fight, ceased functioning as a living wall and melted back into the cleared water.

Joanie climbed as fast as she could, but the trials of the last days, the last terrible hours and minutes, had finally emptied her reserves. Her arms and shoulders were exhausted. She didn't notice the rope swinging next to her until she felt something strike her side, and turned to see that it was Stype. Stype, conciliatory Stype, who hadn't been quite so forgiving after all.

Stype's face was twisted into a rictus of sheer rage.

"Major Stype! Stand down!" Tsiolkovskii roared from above them. Stype ignored him. Joanie saw in that moment that nothing would save her but herself, Stype coming after her, looking for this one final chance to kill the woman who had killed her love.

Joanie saw the knife Stype had slipped from its sheath, held in her right hand as she had twisted the rope around her left wrist, twined it around her left ankle for support as she swung. Slashing at Joanie, slashing at the rope, at anything she could reach. Joanie twisted with all the power in her core, and instead of climbing, spun around Stype, arcing away and then back in fast, feet first, smashing Stype in the face.

Stype slackened with shock and lost her grip. If she had dropped her knife and grabbed the rope with her right hand she wouldn't have fallen over backwards, feet still tangled in the rope, screaming, face now within snapping distance of a leaping grendel. What followed concluded with merciful speed. Joanie shuddered, then climbed.

◆ CHAPTER 63 ◆
AFTERMATH

By the time the last three survivors reached the surface, rescue skeeters buzzed and bent grass and chased away harvesters. They bore armed men and engineers. The injured were already being evacuated, and Godsons who had never faced a grendel were taking command and giving orders to everyone but Anton Tsiolkovskii.

Within another half hour, most of the dust had settled and the worst of the wounded gone. Cadzie found the Russian sitting and watching the action from a folding camp chair, surrounded by the surviving Godson troops. The Russian was wrapped in a greatcoat that made him look a little like an oversized Napoleon. He nodded greeting and shooed one of his men away from a spot beside him.

Cadzie hunkered down. Part of his mind was trying to calm himself, sort through the horror of the last hours, knowing that new nightmares were on the horizon.

But...these demons would find a man who remembered he was a human animal, capable of baring his teeth.

A deep grinding voice interrupted his thoughts. "We will need to lie about what happened," the Russian said.

"Why?" Cadzie asked.

"Because the men who were not here, who did not see, will kill you, regardless of why it happened," Tsiolkovskii said this without emotion. "The Godson troops must never know how many of us died at your hands. The flying things that ate our men . . ."

"Bees," Cadzie said. "We call them bees."

"They don't sting? They bite?"

"Yes."

"Bees, at least, can be a misadventure." His men nodded. All had seen what he had seen, knew what he knew, and had accepted him as their natural leader.

The others, the new ones, had no idea at all.

Together in silence, the two men watched the coming and going of rescuers and engineers for a time. The alien city would have to be cleansed of grendels. Gas perhaps? Or would that risk the lives of their new allies? Smarter men and women than he would work that out. But eventually the depths would be explored, mapped. Perhaps repaired. There was much to do, and despite his soul-crushing fatigue, Cadzie realized that he was damned well going to be a part of that.

Like his grandfather would have been.

"I can live with that," Cadzie replied.

It took four days to convene a hybrid Godson-Avalonian panel. Most of the central colony was present in the main dining hall, and the proceedings beamed to every settlement on the planet.

The Speaker's hologram seemed simultaneously grave and relieved. "Cadmann Weyland Sikes, you are declared not guilty. And this panel apologizes to you for all that has happened. What we see is that communication between human beings united in general intent can still go so very wrong. But you and your people bridged communication between species."

The Speaker spoke on. "We, the Godsons, think of ourselves as great communicators. We were wrong. We thought that humanity was the only group worth saving. What we saw was an alien species, for reasons we do not understand, willing to die to protect us, protect our children . . ." He stopped, overwhelmed by emotion.

Sylvia, a living presence in the main dining hall, seemed tired but intense. Zack's death had awakened her from a long emotional slumber: the colony needed her. "We do not understand their motivations. But a species who treats our children as their own is worthy of respect, study. Friendship."

"Agreed," the Speaker said. "We will continue to the stars. But we will also create a colony here, on the mainland, and with your permission a smaller settlement here on the island where we might retreat in emergency. This is a large planet, and we would like to share the responsibility of taming it."

Tsiolkovskii stood, thick fingers balled almost to fists, scarred knuckles resting on the table before him. "I request permission to remain here. I believe that the risk of another stint of freezing outweighs the benefits of my participation in the establishment of our new colony."

The Speaker looked like a man who had expected a gutpunch but was still dismayed by its impact. A man who knew that he had no real leverage to stop Tsiolkovskii from leaving them . . . completely. This was a moment requiring real wisdom.

"I believe . . ." he said carefully, "that the contingent of Godsons we leave here will need . . . guidance." He paused. "I believe you are not the only member of our inner circle who has made this decision." It was clear that the Speaker was having a difficult time framing his thoughts. "Marco? You wanted to speak."

Marco stood. Beside him, Joanie sat straight and alert, her bruised face no longer swollen, but still a bit discolored. A souvenir of her conflict with the late, enraged Major Stype. Marco bowed slightly to the Speaker, and then to the survivors and colonists. His normal theatricality had returned, lending him gravity. "Humans have always been interested in strangeness, in alien modes of thought. We are hunters. In order to stalk prey, we need to learn how these other life-forms think and plan.

"Human beings have evolved as communicators. We teach our children. We coddle our elderly and listen to their stories. Men and women learn to talk to each other. We tamed dogs and horses. We keep pets. We talk to strangers, we trade, we make treaties. We lie.

"The cthulhus also have learned to talk to dolphins and men. Even so, they can't travel with us. They're linked to one environment. Most of the galaxy's creatures may be chained to some pocket environment, like most of the species of Earth.

"There's no reason to think other species have evolved

to communicate as well as we have. The human race may be destined as ambassadors to the rest of the galaxy."

The Speaker's mouth was a thin line; his eyes were squinted half shut. Marco didn't notice. He finished, "*We did not light the torch.*"

"*And we will not see the bonfire,*" said several scores of Godsons, men and women. "*To Man's destiny.*"

The Speaker said, "Narrator, please see me on my private line."

Marco was still filming several hours later. He finally got to see Joan after nightfall.

"Speaker Gus is kicking me off the ship," he said. "We're not going to Hypereden."

"What? Why?"

"He doesn't like my attitude. The Godsons are sent to conquer, not to be ambassadors to a thousand other species. Also I've interrupted him too often. And if I can't go, you're off too. What I want to know is, will you go over the rapids with me anyway?"

She hugged him. "Idiot. You never got it. I spent *weeks* in free fall, and I *hate* it. I'm terrified of cold sleep. I don't want ice on my mind. I'm so glad, so glad you're staying."

"Good. Good. And I asked for cameras, and I got them. I'll be filming your history as you make it."

Dinner conversation on Cadmann's Bluff was a celebration as well as somewhat . . . elegiac. Sylvia and Rachel and Carlos served, while Cadzie, Trudy, Joanie and Marco were on tap to clean up.

Tsiolkovskii sat by the fire, speaking of Peruvian

cave-diving to Carlos' daughter Tracey. He had butchered the meat personally, and his duties were done for the day.

No one had ever seen such a clean, powerful killing stroke, decapitating the beast before it knew it was dead.

If the pungent aroma of goat ragout disturbed Billy the Kid's appetite, however, he gave no sign. That lucky creature nibbled and wandered where he willed, safe from man or beast on a tamed subcontinent, a talisman for life.

Zack and the other honored dead had been consigned to the soil. The Godsons, settled onto their third of the island, had performed their own ceremonies over what corpses had been recovered, and gotten on with the business of colonizing the galaxy, their industry sprouting up like mushrooms. Replicators had been replicated until half the homes had a miniature, and every shop a full-sized system.

Camelot was reborn.

The dinner was also a good-bye party for Toad Stolzi.

"What made you decide to leave?" Cadzie asked.

He shrugged. "I was raised to be a pilot," he said. "I'm not afraid of cold sleep. I figure if I lose twenty I.Q. points I'll finally fit in with the rest of you." Laughter.

He raised his hand, suddenly more serious. "Really . . . I just can't resist. I can be what our grandparents were. A real spaceman."

His father Mason squeezed his shoulder. His hand trembled with age, his voice with emotion. "I'd say I'll miss you, but all I can think is how proud of you I am."

They toasted the beloved living, and the honored dead.

Just outside their northern window Billy the Kid brayed, as if he knew a friend was departing.

A year later.

Messenger was under point four gravity of thrust, the most it could manage with a full fuel balloon. The Speaker enjoyed that sensation immensely. *On our way.* He stretched in his great chair and released the pause button. "Carlos, we've been sending you what we learn of Tau Ceti's solar system. Of course you had records from your own arrival, but we have more detail. The fifth planet, Shalott, is the only world of which we'll see a close approach. We've seen details of two dozen moons, of which Bree may be worth exploring, even terraforming one day. As for the Kuiper Belt, we'll know more in a few months, but it looks as rich as Sol System's.

"Thank you for the hundred Starchildren you've added to our passenger list. We know you'll treat our hundred well. They'll add to your genetic variety, and God knows you needed that after the Grendel Wars, and the quarrel, for that matter."

The Speaker coughed, then continued. "You twenty-six who remained on Avalon, Godspeed! Your mission hasn't changed. You are still Godsons. As ex-narrator Marco Shantel pointed out before he left the ship, planets must be conquered one bite at a time. Live your lives to make your descendants proud."

Messenger's main recreation room could seat thirty

people, more than were ever supposed to be awake at a given time. One at a time, the inhabitants would be taken to the cryoroom, and there put into a sleep that would last another twelve years, at the very least.

On the main holo stage, Marco Shantel's image was pontificating, as he did so well. More of his native charisma seemed to have returned, and with it the boyish charm that had carried him across trillions of miles of interstellar space.

Toad Stolzi and Dr. Charlotte Martine took a seat at the table where Thor sat with Chief Engineer Jorge Daytona. Two floating cameras framed Daytona. None of them said anything, just watched. Ear buds let them switch from program to program. On one of the screens, the ringed gas giant planet named for the Lady of Shalott was sliding past. On the middle screen the transmission from Avalon continued to stream.

In holographic form, Trudy Sipes held her husband's hand as Cadmann spoke. "Since *Messenger*'s departure Cassandra seems different now. She may be feeling her freedom, now that the last member of the board is dead. Or contact with *Messenger*'s autopilot may have changed her in some way. She's relaying all this to *Messenger*, where it will go to Earth; and to the cthulhus, for whatever they can make of it."

Trudy said, "Zack, and the friends who defended my consort in our recent quarrel, and the Godsons who fought us, will all contribute to the life we brought here. Life of Earth will grow from their bodies, what we were able to recover. Sometimes conquest takes that form.

"Meanwhile we patch the wounds left by our quarrel.

Before its departure for Hypereden, *Messenger* printed out over a hundred of the cthulhu dipoles, the belly magnets. We can print more. The cthulhus are distributing some of them to their cousins below Blackship Island to raise their next interactive generation."

Thor settled back in his seat. "Marco does a great show," he said.

Dr. Martine said, "We're going to miss him."

Harry Dean snapped, "He had exactly the wrong approach. We're not ambassadors, dammit! We're warriors meant to conquer the galaxy! That's why the Speaker tossed him overboard and made me narrator. Which reminds me, we'll have to send them an answer, and relay everything to Sol System."

Stolzi said, "No hurry. We're one and a half light hours away, round trip. Want us in on the interview?" Dean shrugged.

Thor said, "I like Marco's approach. He'll get to practice it on Avalon. Ambassadors to the universe. We humans get to do all the talking. Talk without fighting. You Godsons are entirely too feisty."

Toad Stolzi grinned. Neither Dr. Martine nor Narrator Dean were quite ready to challenge the massive Thor.

And of those present, only Toad and Thor himself knew the Viking was a hollow man.

Skeeter Blue settled on a bare patch below a field of ice on a clear winter day, visibility a full seven klicks of bluewhite frost.

Marco Shantel climbed out first. Three cameras looped

around him like trained doves. He said, "We're here. The weather isn't that cold. Avalon's pole is warmer than Earth's, and the ice hereabouts is patchy, with solid rock underneath. The true north pole is only sixty klicks north of here. The north magnetic pole is directly below us."

Joan climbed out. She pulled a case after her, set it on the water-darkened, rocky ground and opened it. It unfolded itself: Godson magic. A telescope rose on stilts and its lens wandered about, questing.

Marco said, "General Tsiolkovskii, come in."

Static roared. Then, "Tsiolkovskii in Skeeter Yellow. You're fading a little."

"Even so, these new electronics are miraculous. We're right on the mag pole and we can still hear each other and record. The cameras are working. Joanie's set up the telescope and . . . got it, Joanie?"

"Got it. Recording. *Messenger* is approaching Shalott's orbit on course to Hypereden. Shalott is this system's fifth planet, and *Messenger* is dipping in for a spectacular view and a gravitational boost. It's got nice rings."

Marco focused a camera on the telescope's display screen. It showed two blobs, one big and orange, with a barely visible ring and a scattering of dots for moons; the other tiny but brilliant, bluish white on black, and no other details.

"Marco? Want an expanded view of Shalott?"

"Maybe later, if we don't find anything more interesting. Hey, Cadzie. Hey, Trudy. We're sending to Camelot. Come say hi."

Trudy was carrying a conspicuous bulge below her ribs. Cadmann helped her out of Skeeter Blue, being very careful. Cadmann spoke to the cameras. "Hello, Camelot and *Messenger* and everyone I've known. We're in place and looking around. If you're receiving this, stay with us."

He reached back into the skeeter for another case. Joan looked into the cameras and said, "*We did not light the torch—*"

"*And we will not see the bonfire,*" Marco said. "*To Man's destiny*. Cadmann, let's you set up the microwave sensor—"

Tsiolkovskii's staticky voice interrupted. "No need. I have it in view. Can you see me? I'll circle overhead."

Marco and the cameras focused on the sky. "We see Skeeter Yellow—"

"Good, now just follow me down."

Skeeter Yellow sank below a ridge of ice.

They piled back into Skeeter Blue and crossed over a rise. And there it was: half an acre of pale ice, on dark permafrost. You could make out struts and pentagonal blocks, all quite flat, the remains of a blobby dome collapsed across dark rock.

And next to it—Skeeter Blue settled.

Marco walked downhill, all cameras focused ahead.

It was a big, bulky, overbuilt chariot with a bathtub for a belly. The wheels were made of wrought iron, big, solid, ornate, with no spokes. Five wheels included a steering wheel just like the other four.

Tsiolkovskii was standing beside it with Little Chaka. What they were about to broadcast to the planet was something that never would have been said until the Godsons were on their way out of the solar system.

Despite the Speaker's conciliatory words, the Starborn had voted that the total truth should only be shared among those inheriting Avalon.

Family business.

"They did it! The old cthulhu reached the planet's north pole!" Cassandra's translation of cthulhu myths and stories had implied as much. Their new partners in Avalon's future had been more amazing than humans, Starborn *or* Godson, has ever dreamed. Aquatic creatures mastering fire, smelting metals, and crossing the desert was an accomplishment on the levels of humans launching Yuri Gagarin into orbit. "They used a chariot and...that reservoir held ice, right? That's why they were making ice. They'd have found more here. And..."

"Marco, get a view of those struts," said Chaka.

Marco zoomed in. Shamboo bars, weathered, stretched along two long lines. Strands of something that wasn't leather, that hadn't held up well. "We were expecting motors. Or even bicycle gears or a gerbil cage. What is that? How—"

"Harness. It's harness," Little Shaka said.

"For what? Oh my god."

"Grendels. Ten grendels, but some of these are tied off, so they must have lost a few on the way. Their conquest was driven by grendels...big ones, they must have been as big as any I've ever seen. The cthulhus were taming grendels, and it worked."

Cadmann was at work with the microwave sensor. "I've found another chariot, I think. Under the ice. They took at least two, one for cargo, I bet."

Big Shaka said, "It got them this far, anyway. They don't

seem to have gone home. Maybe they never intended to. They built a dome...this low spot could have been a pond."

"No, that dome was an igloo. Ice. They must have planned to stay."

"At least until they ran out of food. That could have been nasty."

"That patch that pokes up out of the dome area, could that have been a forge?"

Marco stepped back out of the discussion. "Calling *Messenger*, calling Camelot, calling Earth. Calling Cassandra, I expect you can translate for our cthulhu friends. We are looking at the remnants of the cthulhu space program..."